BOYS OF LOVE

BOYS OF LOVE

GHAZI RABIHAVI

Translated by Poupeh Missaghi

THE UNIVERSITY OF WISCONSIN PRESS

Publication of this book has been made possible, in part, through support from the Brittingham Trust.

The University of Wisconsin Press
728 State Street, Suite 443
Madison, Wisconsin 53706
uwpress.wisc.edu

Printed in the United States of America
This book may be available in a digital edition.

Library of Congress Cataloging-in-Publication Data

Names: Rabīḥāvī, Qāẓī, author. | Missaghi, Poupeh, translator.
Title: Boys of love / Ghazi Rabihavi ; translated by Poupeh Missaghi.
Other titles: Pisarān-i 'ishq. English
Description: Madison, Wisconsin : The University of Wisconsin Press, 2024.
Identifiers: LCCN 2023053636 | ISBN 9780299349042 (paperback)
Subjects: LCSH: Gay men—Iran—Fiction. | LCGFT: Novels. | Fiction.
Classification: LCC PK6562.28.A25 P5713 2024 | DDC 891/.5534—
dc23/eng/20240409
LC record available at https://lccn.loc.gov/2023053636

For Karl Hoff

BOYS OF LOVE

A ND FINALLY, FATHER SAW WHAT HE WAS NOT SUPPOSED TO. I've already told you about it, haven't I? We had played this game before with our sisters and nieces, at Naneh Reyhan's house, because she was the only one who allowed us kids to do whatever we wanted at her house. My sister Behi and I would sit on two stools, and the other girls would apply makeup to our faces with cosmetics they had stolen from their mothers. They'd turn Behi into the groom because she was older and bigger than me. They'd make her a mustache with a doll's hair. And they would turn me, the skinny, delicate one, into the bride, tarting me up, my lips pink, my cheeks dotted with two red circles, my eyes contoured black with kohl, my eyelids green and blue, my forehead many colors, and on my head a piece of white lace.

Until one day Hamed, who since he was a child had had his eye on Behi, saw us in the middle of all that and told on us to my father, Haji. And then Haji came, with a look of menace and contempt, and not a word. That very evening, he tied Behi and me to the jasmine tree in the backyard, and his wet stick whipped our soft thin calves with pain, burning, and pain again.

At the time, I wasn't used to pain yet. Now, though, pain is woven into the fabric of my body. I should even put *Boys of Pain* on the cover of this book. *Boys of Love* is not the best title for this narrative of pain and violence. Or maybe *Boys of Death*. Yes, this is the title I'll put on the cover once I finish writing, because you, the protagonist of this narrative, are dead. Even though I did not witness your death or hear about it from anyone, I know you are dead, and I am your real murderer. I murdered the one I loved more than anyone and anything in this world; I was cursed to kill the love of my youth so that he would forever appear to me in various shapes and forms, reminding me that I was the one who, with love and smiles, led you to death—like the moment I saw you at that wedding, staring at me with your smile, especially now that I'm sitting in front of the mirror, smearing my face with coats of colorful powder to cover my scars, and you appear to me in the depths of the mirror; or sometimes when I am dancing on the stage, twisting around myself, suddenly a shaft of light shines through the darkness, and I see you in that light, sitting there among the audience, staring at me with a smile.

I wrote that I was cursed, yes, and that is why I began writing this story, so that I can free myself from this curse, if I can ever be freed; either way, I have to ask you to free me, so I resurrect you by writing you, and then I am going to ask you to forgive me, because I was not given the opportunity to ask for your forgiveness in our final moments together. (Silence.) Can you hear me? I just wrote that I was not given the opportunity to ask for forgiveness, and now I am writing what a pity it is that I cannot bring you here, to the present moment and to this freedom, so instead I have to go back to the past, to come back to you, to that dark cage, and describe what befell us and our love.

But before I introduce you, I must introduce myself, because it was I who chose that perilous path, dragging you along with me to the heart of death. Was it I? Anyway . . .

I was born to a dead mother, a mother who was the most important person in my life in my teenage years, even though she had always been dead and I never saw her, only smelled her, because only a few minutes passed between the moment I fell into life and the moment she drowned in death. When my eyes were still incapable of seeing and all life in front of me was simply a thin line of my mother's white skin, as if she were the force of gravity and my head a heavy object suspended in space that had no option but to constantly fall over that body, a flock of sparrows flew to the window of the room and started screaming. It was Naneh Reyhan who told me this. Maybe the sparrows were singing a ballad that to her ears sounded like screaming. Anyway, I was lying on the warmth of my mother's body, on the softness of her breasts, and I could not recognize anything; there was only sound and scent, and all my joy was to rub my body against hers.

Many years later, when I was grown up, I learned a horrifying story. One Thursday evening when Naneh Reyhan was giving out alms (a wrap of bread, cheese, and dates) to remember the dead to neighbors and passersby, I walked in front of her, and she thought I was there to help her out, but truth is I was there to be rewarded for my virtuous act. The wraps were inside a basket hanging from my shoulder; Naneh's eyesight was not strong enough, so she would follow me and my footsteps. We reached Bibi Gohar, who was sitting by a palm tree, basket weaving, as if her whole life went by weaving. "God bless your dearly departed. I was so hungry, I swear to God," she said and laughed.

"Say a prayer specially for Sara," said Naneh Reyhan.

"Yes, I swear to God, you are right," said Bibi Gohar, looking at me with a smile, and adding, "Mashallah, what a handsome son did she leave behind, sweet as rock candy. God himself bestows his special blessings on good people." Holding the wrap in hand, she closed her eyes and said a prayer for the dead, and when she finished, she cast a cautious look around and said, "May those who destroyed such a good woman never have it easy." It was the first time I had heard about this. Then Naneh Reyhan whispered something to me, and I realized Bibi Gohar meant two people, one Zobeydeh Khanoom, my father's older wife, and the other Bibi Saleem, my father's mother. They had told me that my mother suffered from tuberculosis and was so thin that her body could not handle the weight of birthing me, and that was why all attempts to save her were unsuccessful and, a few minutes after my birth, she died. "So full of life and joy, that woman."

Naneh Reyhan was our neighbor of many years and a distant relative of my father's, living in a small house behind our big house, and no one in our household liked me chatting with her. They said she was not in her right mind and spoke nonsense, but I was close to her, and we chatted. Later, when I grew up, I would bring her medication for her eye problems, and sometimes, when I put the eye drops in her eyes, I would open my heart to her, sharing some of my secrets, and she was afraid that Bibi Saleem would bring upon me the same destiny as my mother and order me murdered, but I just wanted Naneh Reyhan to tell me about my mother.

"Always happy? What does that mean?"

"She was chatty and ready to laugh. She liked to play the tombak and dance."

"Dance?"

"Just for herself, and to make others happy."

"Did she dance?"

"Yes, here at my house. She had a small record player and would put in a cassette of happy songs and dance. She said the cassettes belonged to her father, who was also a skilled musician."

The record player and the cassettes had all disappeared, and I never set eyes on them. I only saw the violin that my mother had kept as a memento of her father; during her sick days, she had asked Haji to pass it on to me when I grew up, and my father took good care of that instrument because he loved my mother.

"Yes, he would have died for her. Whatever Sara craved, Haji would give to her with all his heart and soul. Once, in the dead of winter, she fancied cherries, and Haji sent his men all around the city until they finally found some for her. He loved her so much, and that love cost the woman her life."

One summer when my father had gone to Mashhad on pilgrimage (he went every summer), he saw my mother in the courtyard of Imam Reza's shrine and married her by way of sigheh, a temporary vow (what he did every summer with different women), but that summer turned out to be different from the others. The temporary wife of that year was unlike the temporary wives of other years, and my father fell head over heels for her. A luminous seyyed in the shrine's courtyard held my mother's hand in one hand and my father's in the other, listened in silence to their breathing, then turned to my father and said, "This woman carries within her seven sons. If you wish for a son, this woman will give you one every year." And right there and then, my father married the woman for good, and, despite already having two wives at home, brought back my mother as his third wife, apparently granting her special status so that she would give birth to me for him, but the woman's short life didn't allow her to birth the other sons the seyyed had predicted. I, too, would have died immediately after my birth, had it not been for Naneh Reyhan in the room breaking into a joyous ululation the moment I left my mother's womb. She ululated with all the force in her throat to give the good news to Haji, who was pacing back and forth in the yard. Haji kept pacing, whispering under his breath, pacing, and repeating a question, Would I be a girl or a boy? And what was I? Did anyone ask me? Did I ask myself? I don't know, but I can imagine my father in those moments, silently asking, with his eyes wandering around in the air, "What is it?"

He, whom we all called Haji, had seven daughters from his other wives and had had it with having so many daughters, until Naneh Reyhan ululated. An ululation to announce my sex and to sway Bibi Saleem and Zobeydeh Khanoom from their scheme of forcing a pin into my skull and killing me. But little did Naneh Reyhan know that they had carried out their plan to poison my mother (had she made this up, or had it really happened?). "That day, out of fear, I myself washed your body," she said, and once again laid me on top of the body whose warmth was fading little by little, its cold seeping into mine to stay with me forever, until now.

No, I should not say my life has always been cold, because years later, the love of my youth gifted me a pleasant warmth, with many memories, good and bad. That forbidden union had a mad tumultuous beginning, but after we both got used to living in the city, I was happy and warm, with light wings, like a bird that has arrived at its destination, at freedom. I was liberated from that cage, from the village where I was born and raised. (But now I sometimes involuntarily think that village was the most beautiful cage of the world and wonder, What if I could fly from this freedom back to that cage?) With all the limitations my father set around my life and amid all the hardships, the only nice thing he did for me was to send me to school, despite the painstaking commute to the city, so that I learned how to write, so that today I can write the story of what befell us, befell my young life and the young life of another human who would still be alive had I not entered that life; but I did, on the night of that wedding ceremony.

If my father knew that I would someday write these words, he would have never sent me to school. He sent me to school because he wanted his son to become someone. He knew that no matter how much he toiled for the girls, in his words, it would be no use, because, in the end, he had to send them to another man's house, where they would be fucked; again, these were the words he used to describe the future of his daughters. But I was a boy; I was different. Father wanted me to become an educated man and be at his service, and, for him, mastering reading and writing was the pinnacle of education. No one could read and write in the village, or in the communities around us. Even for that very simple goal, Haji had to take special care of me, making extra sure that I did not follow the path of my mother's father, that of the motreb, the lowly musician. But he didn't care about the old violin, and the instrument that had once lain in the hands of my mother's father and, in the words of Naneh Reyhan, that used to create magic, now gathered dust in my room under a pile of other belongings.

Our village was far away from the city, by the river, and my father was one of the wealthiest men of the area. He owned some land and palm trees, several cows and sheep. He once traveled to Mecca and became a Haji, a title he needed, because at that time and place, being a Haji brought high regard. He wanted to be known as a virtuous politician, to be respected by others. He was certain that sooner or later the Iraqi army would enter the country from the other side of the water, liberating the area from the rule of the shah and handing the power to the locals. Haji was hoping to secure a big share of that transition, such as becoming the sheikh of the neighborhood, and he wanted me to get an education to become his secretary and assistant. To reach his goal, he was prepared to do everything, spending as much money as needed for my commute and studies. And in the year when early fall turned the landscape to a beautiful yellow, I was taken to school. That was the very fall when Haji forbade me from playing with girls.

"You are a man now, and you go to a men's school. It is beneath you to create another childish scene with the girls, to do something to make the women and girls laugh at you. You hear what I'm saying?"

"Yes, Haji, I hear you."

He was right. I had grown up and had to behave manly, had to behave manly everywhere, at home and at school, which was in the city, where a driver called Obood would drive me during the winter in a black-and-white Chevrolet. I would lounge in the front seat, and he would drive, and because he had a heavy stutter, he preferred not to talk, instead just looking at me from time to time and asking with a kind smile, "Are you comfortable?"

Years later, when I was older, I asked to be taken to school on the warm dry days by motorcycle, and Hamed said, "I'll take you myself." He was both my cousin and one of Haji's workers. Since his teenage years, he had loved to drive a motorcycle and run Haji's errands. My family even married off my sister Behiyeh, whom we called Behi, to Hamed in her childhood, but Haji said Hamed could have the wedding ceremony only when Behi had reached puberty. Despite this, Hamed often hung around in or outside our house, because Behi was becoming more of a woman every day, even showing off her womanhood to me, the two breasts that were, little by little, swelling under the skin of her chest and revealing themselves more, while their nipples grew a darker brown.

"When these two become the size of pomegranates this big, I will move to Hamed's house." She laughed and hid her breasts from me.

"But why don't mine grow big?" I asked her.

"Because you are a boy, you crazy one," she said.

It took twenty minutes to travel from home to school. I sat behind Hamed and wrapped my arms around his waist. Sometimes, when he wanted to go faster, he told me to hold on tighter. I would hold tightly to his body, and he would speed away. I liked it when we sped through the wind. Then, with one hand, he took one of my hands and guided it through the opening of his shirt and onto the skin of his belly. His skin was cold, very cold. I was terrified that he was driving the motorcycle with only one hand, but I had no choice but to press my cheek against his back and close my eyes. Once again, he took my hand and, this time, pulled my fingers much farther down. My fingers passed beneath his belt and touched the thick rough hair under his trousers. I felt disgusted and pulled my hand out. Then, the next day and the days after, he took my fingers even farther down until they touched his large erect sex. "Do you like it?" I didn't. "You'll get used to it." I didn't understand what he meant, what I had to get used to. I didn't get used to anything; only my curiosity was aroused. Maybe I felt some pleasure too? No.

No, I must emphasize through writing that I disliked him and was afraid of him. But my fear of Haji's status and of losing the joy of riding a motorcycle stopped me from telling Haji that I didn't want Hamed to take me to school anymore. Who else could I have told? My only confidants, the only ones I could open my heart to, were Naneh Reyhan and Behi. But Naneh Reyhan could do nothing more than curse my abusers and burst into tears, crying as much as she could, making me wonder whether those tears were for my grief of the day or for her own age-old accumulated grief. She advised me to be more careful and to not hang around Hamed. The only good that came from speaking to Naneh Reyhan was that she would embrace me and hold me tight. And, with closed eyes, I would let myself go, deeper and deeper into her rosewater-scented arms. "If only you could go somewhere safe, a distant safe place." Her fingers slid into my hair.

"Where, Naneh? Tell me where," I asked.

"No, I should bite my tongue. Don't listen to what I said. I'm talking nonsense. Where can you go, be stranded in foreign lands, you with your soft, gentle heart? No." She kept biting her hand and spitting around in a gesture to ward off evil.

Opening my heart to Behi was also useless, because the bigger her breasts grew, the closer her heart to Hamed's. "What does Hamed even say to you?" she asked.

"He says he wants to show me places I have never seen before, distant bushes and groves, trees full of pomegranates, the other side of the river, rose bushes."

"Rose bushes?"

"He knows I like watching them."

Behi laughed. "Well, what did you say?"

"I said, 'But you are marrying Behi. What if she finds out?' He said, 'She won't, and even if she does, she would like it.'"

"Ha, he is right."

She didn't understand that I could become her rival if I wanted to. I could charm Hamed myself. "But you don't understand what I'm saying," I told Behi. "It's useless. I should tell him." Did I want to tell Hamed that he should choose between me and my sister? But another day, when he tried to get close to me with one excuse or another, I whispered in his ear, equal parts threat and naughtiness, "What if I tell all of this to Haji? Should I tell him?"

He got scared, though he shrugged his shoulders to pretend he wasn't, then walked away from me. But his presence in and around our house didn't fade, because after all, Behi's breasts were now the size of pomegranates, such that one could even notice them under her dress. At that time, Behi and Hamed got married, and she seemingly moved to Hamed's house, a house in the adjacent village, but the two of them were still most of the time hanging out at our house. To avoid any physical contact with Hamed, I would not even shake his hand when greeting him, trying to escape what was nonetheless a common tradition. This feeling was something I had not only toward him but also toward other men. A sense of disgust when I saw men hugging and kissing each other. First, they shook hands and squeezed each other's hands hard, then they would all of a sudden leap toward each other's faces, putting their wet lips on the other person's cheek, sucking in, and then turning to the other side of the face, another kiss on the other cheek. Rough faces of people who did not like each other; I could sometimes even notice hatred in their eyes. What kind of pleasure were they finding in those kisses, or what kind of pleasure were they even looking for? I felt disgusted even shaking Hamed's hand, let alone kissing him or letting him kiss me. I kept repeating this to myself, that I hated him, so I kept my distance from the whole of his coarse body, until that day when I myself went toward his body, but only to save Naji's life. If Behi had not let me know, perhaps Naji would have been killed on that very day of that very year.

I must write about this, too, about Hamed, Naji, and me rolling into the river's waters in the early hours of the morning. It was always Behi who brought me the important news. Like the news of the dancer coming to a wedding ceremony, one of the best pieces of news she ever gave. She knew I loved dance. She had seen the poster of a man dancing that hung on my wall, though it hung there only sometimes, because I had to keep it away from Haji's eyes, or he would tear it apart. Behi said, "The ceremony is at the groom's house, which is in Sabri's neighborhood." Sabri was our elder sister, who had married before I was born, whose children were the same age as Behi and me and had been our playmates when we were kids.

"Are you sure there are going to be musicians and dancers at that wedding tomorrow night?"

"I heard it from the bride's sister," she said, and to build up my excitement even further, she added, "They say the dancer is phenomenal." She knew that I would enjoy watching the wedding dancer, but she didn't know that going there would change the course of my life forever. The life I am going to write about.

"I'll do whatever I can to make Haji let me go to the wedding."

"And I have to haggle with Hamed over this."

Hamed was somewhat submissive to Behi, and it wouldn't be hard for her to convince him, but it would take a lot of effort on my part to negotiate with Haji. He said watching a wedding ceremony was entertainment for the girls only. He said watching a big-bosomed dancer is haram for a boy who has just come of age.

"Come of age?" I asked.

He moved his hand up and down in front of me in a gesture of ridicule. "Mashallah, you, with this height and body and such education, still do not know what *coming of age* means? Holy shit!"

I knew, I understood, but I didn't yet want him to yap on about it. All I was thinking about was watching the dancer. So I didn't give up begging, and, finally, I was able to get his permission to go to that wedding.

When he learned we were Haji's children, the groom's uncle guided us to a good spot to sit. Behi was welcomed in the women's section on the floor, and Hamed and I in the men's section in rows of chairs. The moment we sat in our chairs, a man appeared in front of us with a tray with two coffee cups. Hamed took one, and I the other, but the coffee was too bitter for me.

The musicians finally arrived and started playing and singing. The dancer entered a bit later. On the middle finger and thumb of each hand, the dancer wore a pair of round metal cymbals that looked like two coins and were clinked together, following the rhythm of the song and swaying of the dancer's body. Sometimes the dancer would pause and shake their breasts, and the man who played the tombak would scream, and no matter how hard I listened, I could only hear and not understand him, and the dancer turned toward the tombak player, laughing and presenting their body with such coquetry, and the musician kept slithering his hands on the stretched-out skin of the tombak with more gusto. The two swells under the dancer's tight dress were like two hidden pomegranates that were constantly flaunted, stealing the gaze of the men in the audience. The old men stared with open mouths at the shaking of the two pomegranates that demanded everyone's eyes, except those of the young violinist, who was simply absorbed in his instrument. He sat on his chair, and even the few times that the dancer stepped toward him, bent over, and moved their breasts in front of his face, the violinist didn't do anything but pull back a bit so that his violin bow wouldn't touch them.

The dancer's torso stretched beneath a soft cloth covered with turquoise pearls sewn onto it. I didn't enjoy watching the dancer's breasts but was captivated by their waistline swaying in the yellow rays of the kerosene lamp like a snake of light. The loose skirt was of a thousand colors, lace over lace, and with every sway, the lace flew up in the air like a thousand colorful butterflies, all swirling around each other. The tombak player also sang. He sang of the beloved being unfaithful. He sang, "You saw me standing at the port for seven days and nights, sleepless and without food, waiting to see you. You passed by, not even throwing me a look, my beloved." A woman ululated. The dancer paused and jumped up—a masterful high jump in which their two touching ankles kissed their curvy buttocks. I knew that what the dancer was doing took both skill and strength. Now that I myself am a dancer, I know how hard the move is, and that is why the dancer did it with such pride and joy. Their most beautiful features were their smile and their long slender legs moving underneath the pink pearls of their skirt. The dancer was barefoot. Their toenails were painted red, the same as their fingernails.

The dance floor was a circle whose circumference was marked by the metal chairs arranged around the courtyard, but the dancer sometimes spun their way out of the circle, toward a man they had pinpointed, a man among the crowd, one of those with proper clothing sitting on the chairs, whom you could guess was wealthy, or at least had enough money in his pockets that night. The dancer would first stop in front of him, dance a bit, then turn around and bend backward until their long black hair brushed against the man's face, and then they bent even farther until their forehead almost touched the man's chest, and they shook their breasts and bent even more, so that now, perhaps, the man could take a peek at those bare breasts through the line of the dancer's collar, his eyes hooked on one point, yearning for a moment of touch. I figured that the men were not allowed to touch the dancer, and that gave me some peace, because I didn't want any of those men laying their hands on my dancer. I was happy that the dancer was just to be watched and not touched. The dancer bent farther and farther back in front of the man, staying there until he reached into his pocket, grabbed a bill, and tucked it into their collar, and the moment the dancer got the money, they started their slow ascent to the upright position, without staying motionless for a moment. Their body was under the command of the music played by the violinist and the tombak player. When the dancer reached their usual standing position, they secured the bill inside their dress, put a long kiss on the man's cheek, and returned to the circle until they picked another man in the audience and moved toward him. What is the secret of breasts that puts men under such a spell? I remembered my sisters being told, "Button up your shirt or else your cleavage will pop out like a hooker's."

The chairs were only for men, old and young. Some of the men wore keffiyehs the same color as my father's, but he never went to any wedding. Even when he married his daughters off, he would never allow for musicians to be brought in. He said, "We are Muslims, and for weddings and funerals, we follow the rule of God." So during the weddings of my sisters, only recordings of readings from the Quran were played from the rooftop of our house for three days.

The dancer moved toward me. From the moment they threw me a look from a distance, fear took over my entire body. I looked around for Hamed, as if by finding him, I would rid myself of the fear, but he was nowhere to be found. Maybe he had gone to look after Behi. The dancer looked at me, coquettishly snaking their way to me with a flirtatious smile, turning the eyes of all the men, and perhaps all the women (I could not see the women, because they were sitting on the ground behind the rows of chairs for the men). I just wanted to crawl into a hole and die. The dancer finally reached me, swirling and moving while standing in one spot, and I just looked down, and of all that pleasure, it was only the scent that found its way to me. Did the scent that seductively wafted in the air come from the dancer's belly button, or was it a scent similar to that of my sisters' bodies when they consummated their marriages on their wedding nights? I reached into my pocket for a bill to give to them so they would leave me alone as quickly as possible, though somewhere in my body, I wanted them to stay, to rub their body against mine, but what if Haji saw me in that state? I brought the bill out of my pocket and held it toward the dancer's hand, but they didn't accept it and instead pointed that I should put it inside their blouse myself. I only wanted them to get the money and then to leave as quickly as possible. Their fingertips softly pulled up my chin, offering me a pleasure I had never before experienced. The tip of my nose followed their scent. The pressure of all that weight, as of two

heavy sacks, was unbearable on my head and face. My hand came up
and pushed the bill between the two sacks that were their breasts.

When I looked up again, the dancer was gone, and I could only hear
the sound of the musical instruments, and I could see a group standing
on the rooftop, looking down into the courtyard, and among all the
heads hanging over the edge, only one face stood out, filling the empty
space between me and him, his eyes huge among a shock of hair, and
a smile. I had seen him before, and now he emerged from the fog,
only to stay for a few seconds before once again disappearing into the
fog. Where had I seen him before? I remembered. It was on the banks
of the river. He was cutting the long grass with his sickle, throwing it
to the side and making a pile. I had also sometimes seen him lying on
the grass in his canoe, singing in the wind. I had never stepped forward
to talk to him. Until that night, I didn't even know his name.

"Naji," he introduced himself when I found him on the rooftop.

I realized I had been staring at him in a long silence. I don't know
how long it took me to pull myself together. "And my name is Jamil."

"So your mother knew that you would grow up to be beautiful.
That's why she named you Jamil."

I was shocked. It was the first time anyone had ever talked to me
about my own beauty. I never thought one could call a boy beautiful or
that one could hear it from another boy, let alone from a grass-cutting
helmsman.

"But beauty is for girls, man."

He burst into laughter. I looked down.

"Whose side of the family are you on to receive such red-carpet
treatment, the bride or the groom?"

"How about you?"

He laughed. "If I were someone's family, why would I stand on the
rooftop? With no dinner? We were not even served a glass of sharbat."

"I just came to see the musicians. I'm glad I did. Which one do you
think is the best?"

"I think the three of them should play together to have a good program, but, well, if you only know how to play the violin and have an

okay singing voice, maybe you could pull it off. I don't know. Why do you ask?"

"My grandfather played the violin. I never saw him, because he died young. Just like my mother."

"So you say the violinist is the best of them? Well, of course he is the best."

I didn't say anything.

He continued, "No? Looks like you've liked someone else's performance. Who? Don't you want to tell me?"

I was feeling a trembling at the depth of my heart that I knew I should run away from. I did run away. I went to the groom's uncle and got a large glass of cold sharbat for Naji. He lit up and gulped the drink with pleasure. I told him I had sometimes seen him cutting grass on the riverbank, but because Haji had given me strict orders to never talk with unfamiliar neighborhood kids, I had never talked to him. I told him I would now probably ignore Haji's words and go to the riverbank to see and chat with him. He wanted to know when.

Behi showed up on the rooftop looking for me. Before she could spot me, I managed to say goodbye to Naji and go to my sister, and we went home together. Amid the darkness of the palm grove, Hamed walked in front of the two of us, a flashlight in hand. In that silence was I thinking about the dancer or Naji? Which one did I want to escape from? Which one to find refuge with? I told myself I was thinking about the dancer, who smelled so nice.

"How beautifully the dancer danced."

"Yes, very," Behi agreed.

"Only a woman should be able to dance like that, as skillfully as the dancer did. Wow!" added Hamed.

"The dancer was a man, Jamal. You know that, right? That man danced better than any woman. You yourself saw what he did with his waist," Behi said.

One of my joys was walking along the riverbank during sunset. I walked over the mud platform and looked at the river and at the banks, where sometimes young boys and girls worked. They would cut long grass with their sickles, piling it in one place to then carry to either their own or their master's house. That was where I saw him again. He had pulled his canoe over the mud and was busy cutting some grass that was taller than he was. I stood there. He looked up. When he saw me, he stopped working. For a while we simply looked at each other. I took my shoes off, threw them behind the platform, and jumped down onto the riverbank. He looked at me and laughed. He told me he had been cutting grass since early childhood. He would throw the grass into his canoe and take it to sell to people who needed it for their animals. That day I stayed with him and helped. With one hand, he would hold a bundle of long grass, and with the sickle in his other hand, cut it. The crisp stems of grass would flow down to the ground, where I gathered them, bundled them, and tied them with rope.

"Evening is a time to rest. Why do grasscutters work in the evening when everyone else is going back home from work?" I asked him.

"The best time to cut grass is either at sunrise or sunset. When the sun is up in the sky, you should not bother plants, be it trees or grass. They don't like it at all."

"You mean you, too, think that grass has a life?"

Breathless with fatigue, he laughed. "When did I say it didn't? Of course it does, but that doesn't mean it should not be cut. Right?"

I was staring at the tip of a newly cut stem of grass that I held in my hand. Suddenly I came to myself. It was as if I were just hearing his voice. "No. Then what would we give the cows and sheep to eat to keep them from dying of hunger? Their digestive system is similar to ours, or, even if not similar, it needs food like ours."

He looked at me with confusion and began to work again. The riverbank was covered in soft mud. A bit farther away, a few girls, too, were busy cutting grass among the green hallways. They wore colorful dresses, and, as they worked, they gradually moved closer to us, but I only wanted to look at Naji and listen to him say happy things.

"You did well cutting your hair," I told him.

He removed his foot from the top of the grass bundle he had just tied and, with effort but smiling, straightened his back. "You are only saying this to please me and make me happy, just like my father, right?"

"What does your father say?"

"That a man should always wear his hair short. But I ask him, What if a man wants to keep his hair long? What does it have to do with anyone else? But he only knows to say no. He says a man with long hair is not a man, and when he can't answer my questions, he just says, 'To tell the truth, long hair doesn't suit you at all.'"

"That time I saw you at the wedding, your hair was long, and all I could see were your eyes, because they are huge."

He picked up and carried another bundle of grass to the canoe.

"I want to help you out," I said.

"The way you walk on the riverbank, I can tell you are not used to it, so be careful not to topple over in the mud."

He was right. I was very careful with my steps and kept looking in front of my feet, terrified. My wobbly steps showed that I was not used to walking on the muddy riverbank, but I didn't want to hear this from another person, especially from him. "Are you making fun of me?"

"Making fun? No. Why?"

"Because sometimes the kids in the palm grove say a true man is one who can gingerly climb up the palm tree, cut the date bunch, and throw it down. Then they ask me, 'You don't really know how to climb a palm and cut a date bunch?' They make it sound like they're seriously asking a question about how I can't do such an easy task, something that any man other than me can do."

"But maybe there are things that you can do that none of them can. Are there any?"

"Like what?"

"I know that you can read and write. You can read a letter, write a letter, you can read a book of stories or the newspapers published in town. So which one of them can do any of these things? Right? You tell me, which one of them can, for God's sake?"

"Of the ones I know, none of them."

"Your father was very smart to send you to school, boy. You should be thankful for such a father. Kudos to your dad."

"Well, I am thankful. Yes, I am."

"Do you know how important it is that he simply doesn't let you do any heavy work?"

"At our house, cutting grass is what the workers do."

"I know."

"You do?"

"Well, I heard from Seyyed. One of your father's workers. Seyyed is a good man. A few times I saw him sitting with other men, smoking and talking about his master's house, good things. He said your father is a kind man, treating his laborers especially nice. He said your father wants you, his only son, to become an important civil servant." Naji was standing in the canoe, and I was still outside it. I was in the mud up to my ankles. He kindly looked into my eyes. "You very much look like an important person, an important educated person." We both fell silent for a while. Then he said, "I'm finished with my work here and have to get going to get the grass to someone's animals. What about you?"

"I should go home. They are looking for me by now. But honestly . . ." I didn't finish my sentence. He stared at me to hear the rest of what I wanted to say. His hands grasped the long wooden pole used for propelling the canoe.

"What then? I'm all ears. So go ahead, say it."

I laughed. "No, you know, I wish we could sit in the boat and do a short ride right along the banks, nowhere too far, right around here."

"So what are you waiting for? Hop in."

"But my feet . . . I'll make your boat dirty."

"But mud is not dirty. It's just wet soil. Your feet are not worse than mine, for sure. Now, hurry up and hop in, the sun has almost set." Listening to his kind voice was a new experience in my life. I had never met a boy my own age with such a masculine, graceful, and kind tone. He looked at me as if he had known me for years. I smiled, bent down, held the edge of the canoe, and pulled it toward me, but it suddenly slipped out of my hand, rocking away and almost tipping over with its only passenger, him, standing there, pole in hand. Frightened, I stepped back, covering my face with my hands to block out the fall I had caused. Peeking through my two fingers with one eye, I saw him skillfully and swiftly anchoring the canoe with the tip of the pole, driving it into the muddy riverbank, juggling to keep the canoe from capsizing. It was back in its place. He was standing in the boat, smiling. I moved my hands away from my face. "I'm sorry."

"Back when I didn't know how to jump into the canoe, I would make the same mess. So did this upset you? Were you scared?" He added, "Give me your hand. Now come." I put my hand in his hand. What was this feeling? A fire started burning in his body, its flame blazing its way through his hand to mine, finding its way through my veins to my heart. "Sit tight and we can leave." I sat down on the wooden rod that spanned the middle of the canoe, holding on to it with both hands.

"Are you ready?"

"I am."

Still standing, he started steering the canoe. He dug the long wooden pole into the mud and pushed the canoe away from the riverbank. He kept pulling the pole out of the water and pushing it into the mud at the bottom of the river in another spot farther away. Thus the canoe moved across the water.

Ahead of us, where the sky and the water merged into one, the sun, like a large yellow ball, kept sliding down to hide beneath the water-line. I wished for our canoe to keep moving until the sun had gone down completely. I thought what a miracle it was, the tide, the rising of the water level every morning with the sunrise and lowering every evening with the sunset, leaving the river empty.

"Okay, we have to go back now."

"Go back where?"

"Where we were, where you got in. I have to go that way, and your house, too, is that way. Plus your shoes are there too."

"Oh, I had forgotten."

"Hold on, 'cause we have to turn."

He turned the canoe around, steering it in the direction we had come. We saw the girls on our way. Heading home, they carried the bundles of grass on their heads. Their faces could not be seen. Even the swell of their breasts was hidden under the heap of grass. Naji steered the canoe to the foot of the cement staircase on the riverbank. "Do you remember where you left your shoes?"

"There, behind the docks, under the lotus tree."

"You have to wash your feet before you put your shoes back on."

"I'll walk home barefoot; it would be easier to just wash them there."

"What if your father or someone asks where you were? What then?"

"Well, I'll tell them I was here with you."

"But you should not. Telling the truth is not always the right or best thing to do."

From those early moments, I realized that I had to trust him and his insights. He seemed way more mature and aware than I was.

"So you are saying . . ."

He cut me off. "I say first get out of the canoe and go stand there on the cement platform, that big one." Cautiously, holding on to his hand, I stepped out of the canoe and stood up on the large cement surface he had indicated. "Now I pour water on your feet, and you wash the mud off them and clean up." He took a plastic jug from the canoe floor, filled it up with river water, and slowly emptied it over my feet. My pants were folded up to my knees. "Don't bend. You just stand there, and I wash your feet and clean up the mud."

I wanted to say no, wanted to say I was able to wash my own feet, but the way he bent over and began washing my feet, the feeling of that pleasure in my body and soul made me surrender to his hands moving ecstatically over the nakedness of my feet.

"Was the young woman who was with you your fiancée?"

Why did he ask that? Was he teasing me, or was he trying to get to something more important?

"She was my sister. Behi. Hamed's wife."

"Okay. Hamed is your brother-in-law. I see."

"First he was my cousin. Then he became my father's worker. Now he is my brother-in-law. My father loves him and tells us to learn from him how to make money from nothing, literally nothing. So you, too, know Hamed. How?"

Through the long grass, a pair of large eyes cast their shadow over us. Naji was almost done washing my feet, still touching them. There was still a bunch of uncut grass growing close by, and the girl's eyes stared at us through those stems. "What are the two of you doing with each other?" She didn't wait for an answer, instead started laughing in a pretentiously loud way, then raised a bundle of grass to her head and walked away. The sound of her laughter continued to reverberate.

"Who was she?"

"Sadreh."

"That's her name?"

"Yep."

"That's the name of one of my aunts who thinks she has a beautiful name."

"This girl, she herself is as beautiful as her name."

"Why did she laugh at us?"

"Well, her heart is not as beautiful as her appearance. No, it's not."

"Her heart?"

He pulled a plastic bag out of the canoe, inside it a clean, dry red-and-white keffiyeh. "Take this and dry your feet before wearing your shoes."

"No. This cloth is more useful to you. You are in the water and have to deal with it much more than me."

"You should go up the bank by carefully climbing these cement blocks, otherwise your feet will get muddy again." He treated me as if I were a city child who had never seen a village, but to tell the truth, I didn't mind it at all, because he was doing it with such purity and kindness. "Be careful, since these blocks are not all steady; some are very loose, and if you don't step on them properly, you might suddenly find yourself taking a bad fall. So watch out when you are going up."

I got ready to leave. "So when can we see each other again?"

"The day you come back to give me the cloth, of course." He laughed.

"You mean this will stay with me until then?"

"Until then!" He looked at me with a smile. "So you really want the two of us to meet again?"

"Yes, please."

"Please?"

I felt awkward. "I mean, I have to return this keffiyeh."

He put his hand on my shoulder. "Do you know where the oldest white mulberry tree of the neighborhood is?"

"Yep. By Captain's Daughter Creek."

"That's it! Right there."

Captain's Daughter was the name of a large fish that lived only in the sea and never came to the river, let alone the creek. It was slim and long, sometimes as long as a person was tall. The fish had elongated black eyes, like a girl's beautiful eyes, and that was why the fishmongers called it the Captain's Daughter. True or false, they said one night many years ago (what year, exactly, nobody recalled), a fishmonger had caught a large Captain's Daughter in a creek in our neighborhood, and after that, the creek was named Captain's Daughter.

"So tell me first what is happening there."

"The day after tomorrow, I'm going there at sunrise to cut grass. Some of the grass at the riverbank there is mine, and it will be quite high in two days, ready to cut, I think." He went silent. I continued to look at him, waiting. Finally, he continued, "At that time of the day, there is no one there to see us."

"But that early in the morning I have to find a good excuse to leave the house, a strong excuse."

"Excuse?"

"What if Haji asks where I'm going that early? What should I tell him? That I'm going to pick mulberries?"

He burst out laughing. "That early in the morning?"

I laughed out loud too. "What if I tell him I had a dream of a holy seyyed coming to me and telling me that if I go to the mulberry tree early Friday morning, I'll have a bright future and will surely be happy."

He laughed even louder. "That's good thinking. I can't think of a better excuse. So yeah, just tell him that."

We looked into each other's eyes and laughed. Then we stopped laughing. It had been so long since I had laughed like that. With anyone. "Something in my heart tells me we have to be careful," I said. "Very careful."

"Yeah. So make sure you don't get yourself into trouble."

"And you."

He remained silent. He threw a terrified look around but tried to hide his fear from me. "Now go, go, and see how things work out between now and the day after tomorrow. And if you can't make it, don't worry, okay? We will see each other again someday."

"Why don't you come with me to the end of the platform so that I can give you back your cloth after I have dried my feet, in case you needed it . . . ?"

"It's enough that Sadreh saw us together, and now who knows what she is going to tell others and how she is going to tell it?"

"So you are afraid that others will see us together?"

"I'm not a coward, Jamil. Well, maybe I am, but I tell myself—well, you go now, please, and we'll see what happens next."

It was as if he knew what would happen next, that nothing good would come of it, but he had already become all that I could think of. He didn't ever get the scarf back from me. I would spread it over my pillow at night and rest my head on it. I would wake up dreaming of him and fall asleep thinking of him. Later he said he had the same feelings for me. It didn't matter whether it was the truth or a lie; what mattered was that he spoke it, he put it into words, and that was enough for me, and it was enough that I had discovered in myself the ability to laugh, to laugh from the bottom of my heart.

I saw him again, on other days. In his canoe, we went to the middle of the river, where no eyes could see us from the banks. He was more afraid than I was that we would be seen together. "Well, because whatever happens, no one is going to bother you, because you are Haji's son and have everyone's respect, but what about me? A poor young grass-cutter who is at the mercy of anyone and everyone, pathetic, because he has no one in this world."

I never liked it when he put himself down. "What about your father? Doesn't he love you?"

"He loves me when I bring him money." He sighed. "But if one night I didn't take home some money, do you think he would even want me to be alive? Or he would even put up with me being in his run-down house?"

I thought he was too concerned, but later I found out that he was right. We had slipped into a dangerous game.

On that hot afternoon, every member of our household knew that Father wanted to talk to me about an important issue. And on the rooftop, of all places. Hamed and Behi, too, were at our house. Behi was preparing the rooftop for us, the men. Before taking the carpets to spread upstairs, she swept and watered the floor. She then watered the short walls around the edge of the roof so they gave off a nice breeze, cooling down the area inside the mosquito net where we men, her father, her husband, and me, her brother, were to sit and chat. We three were still downstairs. Haji and Hamed were in the guest room. Hamed was the best person to get Haji's opium setup ready. But Hamed was not at our house all the time. It was Seyyed, the old man who did gardening and watered the vegetable lots, who was in charge of the everyday setup. He grew all kinds of edible vegetables, but his other important job was to set up Haji's opium paraphernalia twice every day, after breakfast in the morning and before prayer in the evening. Then he himself would smoke a few puffs before collecting everything. But when Hamed came over, Seyyed looked after other things. Hamed was in charge of all opium-related tasks for the men of the family. He was the only one who knew where to buy it. And that was one reason Haji was always in need of Hamed. As Hamed himself said, he even had some opium-related accounts with the police. When it was just Hamed and Haji, Seyyed didn't go to the guest room. He either attended to the garden or, like now, wandered aimlessly around the courtyard until Bibi Saleem asked him to go bring a carpet and spread it at the corner of the court-yard so that she could sit on it and witness the event.

I was sitting under the jasmine tree, waiting calmly. Saeedeh Khanoom (Haji's younger wife) was moving around the bread oven. In another corner of the courtyard, one of my sisters was throwing breadcrumbs for the chickens and ducks, and they had gathered around her, making a lot of noise. One of my nephews, a boy of four or five, stood by the oven stark naked with a swollen belly, waving a big matchbox, enjoying the sound of the matchsticks moving.

A black bundle on the carpet, Bibi Saleem sat there and turned the green prayer beads between her fingers. From time to time, she glanced at me, pretending she didn't know anything, even though everyone knew that she was aware of everything, small or big, that happened in the house. Seyyed handed Bibi a clay cup full of water, and she swallowed it, the water trickling down the two sides of her mouth. Seyyed brought a towel and spread it over Bibi's skirt. Whenever a wind started blowing, like a group of white butterflies, jasmine flowers fluttered off the tree's branches, but before they flew away, they, united and mingling, flew downward, landing on my head and face.

Coming down from the rooftop, Behi glanced at the door of the guest room, which was still shut. "What does Haji want with you that he needs to speak with you only on the rooftop?" she asked.

I looked up from the stool I was sitting on. "I don't know. No one has told me anything yet, but I know that you know."

Behi laughed at me with tenderness and stepped closer, so close that I could smell her scent. She brought her hand toward my ear, and her fingers picked something off my earlobe. "Like an earring, it has gone and sat down right there, hanging off your ear." She put the tiny flower with its white petals on my palm.

"It would be nicer if there were two of them."

"Somebody come here and collect these matchsticks!" Bibi shouted.

The naked boy had spread the pile of matchsticks all around. Behi ran over, took the box from the boy, and began collecting the sticks from the ground. And then Bibi produced a satisfied look that she had snatched Behi away from me.

The time for smoking opium ended, and then it was time for the hookah. Haji and I sat inside the mosquito net, and Hamed went to get the hookah.

"So . . . who is this Naji?"

"A hardworking boy. He cuts grass wherever he finds some and takes it to those who have animals. To make money for himself and his old father, who cannot work."

"Of course, we do have animals, and thank God we have our own grass cutter to bring it to us."

"He is not supposed to cut grass for us."

"So what is he supposed to do? To humiliate you in front of others? What would people say seeing Haji's educated son in the boat of a happy-go-lucky idler?"

Hamed entered the mosquito net holding the hookah, having heard all our conversation. Or had he? "I wish this was the only problem, Haji. This idler has other worse issues, too, that I'm ashamed even to say; I'll just say that it is not advisable at all for Jamil to hang out with him again." I knew what he meant by those worse things about Naji. The day before, Hamed had tried to tell me something about Naji's relationship with the fishermen. He had used the word *whoring*, but he didn't repeat that in front of Haji.

"Now, how long have you been hanging out with him?"

"Not long."

"It has not yet been five weeks, of course." Hamed smirked, then threw me a hideous glance. "Has it?"

"Maybe."

Hamed was prepping the hookah for Haji by taking a few hard pulls. The naked doll floating in the hookah water started to dance, mingling with and moving up and down through the bubbles that roared and rolled inside the glass. The red doll had its own orderly movement among all that hustle. With every pull at the hookah, she moved among the bubbles, and, as she swirled, she rose to the top of the water before coming down with the same orderly movement. Was I watching this scene because someone was dancing in it? Or had I become an observer to distract my mind from what was going on around me? I knew that I could not easily cut off my relationship with Naji, even though I had to. Despite all its pleasures, I was carrying a hard ominous burden on my shoulders, and I had to escape that. I knew the relationship would not end well, but my pride didn't allow me to bow down to Hamed and Haji's wishes. I wanted to be the one in charge of my destiny. "It's not like I want to constantly see him. I know he doesn't want that either. I just felt he was a good boy, and now I am certain that he is. I haven't seen anything bad in him, and whenever I happen to be by the river and see him, I just say hi, because we are not enemies, we are friends."

"But Haji wants you to take another step farther away from him." Hamed smirked.

For a while, we all were silent. The only sound was the bubbling of the hookah. The swirling smoke stayed in the mosquito net for a bit, thickened, then gently streamed out through the little holes of the white mesh.

"Exactly what he said. We want you to take a step farther," Haji said. I stared at him, waiting for him to say what he meant by *a step farther*. "You are a people person, a sensible boy who wants to help the poor, but you don't know what goes on in their hearts, how they betray even themselves, let alone those who help them, a simple kindhearted person like you."

"Why would he betray me? We just have a simple friendship. Really, how would he betray me?" I asked.

"Don't repeat what you just said in front of strangers, or the kingdom that Haji has built for him and his family will crumble down and vanish," Hamed said.

"Why? What? What did I say?"

Hamed used a towel to clean and dry the mouthpiece of the hookah, and, before extending it toward Haji, he said, "Being friends, the very fact that you two are friends!" I wanted to chime in, but he didn't let me, adding, "If he didn't hang around with the fishermen, then maybe . . . but to hang around the fishermen . . ."

"Which fishermen? What kingdom are you talking about?" I asked.

Haji took the hookah hose from Hamed's hand and asked, "Didn't you say he is an idler? That he cuts grass for the elders? What does he have to do with the fishermen?" He put the mouthpiece to his mouth and took a puff, and once again I got absorbed in watching the dance of the doll inside the glass base.

"God only knows these fishermen are the worst people on the earth. Or perhaps they just have a bad reputation. Since they are all men, they love to talk dirty. They yap on about anything and everything. God forbid if you suddenly find yourself among them."

"Naji has mingled with the fishermen? How do you know?" I asked.

Seeing how Hamed paused and smiled, Haji turned toward me. "Hamed is everywhere. He knows everything about everyone. It's his job to know anything and everything."

"I know," I said.

Once again there was silence for a while, as Haji and I waited for Hamed to tell the rest of the story. But he didn't seem eager to speak, pretending he was worried about the hookah's fire, fiddling with it and blowing gently to set the coal alight again. Haji looked bored and was on the verge of getting angry when Hamed finally started talking again. "It's shameful for a man to talk about these things, otherwise I myself would talk about them, Haji."

"It is shameful to talk about it, but it's not shameful to actually do it, it seems," I said.

"Wait, do you know what Hamed wants to talk about?" Haji asked me.

"Well, no, not exactly."

Haji looked at Hamed and then at me. "No, my son. It's best that you are not seen with him ever again, not even once."

"I'm just going to see him quickly one more time on the riverbank to ask him whether there is any truth to this talk of him being a whore of the fishermen or whether people are making things up," I said, looking at my watch and pretending that I had to leave soon.

Hamed smiled. "An educated person uttering such words in front of Haji? Wow!"

But Haji didn't buy his smooth talk and asked, "Why would people make up these stories? Why the animosity? No one would make such things up about someone unless they have seen something. Here is one witness, sitting in the flesh in front of you. You yourself can ask him."

I couldn't tell him directly that I didn't trust Hamed, so I said instead, "Well, but some people are hostile to some youth, Haji. These days, being young is a dangerous thing."

"Why?"

"No good reason. And it's not just in the village; it's the same in town too. Right now, there are old teachers in our high school who don't like the younger teachers."

Hamed laughed as if I had said something funny and added, "No. Actually, everyone loves him, old and young. No one says he is a bad boy. He is a good boy, but, well, because his family is poor, he is forced to work at night too. To tell the truth, he used to work at night, and in the past, he made good money doing that for a short while."

Haji turned completely toward Hamed and asked, "Good money?"

Hamed shifted from one knee to the other, trying to get himself together. He forcefully drew his fingers around the contour of his lips to dry them. Haji was waiting anxiously. Finally, Hamed said, "Well, the thing is, Haji, the boy is handsome, and he has a young perfect body, honestly, so much so that he can just make some money off these hillbilly fishmongers." He emphasized with a look at me, "I mean he could in the past." Then he turned to Haji again. "He is a smooth talker too, has a tongue this long." And he laughed.

"What's the use of us sitting here talking about such people?" Haji asked. To reach me, he then bent a bit and held my hand in his. It was as cold as a corpse's. "And Jamil already said that he won't see the boy anymore, no matter what the conditions."

"When did I say that?"

"No, I didn't *promise* Haji that I wouldn't see you anymore."

For our last meeting, Naji took me in his canoe to a faraway village, a village I had not seen before. It had short entangled palm trees. It was greener than our village.

"What did you say, then?"

"I *said* I wouldn't see you anymore."

"But you are seeing me now."

I looked around with fear. "Are you sure no one could see us here?"

"Don't worry. Ghandi is around, and he won't let anything bad happen."

We were inside Ghandi's shed. He was the guardian of a palm grove and looked after some water pumps. His shed was large and open. Sitting in it, you could see outside through the dry branches that made up the walls of the room. The shed was at a corner of the palm grove, and there was a fence built around it, a barrier with a small gate that meant strangers could not enter it; even though the gate would open easily, everything around the shed indicated that it was a private space. Ghandi wandered around with his goats. So Naji said we could sit there in his shed with ease of mind, that it was a safe space for our meeting. Sometimes we would see Ghandi moving from one place to another.

He was Naji's friend. No one knew how old he was. He had never grown facial hair, and he had a small body. The grove's owner fed him, but he provided his own milk. He liked goat milk and kept two goats that roamed around there. Naji brought the goats grass, and that was the reason behind his and Ghandi's friendship.

Naji sat behind me. I was facing the wall of the shed and was keeping an eye out, looking through the dry branches. I hadn't yet gotten used to that space and was still worried. Then I felt the mist of his breath over the skin on the back of my neck.

I wanted to ask, "Why were you a whore for the fishermen?"

"I think our biggest problem here is Hamed, not Haji," he said.

"Because he knows things he should not know?"

"Because I can't curse him strongly enough in front of you."

"You can, as much as you want, but that doesn't change anything."

"It does."

His hand rested quickly on mine, which lay on the straw mat covering the shed floor, supporting the weight of my body.

"Why does he want us to stay away from each other? What's in it for him?" he whined.

I looked at our hands and pulled mine away. "Why should we see each other? What good does it do us?"

I was staring into his eyes, which seemed to reflect a sudden understanding of this new question. What good? Had I really decided not to come see him again? Had I come today to just say that?

"We wanted to be together to start a band. I know someone who can build us a rubab," Naji said.

"But I don't know how to play anything or even make an instrument. And I'm not interested in learning either."

"But you said you wanted to be part of a band."

"Not for the music and the singing."

"Then for what?"

As hard as I tried, I couldn't bring myself to tell him I loved dancing. I didn't know what he would think of me if he heard that; I was afraid that this would affect our relationship. I remained silent. Through the branches, I saw Ghandi's black goat jumping to the other side of a stream. Naji was waiting for me to speak, looking at me with the most beautiful smile in the world. I remained silent. What could I say? He put his index finger on the bulge of my aching Adam's apple.

"What are you staring at like this?"

"At Ghandi's goat."

He took a look through the gaps in the shed wall. "If I ever have a proper house, I'll definitely keep goats too, one male and one female, so that the poor animals don't feel lonely."

"You'll soon have your own house and buy your goats too. You are a hardworking boy, you have everything, and soon your father will get a wife for you to have a home with and be happy with."

Outside, I could see the stream. It wasn't big, but there was abundant water in it, rising and falling. "Instead of talking about going to the stream and jumping in the water," he said, "here you are talking about me getting married. Instead of the two of us getting up and going in the water."

"Going in the water? You and I?" I suddenly got up. "No, seriously, I have to go now." But this was exactly the opposite of what I was feeling inside. My heart wished I would stay. We would stay. Stay to do what? To keep each other company? I had never felt so close to anyone just chatting with them.

Sitting there, he looked up. I could see fear and worry in his face. He was convinced that I was leaving; he looked like someone who had been thrown in the water and was drowning, kicking with his arms and legs to save himself from that perilous situation. "So you believe all that they've said, don't you?"

"I have to go now. That's all I can say. Forgive me."

He got up, too, and stood in front of me. Eye to eye. Locking his gaze with mine. "You aren't leaving because you believe what he said?"

"It doesn't make any difference."

"What doesn't make a difference?"

"Where you go at night and what you do and with whom you do it."

"I'll tell you everything about the fishermen. Not now, but soon. It's from many years ago."

Irked, I said, "So Hamed is telling the truth."

"I'll tell you everything. I know that they've told you too much, both truth and lies. But give me some time, and I'll tell it all myself. It'll be better that way, won't it?"

I looked at him. He didn't know what to do or say. I wanted to be with him, to talk of nothing but the two of us. He put his hand on my shoulder. I lowered my head and put my face on his warm hand. He said, "We are two adult men, and it's not right for others to decide who we can hang out with and who we can't."

"But your situation is different from mine."

"Because you are a rich kid, and I'm not?"

"It's not about wealth and poverty. It's about my father and his excessive expectations of me. I understand why he is like that, I know what he wants of me, but I can't understand what Hamed's motive is. Why doesn't he want to see us together? Perhaps he has some reason."

"I know that money is the most important thing in the world for Hamed; he would even kill for money. I'm sorry to say this about your brother-in-law, but, well."

"I know that myself."

"Maybe he thinks our friendship might harm him financially in some way."

"Maybe you are right. Hamed is getting closer to my father. Perhaps he can gradually start managing his finances. And he doesn't want anyone else to get involved in that area." And finally, I broke down crying. "But we don't want their money, do we?"

There was no way to convince Haji and Hamed. They insisted on separating Naji and me, but we didn't want to be separated. I did actually try to not go see him again, but whenever I looked at the scarf he had given me, I would lose myself like an addict, like a person sleepwalking, headed toward the riverbank. He would take me in the canoe past the white mulberry tree. Our destination was Ghandi's shed. I gave Ghandi a box of chocolates, which made him happy. "You two sit and study. I'm going to be around busying myself with my chocolates." He laughed. Naji told him I was teaching him how to read and write. "May God bless you. Do you know how virtuous this work is?" he said, though you could tell by his kind demeanor that he was aware of our relationship. But why was he kind to us? We weren't sure. Maybe he, too, had fallen for someone in his youth. Maybe our trysts brought to life some good old memories for him. He didn't say anything to us about it; he simply smiled. "Feel at home, and get to your studies peacefully." And today, how joyous it is to write about those days, days during which we studied without the need for pen and paper, when it was all about wanting to be together, to chat and laugh and sometimes touch each other. All that pleasure meant that we wanted to be together, that we didn't take the risk of our trysts seriously, until the day that Behi told me that she had been hanging around outside the room during one of Haji and Hamed's opium sessions and had overheard them talking about killing Naji.

Knowing Hamed's love of killing animals, I had always guessed that it would be easy for him to kill humans too. I had seen how ruthlessly he aimed his air gun at sparrows and rock pigeons, or the day when, to show off in front of Haji, he killed a sickly sheep that had collapsed to the ground, quickly and skillfully cutting the animal's throat from ear to ear. So when I heard this news from Behi, all these images rushed to my mind. I saw Hamed, with his coarse hands, holding Naji against the jasmine bush and cutting his throat with a big knife. I screamed. Where was I? Behi was terrified. The way she took a step back, I imagine my face looked horrifying, impelling her to put some distance between herself and me. She then turned her back and ran away.

I said, "This is the last time, our last meeting, and from now on, I have to prepare myself for the coming school year. I have to finish high school, and if I graduate with good grades, I might be able to talk Haji into letting me go to the university." I was certain that Haji would never agree. No, there was no way. He wanted me to be, like a hired secretary, by his side at all times.

Naji's fingers touched my toes, giving the sensitive skin between them a newly found pleasure. "What long toes! Don't you wish to paint your toenails? A beautiful color, like blue?" He laughed and so did I.

I said, "But it's forbidden to smoke a cigarette in Ghandi's shed." So he put the pack of cigarettes back in his pocket. I cried. I believed that this was our last meeting. "I have good memories of this shed."

"Yep. The lump on my waist underwent surgery right here. I was freed from its pain and suffering, thank God. I mean, I have you to thank." Bringing up that memory made me laugh, the memory of the lump I had found on his waist. Several times, I had noticed him scratching his back and waist, so I asked what was going on, and he said nothing, feeling ashamed to say that for a while an awkward lump the size of a grape had been hanging from his lower back. Finally, one day in Ghandi's shed, I asked him to show me his naked back so that I could see why he was scratching it. He kept saying it was nothing, but, certain that something was wrong, I insisted until he showed me his naked back. The lump was hanging there, suspended from his back by a thin thread of skin. Naji explained that the lump had been there for a long time and that sometimes it was painful, especially at night when he would roll over onto it while asleep.

I immediately realized that the only way to remove it from his body would be to cut it off, but I didn't tell him anything about my plans, because I saw how afraid he was. So the next time we returned to the shed, three days later, I brought with me a razor blade, alcohol, and cotton pads. I told him I wanted to put some alcohol on the lump with the hope that it would fall off itself, but at an opportune moment, I cut the thin thread of skin with the blade, and he screamed, and Ghandi rushed to the shed, worried, and I explained what was going on. I rubbed alcohol on the tiny scar, holding the wet cotton pad there for a while. Naji then put the lump in a matchbox to show it to his father.

I was still laughing. "Now it's really time to go. Let me go."

Suddenly we heard Ghandi's voice, talking to someone, seemingly a stranger, not too far away from the shed. "Hey, salam aleikom, brother. Are you looking for something?"

"I'm looking for my brother-in-law. I want to go look in that shed."

It was Hamed. His voice was getting closer, right around the corner of the fence, or perhaps outside the door of the shed. I got so frightened that I didn't know what to say, what to do.

"For now, get out of here, brother," Ghandi said. "Get out, and we can chat about what you are looking for."

"Out of where?"

"This is private property. My boss is very sensitive about strangers. He has ordered me not to let anyone come onto this property. You know that if the owner is not happy with you being here, well, it is haram to be here without his permission, unless you are not Muslim. But mashallah, I can tell from your forehead that you are a devout Muslim."

We could not see them. They were hidden from us behind a big bush. I don't know what Hamed did, but Ghandi whistled and called his dog over. We heard the dog running, getting close, and starting to bark.

"Okay, okay, okay," Hamed retorted.

His voice moved away. I could now see him standing outside of the fence through the spaces in the wall of the shed. He was smoking and looking around curiously. Maybe he was certain that Naji and I were there.

Ghandi calmed the dog down. "Okay, brother. Who or what did you say you were looking for here?"

Hamed talked loudly once again. It was clear that he wanted us to hear him too. "You said I should rest assured that no one is hiding in your shed?"

"Yes, brother. Rest assured."

"I know your boss, Kamal Baghdadi, a devout man who is originally from Baghdad, but he has lived here for so long that he should be called Kamal Irani. He won't be happy if he finds out that you are doing wrong things here. He might even sack you if he learns that you shelter these haram-doers."

"There are no haram-doers or haram-eaters around here, brother. Ghandi is always alert and ready here with his animals."

"Okay, I believe you, but if it turns out otherwise, it will be very bad for you."

"I know, brother. May God grant you strength."

"Okay, then. May God grant you strength as well. So I should go look elsewhere for my missing person."

"May God be always by your side, brother."

Then a long silence. Frightened, I had moved away from Naji, but he still held my hand in his. "Your hand is trembling." He looked closely at each and every one of my fingers, as if he were looking for a mole or something.

"Well, we're exposed now. We can't come here again. That's a good thing, actually. Now I'm sure that this was our last meeting. Whether we want it or not, everything is over."

But everything was not over. Haji was waiting for me at the palm grove by the house. Seyyed was busy in the vegetable garden. The afternoon was giving way to evening. Hamed was up in a palm tree, cutting the dried branches and throwing them down to the ground. With a book under my arm, I said hi to Haji and planned to keep walking as fast as possible to my room. I knew that if Haji asked about Naji, I would tell him with conviction that I wouldn't be seeing Naji again and that I had nothing to do with him anymore. Haji didn't respond to my greeting; instead he asked me to come close and stand in front of him. Suddenly he raised his arm and slapped me hard in the face. The sound of the slap was the only thing you could hear. Everything went black in front of my eyes. It was as if I had turned blind. I blinked. He was still standing in front of me but inside a trembling halo that constantly shape-shifted his face, a face that had nothing in common with that of a human.

Seyyed and Hamed didn't stop working; they didn't even throw us a glance; it was as if nothing had happened right next to them. A wind of pain was howling in my head. I could see my temple falling into pieces before my eyes. I wanted to run, but I had lost my legs. I wanted to scream, but my voice had left my body. Everyone and everything, even my own body parts, had forgotten me. There was no one to help me. I had nothing to hang onto. Finally, I found my legs again. Haji's savage look was still directed at me. I ran to my room with a face drenched in tears, locking the door from inside. When night fell, one of my sisters brought me a tray of food. I sent it back without touching it. I stayed awake all night long and thought about what to do. I didn't want to stay in that house anymore. But before leaving, I had to kill Hamed. He was the reason behind all my misfortunes. In my dreams, I saw that I had killed him. I saw that I was drowning him in the river, and he kept begging me, but I had made up my mind. The humiliation of enduring that slap in the face had turned into a ball of fire, turning inside me and burning. I owed the courage of thinking about killing Hamed to Ghandi; the way he had talked to Hamed, showing he was not afraid of him, had painted a weaker picture in my mind of Hamed, whom I knew now I could easily kill.

The following day, with the excuse of having to put drops in Naneh Reyhan's eyes, I went to her house. I lay my head on her lap and cried. She advised me to be careful and not to do anything that would end up hurting me. As if she sensed my plan to kill someone, she kept warning me about prison. She said if I killed anyone, I would have to spend my whole life in prison, and I would have no share of life except prison and an envy of freedom. I could even be hanged. The possibility of being hanged terrified me. Its horror was more agonizing than that of any other kind of death. It would be better to stand before a firing squad, to have blood suddenly sprout out of my body and to die immediately. But to be hanged! To have the noose around my neck and then have the stool kicked from under my feet. And that would only be the beginning. They say the dying happens in just one moment, because when your feet start dangling, the veins in your neck are torn, and then death comes, and that is that. But in my nightmares, I experienced a long lapse between the kicking out of the stool and the tearing apart of the veins in my neck. Sinking into my pain and regret, every scene from my bygone life began to roll once again before my eyes. Like the time I was a kid drowning in the river, with no one around to reach out to for help. I had imagined I would be able to swim to the deeper parts. I had followed the older boys, swimming behind them. They were approaching the middle of the river, and I was running out of breath, but I didn't want to be inferior to them. They turned back, and I continued to swim until I made it to the very spot they had swum to. On my way back, I came upon a heavy barrier: my own fatigue. I was out of breath. I began to sink down into the water, and they could not see me. They continued to swim to the riverbank. I was drowning, I mean dying, and watching my own death. First I saw all the images from my present life. Then I saw images from the future. My naked dead body being washed on the mortuary's cement slab, the stretcher carrying my body held over people's shoulders while they recited Allahu Akbar and then let me go into that cold hole all alone.

No, I didn't want to involuntarily fall into those nightmares once again. So what did I have to do? Run away? To where? For now, I didn't have anywhere to go but my small room. A room that was both my prison and the best place in my world. I sat down by my small bookshelf. Most of the books there were bought or acquired upon Mr. Heidari's orders. He mostly liked to talk about contemporary literature. The latest book he had asked us to read was *The Blind Owl*. I was hoping he would be our literature teacher the following year too, so that I could ask him about the secrets of *The Blind Owl*, such as the meaning of the sentence the book opens with: "In life there are wounds that, like leprosy, silently scrape at and consume the soul, in solitude— This agony can not be revealed to anyone . . ."

Was he describing the very pain I was feeling but could not speak of with anyone? Even if someone was eager to listen to them, what could I have said? Where should I have started? Even if I spoke, would the listener understand what I was saying? Why should I even describe my pains to others? Everyone around me in that house lived atop a layer of lies and hypocrisy. Every one of them wore the masks of religion and prejudice, knowing nothing of either, knowing nothing but violence. Every time a sheep was to be sacrificed in the garden, everyone, young and old alike, would gather around and, with the excuse of gaining a spiritual reward, stare at the butchers' hands tackling the poor animal to the ground and cutting its head off. The pleasure of watching blood spurt out. When I was a kid, Haji forced me to watch those scenes, which became fodder for my nightmares for many years to come. Did I have to live in that house forever? If *The Blind Owl*'s painter from Rey had escaped his house, that environment, in his youth and gone to a place where people were even a bit nicer, would he still have lived the same life? Who pushed him to become a pimp? Who turned him into a hoarding old man? People. But he tolerated the people, because he had found not a cure but a balm for his pain, so he spread his bed of calm under the cozy shadow of that pain reliever and was happy with it. But I wanted to find refuge in the sun, in the hottest place in the universe. Perhaps that was why I got burned without even having set out on that journey. I had only walked toward love.

Later, Amrollah Khan would say, "Whenever you two walk into this room, it is as if two love birds have entered. But you are not birds, you are boys of love," and he would laugh. I would have preferred that he call us boys of the sun.

How many days had it been since I had locked myself in my room? Naneh Reyhan would come to my room. I would put the eye drops in for her. Behi, too, would come. They were my only friends, though they said that was not the case, that Haji, too, loved me a lot, and it was out of too much affection for me that he behaved the way he did. Behi said that her mother, my stepmother, loved me too. She pitied me, was worried that something bad would happen to me. "My mother had a bad dream. Pray to God that it doesn't come true. She dreamed that a group of stranger men were torturing you." Behi cried, "But why would they want to torture you, Kaka Jamil?"

I said, "Promise me in front of Naneh Reyhan that if I were ever not around, you would help her with her eye drops every few nights."

Naneh Reyhan laughed loudly. "But people have their own lives. They can't come here all the time to put eye drops in my eyes."

Why did I think so much about Naneh Reyhan's eyes? Was I looking for an excuse to stay? Part of me wanted me to leave, to escape toward freedom and build a life of my own. The other part of me was afraid and wanted to stay alone in my comfortable room, put up with these living conditions, and try to make things tolerable for myself there. Tolerable? No, that wouldn't do. What tasted sweet to me, to my family members tasted bitter, and vice versa. No, I had nothing in common with this tribe, and I was sure that, one day soon, Haji would realize that and do anything to get rid of me. I was constantly occupied with these thoughts. I rested my forehead on the edge of the table. Someone seemed to be knocking at the door. I knew it was one of my

42

sisters. Perhaps she had brought me something to eat. When I opened the door, one of my sisters was indeed standing there, but she didn't have anything in her hands.

"My mother said Haji has asked that you come to the guest living room. He has something important to tell you."

"Who told you to come tell me this?" I asked.

"I told you, my mother."

"Where is Hamed?"

"In the living room with Haji."

"Go tell them that Jamil didn't believe you and that I said if it is true, Hamed should bring Haji's message to me if he wants me to believe it and come. Do you get what I'm saying?"

My sister stared into the void. "Believe?" It was as if she were staring at the blackboard on the wall, calculating something in her head. "Oh, okay." She unwrapped her dark green scarf and wrapped it around her head once again (this time tighter) and left. The best murder weapon I had in my room was a pair of scissors. I buttoned up my shirt. I said farewell to myself in the standing mirror. It might be the last time the two of us saw each other. Finally, there was a hint of a mustache on my upper lip. The black line there was now darker than ever before. The scissors trembled in my hand. What did it signify? Only the scissors trembled in my hand. Naneh Reyhan always said there is a reason behind anything that happens in the world. Why didn't Hamed want Naji and me to be friends? Why did Haji slap me in the face? There wasn't any reason I understood behind anything they did. I could be a good son for Haji and a good brother-in-law for Hamed, who was now gently knocking on my door. "Come in." He pushed the door open and slipped inside. When he saw the scissors in my hand, he stepped back toward the door once again. "Haji has something important to tell you, Kaka Jamil. Thank God that it's a good thing. Just come to the guest living room so he can tell you. I'm going to wait for you in the yard so you can splash some water on your face. You look pale."

I told myself I'd kill him the next time. For now, I was tempted to know what was so urgent with Haji. Then I found out that it was nothing, or worse, something stupid. He told me he was going to get me a wife. The fifteen-year-old daughter of Haj Ghiyas, who had several local brickmaking kilns.

"I don't want a wife now, Haji."

"Why not? Is there something wrong with you?"

"Nothing is wrong with me. It's just that I am studying now and very busy with that."

"Even better. A wife's responsibility is to care for you so that you can do better in your studies."

"Let me think a bit, Haji. I don't want to bring an innocent person here and make them miserable with me."

Suddenly he jumped forward in his seat and grabbed my collar. I stood up. He, too, stood up. I was about to move toward the door when I saw Hamed standing by the entrance, blocking my way out. I escaped to the corner of the room. Haji followed and wrapped his hands around my neck. "What is going on? You have to tell me! Hurry up! Pull down your pants. I want to see whether you are even a man or whether I have been duped all these years. Quick!"

He was shouting. His hands were trembling, and he couldn't hold me tightly. It wasn't pain that I was feeling, it was shame. The shame of being held, in Hamed's presence, by Haji's trembling angry hands, like a mouse curling up on itself in a corner of the room, not seeing anything but darkness. At that moment, I preferred death to that humiliation, and Haji continued to shout. "Is this my bad luck or what? That my only son has no balls?" and still louder, "Oh you unjust God." Then I was slipping out of Haji's hands into Hamed's. His iron fingers circled my neck. Now the shouting came from Haji and the heavy pressure around my neck from Hamed. "Tell Haji," Hamed said. His wild coarse hands were strangling me.

Whenever beautiful scenes from life begin to appear in my mind, I know that I'm stepping into the world of the dead, even though, in my heart or my mind, I know that I am still alive, alive but hopeless. "Let him go!" It was Haji's voice addressing Hamed this time, but Hamed's hands did not seem to hear him and continued pressing even harder around my neck. My tongue was sticking all the way out of my throat. "I told you to let him go, you motherfucker! Let him go or I'll

shoot you in the head!" And suddenly it was all over. The hands fell
away from my neck. I could breathe once again and was coming back
to life. Haji held a gun in his hand, pointed at Hamed's head. Still squatting on the floor, I turned my head to look at the room. Hamed was
slowly walking out of the guest living room. Haji was on his knees
in the middle of the room, still holding the gun. His shoulders were
trembling, the same way Behi's trembled the morning she brought me
some important, though grim, news.

That day, Behi held her newborn in her arms and arrived at our
house with the excuse that the baby had a stomachache and that she
wanted Bibi Saleem to take a look at her because Bibi knew how to
cure babies' stomachaches. But before going to Bibi, Behi rushed to
my room. Terrified and spluttering, she told me that Hamed had
gone to find and finish off Naji. "He wants to drown him in the river. I
heard it myself; he told Haji he would put his head under, told him
to rest assured that he would do it in a way that no one would be able
to find out."

"When is he going to do this, do you know?"

Behi stared into the depth of my eyes. "If he hasn't done it already."

I didn't hear or see anything after that except the beautifully carved
and easy to handle wooden walking stick that Seyyed kept by the door
of the guest living room. My hands picked it up. I could see myself running through the palm grove toward the spot where I thought Naji
would be working. Of course, I had decided that I would not go to see
Naji ever again, but I didn't want him to be killed, especially because
of his relationship with me. If Hamed killed him, how would I, how
could I continue to live my life under such a heavy burden of guilt?
What am I saying? The burden of guilt I am carrying today is a thousand times heavier. The feeling that I was, that I am his murderer, a
feeling I cannot escape and have to carry, with much pain, until the
end of my life. But that morning he was still alive, and I ran madly
through the palm grove, repeating under my breath, "No, no, I won't
let it happen." I kept telling myself this and running. The shape of the
white mulberry tree came into view, the thick sturdy tree standing over
the dock by the river. I looked at the river from the dock and saw two

figures like two whales entangled and fighting. The sound of terror rising from the splashing water. The screams coming from the muddy depths of the water. A drowning person was calling for help. The two of them were close to a small island bulging out of the water. I walked farther, reaching it. Hamed stood torso-deep in the water. Naji surged repeatedly out of the water, screaming, but Hamed's strong coarse hands kept pushing his head under the surface. I walked farther, until I could raise my heavy stick and bring it down on Hamed's head. But the stick slid in my hand—or did I slide it myself?—and it came down on his shoulder, and I could no longer balance on land and stumbled into the water. Hamed had stopped moving, and his hands were no longer around Naji's neck. My stick had fallen from my hand and was now floating in the water. The water was deep where I ended up. When I got tired of treading water, I stood on the tips of my toes in a layer of mud so soft my toes sank into it. My whole body kept spinning despite myself. I was like a doll left in the wind, connected to an invisible thread hanging from my neck. The wind almost turned me upside down. In no time, Naji found his balance. He vomited some muddy water. "The guy is drowning," he said, coughing.

"What should we do?" I said, while I, too, needed help.

"Let's pull him out." First he pulled me toward the shore so I could fully regain my footing. Then together we began to slowly drag Hamed's heavy sapped body toward the riverbank, but his limp form didn't want to cooperate and kept sliding back down into the water. His legs surely reached the muddy layer, because he was much taller than either of us. He kept slipping through our hands like a fish, until we finally managed to pull him out of the water. We laid him on the ground and, putting to use the first aid lessons I had learned in school, I was eventually able to bring him back to consciousness.

He opened his eyes, looking back and forth from me to Naji, and back to me. "Behi told you I was here."

I didn't utter a word and just looked at him.

"I should get going now," said Naji. Then, with his head bowed low, he added, "I won't say anything to anyone," and asked me, "How about you?"

"Of course not."

Still spitting out water, Hamed stood up. "Whether you tell anyone
or not, Haji doesn't want to see the two of you together. And I can't
override his word. I should also tell you this: I'll do whatever he wants."
He turned toward me and quietly added, "Yes, cousin. Do you get what
I am saying?"

He threw a long look at the thick wooden stick with which I had hit
him, still floating over the water. Then, as water dripped from his head
and body onto the ground, he turned and walked to his motorcycle
hidden behind a bush. With his bike screeching, he drove away. We
looked at one another and laughed. Maybe Naji, too, was thinking
about what our next step should be. What should it have been? One
thing was clear—the warning Hamed had given us before leaving.

"Well, I have to leave too. I have to prepare for an important exam.
I'll be so swamped I won't be able to leave the house at all in the next few
months, or I'll get behind in my studies." I didn't let him see my tears,
because he shouldn't have had to bear my tears. "Well, goodbye then."

"He really wanted to kill me just then."

"I told you what a savage he is."

"If he had killed me, he would've ended up in jail, no?"

"No, he wouldn't. First of all, he would pull a thousand tricks to
hide the fact that he was the culprit. And even if the truth were out,
the usual five brothers would gather and confess that they all committed the crime together. Then the court would sentence each to just
six months, a term they can easily buy their way out of like any other
commodity."

"So you are saying that he will eventually kill me?"

"No, I didn't say that."

"Then what? You just said that. You said that he could kill me just
like that, easy. You even heard him say that he would come for me
again. So what do you think I should do? Do you see how I threw
myself into the fire all of my own accord? So what should I do now?"

"It's not like that. I just have to stop seeing you. That's all they want.
I'll tell them that I won't be seeing you anymore. I'll tell them that it's
all over between us."

I started walking away. I was headed back home. He followed me. "Hamed now has a good excuse to get rid of me, right?"

"If there is something secret between the two of you, that's your thing. Please don't connect it to our own relationship. That's something between the two of you that I'm not even aware of."

It was as if he did not hear me, so busy was he mulling over what he wanted to tell me. "Why don't we just run away together?" I ignored his words and kept walking. He skipped to catch up with me. "It doesn't matter where. Someplace where no one can bother us. Just the two of us in a new environment among new people."

"Please stop following me, okay?"

But he kept walking and talking. "My dad can figure out something with his own life. His money is with his sister. He can go live with her and live off whatever he has."

"Okay, goodbye."

He stopped. Stood for a while, in silence. Then he said, in a louder voice, "So Friday morning, after sunrise, in Ghandi's shed, all right?" But I had already put some distance between us, and I could not hear his voice, because his voice was lost among the mass of small palm trees whose green leaves hung down all around them as if they were weeping willows. Late that night I confessed to myself that his voice had not gotten lost among the trees, that it did actually reach me, entered my head through my ears and lay on my heart, with no intention of leaving, and now it was mingling with the sound of my breaths. "Friday morning after sunrise in Ghandi's shed."

It was the middle of the week, and I still had time to mull over and make a decision about a very important issue in my life. I knew I had to push the thought of running away with Naji out of my head and my heart. Going somewhere, going nowhere, going into darkness. I knew that if I left, I had to think of working rather than studying and looking forward to a bright future. Here at my father's house, everything was ready for me, and if I wanted it, I would be the light of his eye. But then again, I thought, yes, I would be, but only to serve a purpose I had no interest in. I didn't even understand what this purpose was, but I had to pretend I did.

Sometimes two clergymen visited our house. Upon Haji's orders, they were given the best welcome. After they had their lunch, they would nap for two hours by one of the shorter windows in the guest quarters, then they would wake up for tea and conversation about politics. During those times, Haji wanted me around to listen to their opinions. They said soon the shah would have no choice but to hand over the rule of the region to the Arabs, but Haji and his people were worried about the leftist youths who were against the shah and who could take hold of the politics of the region, which would be a disaster for orthodox Muslims. Haji said the clergymen were the best publicists because from their pulpit they could explain the country's situation to the people in simple language (by which he meant the language of the public), so Haji took every opportunity to help set up a pulpit for them. He distributed alms, and people would rush with their containers big and small to grab food and drinks. Hamed would shout at them, "The food and sharbat are for after the religious recitations and sermons, for those who sit through the clergyman's sermon, who cry and hit themselves in the head. If you are only crying in passing, you'll just get some tea." These moments were perfect for Hamed, not because he would gain any money, no; he loved being in positions of power and bossing people around left and right, a handful of poor people who had come from far away, roads full of streams and creeks that they had to jump over and over again, roads running along hills that they had to hike up and down over and over again. Hamed told them, "If you are here to fill up your bellies rather than listen to what the clergymen says from the pulpit, then the infidel communists would come and turn everything corrupt halal, then a brother would fuck his sister, a father would fuck his daughter. May God forgive me." That was why the people had no choice but to listen to the preachers' sermons all the way to the end, hitting themselves over the head, if they wanted to go back home with food.

There were other things, too, that tarnished my fondness of that house and my paternal family. Even before these incidents, I had thought about running away and leaving forever. And now, the threat of death, of being murdered, was hovering around my head.

Behi said, "Have you gone mad? Where do you want to go, to foreign lands where you know no one?"

I didn't tell her that I would not be alone; no, I didn't tell her, because I thought I was keeping a secret, but I learned later on that Behi knew everything. I said, "You won't tell anyone that I told you about my escape?"

"No, never. I promise," she told me, but soon after, that same evening, I saw her speaking with her mother in hushed tones, clearly worried that I would be nearby. When I found her alone later on, I said, "I trusted you. I thought you were my confidant."

"I'm glad I consulted with my mother. She doesn't have good news, actually, she has bad news. You know that my mother loves you. She is worried that you would be killed for no good reason."

"Killed? Me? But why?"

"My mother knows what a strict bigot Haji is. She says Haji has heard things about you that there is no way he can tolerate. He has even said that far more good would come from the death of this boy than from his being alive."

"What does that mean?"

Behi was silent for a bit, then she threw herself into my arms, crying. "Kaka Jamil!"

I held her tight. "What has Haji heard about me?"

"My mother is afraid, terrified. She says if you don't hurry up and do something, it might be too late." She pulled back from me and looked into my eyes. It was obvious she had an important message for me. "Run away. If you want to stay alive and enjoy your life, run and never come back here."

Yes, I did want to stay alive and enjoy my life. I had always wanted that, to enjoy my life, from the very first day of birth. But that had not been possible.

While I was squeezing eye drops in Naneh Reyhan's eyes for the last time, she said, "Be careful, my son. Maybe they are planning to send you away so that they can help themselves to all of Haji's inheritance."

But there was no more time to think about Haji's wealth and what would become of it after his death, whenever that might be, and who knew whether I would be alive then or not? "What if they finish me off, Naneh?" I knew she wouldn't have anything to say in response, because she, too, knew how coldhearted Haji could be, so much so that he could spill his own child's blood if it came to preserving his political status among the people of the villages of the region. But, of course, these were all speculations. On the one hand, I told myself that Haji hadn't let Hamed kill me. On the other, I rejected my own argument and considered that Haji had called Hamed off because he wanted to do the good act of killing me himself, to earn the honor of ideological filicide for himself, a quite important honor.

Behi begged me, "Please leave as soon as possible. I know my husband. I know how the djinns find their way into his body, little by little, turning him into a brutal animal."

"Are you saying these words about your own husband?"

"One's brother is dearer than one's husband," she said, staring at me with her small close-set eyes, believing that I was being deceived unwillingly, deceived by her words, which she had grasped from her mother in order to inject into my baffled brain. I would be deceived, but willingly. Like a beloved becoming all ears to be deceived by the lover's praises. I, too, was deceived, not by Behi and her mother but by something much more serious.

"Help me move my stuff out of the house without making any noise, without anyone finding out," I asked her.

"When?"

"Friday, before sunrise."

"Good for you, Kaka Jamil. Lucky you for leaving this place behind." Perhaps she was saying this from the bottom of her heart. Perhaps she, too, wanted to escape that environment and her existence under the stupid reign of the man who pretended he was the neighborhood sheikh, walking and talking and ordering as if he were a powerful, influential man of the state. And people believed him because he had money.

During the summer, Haji had more wiggle room because it was the labor season, the labor of picking and cutting dates from the palm trees.

There was a group of gypsies who arrived in the summer, camped at a corner of his plot, and worked for him. Their pay was lower, because they were given a place to stay and two daily portions of rice and stew. Whenever the gypsies were around, Hamed was happier. In recent years, as I have begun to make sense of it all, I have realized that Hamed took liberties with the women and the young boys. I had even seen things: him sneaking behind a tent followed by the fearful voice of a woman begging him, "No, not now, master. My husband will be back any moment. For heaven's sake, leave."

"Your poor husband is buried under the weight of so much work now. And let's say he does walk in. What is he going to do? Tell me."

And the sound of his guffaw.

The woman cried, "No! No! Leave."

If it had mattered to Behi at all, I would have recounted to her that scene and the others, but whenever she heard such things about Hamed, she would just laugh. She listened and giggled. "He's a man. All men are like that. From what I've heard, they can't make do with just one woman. You'll grow up to be the same, even if you have a wife and kids." She would laugh. "Hamed is a man too. Like the rest of them."

Eventually, Naji and I decided to run away. Not on the Friday that he had picked, but two Fridays later. Behi said, "This is the best thing to do. To escape from this house, to go far away, to be rid of this place forever."

"But I need help. Without help, I can't do anything." She stared into my eyes. I said, "Without your help, I can't take my stuff out of the house." My belongings included two pieces: my backpack and the leather case containing my grandfather's violin, which I wanted to take for Naji. The night before our escape, I couldn't sleep at all. I didn't fall asleep. I kept thinking about what would happen and where we would go. Behi lied and said her child was sick so she could stay at our place that night and so that early in the morning she could hide my backpack under her black veil and take it to the riverbank without Haji noticing. She pretended that she was doing all of that secretly, while everyone in the house (except Haji) knew what was going on, that I was, with Behi's help, running away from home.

"But I don't know anyone in the city. I don't know anyone anywhere. Where are we going?" Naji asked.

"I have a classmate called Ararat whose father, George, runs a pig farm. Maybe if we go to them, they will help us out."

"They are Armenian, right?"

"Christians."

He seemed not to hear me. "Why should an Armenian guy help us out?"

"Don't mind his religion, please. He is an angel. My best classmate. We sit in the same row. Used to sit in the same row. He is one of those kids who I have no doubt will one day become someone, a prominent person, he's so gifted. He is a genius in both math and English. He is so kind that you'll fall in love with him the moment you see him."

We trudged through the dirt and mud toward Naji's canoe. We got on the boat. Behi was standing on the dock, crying, waving to me. I had lied to her, told her that Naji was there to simply take me to the other side of the river. She thought I was headed to Tehran. I, too, imagined we would end up there. Traveling to the capital was the wish of every youth from the provinces. Naji and I were still on the water when the sun came up. I was staring at the village, wondering if there ever would come a time when I could return without fearing being killed, dying for no good reason. The village I loved had turned into a place of horror, unrest, and fear. How had that happened? That had happened because in their eyes I was sick, and Haji had come to the conclusion that there was no hope of me being cured. The son he wanted was not me. He had to let me be in the hands of God, but he could not simply let me go, because I was his son, and he had to set my life straight as soon as possible. The village began to fade before my eyes, lost amid the palm grove. Then we arrived at another sad moment: the moment Naji had to say goodbye to his boat. He cried. He said he had had that canoe since he was born. He said his uncle had given it to him to work with and earn money. Besides, Naji was attached to it, that's why he hadn't been able to bring himself to sell it to anyone before the trip, and now he was acting like a mother who was separating from her child. First, he tied the rope to a tree close to the water. Then he changed his mind and untied it. He said it was better to leave the canoe untethered and push it into the current, so that it could float along until someone grabbed it from the water. He prayed for it to be picked up by someone who needed it. We stood there and watched the boat sway along until it reached the middle of the river. The water, which had begun to rise, carried it even farther away from the riverbank. I kept telling him we should leave. Naji stared at his canoe, crying, unable to move. The boat moved farther and farther away until it turned into a little black dot, until it disappeared from our sight, and all we could see was the muddy water rising and falling in waves.

Once again, I reached for the piece of paper in my pocket with Ararat's address. When we got to the main road, we waved for several cars before one finally stopped for us. And in our very first steps in the new world, we realized that we wouldn't be safe anywhere, that danger would continue to hover around us like an ominous bird, from the moment that junker stopped for us and we hopped in with our belongings on our backs. It was a truck taking bricks from the kiln to the city. The beat up cab had two parts, one where the driver and his co-driver sat, and the other behind them where instead of the seat, there were two low stools, where we sat and told them where we were headed. The driver told us he could drop us off somewhere close to our destination. We went with them. I held on to Naji's hand and looked around at the desert. The driver was looking us up and down in the rearview mirror. "Are you sure you're heading to this place you told me?" he asked. I didn't get what he meant, but it seemed that his co-driver did, because he laughed. The driver asked, "How much? Maybe we could afford you."

"What? What are you talking about?"

"Don't play dumb with us. It's not a shame to have a job. Actually, your job is very nice and respectable. Especially at this early hour of the day, I swear to Abolfazl that there's much virtue in it."

Naji, too, understood what the driver was implying. "No, brother, we are not what you think we are. We are just headed to our friend's, who is waiting for us."

"Friend? This early? And you want us to believe you?" asked the driver.

The co-driver started laughing hard. Naji's face turned red. I pressed his hand firmly and asked him to control himself and stay calm.

"We won't be too much trouble. There is a comfortable space right here in the back of the car to do your business, you can rest assured," added the driver.

I saw Naji's fingers slowly sliding down to the knife he had in his pocket. I was terrified. My legs were trembling.

"Look, sir. Like my friend said, we are not what you think. Maybe you've mistaken us for someone else."

"Both of you, so clean and fresh, so young and bright." The driver pointed to me. "Especially you." He then turned to his co-driver and said, "Did you hear? The boy says we have picked them up by mistake." The co-driver kept laughing as he threw glances at us.

I said, "Please stop right here, sir. We'll just get off here. Thanks."

"I like you better because you know social etiquette."

"Please stop right here, if you don't mind."

"But we haven't reached our destination yet. I'll stop when we get there."

Suddenly Naji pulled out the knife and put its blade at the back of the driver's neck. "Didn't you hear what he asked? He asked you to stop. Right here. Right now."

The driver hit the brake but pretended that the knife had not frightened him. "Well, you pretty little homo with your knife, you could have just asked like a normal human being. Now both of you get lost."

Naji opened the door and told me to hop off first. He was still holding the knife to the driver's neck. The co-driver had stopped laughing. Following me, Naji, too, jumped down. I threw two or three coins over to the co-driver. With that experience, we realized we had to be very careful, because the world we were entering was far more brutal than we had expected. Though we would meet kind souls along the way too.

From the house's entrance, we could tell we had finally found the place we were looking for. There was a bas-relief of crucified Jesus over the doorway, decorated in various colors. Where the nails had penetrated his body, we could see the red blood trickling. Jesus was looking at us, and Naji was looking back, with eyes that were beginning to fill with tears. I don't know what he was thinking of. It seemed strange. I said, "So you know Jesus. You hadn't mentioned it. I didn't know."

"No. This is Christ. My mother liked Christ very much. She said he knew what he was doing as a prophet, but sadly his friends stabbed him in the back. Look how the motherfuckers have pierced his hands with nails."

I looked around, worrying that someone had heard Naji. He was wiping his tears. "Okay, pull yourself together now. We should ring the bell."

He looked at me with a smile. "Sure. Do it."

I rang the bell. "By the way, Jesus is just another name for Christ. They are one person, one prophet with two names."

"Really?"

Ararat himself opened the door. I hadn't seen him since the school holidays had started. He seemed to have grown some beard stubble in those three months. Because he was tall with a large build, he looked older than us. He got excited when he saw me. "Jamil! What are you doing here?"

"I am here just for you," I said, laughing.

I felt so much at peace in that living room with images of the Virgin Mary and Jesus on the wall along with family photographs of Ararat with his father, mother, and sisters. He had three sisters, two of whom were older than him, one younger. One of his older sisters had married last year and was giving birth to her first child, so his mother and other sisters were at the hospital, while his father, George, was at work on an old pig farm outside the city. Ararat came back from the kitchen with three large glasses of tea.

"Do you seriously want to quit school, Jamil?"

"You know well that a high school diploma is only good for someone who wants to go to college, like what you are doing, or any other sane person might do these days," I responded.

"So what do you want to do after quitting?"

"I want to do labor work for a few years to save some money, to migrate, and then continue my studies there."

Ararat wanted to know what Naji's plans were.

"Naji doesn't want to be a grasscutter anymore. He wants to change his life. He, too, should work for a while to save so he can pay for leaving as well."

"Where do you two want to look for work? Have you thought about it?"

"We are not sure yet. Maybe somewhere around here, or we might have to go to Tehran."

"Tehran is crazy. You can't survive it."

"What then?"

"Why not ask my dad? Maybe he has some work for you. You know what he does, right?"

"Yes, we do."

"If you are okay working there."

"We are."

George, too, was an angel. He kindly looked over our birth certificates and said, "You can work on our farm for now, until you turn twenty. But only if you are good laborers and do not cause trouble for anyone. Then you have to go to military service. I mean, I can't keep you then, because if I do, I will be a criminal. You have to serve after the age of twenty; the officers in the barracks are counting the minutes until your arrival. At that time, you have to leave here. Understood?"

"It's still a long while till then."

"A long while or not, I wanted to tell you from the very beginning, so you don't make excuses when the time comes. Agreed?"

"Agreed."

Ararat said, "They don't have a place to stay either."

"One of the rooms in Kheir Abadi's house is still free. They can live there," George replied, and then turned to me. "But you have to be careful there, because the people living there are all either single laborers or those who are living away from their families. Most are here from villages near and far. You two are both young and pretty, so they might cause you trouble. Promise me that you'll do your best to stay out of trouble."

We promised to be very careful. We were so delighted that whatever George asked us, we accepted. We had recognized kindness and safety in his eyes. Maybe it is hard now to imagine such generosity in that country. I know. Maybe today all of this sounds like a myth, but it was not a myth, because back then there was kindness and generosity in that land, there was at least some still.

The farm was big, but there were not too many pigs, and because they were taken elsewhere to be slaughtered, their numbers constantly kept changing. Some of them were there only to give birth. Each laborer had his own responsibilities. One of my jobs was to count the animals every morning when we arrived to make sure none was missing. I looked at each and every one of them closely to report to George if any of them looked sick so he could call the vet as fast as possible. Because I had gone to school, and, in George's eyes, I knew better than others, sometimes I was given cleaner jobs to do, even though no job with the pigs was really clean. Naji was in charge of cleaning the pigsties. It wasn't an easy job, especially on the hot days, or on the cold ones. Our wages were not bad, enough for us to pay the rent for our room, buy food, go to the theater or have some fun on Fridays, and have some money left to save. Naji loved watching Western movies with lots of killing, and I loved Indian romantic ones. The good thing about the theater we went to every Friday was that they often showed two films for one ticket. And the two were never of a similar genre, so they fit both my taste and Naji's.

We went to the theater at noon and first had lunch. We bought two big sandwiches with sodas. Naji liked Coca-Cola and I liked Canada Dry. The taste of coke was too sharp and bitter for me—whatever was in it, I didn't like it. But we agreed on liking one thing, and that was the fresh herbs in the sandwiches. Many years later, when we had to live in a foreign land far away from those lovely flavors, we reminisced about those sandwiches and their fresh herbs. I enjoyed watching the

58

Indian dance in the films. Did they show the Indian films first or the Westerns?

Another thing we did for fun on Fridays was to go to the riverside, where the docks and boats were, where the sailors gathered on a boat sometimes during the sunset to sing and dance in a circle. A little farther away, there were street vendors selling bootlegged foreign products. Sometimes we would find cheap colognes, sometimes different types of soaps, and I once found a pair of sunglasses that I got for Naji. He got me a strange metal box that included a few small knives, a bottle opener, scissors, and a dozen other shitty sundries, all of them in travel size. I accepted it as a gift from him and didn't complain; later on, I realized he had liked the picnic box himself, so I gave it to him, and he always kept it with him until the end. I liked buying gifts for him, and I liked him to buy me things too, but I never asked him to. One day in the street vendors market, he saw the exact same red-and-white keffiyeh that he had given me the first day we met, and he got it for me. The old one was gone. The woman whom Naji was falling for had come and taken it from my shoulders and walked away. What nonsense am I saying? How could Naji fall for a woman? It was not possible, because he reserved all his love for me, and I for him, but I don't know why he liked helping that woman out. Of course, it was just out of pity. He later completely forgot her, but he never forgot the joy of going with me to the theater on Fridays, just as I never did.

Fridays before going to the movies, Naji had his violin class. George had found us the instructor. Amrollah Khan the violinist had been their neighbor many years ago, and George still met with him from time to time at a bar.

"But you have to promise me that you take care of yourselves, because the guy is a drunk, though he is a nice person and an amazing musician. You should just take your lessons and benefit from his skills. You simply want to learn violin from him, and nothing else, my kids." George was worried about Amrollah Khan's influence on us. "It's too soon for you two to start drinking, too soon."

"Rest assured, monsieur. I'll be there with Naji for every class and lesson. That is if Amrollah Khan is fine with it," I told him.

He was fine with it. Amrollah Khan liked both of us. Every Friday, right at nine in the morning, we went to his place with some money and a few packs of cigarettes, and sometimes a gift for him too. Naji had a violin session for two hours. Amrollah Khan held the violin that once belonged to my grandfather and said, "Whoever holds this instrument will become a great musician. This is one of those good old instruments, the kind that are not made anymore. Whoever practices with it will definitely become a musician, though it also depends on the person; one has to practice too, practice a lot."

"I'm sorry, sir, that I won't be able to practice much, because, well, I have to go to work too," Naji told him.

He looked at me as if he was complaining about life, and I felt it was my job to explain the hardships of our life and the reasons behind them, and that it was my job to make him feel at peace. I said, "One must work and make money in order to survive anyway, especially those who do not have anyone to support them, people like us who have to carry the burden of life all by themselves. Right, Naji?"

Squatting, Naji was deep in thought. Maybe he was imagining himself as a famous musician everyone knows whose picture is on the cover of magazines. When he came out of his reverie, he said, "Yes, all by themselves. Amrollah Khan, too, is all by himself, and he is not bothered by it."

Amrollah Khan had a child. A daughter who had once wanted to become a famous singer, but she didn't, and instead she turned into a singer for weddings and celebrations. Amrollah Khan had not seen her for many years. "She didn't become what she dreamed of. You know why? Because she was too ambitious, too ambitious for her own good. Exactly like her father, her stupid father." And he advised Naji to be careful while pursuing art and not to fall prey to promises of performances for radio or television. "The world of art is quite attractive, but also dangerous and cruel. It was this very love for art that ruined my life like this." He didn't explain how, and we didn't ask either.

Fortunately, Naji didn't have such dreams in mind. I mean, I wouldn't let him have such thoughts. I constantly reminded him to think about being in Europe, when he would be able to take his art more seriously, reach the highest levels of playing and researching about the violin. But here, now, never. I didn't want Naji to think that we were at peace here and to forget about moving abroad. No. I wanted him to always think about that trip, engrave that in his mind as our main goal. All my senses had assured me that this was not a place for us to live. My heart told me that we had to escape it. One of the good things about our relationship was that Naji listened to me. Or perhaps this was one of the bad things about it. I am not sure. Today all those standards, whether good or bad, are lost to me. Which one was which?

Amrollah Khan said, "You two seem like one heart in two chests. A heart full of kindness, full of love." Then he turned to Naji and added, "You seem to be a born violinist," and held him in his arms. "Promise me you won't turn out like me. Never. Promise me." He meant that he had failed in his career and now he was a drunk. "Play for your own heart and not for making others happy for as long as you can. Remember that these very people can one day become a threat to the artist. Yes, these very people." Then he turned to me. "You are smarter than him. So you make sure you don't let his art make him arrogant, lead him astray."

I retorted, "I am not the smarter one, sir, but I promise you that I'll do my best." What happened that I couldn't keep my promise? What happened that instead of taking care of him, I led him to such big troubles? Dragged him with me from one fire to another? Yes, that would be a more accurate title for our destiny: *Sons of Fire*. If Amrollah Khan ever learned of our real destiny, he would surely give us that title. He told us about his daughter. "I know where she lives. I have her address, but I don't go check on her, because I don't want to be a bother and make her ashamed of me in front of her child. You know, kids have some expectations of their grandfathers that I'm unable to meet. Knowing that she has a good husband and a beautiful chubby girl is enough for me. If the hand of destiny leads me to her just one more time, I know what to tell her. Just one more time before I die. Then I can leave this world in peace, in much more peace."

Amrollah Khan would say these things after we had finished the violin lesson, after he had become quite drunk. He would start drinking little by little from the moment we began the session. He said, "I should pay attention to this kid's work. I don't offer you any because you two are still too young, but if you want, I can give you one or two shots."

I said, "I'm not into it, sir, but I know that your student here wouldn't mind having a shot or two, but just one or two, nothing more than that." There was a sparkle in Naji's eyes.

Amrollah Khan poured a shot for him and told him, "You're lucky that someone has your back like this." He held the glass out to him and added, "The best gift from God is to have someone who has your back like this."

We met Kavous by chance one day, and I wish we never had. One day George said, "Kids, I have some bad news. The truck has broken down and needs to stay at the mechanic's for a few days. In the meantime, you must find a way to commute to the farm. The mechanic said he might be able to do it in one week. Anyway, see what you can do to somehow make this one week work." The truck belonged to George. Every morning, four of us farmworkers would wait at the town square, and when the truck got there, we just hopped into the back, which was covered by canvas to shelter us and the pigs from wind and rain. The truck would pick us up every morning from the square and drop us off right there every evening, and we would walk the rest of the way home.

In the cab of the truck, there was space only for the driver and George, who was quite fat, and no one else could sit next to him. Sometimes when the driver was not there and George drove himself, he would ask the two of us to sit in the front, and he would talk all the way. While the truck was at the shop, the driver borrowed a motorcycle to take George to and from the farm. When the day's work ended, each of us workers had to find a way to get home. We didn't have any other choice but to wave at every car that passed by us on the road. Of course, we also had to pay the drivers who took us to town or from town to the farm. Most were trucks heading to the other nearby farms or to the docks. In the mornings, we had to wait around until finally someone would stop to give us a ride. The same in the evenings. But Naji never let me get bored. He would tell jokes or imitate others to entertain me. It was the third or fourth day, and we were walking along the road after work, talking about the sunset, how it wasn't funny but strange. The circle of the sun went down slowly, but before it reached the horizon, suddenly it was drowned in an unknown darkness. As if a box of smoke devoured the sun before it reached the horizon. We were busy talking about that strange smoke when a truck carrying three sheep stopped for us.

"Hop on, kids," said the driver. He sounded so friendly that we became suspicious.

"No, thanks. We're not headed anywhere."

"I know you two. You work at George's farm. You know, George is my friend, so helping you is like helping him." He reached for the door and opened it for us. We got in hesitantly and said hi. He laughed aloud and began driving. "Do I look like such a scumbag that I've scared you both so?"

"We weren't scared. Well, why should we be? We just felt like walking a bit. That's it," said Naji.

The driver laughed some more, making it obvious that he knew we were lying to him. "Walk all the way from here to town after you've worked so hard all day long?" He paused a moment before adding, "Anyway, my name is Kavous." He looked at both our faces. "Have you ever heard such a name before?" he asked.

"I haven't, but Jamil should know," said Naji.

"Do you?"

I said I only knew which historical figure the name came from. Then I explained that it was from Ferdowsi's *Book of Kings*, and Kavous, the son of Keighobad, the King of Kian, ruled for 150 years, and I explained how Eblis deceived Kavous the King and sent him to conquer the skies and meet the sun.

Kavous looked at Naji and said, "This friend of yours seems to know a lot. I like that. Like that a lot."

"'Cause he has both gone to school and read many books. You haven't even seen much of it yet."

"If he knows so much, how come he works at the pig farm?"

"Do you see a problem with working?"

"No, of course not. It's actually very good for men."

"So what is the problem?"

"I meant you don't seem to be Armenian or Assyrian. Neither your faces nor your names say so. Am I right?"

"Yes."

"You are Muslims, right?"

"Yes."

"Well, that is the problem, then. I know you are not the only Muslim workers on the farm, but the ones you see who move around the pig's butts and work there are Muslims in name only, not in their hearts. You two seem different from them. You are very different from them, it's obvious."

"But we don't want to be different from the others. We want to be like them. Two cousins like any two cousins who are also friends with one another. Good close friends who have a normal relationship with other people too."

Kavous looked at me and at Naji once again. "You're kidding me. You two are not cousins." He laughed, loudly and pretentiously.

"Why would we be kidding?"

"'Cause you don't look like cousins."

"But we are."

"Well, if you say so. Who am I to say you are not?"

"You didn't tell us whose sheep these are and who you work for."

"They are mine and my business partner's. We trade sheep. We have a space for the animals in the city that costs us a lot, so we are looking for something around here." Kavous paused before continuing, "If we could close down this piggery and instead bring our own sheep here, that would be great, right? That would be better for you Muslim boys too."

"Do you know how many people would lose their income then?"

"We would hire all the workers there. Like, I would immediately hire you two; it's obvious you are hardworking, honest kids."

"Are you sure?" I asked him, laughing.

"I'm thirty-two years old and have been in this work for many years. I've learned the ins and outs of the job and am great at reading people, because I've dealt with all kinds of people, from good to bad, from Muslim to unbelievers to Armenians to Zoroastrians."

"Unbelievers and Armenians seem to be very different, right?" I asked.

"Whoever eats hog meat is no different from an unbeliever, is he?"

I didn't continue, because Naji and I also loved pork meat, and George sometimes gave us salt-cured pork. We remained silent until we arrived in town.

"Thanks for the ride," I said and pulled out some coins I had in my pocket. "How much do we owe you?"

"But we haven't reached your house yet." He laughed.

"We are not too far away."

"I'll drop you off there."

"God bless you. I swear on your life there's no nicer deed in the world," Naji said.

I knew Naji was saying this because he was very tired. I gave him a look that said we should have Kavous stop and let us out, but he didn't notice me.

"No, thank you, Mr. Kavous. We're grateful that you brought us all the way to here. This will do," I said.

"You are tired. You have worked for ten hours. Let me drop you off at your door. It's no trouble for me."

"Honestly, we have to get some groceries here for dinner."

"But you made dinner last night and left it in the fridge. Did you forget?" Naji asked me.

"I'll wait for you to buy your things and come back," Kavous said.

"I think we only need a few sodas, right?" Naji asked.

"You don't know. We need a lot of other things as well," I said.

"What else?" Naji asked.

"Well, a lot of things." I said. I was getting annoyed with him but didn't want to yell at him in front of Kavous. He kept insisting that he would drop us off at our house, and I kept trying to get out of his truck as soon as possible. Finally, he stopped and we got out.

"Okay, so I'll see you tomorrow," Kavous said.

"Tomorrow?"

"I'll meet you right here at seven tomorrow morning."

"Why?"

"To give you a ride to work."

The sheep had started to make a lot of strange sounds in the back of the truck, perhaps because of the darkness suddenly descending as the sun set. Kavous left without taking any money from us.

"I didn't think you would be so stupid," I told Naji, and then yelled, "What were you doing back there? Did you forget what advice George gave us? Didn't he say we need to be very careful with strangers?"

Naji looked down and said in a slow voice, "He didn't seem to be a bad guy."

I screamed, "How did you find out so fast that he's a good guy? Was it written on his forehead that he's a good guy?"

He didn't say a word and stood there staring at the ground under his feet. I dashed away from him. After a while, I heard his steps behind me and then his voice saying, "I'm sorry. I made a mistake. Well, the guy seemed very friendly, but that was not real, it was fake, I know now. I'm sorry from the bottom of my heart. Are we okay now?"

I slowed my pace so that he could catch up with me. I checked around us, and without turning to look at Naji, moved my fingers into the empty space behind me to find his. He then acted like he was a reporter to make me laugh. "Excuse me, sir, can we ask your opinion about the breasts of the woman walking toward you?" I looked up. You could see her buoyant breasts bouncing from a distance. She was fat, but she seemed to not want to accept that and was wearing a shirt one size too small. Her big breasts were trying to jump out of the tight prison of the shirt; they kept jumping up and down to set themselves free but with no success. Even though I tried hard to stop my laughter, the woman, whose hair was thick and blond, noticed that I was laughing at her. She said, "You sweet young cocks are loving this. I know you're getting hard, you pretty little babes with your fresh beards and mustaches . . ."

When we realized that the woman was chill and chatty, we stopped laughing at her appearance and laughed instead at her words and also at her strong Tehrani accent, which sounded odd and funny to us. Such words uttered by a woman her age? She stood in the middle of the sidewalk and talked to us, trying now to make us laugh. "I know tonight you'll have a fight over whose dream I will visit, but don't worry, my pretty ones, I'll come visit both of you in your dreams." She laughed. We laughed too. A few other people also laughed with us without knowing what was going on as they passed us by. The woman left, and we were still laughing as we went on our way. The sidewalk was bright and joyous, or maybe the joy came with the minibus coming along the road behind us, which was full of schoolgirls who seemed to have just come back from a camp or a competition. It seemed that they had won something. Some of them had their heads out of the bus and were happily singing a song. The bare hair of some of the girls was blowing in the wind. Naji, too, was happy and insisted on buying ice cream for me. I think he had a craving himself, because he didn't heed my refusal and pulled me by my arm in the direction of the ice cream shop we knew.

"I'm tired and can't stand outside the guy's shop," I grumbled.

"We'll just go inside the shop and have them served at our table. How does that sound?"

We went in. There were no other customers there. The shopkeeper had his head inside the big glass case full of different ice creams. People usually first checked the glass case and chose their ice cream before sitting at their table, but Naji and I had been there so often, we knew what flavors they had and what we wanted. We always ordered to go and had our ice cream while walking, but this time Naji insisted that we sit and order inside for the first time. Chocolate for Naji and strawberry for me. I couldn't understand how Naji liked the strong taste of chocolate. Strawberry was the king of all ice cream flavors, the taste of heaven. Imagining those tastes in our mouths and our minds, we walked into the store and sat at the table on the metal chairs, waiting for the shopkeeper to come get our order. Two women who seemed older than us, around thirty, walked in. They were carrying a metal pot containing a weeping willow sapling, holding on to two rope handles they had made on the sides to carry the pot more easily. They seemed tired. The shopkeeper lit up when he saw the women. He was looking at either their very short skirts or their bare thighs. The weather was not that hot. The women were wearing coats, as if it was only their torsos that were sensitive to the cold and their bare thighs had no sense of it. With such respect, he gestured to a corner of the store where they could put the plant. The women placed the pot there and laughed and walked toward us. The shopkeeper walking behind them silently mouthed, "Hotties!" I was mesmerized by the woman with the shorter hair, who looked kind and had a smile on her lips that seemed eternal. Suddenly we noticed the shopkeeper standing over us. "Kids, I'm sorry, please go wait outside."

"Why? What's going on?"

"Nothing. The whole store is reeking of the smell of your clothes." Gesturing with his fingers and nose that we smelled awful, he pointed to us to get up, and we got up and followed him out of the store. "Please wait here, my dear ones. I'll put your ice cream in beautiful bowls and serve you in a minute." He was trying to act in a way as not to offend us, but it was too late. Naji was looking at the metal weights next to the scale on the shop counter. Good thing I noticed his look in time and was able to hold both his arms. "I beg you, don't make a scene. Let's go. Let's forget about the ice cream and just go."

Naji muttered through his teeth, "Did you see how the mother-fucker threw us out when he saw two young women?"

"He is right about the smell. Our clothes smell like hog shit. You can't deny that."

Naji was angry. He pulled up part of his dark blue turtleneck to his nose. "So how come mine doesn't smell?"

We laughed. "Thank you, sir. So then all the shit smell in the air is coming only from your humble servant here."

"I'm going to bring all his shop windows down right now," said Naji.

"You are fucking not, sir. Let's go. Don't even think about it. Do you hear me?" I said and pulled him away from the store.

The woman with the shorter hair walked out of the store angrily. "Who talks to people, to his customers, like that? Dumbass!" she said and asked us, "What did he tell you? Was he rude to you?"

"Extremely," Naji said.

"Let's go," the woman said. She went back into the store and came back, dragging the pot out with her. Naji rushed to help and picked the

pot up and held it in his arms. The woman called to her friend and told
her they were not going to have ice cream in this man's store.

The shopkeeper was angry. "What the fuck are you talking about,
woman? You with your barely there skirts. You do not understand how
these two smell of shit. The very smell of shit and nothing else. After
all, I did it for your comfort, you two women, who, even at your age,
seem to have forgotten to wear proper pants."

Led by the woman with short hair, our group had already left the
store by a good distance. "Fucking kidding me. Respecting someone
while putting someone else down is bullshit. This is not called respect.
In our village, that's called being a motherfucker," said the woman with
short hair, laughing. "Am I right, my dear Parvaneh?" she asked her
friend before turning to us. "If he knew what real respect is, he would
be respectful to you guys who are the laborers of this country. You
are laborers, right?" We told her what work we did. Hearing this was
surprising to them, and it was surprising to us that two women of their
age spoke so freely, not shying away from using curses. In our mind,
they were courageous women.

The woman with shorter hair said, "Well, this boy is getting tired.
Sir, please put the pot down while I think of what we should do. I mean
let's see what we can do with it at all."

"It's not heavy," said Naji.

But the woman made him put the plant down. This time, Naji and I
held the handles together and carried it, while the woman with shorter
hair guided us to another ice cream shop close by.

Parvaneh had long straight hair, which she let fall over her shoulders
like a waterfall. She was sitting across from me and kept playing with
her hair. I was worried that a strand would fall into my ice cream cup
or Naji's, but Naji did not mind her hair at all, and while eating his ice
cream, he wanted to know what the story of the plant was. He was
enamored of it.

Parvaneh was not a fan of carrying the plant. An old friend of the
woman with short hair was leaving town for work and couldn't take
the plant, which she loved, with her (her husband didn't agree and
wanted them to get rid of it as quickly as possible), so the friend had

asked the woman with short hair to take it and plant it in her own yard. That was the story of the sapling.

Parvaneh asked the other woman, "Why didn't you tell her that you have a berry tree in the middle of your yard and have no space for this willow?"

"She knew it. She had come to my place a hundred times."

"So why didn't you remind her?"

"I felt shy, and now I've taken it from Maryam. That's done. Maybe we can find some space at the back of the garden. Maybe Saeed will find a way."

"It is as clear as day to me that Saeed, so shy and polite in front of you, will hand it to the garbage collectors at night."

"Shy and polite? Are you being sarcastic?"

"God forbid! But with his bad tempers, if he doesn't like something, even God cannot make him change his mind."

"It's only recently that he acts like that. I swear, he wasn't like this before. Can you believe it?"

"I know. I'm not saying he was born that way."

"Since he has been hanging out with Houshang and gotten involved with this nonsense he keeps talking about, his heart is not even with me anymore. I don't blame you."

Parvaneh suddenly realized that Naji and I were there too, staring at their mouths, listening to what they were saying. "Well, don't think about it now. These things happen. People go through ups and downs in life. Especially in this day and age."

Silence.

The woman with short hair sighed. "What do you think we should do with the plant?"

Naji said, "Just don't let anyone throw it out, for God's sake. It's a shame to let this sapling get mixed with garbage. It's a shame if no one plants it to grow and become a beautiful tree."

"I'll plant it. Parvaneh keeps talking nonsense because she is too tired to walk. Don't think we've walked around the town with this plant, no, we just picked it up from one of these back alleys and are headed two streets down. That's all."

Naji got excited. "We'll bring it for you. Don't you worry, Ms. Parvaneh. I can carry it all by myself. It shouldn't be more than a few minutes away."

Parvaneh said, "I'm not worried about the distance and being tired. I know that this poor sapling will go to waste at this lady's house. It will either get crushed in the garbage truck or die in a corner of the yard."

The woman with the short hair kept laughing at Parvaneh's words. Naji paid for all our ice creams. The women were really touched by his gesture. Even though I was tired, I followed them around because I could see that Naji was enjoying their company. Luckily walking along with the women was not hard because they were wearing high heels and couldn't walk fast. Every minute or so, one of the women's feet got loose in the shoe and twisted, and she stopped to find her balance before continuing.

The woman with short hair asked us, "Do you have a garden?" Naji and I both responded at the same time, except I said no and Naji said yes. The woman laughed. "Which one is it then?"

I asked Naji, "Excuse me, but where is this garden that I don't know about?"

"I'm talking about the empty bed in the middle of the courtyard of the farm buildings. Can you imagine how beautiful it'll be if we plant it there? It would be amazing, right? Don't you think so?"

I realized Naji was so enamored of the plant that there was no room for any discussion. George would probably let him do it. Maybe playing around with the tree could cheer Naji up. The women, too, had understood that Naji had fallen for the tree. What joy there was in his eyes. Why? What was it about the sapling that was so charming to Naji? The women, too, seemed to be looking for answers to the same question. The woman with the short hair, who knew the area well, took us to a green park with a small pool around which children strolled with their parents. We sat on the lawn. The willow sapling was close by. The woman with the short hair said that if Naji could give some good reasons for his love for the plant, she would give it to him. The women, because of their skirts, had no choice but to sit on their knees. We could see their bare thighs very close to us, but we had no sexual desire for them. I mean I didn't have any, and I hoped that Naji didn't have any either. He didn't. The women were simply interesting to us, because they were different from the kind of women we knew, very different, full of novelty.

Naji started his story like this: "A year had passed since the death of my mother. One Thursday afternoon when I went to Naneh's grave, I saw that the soil on top of it was cracked. I brought a few buckets full of water and poured them over the grave, from the top to the bottom, but the water was not enough; the soil drank all of it. I noticed that people had planted bushes and flowers around some of the tombs, but around my Naneh's tomb the earth was all dry and empty. I sat down next to the grave to cry, but no tears came to my eyes. I felt devastated. Suddenly I noticed something moving around. I looked up and saw a guy planting something near his own mother's tomb—he told me it was his mother's tomb. He was planting a crazy willow sapling above the tomb and was busy digging in the earth. When the hole was ready, he put it in. Now the sapling wasn't a sapling anymore, it was a little weeping willow tree. The man began watering the newly planted tree. I wished I could plant one by Naneh's tomb. The man told me he had bought the sapling at the gate of the cemetery, from a guy who sold them to people from his truck.

"Happily, I set out toward the gate. I noticed a few other people here and there who had bought willow saplings and were busy planting them near their loved ones' tombs. I thought about having to come a few times to generously water the tree. I thought about the tree growing so tall after two or three years that its shade would cover the whole area. My Naneh's tomb would be covered from head to toe with the shadow of the weeping willow. What calmness my Naneh would have, under the shade of the willow, surrounded by its beauty. The sun could no longer crack the soil of her grave. I was deep in these thoughts when I got to the truck selling the trees. There was only one sapling left in the back. I fell in love with it, so much so that I forgot to first ask its price and was simply standing there admiring it. Finally, I asked how much it was. The seller's answer was like a kick in my chest. He had a large build, and, standing above me in the back of his truck, he gave me a look of disdain, because he was sure that I, at fourteen, didn't have that much money.

"He shouted that he was leaving for town, that if there were any passengers, they should hop in the back of the truck. There was a long straight road that ran from the cemetery to the town, all the way to the town center. Some folks jumped up into the back of the truck. The man had given up on selling his last tree. It was so expensive that I would have had to work for several days to save the money to afford it, if I could afford it at all. The man told the passengers who were hopping in the back of his truck to be careful of the sapling. Finally, there were five or six passengers. The seller asked one man to hold the pot firmly with both hands, and he did. The seller then sat at the wheel, turned the car on, and drove off. As the truck and its passengers drove away, my sapling, too, got farther and farther away from me. And I, ashamed of myself for letting my Naneh down, couldn't bring myself to return to her tomb, so I just stood there, staring at the truck driving away on the straight road, staring until my seedling got smaller and smaller and finally disappeared, and now it is here, appearing once again. That is my story."

The women had been crying and were wiping their tears with tissues. I didn't believe Naji's story, because I knew he sometimes made up stories in order to get what he needed, but either way, the women decided to give him the tree.

"Instead of the courtyard, why not take the tree and plant it where it needs to be, right next to your mother's grave?" I asked him.

"Don't even mention it."

"How come?"

"Because Naneh is very far away from here."

The next morning, we were happy to have a good excuse to sit in the back of Kavous's truck. Seeing us with the weeping willow pot would be enough for him, I thought, to let Naji and me sit in the back to hold the plant instead of sitting in the front right next to him. But instead he secured the pot in a corner of the back section of the truck and fastened it tightly so that it didn't need any special care. While he was putting the rope around it, he told Naji to test it to make sure it was fixed, and then started to laugh.

"It's brilliant, super, super brilliant, our dear Naji's young tree." Kavous insisted on calling it Naji's tree. "But just between the three of us, how could you take this lovely tree of yours and plant it in the middle of a pig farm?"

Naji said, "It is meant for the middle of the farmhouse courtyard. When it is all grown, the workers will sit under its shade at noon and have their lunch. I might not be here that day, but I know there will be someone who would remember Naji kindly and say, 'Thanks, man, for planting this weeping willow for us before moving on.'"

Kavous was staring at Naji's mouth. "How lucky to have such beautiful love for a plant, bro. It shows what a pure heart you have in your chest. If you allow me, I'll come and plant the tree myself and do it so firmly that no one can ever pull it out."

Of course, I had warned Naji beforehand to not get excited and suddenly invite Kavous to the farm. Under no circumstances. Because George would not like that at all.

As he was driving, Kavous craned his neck and stared at Naji's face. "Only a coldhearted man would refuse you permission to plant your tree on his land. If I had a plot around here, I promise my workers and I would take care of your plant forever. I'd even show you how." He was trying to send love messages to Naji.

Actually, George welcomed the planting of the willow in the middle of the farmhouse courtyard. So the first thing Naji did that day on the farm was to find a shovel and dig a hole in the middle of the courtyard. He then put the sapling in there, filled around it with soil, and watered it as much as he could.

George kept checking the newly planted willow and asked Naji, "Do you think it will survive here?"

"Of course it will. Why should such a fresh and lively tree die?"

"I mean because of all the shit smell around here."

"That's exactly why we need a plant, because there is a bad smell."

"Really? How come?" George asked.

Naji looked at me. "Jamil knows well and can explain it to you."

But I was in no mood to explain, and George, too, didn't seem to want to listen. "If you say so, then it will surely stay alive. Perhaps you have experience in planting trees. Either way, thank you, my dear boy, your tree will bring some life to the empty courtyard."

"If no hand intentionally removes it during the first two to three weeks, before the root is fully settled in the soil to hold the tree down strongly. Only if this period passes will it become a thick tree that can't be easily uprooted. I mean it can be uprooted, but not easily."

"Why would anyone want to pull it out?" asked George.

Naji grimaced as if he was complaining about someone or something. "Well, monsieur! Sometimes people do things that make no sense, I swear to God, but they do them just to enjoy themselves or to break someone else's heart." It seemed that he was trying to sadden George with his words, but George started laughing out loud and continued to walk away from Naji to check on the animals. Naji stood there with the shovel, looking proudly at the new tree he had just planted. "You like it, right? Isn't it wonderful?"

I didn't have any desire to take Kavous's truck to the farm, and Naji had to agree with my wishes, otherwise he would have to put up with my rapid-fire grumbling. But when we got to the town square, Kavous was already there, standing outside his truck, looking around, waiting for us. So that day, too, we had no choice but to go to the farm with him. On the way, he first asked about the tree, and when Naji excitedly described the whole process, he said he prayed that the tree would remain healthy and lively forever. He was waiting for Naji's story of the tree to end so he could start his own and tell us what he wanted to tell us. When we asked him how he was doing, he said, "I am very sad. They are pushing the country to extreme corruption, but somehow that's a good thing, because this level of corruption can lead to positive events. You know, it can accelerate the Agha's arrival, make it happen much sooner than is promised." We didn't respond, because we did not know what he was talking about.

"Did you see what was written in the papers yesterday?" asked Kavous.

"We don't buy the papers. I mean, whatever they write has nothing to do with us. I'm sorry," I responded.

"But it does have to do with you. You are the youth of the country. Whatever happens here has to do with you, with your life, your morals, your religion, whether you like it or not. I mean, it has something to do with all of us here," he explained.

"Tell us why you are angry now," I said.

"If you read the papers, you would know how the clerics, especially the Agha, are being insulted. Do you know why him? Because he is against corruption, against the shah himself. The shah, who is supposed to take care of people, provide jobs and safety, only knows how to spread moral decadence, support the fags, and make the country lean more toward the West," said Kavous.

"Sorry, but why are you worried about this?" I asked him.

"Looks like you're completely clueless. You don't know how the people of Qom are fighting with the newspapers because these papers are the main force behind faggotry; but as long as there are people like me in this country, we won't let this happen. I myself am looking for an opportunity to reach Tehran to find those two fags and hang them with my own hands." He looked out the car's window and sighed, "Oh God, would I be honored to put the noose around their necks with my very own hands."

"Oh, watch out!" I snapped.

"What?" he snapped back.

"Nothing. You were just swerving off the road and killing us."

"You don't believe what I'm saying."

"We do, but excuse us, we don't know who you are talking about."

"So I should bring the newspaper for you to see," said Kavous before dropping us off.

At the end of the day, when we arrived back at the square around sunset and he picked us up, he continued where he had left off. "It will happen. Do you know when?" We just looked at him. "The day this statue is brought down by the people. Just like years ago, when my uncle was a kid and saw how the people pulled it down, but alas, the very next day, it had gone up again."

Early mornings when we stood in the town square waiting for George, I would get bored and whine for no reason, but Naji tried to make me laugh by pointing to the shah's statue in front of us. He said, "Begging you on Prophet Abolfazl's grave, take a look at this statue." The statue was right in the middle of the square, and cars drove around it. The shah was standing tall on a rock column there. His hat at the highest point. His right arm up in a military salute, with the tip of his middle finger touching his temple. His left hand, though, was hanging next to him, with his wrist bent in a way that made it seem he was pointing to his sex, and this had made the statue a laughingstock for Naji: "Look how he is offering his penis and balls to the nation!"

I would laugh. Naji would give a military salute and position his other arm similar to the statue, slowly swirling his hand around. "Ladies and gentlemen, please come enjoy these majestic genitals." I would burst out laughing. Sometimes he entertained me there in the evenings as well. The ground around the statue was covered with grass, and at night the fountains surrounding the rock column turned on and sprayed water into the air. Sometimes when the wind was blowing, we would walk to the grass to wet ourselves with the water drops, but I don't know why the blue-uniformed police officers didn't like seeing people on the grass at the foot of the shah, and even when they were distant, they would pull out their batons and gesture to us to leave the grass and return to the asphalt. Unlike me, Naji wasn't afraid of the police officers and stood there as long as he could, in the path of the wind and the water spray, facing the statue. "Mashallah to the grandeur of our rock shah."

And if he was drunk, he would burst out laughing loudly. Afraid, I would try to pull him toward the street to avoid facing the police officers. The police officers at that time were quite foul-mouthed, cursing people, especially young men like us, with profanities, and I was really anxious about being cursed at. Until that night when Naji got pretty drunk. It was Friday night. We had our violin with us. Whatever I did to stop him from getting close to the fountains did not work. In the blink of an eye, he handed me the instrument and ran in the direction of the statue, taking his shirt off and throwing it to the side, running drunkenly in between the fountains, screaming, his body getting more and more wet. I was standing at a distance when I noticed two police officers walking toward Naji from the other side, and there was nothing I could do as they pulled him away from the fountains. One of them started talking to Naji, and the other one went toward the column, looking for something on the ground. I stood there, frozen, thinking they'd let him go now, but I saw the police officer who had paced around the statue and hadn't found anything there walking to Naji and smacking him in the head. Finally, I walked up and told them I was his cousin. They asked me where his shirt was, and I found it somewhere on the grass and had him put it back on. The two officers, who had handguns on their belts, spoke to one another in low voices. Then one of them set off toward the navy Jeep, and the other one told us to follow him. He took us from the square to a quiet corner on the sidewalk and asked how much money we had. We had just been paid our wages by George and had a good sum of money with us that we had to give the officer. He took all our money, not even leaving us our taxi fare to go back home. He told us he was going soft on us by not taking us to the police station, otherwise we would be in big trouble. But as he was telling us to leave, his colleague arrived and said, "Hey, Goudarzi, don't let them go. The captain wants to talk to them. Bring them. Bring them." The officer who had taken our money said, "It's out of my hands now since the captain has seen you and needs to ask some questions. There's nothing to worry about. He'll let you go soon."

As the other officer was taking us to the car, he asked us if we had cigarettes. Naji pulled out his pack that he had just bought. The officer took the whole pack from him and said we were still kids and should not be smoking. He lit up one for himself and put the rest in his pocket, adding that we would thank him when we grew up for what he had just done. Then, in the navy Jeep, they took us to the station. An officer who was clueless about the situation and was simply wandering around in the station courtyard walked up and slapped Naji in the face and turned away without a word. When Naji asked why, the response was,

"You mean you don't know? You really don't? Okay, then. You'll soon find out, then." Another officer took us to a small room where there were only three chairs. No matter how much I insisted that we had done nothing, no one listened. In the room, an officer silently took a set of handcuffs from his belt, inched forward to us sitting on the chairs, and locked one cuff around my ankle and the other around Naji's, then told us to just wait there and left. The fear and the slap had sobered Naji up. I, too, was so frightened that I couldn't even curse Naji. We were devoured by fear. If it weren't out of respect for Naji, I would simply call this story of ours *The Boys of Fear*.

A large man in plainclothes entered the room, threw a glance first at us and then at the folder in his hand. "Which one of you is Jafar and which one Reza?"

"I am Jamil, and this is Naji, Officer," I responded.

"Wait a minute, how many names do you two have?"

"We have always had only these names, Officer. You have to believe us."

"Okay, that doesn't really matter. Where did you put the watches? You haven't sold them yet, right? Here it says you haven't. Is that right?"

Naji had become mute. Later on, he said he didn't talk so he wouldn't enrage the officers even more with his breath reeking of alcohol. I told the officer we knew nothing of the watches. Still sitting, the man kept kicking at our ankles with the tip of his shoe. It was very painful. I cried and swore that we didn't know what he was talking about. After a while, he seemed to begin to believe us and left the room, leaving us there. Once we asked a guard to take us to the restroom, and he took both of us together. We walked slowly. It was hard because Naji still staggered drunkenly and couldn't quite keep it together. Any guard who saw us in that state seemed to be tasked with either swearing at us or hitting us in the head. Afraid and humiliated, we couldn't even feel the physical pain. The main interrogation was done by a young officer. It was after midnight. He wanted to know who exactly we were, what we did in life, and what we were doing there.

I had copies of our monthly pay stubs that George had given us in my pocket, which I showed the officer. Also, because of the violin we were carrying, the young officer thought we were artists and treated us with some respect, not kicking or slapping us, not cursing us, just asking questions. He asked our opinion about government opposition groups, and we told him we didn't know anything at all about them. He wanted to know what we thought about some thugs associated with the Islamic Marxist group, whose trial had been broadcast on TV a while ago. But we hadn't seen anything and didn't tell him that we had heard some things about it from other workers on the farm. He wanted to know whether we had seen others hanging around the rock column while we were playing around the fountains. He kept asking questions, staring into our eyes. He then left us. Very early the next morning, an officer we had not seen before came and sat on the chair in front of us and read us a statement that said we swore to never be seen around the statue again and that if we ever saw anyone taping political leaflets to its column, we would immediately report it to the police, otherwise they would do something unspeakable to us. The officer read the whole statement to us and took our fingers one after another, pushed them onto the wetness of an ink pad, and pressed them at the bottom of the paper. Then he uncuffed our ankles and told us we were free to go.

When, fearful and worried, we were leaving the police station court-yard, suddenly a hand slapped Naji on the back of his neck unexpectedly and forcefully, followed by the disgusting voice of an officer laughing. "You motherfucker, you had it easy this time."

"Where have you been, you two fine young men? Why did you dis-appear these past few days? Inshallah, it has been for good reasons."

"These past few days, we had to go to the farm very early, because we had so much work to do," I said.

"I'd say the monsieur has been exploiting you."

"Not at all. We wanted to get there early ourselves."

"If you want, I might be able to find you a better job."

"No, thank you so much. We are really happy with our job."

Kavous forced us to hop onto his truck. We had been waiting in the square for George, who was delayed, but he had told us that, in case of delay, we should take any car that went in the direction of the farm. We had little choice but to get into Kavous's vehicle, despite my own wishes.

"Where have you been?" Kavous asked again.

"George's car is now repaired, so we don't have a problem commuting anymore, as we prefer to go with him," I explained.

He seemed to not have heard me, or he acted that way. "I've brought you the piece of newspaper I had promised you so you can see with your own eyes and believe me; otherwise, I swear on your lives, it's totally unbelievable." He showed us the newspaper clipping dated a month ago. "Here you go. Look at this, proof of this horrible shit." He passed it to me. He was pointing to the picture of two men standing next to each other and laughing. One of the men wore a tie and the other a bowtie. The news article was about the two men's marriage. "Please read it for your friend too." I explained to Naji what the picture was about. Kavous added, "Tell him the date, too, so that he knows where he is living."

I did. "February of 1356 [1978]."

"What day?"

"That part is erased."

"Can you believe that two men could get married? I mean, how can it be that instead of a man being the groom and a woman the bride, both the groom and the bride are men?" He burst out laughing. "Can there be any vice more serious than this?" He stopped and murmured something in Arabic to ask God for forgiveness. "You don't see anything like this anywhere else in the world, kids. Believe me when I say it. I have traveled to many places—Germany, Italy . . . Where else? Japan, and some other places. But I've never heard or seen anything like this anywhere else in the world. That means our country is number one in spreading vice and corruption, as those who live in the capital think that being civilized means that a man should fuck another man in the ass and then that the newspapers should proudly publish their picture with the news. Don't you think it is time for the Agha to appear?"

We didn't say anything, and he kept going, "But they will pay for all these things, you'll see. Do you know how many towns have already risen in protest? If only the people of our town, too, would show some

courage. The people here and in the capital will come to the streets one
of these days and prepare things for the Agha's appearance."

Naji whispered in my ear, "Who is the Agha?"

Kavous heard him and asked, "You don't know who the Agha is?"
He then turned to me and said, "You who have gone to school and
know everything should tell your friend who the Agha is and where
he is now."

"I studied for a few years, but that doesn't mean I know everything,"
I replied.

"But you know who the Agha is, right?"

As we did every Friday morning, before work we had gone to Amrollah
Khan's place and knocked at the door. A young man opened it. We
had seen him before in the courtyard, washing clothes or dishes in the
small pond, but he acted as if he had not seen us before, as if we were
total strangers. When he saw the musical instrument in Naji's hand, he
asked, "Are you here for Amrollah Khan?"

"Yes."

"I don't think he's home."

"But of course he is. He knows we come to him every Friday at the
same time."

The young man pulled the door toward himself, opening it for us to
enter. "He hasn't been around for the past few days. If you want, you
can go to his room and check for yourself."

We crossed the courtyard toward the staircase and went up the narrow stairs. The staircase was darker than usual and smelled of dampness. We knocked on his door. The landing in front of his room was
quite small, and you had to be careful not to stumble, otherwise you
would fall down all those narrow sharp-edged stairs. Amrollah Khan
had told us how, the first year he had rented the room, he had fallen
down the steps once or twice, though not too terribly, and then he
had gotten used to the stairs and the landing and had never fallen there
again. We asked him why he didn't ask the landlord to give him another
room, and he told us it was because that room was the only one in the
house that had its windows open to the sky. The windows in the other
rooms either opened onto the wall of the huge building almost attached

to the crumbling house or onto the courtyard, so in order to have a piece of sky through his window, he had accepted the risk of falling from the landing. We knocked on his door again. This time even harder. Finally, he opened the door. His body was hunched inside his ragged cloak. He moved his hand from the doorknob to the edge of the door, looked at us with kind but listless eyes, and smiled. "Oh, my kids, you have to excuse me today."

The edge of the door slipped out of his hand, out of the path of his body, which tried to lean on it, and then, as if he were a candle suddenly melting away, Amrollah Khan spread out on the ground right before our eyes. We jumped inside and took him in our arms. Naji called out to some of the other renters in the house. A few came, and everyone offered one suggestion or another. Amrollah Khan's mattress was spread on the floor of his room, and we helped him lie down there. The neighbors said he had to be taken to the hospital, so Naji and I decided to get him there somehow. Amrollah Khan opened his eyes and looked around him.

"What good neighbors I have. May God grant you longer lives. But I beg you not to take me anywhere. At least not today. Just let me lie down in my bed. And if anyone wants to help out, please just make me a glass of lemon sharbat. Then let me stay with these two young men to give them their music lesson."

A young woman wearing a thin black-and-white veil said she had lemon sharbat at home. She went and made a big jar and brought it back. The reason I remembered her face for so long after that day was that she kept smiling at Naji, and, with every smile, she adjusted her veil, but Naji just blushed and focused on doing something for Amrollah Khan. Eventually, we went ahead with our plan—but not to take him to the hospital or to go after a doctor or medication. No. We simply did what he asked of us, what we thought was best for him too, and that was to go tell his daughter of her father's condition. We thought that if we could talk his daughter into visiting Amrollah Khan, we would have done something really meaningful.

All day long, we waited for a good moment to tell George the story of going to Amrollah Khan's room and seeing him in that condition, but George seemed quite busy. The moment I thought I could tell him, someone would come and ask for an animal, so we had to go drag the animal out of the farmyard and load it into the truck.

At lunch, when, like every other day, we were sitting on the large bench placed in the courtyard for the workers, I pointed out to George that I wanted to tell him something. He said it should wait. A while after lunch, I noticed he was slowly raking the hay that was spread around in the courtyard and stuffing it into a sack. It seemed no one was in the mood to do real work. It was either the heavy lunch we had had or some unknown reason robbing everyone of their energy. An invisible melancholy was lurking around. When George saw me, he called me over. When I went to him, he asked, "Where is Naji?"

"Mixing and preparing the animals' food."

"He is such a clever, hardworking boy. I like him. You, too, are pretty smart on the job. In the short while you have been here, you both have learned all the nuts and bolts so well that you could run a pig farm, the two of you."

"It is not such a short time that we've been here at your service, monsieur."

"May God keep away any incidents that might take you two from me."

"Has something happened, monsieur?"

"No, nothing yet, but I don't know why my motherfucking heart has been constantly worried that something bad is going to happen."

"Nothing will happen."

"I didn't call you over to say this. I wanted to know whether you two can stay at the farm tomorrow night. I believe it is your shift." Each one of the laborers had to stay at the farm all night long every three or four weeks. There were two people for every shift, and George scheduled Naji and me together. There wasn't any work to do; we just had to stay at the farm.

"Of course we can do it."

"Tomorrow, you don't need to do any heavy work. Just find a quiet corner and rest during the day." Then he asked me, "What did you want to tell me?"

"I wanted to talk to you about Amrollah Khan," I said, and I told him what had happened and that Amrollah Khan had asked us to go find his daughter; but the address he had given us was wrong. Not wrong really, but we learned from the current residents at the address and the neighbors that she had moved many years ago. I told George that we felt one of the neighbors knew things, but he didn't want to share with us whatever secret he knew, no matter how hard we insisted.

"He didn't want to tell you that the girl has been in a brothel for many years," said George.

He had heard this from one of the old neighbors. I told him I was looking for a current address. George said he would try and find it for me, that he would contact some people in the next few days and let me know.

⁓

"Hamed liked young boys more than women," Naji told me.

"Stop sidestepping the topic. You promised you'd tell me the story about you and the fishermen. You said so yourself," I said.

"What good does it do to review a bitter memory from the past, from the distant past, huh?" He feared that telling me the story would affect our relationship, but the night of this conversation, we were so happy with one another that nothing, no power, could upset us.

"I'm just curious, that's all." It was one of those nights when people had come to the streets to protest the shah and the monarchy. Their shouts of *Allahu Akbar* reverberated in the air. We stayed home that night, as we did many of those nights. We were afraid of going out, because the crowds were quite big, and people gathered from all around, so we were afraid to see familiar faces or for them to see us. I was especially afraid to see one of my brothers-in-law, as we assumed they, too, like the other men, would be gathering in the streets. We *didn't want* to be seen. We *shouldn't have* been seen. So we stayed home in the evenings and tried to entertain ourselves. Naji would drink, but I didn't let him drink just anything. I got him whiskey, often from George, who didn't drink anything but whiskey. When he got drunk, Naji at first said funny things and made me laugh, but as he got more and more drunk, he talked of the old times. That night he was pretty drunk. "I was thirteen. Yes, I must have been thirteen. My thirteenth year was a year of misery and misfortune. My mother got sick. My father sent me to Hamed. He told me he had work for me, a job with the fishermen, a night job. Hamed was not a fisherman himself, but he hung out with them a lot. He looked me up and down, said, 'Mashallah, you are quite sturdy and fresh too.' He then asked how my mother was doing. He said, 'So your only problem now is money.' He said, 'We have to go somewhere quiet to talk, where no one can hear us.' He said, 'Let's just go ride in a boat for a bit.' We rowed to the middle of the river. The image of the moon was reflected on the waves, constantly moving up and down. He said, 'Swear on Shah Cheragh's grave you won't tell anyone I helped you come up with the money for your mother's surgery.'"

The shouts of *Allahu Akbar* had grown so loud and angry that Naji became terrified. He stopped talking. I didn't like it when Naji talked that way. When he said disparaging things about himself and his family, I felt his grandeur diminish in my eyes, but what else could I do but look at him with a smile and listen in silence? Then suddenly a voice from beyond the door of our room said, "Hey, you two gentlemen, aren't you Muslim? Don't you want this monster to leave the country, to make room for an angel? Why aren't you coming out to join the rest of the Muslim kids?"

It was the voice of Amir the Troublemaker. He was talking to Naji and me. He, too, worked at the pig farm and rented one of the seven rooms in the house in town. The workers at the farm called him Amir the Troublemaker because he was constantly looking for trouble and liked to start fights. George had threatened to fire him a few times, and, every time, Amir said he didn't mean to get angry, that he just acted on impulse. He had signed an agreement and assured George that he would stop fighting with and insulting the other workers. So when the revolution started and the time came for shouting in the streets, Amir had a blast, as he could shout and curse as much he wanted, without anyone being able to tell him to stop. When people started to freely curse the shah, Amir the Troublemaker cursed the shah's older sister instead, saying Ashraf was the reason behind all the existing corruption, that she was the head of all drug traffickers. We didn't know how true his words were, but either way, we listened to him and laughed. He said one day we would all realize that he was right.

In his drunken state, Naji said something in response he shouldn't have. "If you are a true Muslim, why do you work on a pig farm, my brother?" he asked Amir the Troublemaker and burst into laughter.

Amir did not laugh. "If a Muslim is forced to do something he doesn't want to do, God will forgive him. Speaking of which, this farm will soon go up in flames."

I nudged Naji to communicate that he shouldn't have agitated Amir. "Don't you get it? There's a reason he is called Amir the Troublemaker. It means he looks for the worst in everything. If George hears that you are making such jokes with the guy, he won't like it. You know that we shouldn't annoy George in any way whatsoever. He has really helped us out."

"I'm sorry."

"You have to apologize twice more so that you remember not to joke around with Amir, who is nothing but trouble from head to toe."

"I'm sorry, once. I'm sorry, twice."

"You can see how much George and his farm are at risk. With the mullahs beginning to take over everything everywhere, and with how they can't stomach the Christians, if they have the chance, they'll burn down all their property with all their possessions inside, including this very farm. What would we do then? Where could we find such a good job with such a kind employer?"

"I'm sorry, three times."

I was mad at him because this was not the first time he had joked around with Amir. Another time, when Amir was talking to other workers about religion and its benefits, Naji walked up to him and said, playfully, "A real Muslim wouldn't be wearing such colorful T-shirts with Ray-Ban sunglasses, like the ones you are wearing!"

Amir wore T-shirts in hot and cold weather. Imported colorful T-shirts. He had said that one of his relatives was a boat captain and that every time he traveled to Arab countries, Amir would give him money to bring him T-shirts, every time of a different color. Amir was infuriated.

"What are you saying, man? What does religion have to do with my T-shirts? With my Ray-Ban glasses? Religion has nothing to do with what one wears, dude. If you are ignorant and don't know anything, you should ask your smart-ass friend, you idiot."

I wanted to tell him that, as far as I knew, religion did have something—actually a lot—to do with what one wears, but I stopped myself to avoid inflaming the argument. That day, Amir and Naji almost got into a fist-fight, but the other workers and I got involved, to prevent anything bad from happening. Over lunch, George had them make peace, forcing them to apologize and kiss each other on the cheeks. The funny thing that day was that Amir didn't want to kiss Naji at first and kept pulling away, but George and the other workers teased them and brought them closer together. With a smile, Naji quickly kissed Amir on both sides of his face, but Amir hugged Naji and kept kissing him without letting him go. I waited for him to let Naji go, but he didn't, and in the end, I had to get between them and pull their shoulders apart. "Hey, that's enough, the peacemaking has already happened." The workers laughed. The next day, Amir gifted Naji a beautiful blue T-shirt. We bought Amir a case for his sunglasses from the bazaar by the river so that he, like Naji, could put his glasses inside and hang the case from his waist.

There were other nights, too, when Naji got drunk and told stories. I would lie down, gently put my head over his legs, and tell him, "George really likes you. He says you are very capable. I like it when he says such things about you."

He said, "So you mean I wasn't capable enough to save my mother from melting away, from dying so young right in front of my own eyes with so many of her dreams unfulfilled." I tried to calm him down over and over, telling him, "You did all you could, my dearest dumbass, more than what any other child would do for their parents. You suffered trying to save her life. But it just didn't work." When he got drunk, he talked a lot of nonsense, and I laughed and called him "my dearest dumbass."

He said, "Hamed told me that everyone knew I hung out more with the girls. Well, the place I went to cut grass, there were mostly girls there. So what was the problem, then? Actually, it's better to be a girl, isn't it? Men always suck up to them. This was what Hamed said. He said, 'I won't let the fishermen do to you what men do with women. No. You said you're thirteen, and it's too soon for you. And if any motherfucker wants to forcefully pull your pants down, run and tell me. No one should have anything to do with what is inside your pants; you should just use your mouth and your tongue.' I kept seeing the shadows of the fishermen moving around in the water near the shore. Hamed said, 'You are going to only lick and suck. Each man should take three to four minutes at the most, but you can learn the skill of how to make them finish faster.'"

I said, "Your words are making me sick. You are getting sleepy now. Come see what a warm bed I've prepared for you. Come slip under clean sheets."

Even after he got into bed and I had turned the lights off and the room was drowned in complete darkness, Naji went on. "Hamed told me he'd give me a quick free lesson on what to do. It was total darkness between our boat in the middle of the river and where the fishermen were. He said, 'No need to worry, they can't see what we are doing here. If you go down like this and kneel between my legs, it seems that you are not here at all. On the floor of the boat, on your knees.' He then unzipped his pants, the motherfucker." Then Naji fell asleep, and I sat there in the darkness crying, thinking how cruel it was that even after enduring such shameful denigration, he had not been able to save his mother from a failing kidney. But I put all my energy into encouraging him to forget about the past and reminding him how strong and brave he was now. Honestly, one of the qualities I loved was his courage. He could do anything he put his mind to. For example, sometimes when we encountered nasty people who wanted to make trouble, Naji would step forward fearlessly and refuse to let them take over the situation. He told me, "The main thing in a fight is how your opponent sees you. If he realizes that you are afraid, you are done. But if he sees that you are not scared of him, he'll try to pull away, even if he is much bigger than you. These types of street fights don't have anything to do with how big or small you are." This was how he comforted me so I would not fear anyone. George told us to stay away from trouble, especially street fights, but knowing that Naji had my back, I had found a strange courage. Maybe I loved him because of the sense of security he gave me. I really was a different person with him. I was not afraid of anything. With him, I had a supporter who was willing to do anything to keep me safe. And that was a huge blessing from God, and for that I was grateful.

But George. Poor George. What fire burnt his soul. What flames burnt his life down, turning it into ashes. *"You two are truly the best workers in my farm."* But what use were we when we didn't do anything to stop the fire? Could we have stopped it? A fire that had started elsewhere, beyond our power to control. If we had handed Kavous to the police, wouldn't we have stopped the first fire in George's life? We were afraid of Kavous. That was clear. We were afraid for our own lives. We convinced ourselves that a fire at the farm was in the making and that whether we turned Kavous in or not, it would still happen. Actually, the blurry news of the event encroached on my dreams. That night, I was startled awake. I think I was mainly worried that I'd fallen asleep during my night shift, even though I knew Naji and Zaal, who never really slept, were both awake. Naji was sitting on a stool and was taking his black boots off to put on regular shoes. "Between the two of us, you snoozed quite nicely," he laughed.

"What is going on? What happened?"

"Is something supposed to happen?"

"I have a feeling it is. Where is Zaal?"

Naji pointed to the window. "There. He is wandering around the courtyard." It was still dark, but a lead-colored dust pouring down from the sky diminished the intensity of that darkness. Zaal stood by the weeping willow in the middle of the courtyard with his back to us. He carried a big wooden pole across his shoulders and had his arms draped over it on either side, looking like Jesus carrying the cross. Perhaps he was gazing at the horizon, waiting for the first rays of sun, what I, too, did on the mornings of my night shifts. George felt assured about the nights because Zaal lived on the farm. Of the two rooms at the end of the courtyard, one was Zaal's alone, and the one we were in was public and meant as a resting place for the workers who stayed overnight.

Zaal was almost two meters tall, with a big sturdy build and very big hands. One of the things that sometimes entertained the workers after lunch was to cheer him on to crush an empty can with just one hand. As the lead-colored dust now poured over Zaal's body, suddenly we heard a gunshot. Just one, from a distance. Naji had his shoes on and was ready to go. Zaal didn't react to the sound, because he was deaf. I jumped down from the bed, and Naji and I walked out of our room and toward the sound. There were short walls all around the farm, the top of which were decayed and in ruins, so it wouldn't have been too hard if someone wanted to jump over them into the farm. We heard someone shouting, "Allahu Akbar!" Not too close. I turned to Naji and said, "We better let Zaal know. Please put the club away. If these guys are armed and see you holding it, that would make them even more angry."

Naji moved the big wooden stick back and forth from one hand to another. "You shouldn't worry. It might come in handy. So go ahead and find Zaal. Stay right where he is, so no one can attack you out of the blue." On the one hand, I liked that he looked after me like that; on the other, I sometimes felt that he saw me as a defenseless child, and I didn't appreciate that. Still, I said, "Okay, I'm going, but only to let Zaal know," and I went looking for him.

"Stick with him until I'm back."

Zaal was truly faithful to George. When he spoke, he uttered the words heavily, so if you didn't know him, you couldn't understand what he was saying. You also had to watch his lips. He told me he had seen a few shadows moving around beyond one of the walls. He pointed in the opposite direction Naji and I had gone. He was worried for us and decided to take the dogs and look around on the other side of the walls. When he started off, I heard a sound from where Naji was.

One of the dogs ran in that direction. Zaal and the other dog went out the gate at the entrance to the farm. I was left there wondering what to do. I really didn't want to come face-to-face with strange men who were either moving smuggled goods or had come to rob us. I could hear the pigs breathing, coughing, and sneezing, crickets chirping, the dogs barking, and worst of all, the clump of unfamiliar feet running. Maybe it was the police officers who could often be heard around there at that time of the morning, looking for the men who had biked to the port at night and returned at dawn, before sunset, with smuggled goods, such as tea or cigarettes or sometimes clothing, tied to the backs of their bikes, heading to the town to sell them. The barking of the dog who had gone in Naji's direction grew louder. When I walked toward him, I saw Naji holding the dog's collar and pulling it away from the pig den by force. All around the stable, there were stalls, small and big, where we kept the pigs at night. Some stalls were big enough for just one pig, since sometimes, because of sickness, we had to quarantine them; and some had space for three or four. Now the dog kept trying to move toward one of the small stalls, but Naji had stopped it and kept pulling it in the opposite direction. Outside the farm gate, two police officers were trying to talk to Zaal. There were just regular police officers from the local station and said it wasn't anything important, just a few petty cigarette smugglers who had escaped but would soon be arrested. But the plainclothes officer said something strange: "There is a group who came to set fire to the farm." We asked him why, and he explained, "Because there are some quite conservative Muslims who say pigs are haram and harmful. They also believe this farm is a sign of the presence of infidel foreigners, such as Americans and British. Can you believe that such people live in this country?" The man had arrived in a spotless Jeep with a solid high-quality body that bore no likeness to the vehicles driven by the local police officers. By then, it was day, and the sun had completely risen above the horizon. Seeing that Jeep, the police officers had quickly composed themselves and pretended they were in control, holding their guns firmly. The man pointed to us and asked the police officers, "Are you sure these two are not with them?"

"They are from this farm, sir. They are laborers."

The man stepped toward Zaal and looked him up and down. "So who is he?"

"His name is Zaal, sir. He, too, works at the farm."

The man asked Zaal, "Tell me what you saw. I'm sure you know them, right? They were your friends, right? If you've hidden any of them, tell me where." He then turned to the police officers. "Why is he not talking?" Without waiting for an answer, he walked to us. "What about you two? Where is this smell of gasoline coming from? Tell me what you've seen and what you know, otherwise this country will be taken over and shat on. Who here smells of gas? You two are young and can be easily deceived."

He stood right in front of Naji, "Are you the driver here?"

"No, sir."

"How come you smell of gas, then?"

The man sitting at the wheel of the Jeep craned his neck out of the car window and shouted, "Farshid!" His eyes were hidden behind tinted glasses.

The man questioning us walked toward the car. The driver told him something before he came back to us. "Okay, so just be very careful. A few of them have already been arrested. We won't let them get away with anything, but we are counting on your help. Report to us whatever you see or hear, otherwise you yourselves will be in trouble. Don't tell me I didn't warn you." He then turned to the police officers. "May you all stay strong. I hope you know what a sensitive time we are in in the history of our country." He kept staring at them, waiting for them to respond.

"Yes, sir, we understand."

"Good," the man said and left us.

There was silence for a while. Then one of the police officers turned to us and said, "Don't believe what you just heard. Who would want to burn down this farm? These are hallucinations. Surely SAVAK knows what they are doing, but, in this area, we only have traffickers to deal with, not crazy people." He turned to his colleague. "You tell them. Am I not right, my dear Jafar?"

"Yes, you are. Instead of increasing our salaries to better fight the traffickers, they have sent a group of SAVAK agents here, to a place they know nothing about. May God help us."

"So now that I'm telling the truth, pass me another cigarette to recharge me."

The second police officer pulled out a cigarette from his pocket and told us, "You two get back to your work, and if you notice anything suspicious, let us know."

Well, the suspicious thing I noticed was that Naji did smell of gasoline. Later I realized what a dangerous thing he had done that night. If it was revealed, we, too, would be in trouble, because with all that was going on, after word was getting around about vandalism and subversives, those plainclothes men looked for any excuse to arrest people and hand them in as vandals to the central office, and we, being young, could be good baits to be arrested for collaborating and hiding the vandals. It was strange that I had not seen any sign of fear in Naji's face. If I had been him or if he had told me that while the police officers and the men from the city were there, Naji had hidden one of the vandals in a pig pen, I would either have confessed or trembled so much that they would have understood that something was going on. Even though, afterward, I scolded Naji for what he had done, I eventually thought he was right and that he could not have done anything else under the circumstances. Maybe if it had been me who had seen Kavous jumping over the crumbling parts of the farm wall, looking for a place to hide, terrified and carrying a plastic bottle full of gasoline, I would've hidden him, because if he had been found by the police officers, who knew what was going to happen to him? Behind Zaal's back, we told Kavous to come out to the pig pen. The dust had settled, and there was no one around except Naji and me. Kavous's clothes were covered with pig shit.

"Thank you, brother. Inshallah, I'll make it up to you for having my back."

Naji said, "Your gas bottle is all empty now. Look how it poured all over my clothes."

"I'm sorry. I'll return the favor."

I went to keep Zaal busy until Naji could send Kavous away from the farm. Kavous left that night, taking with him the smell of the pigs, but that was not the last time we saw him.

Except for Ararat, who had come to our place in town, no one knew where we lived. But one early morning, we were surprised and frightened to find Kavous at the door of our room. One of the other renters had opened the door to the house for him when he said he was a relative looking for us. He had a big box of sweets with him. The neighbor had showed him to our door. We were quite shocked. We really didn't like him coming to our door, but there was nothing we could do about it. He said he had to ask around a bit to find us. He put the box of sweets in front of us. I made him some tea. He had come on the pretext of thanking Naji, but when he started telling us about his life, little by little, we realized he had other intentions. He said he had a wife and three daughters and that he wished at least one of them could have been a boy. He said he didn't have any sexual relationship with his wife, that he didn't enjoy being with her. Between his words, he made us understand that he had fallen for Naji and would do anything for us. He wanted to give us some cash, which we rejected while offering a false narrative: Naji was engaged to our cousin, and they planned to get married after Naji did his compulsory military service. Kavous didn't believe us and implied that he knew everything about our private life. It was obvious that he had worked hard to find information about us. We went through quite a hard day until we could send him away with one excuse or another. We asked him to not meet us there again, telling him that the landlord had prohibited us from having guests. He laughed and wondered how we could be barred from having guests at our own house, but we said it was one of the conditions of our rental agreement, and there was nothing we could do about it. That day, he did leave us, but he was very persistent in the days that followed. On several Thursday nights, we saw him standing around the corner of our street with either a fruit basket or a bag of nuts. All Naji and I could think about was how to get rid of him. Naji didn't think that it was right to tell George about it. He said Kavous was a dangerous person and warned against doing anything to vex him and cause him to seek revenge. What was the solution then? In retrospect, however, the best choice would really have been to let George know. If we had done so, at least we wouldn't have had to carry so much guilt afterward. Even though it would have been dangerous for us to do anything against Kavous, at least we would have felt easier knowing that we had given George the heads-up. About that disaster that befell us.

Zaal had tried to tell George about the police officers and the plainclothes officers. We tried to downplay it by saying they were looking for traffickers and had nothing to do with the farm. We were afraid that if he learned about the events, we would have to tell him about hiding Kavous. But, of course, we had to warn him that danger was lurking around the corner. Yet we didn't. Then came the morning we saw Zaal looking like he was leaving a coal mine. We didn't really need to ask what was going on. We had been looking at the sun. It was completely risen and round, but it was cut through with black clouds that looked more like smoke than clouds, smoke rising from a fresh fire. The yellow pieces of the sun kept shifting, kept growing and shrinking, but they couldn't free themselves from under the black clouds. There were four of us sitting in the back of George's truck, as on any normal day, headed from the town to the farm. One of the workers was singing a sad song. If it were a cloud, why did it keep curving and twisting? If it were a cloud, why did it smell like burning? Naji said, "A burning smell? Is something burning? No. I can't figure it out." Even though Naji and I were whispering in each other's ears, the worker who was not singing put his finger on his nose, signaling us to be quiet, for he was listening to his friend's singing. Naji was so angry he wanted to pick a fight with the guy. Hidden from the eyes of others, I held his fingers in mine, caressing them, and he, sitting next to me, calmed down. The worker was now looking down and simply listening to the song. Naji stared into my eyes. His eyes were light brown and big. His eyebrows looked as if they were shaped by the best stylist in the world. I had trimmed them a bit with scissors, but I never cut them; I just cut some of the long hair dropping over his forehead, nothing else. That way, his eyes were better exposed, and it was the beauty of his eyes and eyebrows that drew men to him. Now I couldn't stare at that beauty anymore, because the driver suddenly and fearfully slammed on the brakes. We had arrived at the farm. Someone asked, "What's going on?" Another blurted out, "Oh, my . . . Oh, Fatemeh el-Zahra!" We jumped out of the truck, and there he was, Zaal, standing there under ashes and smoke, his heavy body frozen in total shock.

George said, "Oh, Sacred Mary!" He drew a cross over his chest and went into the courtyard.

Naji cried, "My tree!" and suddenly he was not next to me anymore. Ashes had covered everything everywhere. The pigs had escaped toward the river. The fire had started during the night, when there was nothing Zaal and the night-shift worker could have done. They were taken by surprise. The arson attack had been carefully planned. They had first poured gasoline over everything and started the fire in the straw warehouse. By the time a dilapidated fire truck had arrived from the town, nothing had remained to hose down. Eyewitnesses said they had seen the pigs running like fire balls toward the river, as fast as possible. How did they know where the river was? From the smell of water or that of life? The river was far from the farm, out of sight. But when it comes to life and death, both humans and animals find some way to survive, led by instinct, the instinct for the joy of existence, the joy of being alive and living a good life. Naji was with his willow tree, watering it amid that gray chaos. I thought George would be mad seeing him like that, but he looked at him and said, "Poor tree. It must be terrified by so much fire. Thank God it is still alive."

Then he squatted in a corner of the courtyard and held his head in his hands. "See how my whole life has gone up in smoke for nothing?" George did not own the farm; he just managed it. It belonged to a group of foreigners, and its products were used by the foreign residents of the town. George had told us this before and said how he was happy with his job, but now he would be unemployed. As would we and the rest of the farmworkers. There was no hope of finding jobs in factories. Every day, one factory or another closed down by demand of the workers, and the newspapers kept announcing more and more strikes coming. The money I had saved helped us a lot in those days; otherwise, we had no idea what to do. But Ararat always had our back, and, eventually, he found us work at a print house with his fiancée's uncle. Print houses were among the rare professions that were busy in those days. People were either marching in the streets or reading newspapers and books. Our job was to bundle and take the newspapers to the delivery trucks. It was a strenuous job, but our employer, Suren, was kind to us. He even invited us to his office a few times for lunch and fed us chelo kabob. There were a few framed photos on his desk, one of which was of Ararat and his niece, Ararat's fiancée. Suren told us that, since he didn't have kids himself, he loved Lily, Ararat's fiancée, like his own daughter. He, too, like George, believed that Ararat would have a bright future with his wife, and whenever they came up in conversation, he said, "Though if they were to listen to me, I would tell them to leave the country as soon as possible."

Before Ararat and Lily found the opportunity to leave the country or, as Suren said, "move to the other side of the water," another fire burnt down what remained of George's life. This fire was bigger and more devastating. We learned about it the day after it happened. We were headed to the print house when we heard that, the night before, a theater had been set on fire, and some people had been burnt alive in there. Some said the fire had started because of electrical issues, but others believed it was arson. But who would do such a thing and with what intentions? Everyone had their own hypothesis. It was said that around a thousand people had died in the fire—women, men, children. The same theater where Naji and I had seen such good films, had so much fun. When we reached the print house, one of the workers told us that Suren's niece and her fiancé, too, had been at the theater. First I remembered Ararat's kind face and then Lily's beautiful smiling face. We had met her when we had gone with Ararat to the pool.

For a while, Naji had been saying how much he missed swimming, but I didn't heed him at first, because I didn't know where there was a pool in the town, until Naji's desire became so strong that I asked Ararat if he knew of a pool somewhere. He told us we had to have swimsuits. We bought them, and he then took us to a pool. Lily was there too. It was the end of summer. They were members of the club and could take us as guests. There were two pools in a large space, one for men and the other for women. The men were not allowed in the women's and vice versa, but we could hang out together around the pool. It was the first time we had seen women in swimsuits up close, sitting with each other in their swimsuits and drinking soft drinks. Lily wore a two-piece swimsuit, and its blue color really looked good on her. She was tall and skinny and had small breasts. She laughed and asked us whether we liked it there. And there we were, simply enjoying the experience, pure joy and nothing else. Now we were thrown from that joy by the sudden painful shock of the present, hearing the news of the theater fire. Naji and I ran to the theater. People were pacing around, stunned. Some women were slapping themselves in the face, madly walking back and forth and moaning. The exterior of the theater was covered in soot. Police officers in blue uniforms with gun holsters at their waists had formed a human chain around the building and did not allow anyone close. Men were pacing and smoking cigarettes. No one was allowed to enter the building, except the rescue team, who wore white clothes and white masks covering their mouths and noses. Eventually, one of them stood on a platform and announced, "Ladies and Gentlemen, the bodies will be transferred to the cemetery. Anyone looking for their loved ones should go to the mortuary. There is nothing for you here, so no use standing around." Naji grabbed my hand and pulled me to the side. He had noticed George slouching on the sidewalk, smoking. It was the first time we had ever seen him smoke. We walked toward him with uncertainty and fear. He looked at us as if he did not recognize us. His eyes red, his face dusty, he just stared at us. We figured he was shaken. We went and squatted next to him. "See what has befallen me? You are witness that this was not my fault. Not my fault," he said. A man behind us said, "It was all the theater owner's fault, who, in these conditions, continued to show films and bring people into this tight dark sinful space, just for money."

Someone else said, "It wasn't all for money, man. It was to cheer people up. It was for entertainment, not for sin."

A woman screamed, "Who did this? Who? Someone tell me who did this."

Everyone was asking the same question, and nobody had an answer. Suren, too, came over and quietly sat down next to George and started crying. His key chain slipped out of his limp hand and fell to the ground. Among the five or six keys, I noticed the key to his Jeep. He had sometimes given us the key to either bring something in from the car or put something in it. Naji and I both liked Suren's yellow Jeep. We had moved newspapers with it several times, because the back seats could be folded down to turn the back into a covered truck, and then Naji and I would sit on top of the papers while Suren drove the Jeep and Kazem Agha, who oversaw the purchases of the print house, sat in the passenger seat. And what a joy it was to watch people through the small window and laugh at them while they tried to rush across the street. They looked funny, I mean the way Naji described them to me. Agha Suren asked Kazem Agha, "What are those two laughing at?" Kazem Agha quietly, but with a smile on his face, struggled to turn around (because he was fat and had a thick neck, it took a lot of effort for him to turn around, and this, in turn, made us laugh even harder, especially since he also had a thick mustache), and finally, he turned his head around and looked at us, and I burst into laughter, at both how Kazem Agha turned and how Naji tried to remain serious. Kazem Agha said, "Swear to God, I have no idea, monsieur. The youth these days are all like this, happy and upbeat, unlike our young days, when we were reserved and grumpy." As he continued driving, Suren added, "We didn't even know what the fuck was going on with us, and there was no one there to tell us. God bless the party for guiding us out of our puzzled mood."

Now George looked at Suren collapsed there on the sidewalk as if he didn't want anyone to sit next to him, but Suren kept weeping loudly as he held his forehead. Naji picked up Suren's keychain from the ground but didn't know what to do with it. I told him to hang it on his belt for now. Then, the corpses were brought out of the theater one by one and put in cars. People tried to run toward them, but the police officers stopped them. One car carrying corpses left. We were told it was heading to the cemetery. We held George by his arms and helped him onto the bus that was taking people there. On the way, we could only hear shrieks and whimpers and incoherent words from the other passengers.

George kept saying, "It's good that your mother has not yet heard the news . . . she has not yet heard the news." Ararat's mother, George's wife, was on a trip and had not yet heard about what had happened. Suren, too, was on the bus, but he wasn't saying anything; he simply continued to cry. In the cemetery, we were joined by one of Ararat's sisters, who threw herself into her father's arms the moment she saw him. Most of the bodies were so badly burnt that they could not be identified. They were all buried together in a mass grave. Naji and I tried hard to find Ararat's body, but we failed, and he, too, was among the group buried en masse. I remembered Lily's long blond hair. Were all those beautiful strands of hair now burnt? George said, "I told you to be careful. I told you these were bad times. Didn't I? No, you tell me, didn't I?" Facing no one, he was talking to Ararat. We were all sitting around the open-mouthed mass grave, watching one body after another wrapped inside a sheet thrown in there. George walked to the mortuary where the corpses were being washed and talked to a man who seemed to be among those in charge. The man moved his head, stepped away from George, and walked back into the building. Alone, George walked toward a corner with more privacy, away from the mass grave. Naji and I went to him. He first asked us for a cigarette. Naji lit one and handed it to him. George said, "Ararat is not among them. The man promised to give me his body, so I can take him to our own cemetery." He meant the Christians' cemetery on the other side of town. He seemed to be talking in his dreams. "You two saw that the guy in charge of the mortuary told me this, right?" We didn't know what to say. He said, "Didn't you just witness what the guy told me? If you did, why do you keep staring at me like the deaf and mute? You seem like you didn't hear him."

"Yes, monsieur. We saw and heard what he told you."

"Go and find Suren and Jacqueline and tell them we don't have anything else to do here and we can head back home. I'll take care of the rest myself." We went and found Suren and Jacqueline among the crowd and told them George wanted to talk to them. Jacqueline was George's older daughter. The moment she reached him, she threw herself over a muddy grave at George's feet. Suren listened to George but kept looking at him in disbelief. He told Naji and me that we should go back to the printing house and do our work. Naji gave him back his keys, and we got going.

A few days later, Suren summoned us when we were busy at work at the printing house and told us that George had called and asked that Naji and I go to his house. He shook his head and said, "The man has gone mad. He has completely lost it." The two of them were old friends. "I fear that he will get worse. I fear that this sweet man, this gem of a man will be forever lost to us."

When Naji and I got there, we saw Ararat's mother sitting like a statue on the couch. She wore a black dress and had thrown a large black piece of cloth over her head. There were now many more pictures of Ararat on the wall. One in which he was beaming with laughter. George said, "So tell me, kids! Weren't you there when the mortuary guy told me they had recognized Ararat's corpse?"

We didn't know what to say or do at first, but then we realized that we had to simply confirm whatever George said. He continued, "Didn't you hear with your own two ears that the guy told me so?"

"Yes, monsieur, we did hear that."

George talked to his wife in Armenian. She asked him something, and George responded. He then turned to us and added, "So I didn't wait around and immediately took my Ararat to our own cemetery and buried him in the grave I had bought for myself. Now, my own grave is going to be a little bit farther away—but still close to my own Ararat."

He continued to talk to his wife in Armenian and kept pointing to us, which meant he was taking us as witnesses. "I'm going to take her to see Ararat's grave tomorrow." The woman kept staring at the photo on the wall. George said, "Thank you, kids, for coming and helping out; otherwise, this woman wouldn't have believed me." He went to bring us some drinks. His wife asked us, "Do you know who set the theater on fire?"

"People are saying different things. Some say they were extremist Muslims. Others say the government did it itself to blame the Muslims, but no one knows who is telling the truth."

"What do the Muslims say? What is it that they want?"

We didn't see Kavous with his truck anymore. Now he had a motorcycle and wandered around the town. He said he was everywhere, and he was right. We, too, learned that he was everywhere. It was Friday. Naji and I were returning from Amrollah Khan's. Buses were on strike, so we decided to walk slowly home. We couldn't go see a film, because, after the fire, all the other theaters around town had closed out of fear. The pool, too, had closed, even before the theaters. All of the town's entertainment centers had closed, one after another. Even the town's National Garden was not safe for an outing anymore and had turned instead into a gathering spot for political activists and various speeches. You couldn't even find an empty bench there. The swing sets had been completely disassembled. The slides were peed upon. You could hear shouts from every direction. A thick smoke rose to the sky from burnt tires. We heard a group of motorcyclists approach from behind and then pass us by. They wore khaki clothes and seemed to be rushing to set something on fire, or maybe they were coming from the place they had already set on fire. We were still far from home. We kept talking to one another to make the distance feel shorter. Because Naji was illiterate, he wasn't in the know about a lot of things. He hadn't understood what Suren meant when he had said, "But I'm a socialist. How can I believe the nonsense George says and act the way he wants me to?"

Suren was referring to George's delirium about Ararat's grave. Every Sunday, he went to the Armenian cemetery in town and sat down at a tomb that he said contained the bodies of both Ararat and Lily. He had even persuaded his wife and daughters that this was true. But Suren had not believed George's words about transferring the bodies. He said, "Ararat and Lily are not anywhere other than in the mass grave in the Muslim cemetery." He said George had made up these things because he had gone mad. We asked, "Now that these two young people are dead, what is the difference where they are buried? What does it really matter if George wants to think like that?"

"You can't just accept such nonsense, my dear kids. I wasn't born yesterday or in a nuthouse. I have for many years studied socialism and science as a member of the Tudeh Party, learned that I should be realistic and not superstitious. It is because of these very superstitions and delirious thoughts that our country is where it is today, suffering such cultural poverty."

Naji had not understood some of Suren's words, and now I explained to him what the Tudeh Party and socialism meant. Sometimes I read the political flyers on the walls to him. It wasn't clear whether the information I was passing on to Naji was correct, because there was a lot of contradictory information in flyers and newspapers, and I didn't know which was true and which false. Still, we read some of them that were printed at our own printing house, just for fun. Naji wanted to know why socialists didn't believe in God, and that was something I, too, wanted to know.

"So how come you didn't ask Suren?" he asked me.

"I'll ask him next time. Right, I should ask him. That's a very good question. Really, why? If socialism is a political path to improve people's lives, why then does it not include God?"

Right then we heard a sound behind us. "Hey, you two lowly musicians!" It was a horrifying sound. I quickly turned around and saw a man in khaki clothes. With glaring repulsive eyes, he pointed to Naji's instrument case in his hand. "What do you have in there? Instruments of evil pleasures? Show it to us."

"No, brother. The case is empty."

"I need to check it."

Naji whispered to me, "But you know it's not empty."

"We have no option but to run."

The man was still some distance from us. He figured we intended to run, so he called for his friends who were on the other street nearby.

"Brothers! These two lowly monarchist musicians are trying to run."

We heard footsteps and had no choice but to run, without even knowing why. We just didn't want to lose the violin that was so dear to both of us. We kept running as the sound of footsteps followed us. We could tell there were many of them. First we ran along the sidewalk of the main street, but then a group of motorcyclists appeared in front of us. "Arrest these lowlife musicians, brothers!" We didn't know how to get away, didn't know which way to turn. We ran into an alley, thinking it would lead us to safety, but it was a dead end, and we had no option but to surrender. We leaned on the wall and squatted down. With their black boots and black smiles, the men walked toward us victoriously. Naji began to moan, almost crying, holding the instrument case tightly in his arms. "My violin." We knew that the moment they reached us, they would pull the instrument out of Naji's hand and break it into pieces. While the bearded men got closer and closer to us, I couldn't do anything but blame myself for not taking Amrollah Khan's advice seriously. "Be very careful in the streets, kids. There are sworn enemies of all music and art out there. They are determined to break and ruin everything." I thought he was exaggerating. I thought the men were into politics and after the shah and his followers, so I never suspected that they would care about a detail as minor as our musical instrument, but now this experience had proven to me that they did indeed care about our instrument. They were getting closer to us squatting there, like two mice cornered by several cats, their shadows throwing their weight over our bodies, until suddenly a savior's voice from the skies came to our rescue. "Stop, brothers! These two are with us." We looked up and saw Kavous getting off his motorcycle. It was the only one in that narrow alley. He parked it and shook hands with the men, and they quietly exchanged some words among themselves. He then came and stood over us and smiled.

"What are you doing here, brothers?"

We didn't know what to say, so we just stared at him. We felt as if we had fallen to the bottom of a pit, and he was up there on the ground, our only hope for escape. He turned to the others and said, "You go ahead and I'll bring them over to the station myself." The other men threw us a look, turned around, and walked away. Kavous called to one of them, "Balal, you stay here with me. I need you for something." Now in the alley, it was Naji and me with Kavous and his friend. "Did no one give you the heads-up to not carry instruments in public under the current conditions? I should have told you myself. You were lucky it was Balal and his boys. Come on, now, get up; we'll give you a ride home. You sit behind Balal, and Naji, you sit behind me. Don't worry anymore." But I was really worried and didn't want them to give us a ride home at all, but we didn't have any other choice. I was afraid that if we objected, he would make things worse for us, so I sat behind Balal, and Naji, with his violin case, sat behind Kavous, and we started off on their motorcycles. Kavous and Naji rode ahead of us, because Kavous knew the way to our house. Even though the case sat between Naji's and Kavous's bodies, I still felt sick and mad with jealousy, seeing how Naji's hands were thrown around Kavous's waist, and there was nothing I could do but to endure that disgrace. Kavous kept turning his head to talk to Naji. I don't know what he told him at one point that caused Naji to rest his cheek against the back of Kavous's shoulder, and then his motorcycle continued on its way, faster than before.

At home, I couldn't talk to Naji for a while. I had an uneasy feeling, as if he had betrayed me. Even though I knew that such thoughts were ridiculous, I had a hard time getting back to my normal self. At last, I asked, "What was Kavous telling you on the way here?"

Naji said, "He's right. We are really lucky that he got there in time to save us; otherwise, what would we be doing right now? Nothing. We would have just had to sit here and mourn the loss of the instrument— that is, if we had made it out of there alive."

"Well, you already said this a few times. What else did he say?"

"He was kind of threatening us. He said he knew we worked at a print house with a boss who is an Armenian and a communist. I was so stupid that I told him Monsieur Suren is not a communist but a socialist, and he laughed and said they are the same thing. He said we better leave the job as soon as possible before something bad happens to us. I asked him what he meant, but he didn't give me any more information. He said the true men of God would not tolerate a communist print house in the middle of the town and let it print whatever it wants to. He said, 'You two need to get out of there as soon as possible if you don't want to burn in that fucking guy's fire.'"

"You mean they want to set the print house on fire too?" I asked.

"No, he didn't say that. He just doesn't want us to go down with Suren. He meant a real fire."

I got angry. "So all the fires set around town so far have been fake? How did they destroy George's life then? With fake fire? How did they knock off poor Ararat and his fiancée? But this time we must do something. We must tell Suren that they plan to set fire to the print house."

Suren asked, "What is your source for this information?"

"Source?"

"I mean who did you hear this from?"

We panicked. Naji didn't say anything. I responded, "We heard it in the street. That they are planning to set on fire print houses run by socialists."

"But nothing about our particular print house?"

I lied to him. "No. Not exactly about ours."

I lied because if I had told him we had heard it from Kavous, Suren would get suspicious of us too, thinking that we had something to do with the group, and we might have lost our job.

Suren said, "It's true that we are socialists, but we are different from the others. We are official members, part of the Tudeh Party that has been active in our country for a long time, especially in our industrial town. Whatever real culture there is in this town, we owe it to the party. Their type won't do anything to our official party. Remember that. Even the baton-carrying crooks in the streets know how important the Tudeh Party is and how much it has served the country. Their leaders, too, know that the revolution wouldn't succeed without our support. They only attack those who have just hatched out and call themselves socialists but don't know anything about it. Our party leaders and the leaders of these thugs share similar beliefs. And you two good fellows, if you want my advice, you better study the party books and join it before it is too late. I'll tell Kaveh to give you some good books in simple language." Kaveh was one of the workers at the print house, a nice guy, but Naji was not able to read, and I had no interest in reading political books. I just wanted Naji to become a good musician as soon as possible and for us to save enough money to be gone from the country and reach Europe. And there, I, too, could start doing what I loved, which was to dance. And we were happy that Naji was really becoming a good musician, and every Friday, we would find a way to hide the violin, carrying it in a way that no one in the street could identify it as a musical instrument. Sometimes we put it in a suitcase and sometimes wrapped it in a bundle of clothes and sometimes hid it in a long pillow we had.

Amrollah Khan was feeling worse every week; he had stopped leaving his house completely, and we did all his shopping for him. One Friday, he was doing especially poorly, longing for and crying out for his daughter, Mahin. We had found out where she lived but had not yet told him anything. On our way back from his place, we decided to go tell her of Amrollah Khan's condition however we could.

The neighborhood Mahin lived in was called the Doub, a word whose meaning we didn't know; we simply knew that it was the town's red-light district. It was a sunny Friday afternoon. If not for the smoke and the smell of burnt tires in the air, you could say it was a beautiful day. As we walked across town, we talked about the theaters and what lovely films we had watched in them. Naji loved Fardin's voice, and he was amazed that it was the actor himself singing, but he was just lip-syncing, and the real singer was Iraj, or sometimes Aref. Even his speaking voice was dubbed. Naji asked me, "So you mean someone else speaks for Fardin? You're not serious?"

"Someone speaks for both Fardin and the other actor, Behrouz Vossoughi."

"Don't tell me that someone else is also dancing instead of Forouzan!"

We kept the conversation going to make the road seem shorter. We were told that the Doub neighborhood was close to the river. We asked passersby as we headed in that direction. One of the boys we asked laughed and said, "But you are late, my brothers. They have closed their doors, and the women do not dare work anymore. So you have to find another solution for your thing. Maybe it would be best to go back to using soap." He laughed at his own words as he walked away. What mattered was that he had shown us the way, and we continued in that direction.

The whole neighborhood was made up of two connected dead ends with a shared iron gate. It was open now, and a group of women were running out through it because the neighborhood was on fire and covered with black smoke. You could only hear shouts and screams, followed by the piercing sound of a gang of motorcyclists who shouted, "Allahu Akbar!" as they rode through the iron gate. They looked like the ones we had seen before elsewhere. It seemed as if we were watching a Wild West film. The motorcyclists were like white soldiers on horses attacking the shelters of defenseless unarmed natives who had no option but to run in fear. Women and kids ran out of the neighborhood, screaming, and every time one of them was knocked down by one of the bikers, she rose and kept running, haphazardly, to nowhere. I turned to Naji and said, "Let's hide, because Kavous might be among them." We jumped behind a column. No one could see us, and we couldn't see anyone either. It was all sound now: the sound of panic and the motorcycles and the joy of the group causing the panic. Women were screaming nonstop, but the sound of the motorcycles kept getting more distant until it stopped.

We walked out of our hiding spot and into the street. The doors to most of the houses were closed. Through the half-open doors of the houses, we could see men and women salvaging their burnt and half-burnt belongings. We could hear fire truck sirens in the air, but there was no sign of any trucks. Only the sound. We kept checking the numbers over the doors, looking for Mahin's house. An old woman rushed out of a house, frightened, with disheveled hair and bare legs. She looked at Naji and said, "You finally came back, Abbas? You are here. Thank God." She opened her arms and moved closer to him. Terrified, Naji took a step back and started running, and I followed him.

We found Mahin's house in the back street. A young woman was squatting at the door and, with her hands on her head, she was staring into an unknown spot in the distance. We asked her about Mahin. She laughed and said, "I know Gholam has sent you. I know that asshole is still looking for me, and he is the one who sent these men to set me and my whole life on fire. The fire will burn him too, eventually. If not today, tomorrow."

When we made sure that she was Mahin herself, we explained to her that we had come from her father. She asked us for water.

I told Naji to stay there and went to the house courtyard, which had a plastic roof. It looked as though I had entered a box of smoke. In the middle of the yard, there was a tiny pond with a water tap. I looked around for a bowl or another vessel. There was a ceramic one on a table that looked like an office desk covered with a large sheet of glass. Underneath it, there were pictures of either several kids or all of one kid. I walked back to the water tap. I noticed the curtain of the room at the end of the yard shifting. I looked and saw a man moving around who retreated behind the curtain the moment he saw me. Frightened, I filled up the bowl with water and went back to the street. We had Mahin drink the water. Little by little, she felt better and began to believe what we were telling her. She asked us how we knew her father, and we told her. She asked us, "Are you sure he wants to see me, that piece of shit?" We assured her that he did. She said, "I'm now a violent mad woman. If you have messed with me, I swear to God, I'll pull out your insides with my own hands, whoever you are, Muslim or not."

When she finally agreed to come with us, she asked if we had a car. We told her we didn't. She said she would go in to find her veil. We heard her calling a man named Farrokh. "Come out. They're gone. Come take us to wherever these boys tell you to go in that rattletrap of yours. In place of what you owe me. All of it. A gift from me to you, a tip for how well you took care of us. Of me and Mom. Now come out of your hiding place. It is all safe now." She put on a black veil covered with flowers that were all in black too, so you could only see that they were Ispahan roses in black if you stepped closer to her. Black roses delicately embroidered or grown on the black veil fabric, now framing Mahin's round face. We carefully followed the man along the labyrinthine streets to reach his car so he could take us to Amrollah Khan's house.

We knocked a few times and entered. Amrollah Khan sat up halfway on his mattress and looked at us in awe. He did not yet believe his eyes. Then his lips laughed, and his eyes cried. Mahin sat down next to the bed and hid her head in her skirt. We sat in a corner of the room. Amrollah Khan started talking. "These past few days, I've been obsessively thinking about your mother, you, and your daughter. About your daughter's name that I don't even know. What did you eventually call her?"

"Hasti," Mahin replied.

"What a beautiful name. 'Life.' You did well. Where is this life of mine now?"

"She is with Auntie Zari. Thank God Zari and Hasti love each other so much."

"Your mother, too, loved you so much. It's so sad that we lost her for nothing. Had it not been for you two, my life would have been a disaster. She was the best, wasn't she? Didn't she have a unique heart? If only I were human enough and had realized the value of all that she had. Mahin, my dear, your father failed to understand. Now, come closer. Come, let me look at you closely one more time."

Mahin moved closer and sat near him. She gently caressed her father's long beard and then moved her fingers over his bald head and seemed to laugh. "Is this really you, Amrollah Khan? How have you changed so much? It's not that you have aged, not that you've lost weight, not that something about your head has changed, or the skin of your face. But something in your eyes has changed, the eyes I remembered have changed. They are not the same eyes."

"Something worse, far worse."

Confused, Mahin asked, "No . . . what are you talking about?"

"Time changes us. You are still young and don't understand how time changes us, so much so that we don't even recognize ourselves in the mirror."

"I'm not afraid of time, Father. No, not anymore, but I'm afraid of fire. You think I'll eventually burn in a fire and die?"

Amrollah Khan pulled her into his embrace with all the strength he had left. "I won't let fire or any other horror find you. You are now in your dad's arms, your dad who didn't do much in his young days is now holding you as close as he can to his bones, the very bones he sold to his art, though no one had rolled out a red carpet for him; who sold everyone around him out to this art in the shadows. He was lost until he found you. These two young men, God bless them, found you and brought you to me so that I could clear up, my dear daughter, any possible misunderstandings that you, too, might have about me, about Soghra, for whom you, your mother, and everyone else thought I had left my whole life behind. No, it wasn't like that." He coughed, and coughed some more, and moved his face away from his daughter's ears before coughing even more. One of us got up to bring him some water, but the moment Amrollah Khan tried to put his lips to the bowl, he coughed again. His coughs didn't allow him to do anything, and his hands, which had been tightly holding onto his daughter, were beginning to loosen up.

"It's the end. His eyes are going, even before him, even before his heart. He is dying in peace."

Amrollah Khan asked for water. Once again, Naji put the rim of the bowl to his lips. Amrollah Khan sipped water, and it dripped down his mustache and his long beard, and he kept laughing through the water dripping down, and we had never before seen such laughter.

Mahin said, "Thank God he is feeling better. You were going to give me something, Amrollah Khan. What was it? Give that to me before you die, Father, as I'm in need. Your daughter is in need." Her black veil had spread around her body on the ground.

"I wanted to tell you about the innocent Soghra. You and your mother and everyone else assumed that she was the one who pulled me into the world of madness, the world of love, but it wasn't her, not her, it was not her at all." He pulled himself away from her and leaned on the wall. He was halfway under the blanket, which had a peacock design. The peacocks were sitting on Amrollah Khan's body with their wings displaying hundreds of colors. "I think you met Kamal. You had seen how he looked like the actor Fardin. Kamal, Soghra's brother, who had a broad chest and above his chest, from right here, had a line that went up along his neck all the way to the bulge of his Adam's apple that kept moving up and down. What a beautiful scene that was to watch. And to watch Kamal, he who owned all that beauty. I'm telling you this so that you don't carry the weight of a sin Soghra never committed. I looked for you for many years to tell you this. I did try to tell your mother too, but she didn't let me; she didn't want to hear it, and she took the weight of poor innocent Soghra's unproven sin to the grave with her. But you are still young, have many more years to live, and I don't want you to carry the weight of someone's sin on your soft delicate shoulders and not realize where that weight is coming from. What I'm telling you is out of my love for you. It was also for the love of your mother that I wanted to tell her too, but she didn't want to hear any of it before dying."

Mahin laughed. First quietly, then louder and louder, like a mad woman, and she kept turning around to look at us. She had big strong teeth that had nonetheless turned yellow. She tried to say something, but her laughter did not let her. We just kept staring at her mouth. Finally, her words began leaving her mouth, bit by bit, letter by letter. "See what the world has come down to! Father and daughter both fell for one person. I, too, was in love with the man my father longed for. But how old was I? Do you remember? Fourteen? You are right, it was because of him that I kept taping Fardin posters to the walls of my room. I think love is the first beautiful thing that comes into teenage girls' lives; it comes like a falling star and leaves like a falling star. He, too, was gone, him and the thought of him. Did you say he was killed? Who said it?"

Amrollah Khan looked down and said in a low voice, "It's a long story."

Mahin turned to us and asked, "Boys, do either of you have cigarettes?" Naji gave her one.

It was decided that Mahin would stay for a few days with her father and take care of him. Amrollah Khan had some money in his chest, all

of which he gave to Mahin. In the chest, there were some other valu-
ables too, like metal frames and pottery that could perhaps be sold
for some money. Amrollah Khan wanted Naji and me, too, to stay with
him as much as we could. He said he wanted to play some music for
his daughter one night. And that night did come. It was a beautiful
night. Even though all the liquor stores had closed, Naji found a bottle
through Suren, and we headed to Amrollah Khan's house. We had hidden our musical instrument and the bottle inside a black plastic bag, as
if we were carrying old clothes. Amrollah Khan had some newfound
life in his veins and looked much younger. "The joy of these few days
and nights is worth the misery of the past few years, misery that is
coming to an end." He raised his glass of arak to our health. Naji and
I felt very proud for bringing joy to the father and daughter. While
Amrollah Khan played, Mahin gradually started singing. She was drunk,
and her voice kept getting louder little by little. What a voice she had!
It was as if her voice rose from the wet flowers of the desert and came
toward us. The sound of the music also kept rising. Father and daughter knew the song inside out. It was as if they had performed it together
a hundred times before. They hit a few back-to-back crescendos together.
Then the diminuendo of her voice, the softening of the music. And then
the silence. Amrollah Khan first leaned his head on the wall, then his
whole back, smiling at us before closing his eyes. Naji said, "He's fallen
asleep." He moved Amrollah Khan's body to the mattress and pulled
the blanket over him. The violin and its bow were still in his hands. Naji
tried to pry them out of his fingers, but with no success. I didn't drink
and felt more sober than the two of them, so I stepped forward and
pulled the violin through Amrollah Khan's fingers, which were loose by
that point. "Amrollah Khan is dead."

"Let him sleep."

"It'd be nice if I lie down to sleep next to him for a bit. You two find
a spot for yourselves to sleep." Mahin crawled under the blanket, put an
arm under her father's head and the other on his chest, and closed her
eyes. A moment later, you could hear her snore, but Amrollah Khan
made no sound. Something leaned on my chest. It was Naji's drunken

head. I pulled his shoulders toward me and tucked him next to me. He opened his eyes, looked at my eyes from beneath my chin, and said, "Amrollah Khan said the safest place in the world is here, right?"

Suren, too, had thought that the safest print house in the city was the one he ran. In Amrollah Khan's funeral procession, Suren walked alongside George. They were stepping around old tombstones with their cement tops chipped. Maybe Suren was talking to distract George from thinking about Ararat.

"It's not that all the religious fighters are wrong. They are right that the country should pull itself out of the shadow of American imperialism. Well, that is what we are saying too. Then they will realize how the Soviet Union has our people's back, if only these deceived Maoists could shut their mouths." Hearing these ideas was surprising to Naji but familiar to me, since I had read some of them in books or heard them among educated people, but I could not tell who would be winning over whom. Maybe I should have known. If I had paid closer attention to the coverage of that foreign radio station, which was the key news source for Iranians back then, I would have understood that the only people who mattered were the devout Muslims, and all others were beside the point. And, eventually, it was they who made the first mark with their shouts and the raucous screams of their motorcycles amid their Allahu Akbars. At that point, Mahin came and said the body was ready for burial. We stepped forward and held the stretcher over our shoulders, walking from the mortuary to the grave. My gaze kept inadvertently going to a woman, an old woman, whose black veil was short for her tall body. Maybe it was her old-style worn-out shoes that made me think she was old, otherwise her body was still fresh and upright, and so smoothly she walked between the tombs as if she were stepping onto the stage in front of an audience. To do what? She was one of a group of eight of Amrollah Khan's friends. Other than Naji and me, there were George and Suren, who knew him from a long time ago, respected his art, and for years had gone to taverns with him. The other two were two old men who were his colleagues. Mahin, too, was there, and that tall woman.

Suren moved his head left and right. "Alas. Amrollah was one of those artists who didn't understand his own art and destroyed himself, like many of this country's artists, from poets to musicians. The moment they receive the smallest praise, suddenly they find more joy in drugs than their art. How easily carried away we humans get."

George shook the hands of the other two old men and smiled. "I know you two." They, too, smiled, but it was obvious that they had not recognized George. "Well, I wasn't on the stage for anyone to remember me. I simply came to see Amrollah perform, which was a miracle to my ears." And he recounted to us that one of the two men played santour and the other tombak, and the woman danced among them. Sometimes wearing women's clothing and sometimes men's clothing with hats, and the men loved her either way.

I assumed that Suren had paid a large portion of the funeral expenses, even though we each paid something too. The gravedigger threw back the soil he had just pulled out of the grave over Amrollah Khan's corpse. We sat down around the grave. I was the only one who knew how to recite the Fateheh prayer for the dead.

Mahin simply kept brushing her fingers over the cold wet soil covering the grave. "You were a good person, though not a good father. You were a good lover, though not a good husband. You were a good musician, though clueless about this world like a child and lost the game, though you yourself thought you were a winner. You took flight into the free skies when others were held in their own prisons, and now, you are completely free."

The old woman raised her head, and, with tearful eyes and wet cheeks, said, "Amrollah's spirit is in the heavens tonight, because he lived free and died free."

One of the old men said, "Lucky him."

George added, "Lucky you, Amrollah, for being rid of this burden. May you guide us who are imprisoned in the cage of this life."

On the ride back from the cemetery, Suren sat next to George in the minibus and counseled him. "It's time for you to get back to life. We must put that incident behind us. Do you know how many of the youth of this country have been finished off by the shah and his American bosses? Well, our kids were just two among those. Also, the case of their murder has not yet been closed." In silence, he puffed at his cigarette and continued, "Instead, the situation is going to change. It's going to change once and for all, and people's lives will be straightened out. We witnessed how the shah had to escape the country with his tail between his legs. And soon enough, Imam Khomeini will return, and we will be far better off. At least then people can choose their preferred party freely and without fear and use its theories as the guiding principles of their lives."

George shook his head and calmly said, "Lucky you who are so naive. I wish I could be like you."

"How so?" Suren asked.

"One's preferred party, principles, better living conditions."

"I know you won't believe it until you see it with your very own eyes, but I'm talking from experience."

George grimaced. "Mainly because you think the theater was set on fire by the shah's people themselves."

Suren didn't say anything. He pulled a pack of American cigarettes from his pocket and offered one to George, lighting it for him as well. Gray smoke quickly filled up the whole minibus, especially since Naji, too, lit cigarettes for himself and Mahin. The two old men, too, lit their own. It was only the dancer and I who didn't smoke but unwillingly inhaled the smoke and kept looking at one another.

When we arrived home that night, Kavous was sitting at the corner of our street on his bike waiting for us. He jumped off the seat and headed toward me furiously. "Hey, you, Jamil! I tried so hard to make you realize you are putting Naji's life and your own in danger, but you just don't get it. You either don't get it or don't want to. Maybe it's because you yourself are one of the fervent members of the Tudeh Party. Of course you are, and I can't do anything for you. I mean, only God can save you, but as for Naji, he is pure like his mind, like clear waters. If he is polluted, that means you've polluted him. You agree, right?"

"Me? Have I polluted him all by myself? Who am I to do that?"

Naji stood there, merely watching us. I turned to him, "Why are you acting deaf and dumb then? Say something yourself. What is this guy talking about?"

Naji stuttered and then quietly said, "What should I say? I don't know."

"Tell him he is wrong. Tell him that the two of us are together to help each other out and be together."

Kavous asked, "Help each other how? You yourself are full of faults. It's not clear yet what your position is with these movements and in relation to the revolution. One day you hang around the Armenians, the other with the communists. And now you have made friends with pimps and whores. All the comings and goings of our youth, who put themselves in the line of the bullets of the monarchy to cleanse this country of such vicious people, then you take the hand of this clueless young man and lead him right to these immoral people whose blood God allows us to spill. What does all this mean, my brother? Can it mean anything other than that you oppose the people's righteous movement? Isn't it so? Speak up if you dare, you who call yourself an intellectual. Please just answer this one question of mine."

I was frightened. It had gotten dark, and no one else was around. I was terrified, thinking that any moment now, he would whistle to summon a group of his fellow motorcyclists to finish me off and send me to the other world with one or two flips of their knives.

Kavous told Naji, "Speak up. Don't you think that a suspicious bunch are leading you astray? To a path that leads to nothing but a shameful death? One that will have you spiraling into the fire of hell, with no questions asked? Huh? Do you want to have such a death await you?"

Horrified, Naji said, "No. Of course not."

"Jump up behind me on the bike."

Naji was dumbfounded. He kept looking from me to Kavous and back without knowing what to do. "What? When? Where do you want to take me?"

"Don't be afraid. We won't go anywhere far. We'll just do a lap around your neighborhood and come back."

I said, "What if he doesn't want to come with you?"

Kavous looked Naji up and down and with a smile that looked like one frozen on the lips of a dead person, said, "Of course he wants to come."

After Amrollah Khan's death, Mahin kept the key to his room for a week or two so that she could take the furniture she wanted from it. One Friday, we went to help her out. Then I had the thought that Naji and I could move into that room. We discussed it with Amrollah Khan's landlord, who didn't have any objections, so we moved into the new house, into the room that had been Amrollah Khan's home and was now ours. I thought Naji would appreciate our move, because it would be to a place of good memories for him and we would be able to get rid of Kavous. But Naji was not comforted by the move, and I was worried about him. He had become fearful, and he looked over his shoulder for no reason whenever walking in the street. It's hard for me to write about those days, when my fear of losing him had overtaken my whole life, when I felt some force was pulling him away from me, spreading in my heart the horror of the possibility of life without him. And all I could do was try and keep myself busy to avoid thinking of that fear.

The other advantage of the new house was that it had a window with a view of the desert, and I would eagerly open the window at night and stare at the desert, but Naji insisted that I keep the window closed and pull all the curtains shut. He reasoned that mosquitos would fly in or that it was too cold, but he really was afraid of something that he didn't tell me about.

I said, "Okay, let's keep the window and the curtains shut. You know that I am always of the same mind as you, that I am there with you. I have been since the beginning and will be till the end." I kept moving my lips all over his arm. "But what about you? Do you feel you'll be with me till the end? That no one will pit you against me, push you to leave me? Leave me for I don't know where, but leave me regardless. Now that you've learned the ins and outs of city life, now that you know you are much worthier than you thought, might you come up with an ending for our relationship like those in tragic books?"

"I haven't read books, so I don't know how to write tragic endings."

"It's very simple. One of the two needs to leave forever. Don't take it personally, but it's always the one who, in the beginning of the relationship, was more heated as well as more dependent. One can guess why this is so. Perhaps it's because the person was, in the beginning, just in need of the other person, had not much choice, just wanted to find an escape from their situation, and then, these conditions, along with a bit of love, went hand in hand to fire up the person's passion, so much so that the person imagined he was the one more in love than the other person, who had not been as dependent and who had had more choices."

"You are talking about me?" he asked.

"Yes, I mean exactly you," I said.

He laughed pretty hard. Then he added, "We will always stay together, until death do us part."

My whole speech was meant to draw those words from him, those most beautiful words, but our real life was not as beautiful as I had imagined it to be. Perhaps all our troubles began when Naji started going to visit Kavous and lying to me that he wasn't seeing him.

After Amrollah Khan's death, we didn't have anything else to do on Fridays, so we simply stayed home. Most of the time, Naji busied himself practicing violin. It had become dangerous to go out on Fridays, especially since the revolution had succeeded and the religious Hezbollahis had won, and now every Friday, they poured out of their homes with the excuse of the Friday prayers, which was great entertainment for them; while they all looked at others around them, they zoomed in on you, searching for a suspect to brand anti-revolution, to jump, to punch with joy and jubilation before leaving his listless body and walking away from the scene with the same joy and jubilation. In that climate, though, Naji did go out. "If you would like, you can come and see where I go."

"Well, where do you go?"

"To watch the shah's officers and uniforms being executed. You can't imagine how amazing it is to watch them all, early in the morning, being lined by the wall and fired at with machine guns. Rat-a-tat-tat."

"What's enjoyable about watching a bunch of tied-up people mowed down by bullets, their blood spilling all over the asphalt?"

"Tied-up people? Don't you remember how they beat us that night? When they were not tied-up?"

"Either way, I know that watching such scenes is not healthy. They impact your mind and can over time irritate you and become nightmares, because you are not a murderer, these things are not normal for you, will never become normal for you in the future."

"If necessary, one could kill, too, for his beliefs, what's wrong with that? Well, little by little, that can become normal. A man should not be afraid of blood; seeing blood makes one brave."

I turned away from him. "Please don't speak to me about this. Be a man and become brave all by yourself."

"I go there to watch because I might see the police officers from that night; doesn't matter which one. For example, the one who slapped me last. Oh God, would it be possible to see him standing by the wall begging?" He then started talking to an imaginary convict, ordering him around as if he were right there. "But it's over and done now, you little boy. Now stand up straight, you fucker, so that your share doesn't hit the other one by mistake."

He guffawed, invoking in me a strange feeling toward him. A kind of mistrust. Naji had changed, become violent, and this was painful. I thought that, despite what he had said about our staying together forever, these were our final days together. Our time together was spent in silence. I wondered what could be done to bring him back to normal life.

I had no idea what he was thinking about. Sometimes he left the bed in the middle of the night, sat by the window, and smoked, blowing his smoke outside through the pulled-close curtains.

One day, Suren introduced us to his so-called Tudeh Party friends. After lunch at the print house, he told Naji and me to stop our work for the day and get ready to leave. He had us join him in his beautiful Jeep (both of us sat in front next to Suren, because Kazem Agha was not with us) and took us to a weird part of town. A neighborhood behind the grain silos, a few rows of affluent houses along tree-lined alleys. Our car passed by a few alleys, turned into one, passed a tucked-away yellow phone booth, and finally came to a stop in front of a building with two tall palm trees on either side and a sign over its door that read, "Revolution Nursery."

We got out. Suren didn't want us to linger and look closely at our surroundings; he kept looking around him and saying, "Hurry up." He took us inside a house with a brown iron gate. There was a big hall full of all types of kids' toys. Through the large windows, you could see the courtyard, with five or six little kids playing there and a young woman looking after them. Suren explained that even though no one had any issues with the party, it wouldn't hurt to be careful. A few blackboards and some pens and chalk and notebooks were lying around. We moved through that room and entered a small room that looked like a newspaper office—stacks of papers on the desks and newspapers and magazines dispersed here and there. Newspaper clippings hung on the walls. We hadn't yet settled in the room when a woman appeared and walked over to Suren, said hello, and kissed him on the cheeks. She was Comrade Roudabeh. We then realized that at the far end of the room, there was an entrance to the basement, where a group of people were busy working. But what kind of work were they doing? Suren didn't say and didn't take us into the basement, as though he didn't want us to know what was going on down there.

Comrade Roudabeh pulled the chairs forward, and we sat. Suren introduced us. The people who came from and went back to the basement all treated us quite nicely. They offered us soda with lots of ice. Agha Safa, who had a bushy mustache, insisted that we accept books and newspapers to read. Naji had the good excuse of not knowing how to read, and I made a case for having too much work and too little time, but the man still gave me a few books and magazines, and I took them. Comrade Roudabeh told us she had been a teacher for many years and volunteered to teach Naji how to read and write. I exclaimed, "What an opportunity. You are lucky, man!" Naji, too, welcomed the idea, and, beginning that day, he started to study with her; later, this became his best excuse: he would visit Kavous but tell me he was going to Comrade Roudabeh's to study. I figured it out when I didn't see any improvement in his reading. Suren had us promise not to share with anyone that we had gone to that house, nor the house's location, and we didn't give that information to anyone, until the day I owed my life to that very information.

One day Suren invited us into his office for lunch and told us that he had introduced Naji to the party's music group and had told them that he was a skilled violinist. But Naji was not pleased by this news, I mean he didn't seem to be in his natural state. That day, whatever he was told, he would simply say, "What?" staring at you befuddled. After lunch, no matter how much I questioned him, I couldn't find out anything. It seemed that Suren had forgotten the pain of having lost his niece. "We have to think about the living and help them out. About young people like you who are the most important assets of this nation, our future politicians." He was preparing us to become active members of the party. "What is interesting is that you each have your own capabilities and each of you can serve the party and this nation in your own way. I know that one day when I'm here no more, you'll remember me and thank me."

In the evening, when the workers left the print shop one by one, Nad Ali, who was both the caretaker and the guard of the print shop, was anxiously wandering around, asking whomever he met, "Have you seen my keychain around? A very big one?" Eventually we learned from Suren that the main keychain for the print shop, including the key to the entrance and all the other doors, had gone missing, and Nad Ali was troubled about it. Suren said, "You must have just put it somewhere around here and forgotten. Now go home and come in early tomorrow morning and look for it." But Nad Ali, who had been at his job for many years, felt that the lost keys were not a good sign. He said, "I'll stay at the shop tonight and just sleep in a corner."

Suren said, "Don't worry for no reason, man. You are old now; you might simply have forgotten where you put them. Things like this happen."

"Still, I'm going to stay. Better to be safe than sorry." But he didn't know that there was no way to be safe. If he had, he wouldn't have lost his life there that night in a fire.

The next morning, Naji said he had a bad headache and couldn't come to work; he wanted to stay in and rest. So I went by myself, and the first thing that grabbed my attention when I approached the print shop was a red fire truck. Then the black exterior walls of the print shop. A corpse lay still on the ground, under a gray blanket. A crowd of people gathered around, and some wanted to go inside, but several of the print shop workers were standing in front of the door and didn't allow anyone to enter. A man shouted, "Now that it's done, let us go inside, brother, and see what kind of spying documents these Soviet-serving folks were printing in there."

One of the workers said, "What documents are you talking about, sir? You talk as if this was a spy den."

Another voice said, "If it weren't, why has it been set on fire like this? Huh? It was a spy den."

The worker said, "The owner was a Christian. That's why it was set on fire."

A few men burst out laughing. "That is reason enough. What other reason do you want?"

Suddenly, the men, as if they had planned it all along, charged through the entrance to the print shot. The sounds of men's angry howls filled the main hall. It was only then that I noticed Suren squatting in a corner, smoking. I walked toward him. He raised his head and observed me in silence.

"That's Nad Ali's body there, isn't it?" I said.

"An ambulance was supposed to come, but there isn't any sign of it yet. Poor Nad Ali thought he could stop them. You all were witness to the fact that I didn't want him to stay here last night. I told him not to stay. I told him to go home and not to worry. But he did worry. I mean, it was him who was worried and who, as a result, fucked up his life. It was not my fault."

"Do you want me to bring you something, Agha Suren? Water? Some soda?"

"Yes, please. Some water would be nice."

I went and bought a water for him from a store around the corner. I brought it to him, and then there was nothing left for me to do but to sink down on the ground.

"Where is Naji?" he asked. I told him he had a headache and hadn't been able to come to work. He reached into his pocket and pulled out a few pills. "Give these to him when you go home. These are the best for headaches." And I did as he asked. Naji wanted to know why I had returned early. I told him that the print shop had been set on fire. Whoever had started it had easily entered the premises, because there were no signs of them breaking in. It seemed they had had the keys to the main door. Nad Ali had tried to stop them, but they had thrown him into the fire without a hint of conscience and written, "Death to the communists serving the foreigners. Death to the Soviet Union."

"Well, it was clear that they would one day come for the print shop. Agha Suren should have thought of that," I said.

"But Agha Suren had no clue whatsoever. You heard him yourself."

"Agha Suren is too starry-eyed. I mean, he should have known because he is a communist and he publishes communist books and newspapers. Isn't that so? You know better; you can read. Those kinds of texts encourage people to become servants to foreigners, meaning they have to accept whatever the foreigners say. Why did the people revolt? So they could free themselves from the rule of foreigners, whether the US or the Soviet Union. A foreign government is a foreign government. Don't you think so? Of course, you do."

"I never was or will get mixed up with such things, but it wasn't fair for them to do that to Suren. Such a lovely man who has been so good to us, who has helped us so much. It wasn't right for them to treat him like this. Don't you think so? I'm sure you do."

"I don't even know enough to be able to agree with you or not. I'm not even literate." I stared into his eyes. He got furious. "Why do you look at me like that? Fuck off, you and all the rest!"

I didn't say anything more, because I didn't want to make him angrier. I knew he hadn't touched food for the past two days and was hungry. He had lost his appetite, that's how frightened he was about the

way things were going in the town. In the evening, I made a nice dinner. Cutlet and fried tomatoes, which he loved. We ate in silence. Before
going to sleep, we talked a while in the sheer darkness of the room.

"We better leave here. Clear out as soon as possible," I said.

"Where to?"

"One of the print shop guys is taking me to talk to a smuggler he
knows. He says the smuggler will first take us to the Emirates. We will
stay there for a few days, and then we will be sent to Europe."

"What about the cost? Where do we find the money?"

"I told you that I entrusted our money to George. It should now be
enough to get us out of here and to a safe place. You have some too,
enough for this journey."

"Honestly, it's safer for me here. You should go by yourself. How
can I say this? That's it. I'm out."

With his words, I felt the sky tumbling down onto my head. I imagined the rest of my life without him. It was so hard. Still, I had a flicker
of hope at the bottom of my heart that he would change his mind and
come with me. "How did you come to this conclusion all of a sudden?
I thought you said we would be together until the end of our lives. Or
that at least we would travel together?"

"Well, people change. I mean, if you look around you, you see that
many people have changed. Also, when you can stay in your own country to work and live, why should you become a nobody in a foreign
land, especially in the West, where all hell has broken loose and everyone only thinks of himself?"

"Has Kavous taught you all this nonsense to regurgitate to me?
Do you really believe his lies? Can't you tell from his character what
kind of a man he is? Listen closely so I can tell you. He'll stay with you
for a bit and enjoy you to the fullest, then when he is bored with you,
he'll pass you on to his friends, who, one after another, will have fun
with you for a bit, and then, when they are all done with you, they'll
hand you in to the authorities, and you'll hang for the crime of moral
corruption. As simple as that. You'll see."

He simply laughed and didn't say another word. Through his laughter, he wanted me to know that he understood I was saying these things

out of jealousy. I added, "What would I need you for anyway? I'm
not lame or anything. And you know what? There are so many nice
new people out there to befriend. This time around, I'll find someone
who is worth it. I have to go to sleep now, because I have a lot of work
to do tomorrow."

The following week, I went to meet with the smuggler. He asked
me how many of us were escaping the country. At first, I said two, but
then I immediately changed the number to one, and then said I was
not sure. He told me to go figure it out and then come back. Right then
and there, I made the decision for us and said it was just me, just one
person. My next meeting with him was at a travel agency. After meeting there with him a few times, it was decided when and from where I
would be leaving. I paid two-thirds of the money, with the rest to be
paid later in the Emirates. Then I exchanged everything I had to American dollars, because I had heard that Iranian money had no value on
the other side of the water, which was true. While I was taking care
of these details, preparing to leave, I didn't share any information with
Naji. Neither did he tell me what his life plans were after I left. On the
first day of the month, we informed the landlord that it would be our
last month there. Naji had decided to move after I left. He didn't say
where he would go, and I assumed it would be to a place Kavous had
set up for him.

"Thank God you at least have a good caretaker who both wants
you badly and has a lot of say in the new government. I wish you the
best from the bottom of my heart," I told him. He didn't say anything.
It was as if I were talking to a piece of rock. I cried out of his sight, all
alone. The last three weeks of our time together, we lived under the
same roof but separate from one another. During the day, he went out,
and I knew that he spent his time with Kavous and his gang. At night,
we spent our time in total silence. I considered him gone. He was gone,
and there was nothing left between us, and I was no longer thinking
about him returning to me. He had stopped shaving his beard, and
the style of his clothing had changed. He had become careless, and like
Kavous and his friends, Naji had started wearing loose and ugly clothes,
and now he shaved his hair, which he very much liked to keep long,

to a buzz cut. I was so irritated to see him with a shaved head. I had been stupid to buy him different types of hair care products, which he seemed not to see anymore, washing both his body and hair with soap. I decided I would not intervene in anything related to him, nothing. Even though I still cared what he wore and how. I cared because I had made a habit of it. Every time we were to go out, I would pick the clothes he would wear, iron them, and have them ready for him. That was a pure joy I had now been deprived of. But that night, I couldn't stop myself from commenting, and I'm so happy that I did. I noticed that he came home wearing dusty clothes and was going to bed wearing the same clothes.

"It's none of my business, but it's not right to sleep in these dusty clothes. You'll get sick, breathing the dust in your sleep."

"No, that's okay. I'll change tomorrow morning."

Still, I got out of my bed, found a clean shirt among his clothes in the closet, and handed it to him. "Wear this." He was so reluctant to take off the shirt he was wearing that I became curious about what was going on and insisted until he had to take his shirt off, revealing a big fresh wound on his arm, as if he had been dragged on his arm over the asphalt. I told him, "This wound has to be immediately washed, or it might get infected." And without asking him whether he would let me wash it or not, I boiled some water, washed the wound with warm water, and then cleaned it with a cotton ball soaked in alcohol. As I cared for him, Naji told me that Kavous had taken him to a fight with the communists, who had cornered Naji and given him a good beating, away from the rest of the gang.

"Why do you do these things? Do you even know what the communists say and what they want?"

"Of course I do."

"Can you please enlighten me?"

"They want to bring pure vice into our society."

His words made me burst out laughing. "Okay, now be careful not to turn over onto the wound to let it dry until the morning." Then I continued talking to him, telling him, little by little, things that might warn him away from what he was doing with Kavous's gang and smooth-talk him into making the trip with me, to no avail. He had made up his mind to stay and live right there. "You see a bright future for yourself here even though it's not clear what is going on?"

"There's so much hope here, so much light everywhere. If you open your eyes wide enough, you'll see the light that has spread across this land. Our country is a country of light now."

I couldn't find it in me to fight with him about it anymore. "Okay. Just be careful one of these brothers of yours doesn't rob you and take away your light or kill you with the electricity you are talking about."

"What did you say?" he asked.

The month came to an end, and the day arrived when we would say farewell. We had packed all our belongings. I had put all my possessions in a backpack. A taxi was supposed to pick me up at nine in the morning at the corner of our street and take me to a village close to the border, where I would be joined by a few others who, like me, planned to leave the country.

"I'll help you take your stuff to the car," Naji said. That was the best thing he had said to me so far that day. It meant that he still cared for me.

"It's still early." Our eyes locked. If begging him would have changed his mind about coming with me, I would have done it. Our eyes remained locked, and he, too, seemed to want to take me in his arms one last time. Or was I the only one who felt the heat of that moment? Suddenly, we heard the quiet tapping of fingers on the other side of the closed door of our room. We knew that no one else was in the house. The men who lived in the other rooms had either left for their villages or gone out early in the morning, and it was strangely terrifying that someone was at the door now. Or maybe it was just I who was afraid and Naji didn't fear anything anymore, because he imagined he had solid support now. He went to the door. "Who's there?" The person at the door didn't respond, instead pushing the door open and entering with his black horrifying boots.

"May God give you strength, brothers. I'm sorry to drop by unannounced, but we are here to pick up this young man. We have so much to do." It was Kavous, and by *the young man*, he meant Naji. Kavous was the last person I wanted to see at that moment, and it seemed that he had been sent by the devil to bring some disaster upon us. In his eyes, I could see that both of us had reached the end of a path, but what path? It wasn't clear yet. He stood in the middle of the room and turned to me. "I heard you are leaving. May God's hand be with you. Naji said you are leaving but didn't say more. Well, where are you headed? Inshallah, it's for the best."

I tried not to lose face. "I'm headed to Bandar Abbas. I have friends there who have found me a good job."

"At least you could have stayed in your own town to celebrate this first spring of our liberation with your fellow townspeople. Our first spring of victory. Who would have believed it? Our infidel enemies were taken by surprise. Sons of bitches didn't know what to do but to run for their lives."

"Bandar Abbas is a town in this country too. It's all the same."

"Well said, that's true. May you be successful, brother," said Kavous, not knowing what was awaiting him.

I realized then that spring had truly arrived. The spring always came after a heavy winter, but how come I hadn't felt the winter that year? It seemed that no one had felt the winter that year, and we had many times heard people chanting in the streets, "Let the shah eat his heart out! The winter, too, is now spring!" They meant that it wasn't cold. Did they truly mean that the season wasn't cold, or was it that they hadn't felt the cold because they were all over the streets, protesting, running, and chanting? We, too, had been out in the streets many days that winter. It was winter when the shah left the country. The night before his leaving, we watched him on TV. Those of us who didn't have TVs at home went to cafés to watch him. Naji and I went to the big café in the town square, and we had to keep ordering tea, otherwise the server would have thrown us out. The shah appeared in a formal army uniform with dozens of badges and medals hanging from it. He said some words and then cried, as if he were begging the people to forgive him, not knowing that it was already too late for such gestures. The following day, with the largest headlines possible, newspapers reported, "The Shah Is Gone."

People poured out into the streets and celebrated and showed the newspaper headline to one another. Some of them had crossed out the words *Is Gone* and replaced them with *Has Escaped*. Cars honked and people jubilated. The streets looked like this once again soon after that, when Imam Khomeini arrived in the country from his exile abroad. It was still winter. This time, not only cafés but also stores that had TVs had switched them on and turned the sound as high as possible so we could listen without having to order unwanted teas, learn that the Agha's airplane had landed at the Tehran airport, and see Tehrani people gathering from the airport all the way to the main cemetery of the city. When the Agha's car reached the streets, people gathered around it in a frenzy, accompanying it all the way to the cemetery, and I wondered why the cemetery. I heard that the Agha wanted to pay his respects to the blood of the martyrs. When he arrived there, he gave a speech. Naji and I were not able to watch the whole event live; walking in the streets, we caught glimpses on different screens of people waiting for the Imam's plane, of the clergymen gathering at the airport. We had gone to the town square that day to comfortably sit and watch the whole event, but everything changed the moment our eyes fell upon the woman with short hair.

"Look, Naji, isn't that the same woman who gave you the willow tree?"

"Right. Why is she standing there all by herself? Where is her friend?"

"She seems very anxious. Maybe she is waiting for her friend Parvaneh."

"I'll go ask her what she is doing here."

"I'll go with you."

We walked up to her and said hi. She was happy to see us. This time, her clothes were long, covering her body, leaving no part naked except her short black hair. She seemed to be looking for someone to stand there by her side. We were right; she was waiting for Parvaneh, even though she wasn't too hopeful that she would come.

"For two reasons, I don't think she will. First, she loves to just sit and stare at the TV these days, and second, she doesn't agree with what I want to do, wants to stay out of it all, because she thinks I'll soon regret actions, but she doesn't know how determined I am to take care of it, take care of it today."

"May I ask what you are talking about?" I asked her.

She looked at her watch. She looked pale. "No, she won't be coming." She looked around her. "I'm going to call her one more time. If she plans to come, I'll wait for her; if she doesn't respond, I'll just get going myself. I have the address, so I'll find it somehow." We couldn't understand what she was talking about. She asked us to accompany her to the public phone booth on the other side of the square. She went inside and called Parvaneh, but no one picked up the phone. She banged the receiver down angrily and came out of the booth. "Whore."

"What happened?" Naji asked.

"We still don't know your name," I added.

"Mehri," she said, looking like she was going to burst into tears. "It's okay, I'll just go by myself. Well, I must find a taxi now."

I wanted to part ways with her as soon as possible and go to the café, but Naji would not let her go, wanted to know what was going on and insisted on helping her out. "Do you want us to come with you instead? Well, we'll come. We don't have anything important to do now." He turned to me and said, "We don't, right?"

"We came all the way here to sit in the café and watch the Agha arriving in the homeland live on TV, and now you say we don't have anything important to do. What is more important than this?"

"They will repeat the program a dozen more times, you'll see. You know that too well yourself."

"What a dumbass you are. I'm talking about a live event, direct broadcast."

Mehri kept looking back and forth between Naji and me. "No. I'm not asking you to come with me. I'll be going alone."

"Also, we don't really know where you are headed. It's also none of our business."

"A neighborhood on the way to the cemetery."

"Cemetery?!"

"No, not there, on the way there, before we get there." She pulled a piece of paper from the pocket of her long navy coat and held it in front of me.

Naji brought his head forward close to the paper, as if he wanted to read it. I gave it to him to tease him. "Here you go, take it and read it to see where the address is." He realized I was teasing him for his illiteracy and pulled away. I read the address out loud. Naji said he knew where it was. But we still didn't know why Mehri was headed there and what she wanted from us. I decided to go along with whatever it was for Naji's sake. Finally, Mehri confessed to us as we set out for the address. We were silent and she cried. "Do you two know what abortion is?"

Naji had not heard the word, so I quickly explained to him what it meant, then I asked Mehri who she was talking about, and she told us that she was pregnant from her husband, Saeed, but did not want to keep the baby, because their relationship had come to a point at which she had no option but to separate from him.

"If I keep the baby, then I'll have to rely on him forever and put up with all kinds of disgrace. I also know what happens in cases like these when it comes to the baby's custody. Because he is a man and a father, the law gives all the custody rights to him, so I'll have to beg him and his family even to see my own child. No. Parvaneh doesn't understand, but I have my own mother's experience in mind—my heartless father oppressed my mother, who went through hell for me after her divorce, because of the fucking guy who called himself my father. Not that he treated me badly or denied me anything, no. But he did my mother as much harm as he could because, as he himself claimed, he loved her, but what a joke. What do men know about love? I'm sorry, I don't mean you, I mean men like my father and now my husband, who has had someone brand his forehead with a mark the size of a coin to fool others into thinking that it's the mark of a prayer tablet, from having prayed too much. May his prayers and the prayers of anyone else who is not man enough to respect his wife go to shit."

"But this is not a hospital address. Where is it?" I asked.

"You can't do this in the hospital now. With what is going on, you never know who is who. A few doctors I visited said they are afraid of doing it because in Islamic law, abortion is a big sin, similar to murdering an adult, so they are afraid to be exposed and have the devout Hezbollahi brothers attack their offices out of nowhere and all of that. A nurse gave us this number, that day Parvaneh was with me. She said this was the number of a midwife who would do it, illegally and for a lot of money. Then we contacted her, and she told us to go there today to take care of it. Now she is waiting for me, and I have to go." She wanted us to accompany her because she was all alone. Naji, too, wanted to go with her. For support or because he was attracted to her? No, let's just say to offer a friend emotional support.

"But it would have been better to wait for Parvaneh, because she is a woman, after all, and knows better what to do in these kinds of situations," I said.

"Parvaneh has the address, so she can come if she decides to."

I had no choice but to go along with Naji and the woman. Naji hailed a taxi and gave the driver the address. The driver looked Mehri up and down and said, "I have no problem taking you, but I have to think about the safety of my car too, kids. A lot of people are headed to the cemetery now to be there for the Agha's speech."

Naji jumped in and said, "No, the Agha won't be giving his speech there. He is doing it at that cemetery in—"

This time the driver cut him off. "I know, boy. If you let me finish, I'll tell you. The thing is, some people are headed to the cemetery here so that when the Agha gives his speech in Tehran's cemetery, they can listen to him there, because they believe it'll be more virtuous."

Naji laughed. "You are pulling our legs, sir. So the Agha's voice will reach from Tehran to where we are headed? From 1,200 kilometers away? Ha!"

The driver turned to me where I was standing next to Naji. "This friend of yours seems to have just left the caves. He doesn't seem to know that there are TVs and radios in our world now that broadcast sounds not just thousands but millions of kilometers away." He laughed. "Anyway, I have no problem taking you there, kids, but on the condition that you throw a scarf over your sister's head, so we do not draw the attention of the fanatics. If you agree, hop in."

Mehri said, "He's right, kids. Why was I so stupid to not wear a scarf and came out with my hair showing?"

"How about Jamil's keffiyeh? Would it be okay if she wears it to cover her hair?" I was wearing around my neck the red-and-white keffiyeh that Naji had gotten me in the market to replace the one he originally had gifted me. I was stunned by Naji's suggestion and didn't know what to say or do. The driver asked us to hurry up and get in. We jumped in, and I hesitantly took off my keffiyeh and handed it to Mehri; she arranged it like a headscarf and checked herself in the rearview mirror. The driver set off while singing. He had been right about people heading to the cemetery. With whatever means they had, they were getting themselves there. Some in their cars, honking nonstop, others on motorcycles and bikes; we even saw a few people on donkeys; and those who had found no other means were on foot, whistling and letting out cries of joy that we didn't know the reason for. Naji was so excited that I had to whisper in his ear without Mehri hearing, "We are not going to pay for the taxi, don't forget." Then I laughed for no reason so Mehri thought I had told him something funny. Naji smiled sadly, but when we got to our destination, he still paid for the taxi. Sometime later, when I took issue with him, he said, "It wouldn't have been right for us, two men, to just stand there and watch a woman pay for our taxi, would it?"

"Were we headed to my aunt's or, God forbid, to your grandmother's? There was no reason for us to pay," I responded.

The house we were looking for was an old one. A young woman opened the door for us. Her face was full of small scars from a skin disease. Mehri told her who we were, and she guided us inside. We crossed a courtyard and entered a large cement room with a few chairs and a small TV on a table. After a while, a tall wide-shouldered woman who looked like a man came through a small door at the end of the room and asked loudly, "Are these men here with you?"

Mehri responded, "They are my cousins. I needed their help."

"Inshallah, you have the money with you."

Mehri squeezed her purse in her arms. "Yes, ma'am."

"Okay then, come inside, with your money, without your cousins."

Frightened, Mehri looked at us and followed the midwife through another door that looked more like the entrance to a cave. The TV was showing the live broadcast of the Agha from Tehran, but we couldn't hear anything and didn't dare ask them to turn it up. Now the airplane was landing on the runway. The young woman entered with a tray, carrying two glasses of tea and a bowl of sugar cubes on the side. She held it in front of us. We took our tea with a few cubes of sugar. We then asked the woman to turn up the sound on the TV. She said she had to ask the midwife, who was busy with work now and couldn't be bothered, so we had to continue watching the TV without sound until further notice. The airplane came to a stop. Scenes of crowds of people in the streets, scenes of the faces of clergymen who were crying of joy, scenes of crowds of people dancing in Shahyad Square, the muted sound of Mehri's sudden scream from behind the other door, and the voice of the midwife, who asked, "What happened?" Mehri probably said something in response, but we couldn't hear her; her voice didn't reach us. The midwife said, "When you held your legs up in the air for the fucking guy, you had to think of this day." The door of the airplane opened, a long silence. The young woman had left the room, and there was no one around for us to ask about the volume on the TV; we didn't dare turn it up ourselves out of fear of the midwife, so we simply continued to watch the scenes on mute. Finally, the Agha appeared at the airplane door, at the same time that Mehri's scream came through from the other room, followed by the midwife's voice, which said, "Stop being such a spoiled bitch, or I can't do my work." Silence again. The midwife's voice once again, "What did you say?" The pilot had the Agha's hand in his, guiding him down the plane's staircase. Mehri's crying. The midwife groaned, "Oh, the young women these days." Journalists and photographers were swarming the airport. The photographers took pictures of everything. Someone knocked. We were terrified and didn't know what to do. We heard the footsteps of the young woman from the courtyard going to open the door, and a little bit later, she entered the room with Parvaneh. She had her hair covered with a black scarf and was panting; she was surprised to see us there but came and sat next to us. The young woman left the room. Quickly and in a very low voice, I explained to Parvaneh where and how we had chanced upon Mehri. She too quickly told us that she had left Mehri hanging in the hopes that she would change her mind and keep the baby. The young woman brought Parvaneh some tea. A long time passed in silence once again. Then I asked Parvaneh, who was staring at the TV, "Where is her husband?"

"Mehri's?"

"Yeah."

"I'm looking for him too. Can't you see how I've been staring at the TV? He hasn't appeared yet."

Naji, too, was surprised by her words. The people surrounded the Agha's car, moving forward along with it.

"Why is everyone teasing us today?"

"Who? Me? I swear on your lives that I'm not teasing you. Didn't Mehri tell you where her lovely Saeed has gone?" And since she didn't get any response from us, she continued, "He has gone to Tehran to witness the Agha's arrival. He said he was going to both see him and touch his car for blessing. Perhaps he is now among the people who are with the car." We, too, focused on the screen, hoping to spot him, but then we remembered that we hadn't even met him to recognize him. The midwife called in a loud voice, "Touran! Where are you, Touran?" The young woman entered the room, threw us a look, and went to the midwife. "Help take her out, then come back here to clean up. Get up, young lady, get up and put on your clothes and leave, it's all done now." We got up from our seats. The Agha's car was almost at the cemetery. The midwife came out of the room, counting a bundle of cash.

Parvaneh ran forward. "Can I go in and check on her?"

The midwife stopped counting and looked Parvaneh up and down. "Why go in there? She'll come out in a minute. Why has she brought along so many people for such a simple surgery?" She pulled the door handle to make sure the door was closed, then continued to count the cash as she left the room we were in.

We were still standing there. Now the Tehran cemetery was the busiest place on earth. The Agha's car had entered the cemetery. Mehri came out of the room, tired and worn out, and smiled at us. She was very happy to see Parvaneh there. Parvaneh rushed toward her, hugged her, and guided her to a chair. Mehri rested there for a few minutes until Touran came and told us that we should be on our way as soon as possible, because the midwife had another customer coming. Parvaneh helped Mehri to freshen up by splashing some water on her face from the faucet in the courtyard.

The midwife asked us where we had parked our car. We told her we didn't have one. Naji said he would go to the main street to grab a taxi and bring it there for Mehri to get in, but the midwife told us we were not allowed to bring a taxi or any other car to her door, so we had no choice but to walk Mehri to the street and find a car that would take us back to town. Naji tried to get an address or phone number from Mehri, but she refused to give Naji any information to trace her; instead, despite her ailing state, she asked Naji about the willow tree, whether it had grown or not, whether the farm owner had agreed that he plant it there. Naji eagerly answered her questions. When we got back to the town square, Parvaneh let us know that there was nothing more for us to do there. She told us she wanted to take Mehri to her house with that same car so she could rest a bit and asked us what our plans were. Naji didn't understand what Parvaneh was implying and kept saying we would go with them, so they were not alone. I said we planned to go to the café to listen to the Agha's speech. Mehri laughed and said, "You should tell us later what the Agha said in the cemetery."

"When?" Naji asked.

"Next time we see each other," Mehri responded. She coughed. It was still hard for her to talk.

"When?" Naji asked again.

"I'll tell you later, my dear Naji. Now, let's get out of the car so people can be on their way and take care of their lives."

The two women laughed and thanked us once again. Naji and I got out, and the car left as Mehri and Parvaneh waved at us, smiling.

"You seem to have fallen for the bitch," I said.

138

"Me? Fall for a woman? Am I crazy or something, huh? I just enjoyed hanging out with them. I mean, women are really fun to hang out with, to talk nonsense with, wouldn't you agree?"

"Oh . . . Did you see what just happened?"

"What?"

"They took my keffiyeh with them."

We walked through the streets and took sweets to eat from people who were handing them out. The first few minutes, Naji was sad that Mehri had left, but a little bit later, he forgot her among the crowd, and we tried to have a good time, the two of us together. We laughed so much that day. How can you not be happy when people are dancing for joy in the streets and jumping up and down and doing all they can to be happy and remain happy? But how long did that joy last? How could it be that joy and elation turned to mourning and sorrow for some in no time?

Kavous continued to stand there self-righteously in the middle of our room in his big black boots. "Well, anyway, the celebrations for the first spring of freedom are going to be held here in perfection, as is deserving of our revolution. Only if these little God-unfearing communists allow people to celebrate and not cause trouble." He then turned to me and said, "May you be happy and successful wherever you are headed," before turning to Naji and adding, "We should run. Are these yours?"

Naji, too, had put all he had in a backpack. "It's just this backpack."

"Just this? Where is your instrument? You should be very careful to hide it from the brothers in the streets. Of course, they have every right to get upset by such instruments of evil entertainment; they have sacrificed so many martyrs to break down tools of sinfulness in our land. But well, since it means so much to you, I won't let any harm come to it. Just hurry up. I've parked the truck at the corner; it's not the best place. I couldn't bring it closer. The streets here are too narrow to drive in to."

"How did you get into the house, Kavous? There was no one inside to open the door for you," I asked him.

He laughed and jiggled the key ring in front of me before moving to pick up Naji's backpack. Naji ran after him and didn't let him do it. "Be careful. My violin is in there." Kavous stepped back. Naji added, "I told you I'd come to your office at noon. I didn't want you to come over. I want to be with Jamil until he gets in the car and leaves. I want to help him carry his stuff. I didn't think you would be coming here, I mean, that was not our plan."

Kavous tried to lighten up the situation by laughing. "Oh boy, what plan? Our plan was for you to come to my office. Was I wrong to come pick you up so you didn't have to walk and also so you didn't, God forbid, have your instrument taken from you on your way?"

Naji was not buying it. He continued to talk to him with bitterness. "First of all, there's still a lot that Jamil and I have to do. Second, I can take care of my instrument myself."

I intervened to put an end to the quarreling. "If you are fighting over me, please stop, because I do not need any help. I can carry my backpack by myself."

Kavous pointed to my backpack, which was still on the ground. "This is nothing. You know what, we will give you a ride. So there is no problem anymore. Hurry up, get going before it's too late. Where did you say you were headed, Jamil?"

"No. I won't bother you. I'll go myself. You two get on your way. May you be healthy and happy." I extended my hand to say goodbye to Naji, but he refused to shake my hand.

"I'm coming with you."

Kavous burst into a fit of anger, like a husband getting angry with his wife. He grabbed Naji's hand and pushed him toward the door. "You're out of line now. You know that you are dear to me, and I'll do whatever you want, but you, too, should promise not to talk over me. And now, get going, we don't have time for this." This time, he pushed Naji harder, and if Naji had not controlled his forward momentum, he would fallen through the door of the room onto his head. Kavous picked up my backpack from the ground and turned to me. "Let's go,

Jamil. You have a brain, so you must know better than to not follow my words when I have such high regard for you."

"Yes, of course, but no thanks, Kavous. I'm grateful to you, but please let me go by myself. I'm not being modest."

"Okay. As you wish, brother. But know that our intention was nothing if not to help, to help one of our compatriots."

"I know," I said, then looked at Naji, who was standing at the threshold with his head hanging low, wearing a hangdog look like I had never seen before, as if his whole body was trembling with shame. A few teardrops rolled down his cheeks.

Kavous once again turned toward me. "I swear on your life, I'm putting my whole life in his hands, letting him manage all the sheep. He knows himself how many are going to be sacrificed tomorrow, and he needs to look after them, because I can't be both at the office of our newly formed Sepah forces and at the sacrifice lot. And now that spring has come, there are a hundred other jobs to be done too. Under such circumstances, this guy is acting like a pampered kid, standing there with his head hanging low, as if I'm the guilty party here and not him. Do you see that, Jamil?" He then turned to Naji and continued, "Okay, enough of your waterworks now, keep moving and lead us down the staircase, or else, God forbid, we might fall down headfirst." He laughed and turned to me. "Honestly, dear, swear to God, you never know."

With a low tearful voice, Naji said, "You go first so I can watch you from behind," and moved to the side of the door.

"May Imam Ali watch after you, brother Jamil. Wherever you go, may God watch your back," said Kavous, then he stepped outside the door, standing there on the landing with his back to us. "And what a dangerous staircase it is too." Naji suddenly rushed to the threshold and pushed Kavous on his shoulders with the palms of his hands. I ran forward to stop Kavous from falling, but it was already too late. Kavous had fallen from the top, screaming, cursing, and shouting with pain, his big body thumping and tumbling down the stairs, and I couldn't think of anything other than to run away from the house with my bag on my back. Kavous lay at the bottom of the stairs, not moving at all.

Alive or dead, we couldn't tell. His handgun was there on one of the stairs. I didn't run into the street for fear of raising someone's suspicion. I felt I was plunging into the ground out of fear. If I were arrested, Kavous's friends would no doubt send me to the firing squad right then and there. The sound of footsteps coming from behind heightened my fears a hundred times. I told myself it was best not to turn around. The sound got closer until it reached me. "I'll come with you. Wherever you go, I'm going to be there with you, wherever."

"Now that you don't have any other choice? Now that you are a bomb of disaster ready to explode at any moment? Do you want to get me killed?"

"I think with the money I have, we can find a way; you know better than me." No matter how hard I tried to push him away, he didn't leave. Honestly, I didn't want him to leave either. I wanted him to stay and be with me on that journey; I didn't know where it was leading me, and I only had a vague description that I had heard from the smuggler. He had told me that I was first being taken to one of the countries on the other side of the Persian Gulf and, after a while (one to three weeks later), I would be heading to Europe. That was all, and now I didn't want anyone else to travel with me but Naji, even though I was afraid of him too, especially after I found out that he was carrying a handgun, which he didn't tell me about until we were on the boat on our way to that unknown land. There were seven of us, five travelers and two guides, whose orders we had to follow. When they saw I had someone with me, at first they gave us a hard time and told me we couldn't take him, but as a result of my insistence and a good sum of money, they finally agreed to take Naji with us. If they knew that Naji had a handgun, they would definitely refuse us. Naji clued me in that it was actually Kavous's gun that had fallen on the stairs. I was terrified and he only smiled. He wanted me to stay calm and quiet and not show my fear, but my only thought was that the gun would eventually cause us trouble, so we had to get rid of it as soon as possible, and yet, no matter how much I signaled to him to throw it into the sea, even though he kept smiling and nodding as though he would do it, he didn't, and, soon, everyone on the boat knew about it. When we got off the boat, the sun had set, and there was a desert in front of us and nothing else. The two guides told us that we had to walk for two nights and two days. During the day, we lay down on the ground so that the border patrol would not locate us, and at night we started walking, tearing through the darkness, all the darkness around us.

During the last hours of the second night, we saw three huge men emerge from the darkness. We were exhausted. We could see the light of day in the distance, but we hadn't yet reached it, or it hadn't yet reached us. Three men who pretended to be more violent than they were had appeared in front of us. The glare from their knives' blades frightened us. We all had knives in our backpacks but not something to compare with those sharp blades rising from the black handles held tightly by those tough masculine hands. They told us to hand them whatever money and gold we had. It felt so cruel. The guides tried to stop the bandits with threats and foul language, but to no avail. After a long verbal quarrel and threats of bringing over the border officers, we decided to give the men our money and gold. Two of them stood over us, threatening us with their knives to make sure we wouldn't trick them, while the third one came over to collect our money. Just as we were looking into our bags and backpacks, Naji pulled out the gun, jumped a few steps back, held it toward the bandits, and told them to leave as fast as possible. We all stood there, shocked and terrified, staring at Naji's gun, not knowing what to do. The three men, too, paused, surprised, until one of them stepped forward jokingly, approaching Naji and implying that the gun was empty. Naji jumped back again and said that if he took one more step toward him, he would shoot, and the man froze. We saw that the man was scared, even as he was telling us that they knew we had entered the country illegally, and if we shot, the sound of the gun would draw the officers there and mess things up for us. Still, Naji stood there firmly, with the gun in hand, and told them to leave, threatening to even take their knives from them if they stayed a moment longer. The men seemed alarmed, and, after much threatening that they would come find us again, they left us to ourselves and walked away. We continued on our path, and the following evening when we saw the village we had been aiming for in the distance, the two guides asked Naji to bury the gun somewhere around there. Naji said he would but didn't.

The two guides handed us off to a fat man who said he was Iranian but had been living abroad for many years. Naji asked him how far he would take us. The man introduced himself as Sardar and told us to address him by that name, but everyone called him Chief Sardar. He explained that he was not taking us anywhere, that he would just find us good jobs, physical labor with good wages. He said that this village was the end of the line. He was right, and we were thrown into a world that I wish I did not have to remember by writing about it—the extent of violence, strangeness, and fear of the other, fear of those who were your coworkers, even fear of the one you deeply love—but I have to recall that time and write about the strange things that happened to us there, in that environment that turned us hard, rough, and emotionless like itself. I have to write about it and ask for his forgiveness for having pulled him along with me to such a hell.

Naji said, "We haven't come here to work. We're passing through on our way to Europe. We were charged to be taken there. That's the end of our journey, not here, this empty desert."

Hopelessly, I asked him to not lose hope, because the smuggler in the country had told me that, in a few days, another smuggler would come and take us away from there. Or maybe a few weeks. And during this time, while waiting for him, it was best to not just hang around idle and raise suspicion but to mingle with the other laborers and work alongside them, saving some money as well.

Sardar wanted to keep Naji and me as his own laborers because we knew Arabic, and he preferred to speak Arabic himself. He said, "People come here to work, my brothers. Work and make good money and live a good life, or as people today might say, a high-level life. All the brothers here pay a little amount for boarding. For food, they themselves decide what price is more affordable to them, to cook separately for themselves or collectively with others. You also pay us a small percentage for having found you a job. It's not that much. Just 30 percent. The other issue I should point out to you, brothers, is the attitude of the laborers who go to jobs on our behalf, an important point, quite

important. If a worker is not good at the job or not well behaved with
the head engineers, their complaints will be sent to us. That would be
a problem that we then have to take care of. Thank God our Iranian
workers are well behaved and good at their work. Inshallah, there will
be no problems. No, there won't be."

Naji was really down, and in our solitude, he kept snapping at me. He
said our goal was something else and kept reminding me that we had
paid to be taken to Europe, not be brought here to slave away. For
hours, I tried to make him understand that we didn't have any other
options but to adjust ourselves to the situation until we met the people
we were waiting for to free us from captivity. I was sure that someone
would soon come for us; that was what the smuggler in Iran had told
me. I mean it was part of our deal; that was what I had paid for.

We started working at the construction site. A few days passed, and
no one came for us. A few weeks passed, and no one came for us. It was
becoming clear that the two guides had brought us here and left themselves, going where, we didn't know. Before we knew it, we had turned
into two hardworking illegal workers in a foreign country, with the
shadow of arrest and imprisonment hanging over our heads.

Every morning, we woke up with the azan rising through the half-
built buildings, calling people to prayer. We had breakfast, and then,
with dozens or maybe hundreds of other laborers, like the slaves we
had seen in films, we climbed the staircases that were not really stairs,
because one could fall off them at any second, and trudged up and down,
carrying bricks and mud and soil, and the only thing around us, as far as
the eye could see, was desert, no beginning and no end. Sometimes we
noticed hills in the distance, but they were not there all the time, hills
that appeared and disappeared, and patches of buildings under construction. We were told the site, in seven or eight years, would be a large
shopping center or a commercial town connected to the main town
with asphalt roads. The project was assigned to different contractors,
each of whom had one or several foremen, who called themselves
head builders. Men from different countries, each with a group of slave

laborers. Naji, I, and dozens of others were Sardar's slaves, which meant that he was the one deciding which employer we had to work for. Sometimes, without even knowing what was going on, we were transported from one construction site to another, because we had been sold off to another employer. It all depended which employer paid Sardar more for us. The employers had different temperaments, some nice and some nasty. Because Naji and I were young, all the employers wanted us, but some of them didn't like Naji's fury and his constant objections, or perhaps they were afraid of him, so we kept being moved from one job to another. Sardar advised me several times, first indirectly and then directly, to separate myself from Naji. He even told me that if I did, he would help me out more, but I had no intention of cutting myself off from Naji, for a thousand and one reasons but most importantly because he was the light of my life, a hope shaping my future in my mind, a future I was certain was more attainable with him by my side. Besides, I loved his courage; he was brave and unafraid, what I was not.

The rooms of the laborers were scattered all around the various floors of the buildings under construction. The cold wind blew through the yet-to-be-installed doors and windows. At night, we wrapped ourselves in blankets. We had to share rooms, each pair of us or a few of us together. Naji and I had one room. At night, we didn't have electricity; it was just available during the day, produced by large generators for work. The builders and employers who went back to the city after work, to their own houses where they lived with their families, believed we didn't need electricity at night. Sometimes, trucks brought us wood to make fire for cooking or warming ourselves. Every few workers paid one person to cook for them, but Naji and I did our own shopping and cooking. Fridays were our day off, and that is when several trucks came to the site to sell workers groceries.

Our whole life was limited to that desert, a land that was sometimes freezing cold and other times extremely hot with hot monsoon rains pouring over our bodies. Our spectacular view was simply of the building changing from one day to the next, or new buildings in the distance that kept growing out of the ground. But we also had the stars and the sunrise and the sunset; we had them all the time, because the sky was clear and blue most days, and the nights provided a blanket of stars to cover us. Naji loved watching the sunset. On weekdays, we couldn't do this, because we had just finished working as the sun set, and we were too exhausted and hungry to really think about enjoying it; at the most, we could enjoy the stars. Fridays were better.

In addition to the employers and the builders, we knew some of the laborers who also went back to the city, but only on Fridays. They said their residence documents were in order, and the police didn't have anything to do with them. They wore clean clothes and headed to the city we hadn't seen and could only imagine, a place where real people lived, men and women and kids and families in houses with amenities, with beds and bathrooms and kitchens and heat. Whatever we dreamed of having, they had. Walking along well-lit streets and sitting in cafés and restaurants that served hot food and watching women dance and sing-ers sing on TV screens and sitting in the park during the day in the shade of the trees. In that desert, we had only the shadows of walls and cement columns. The workers who could go to the city spoke of fancy shopping malls, of going to secret neighborhoods to pick up women and men.

For those of us who were illegal, who didn't have the proper permits and wouldn't dare to go to the city, Fridays were all the same. Putting a pot full of water on the fire, doing laundry, hanging our clothes on the rope clotheslines, then washing our own bodies, which was more fun, and we would pour water on each other and laugh. I cooked the best food for lunch, and we enjoyed having it together. In the evenings, we found a hill far from the construction site, sat on top of it, and Naji would play music. I might have sometimes cried, maybe when the round face of the red sun gradually crawled down toward the horizon and night once again descended on the desert, reminding us of the day soon to be upon us, a workday filled with constant unwilling climbing up and down and our inevitable breathless exhaustion. Naji stopped playing, "I'm tired of this place. When are we leaving? When are we done with this good-for-nothing desert?" Maybe it was then that I cried, feeling deeply guilty for having dragged him to this no-man's-land in exile.

"When we have enough savings, we will look for another smuggler to get us out of here and take us to Europe."

"I wish we were at least members of a religious minority group."

"You're right. If we were Bahá'í, the UN would send us a car and take us straight to Australia."

"Australia is part of Europe?"

"It's not part of Europe, but well, it is similar to it. Its capital is Sydney. I think it is like London or Paris or any other capital in Europe."

"You know every place. That's nice."

"But what use is it? They are all out of reach, and I just know their names. That's all."

"You're wishing we were Bahá'í, right?"

"But we are not."

I looked into his eyes. I saw a smile blooming and opening little by little on his lips, and he moved his head toward my chest, closer, and closer, rubbing his forehead on my chest with pleasure several times. Then I noticed the man standing on the cement column watching us. Naji started playing music again. This time a sad song, a very sad song.

We spent our days and night as slaves who had lost their way. We had no choice but to stay, hoping to save enough money to one day be freed. We changed our money to large bills whenever we could, so they were easier to carry; we always kept them with us, since it was impossible to leave them in rooms with no doors or locks. There were always people lurking around to steal others' money. Even though the bosses seriously threatened the workers, saying that if they stole each other's money, this or that could happen to them, the threats didn't make things any safer. We were all afraid of one another. No one lent money to anyone else, because if the other person did not pay you back, there was no law to defend you. The older men were also always looking to flirt with younger men; they were even willing to pay good money for a certain kind of company. We heard that in the buildings a bit farther from us, there were a few young men who, besides their day jobs, worked at night as prostitutes. We never saw them, but I had heard from one of the workers that a guy named Yadi had brought the young men to the area for this very purpose. When I told Naji about this, he didn't believe me. "Don't believe such things. Agha Yadi is not like that. The builders make up these rumors to ruin his image because he unmasks their swindling. But he is such a nice guy, really caring."

I was the one who saw Yadi first, standing there on the cement column that evening during sunset when Naji rubbed his forehead on my chest and played the violin. Yadi said, "I know you two. You are that idiot Sardar's workers." He laughed at his own statement. "What beautiful music you play! Damn it, man. What if I take you someplace where they'll pay you well for your music?"

Naji looked at me. Someone close by whistled. Yadi waved at a person in the distance whom we didn't see and then turned back to us. "I'm here today by chance, because the generator is out of order. I'm an electrical engineer." He made it clear he was only addressing Naji. "I'll come see you later. I'll find you if you are Sardar's worker. You are, right?"

Naji looked at me once again. Yadi didn't want to look at me, kept staring at Naji for a response. Naji threw his shoulders up to say yes. Yadi jumped down from the column and rushed away. A week later, a very tall man came to our building looking for Naji. He said he had come to take him to Yadi. Naji went with him, telling me that he was going out of curiosity, to see what Yadi had to say and what he wanted. Yadi had told him that he would take him to the sheikh to play music and make good money, but his first condition was that I shouldn't be there with Naji. "I wish you could come too, but well, Agha Yadi said that's not possible. What a pity."

"Doesn't look like you really want me there."

"You don't believe that I would like you to come? I swear on our friendship that I really want you to be there."

Whether I believed what he said or not, it didn't really affect our relationship or his decision. I had no choice and no safe haven but his chest, to rest my head and rub my face against his chest, feeling calmed by the scent of sweat amid the springy hair that grew there. We were surrounded by darkness, by rooms with three walls filled with the sounds of exhausted men in deep sleep, the sounds of their breath, their coughs, their groans, and sometimes their terrible snores. But, with my head on his chest, I was sound asleep, perhaps dreaming or wishing to dream that he and I had escaped that desert. Where to? We didn't even know. We knew we could go back to Iran, but when we remembered that no one was there waiting for us, and with the terrible news of all the killings in the streets, we knew we would not be safe there, especially if Kavous's murder had been discovered. That day, he had fallen down the stairs so horribly. The last image I had of him was his body at the foot of the staircase with his bloody face pressed against the wall. He was facing the wall, kneeling, and not moving. He didn't seem as though he could see me, even though his eyes were open. Had he died of his injuries? Certainly the accident had been investigated by now, and traces of Naji's and my presence there had been found that implicated us in his murder. Besides, I was determined to get to Europe; that was where I needed to be. So I thought not about going back but about the road ahead, a road that was, for now, blocked with huge barriers, and now that I had lost my only joy here, I felt I was buried alive. Fridays meant nothing without him, were gloomy and heavy. I wished I were a smoker so that I could at least walk by myself in the desert and smoke. From dawn to dusk on Fridays, I wandered around those cursed buildings, wondering what kinds of people would work there in the future. Would people coming there to buy clothes or jewelry consider, for even a second, who had built the place? Wretched enslaved men who for years had moved rocks up from dawn to dusk, tripping on the slippery stairways, only some of them having the chance to go back to their homelands once a year. We knew a few Iranian workers who traveled to Iran and brought back with them horrifying news.

If my residence papers had been in order, I, too, could have gone to the city on Fridays, but I couldn't get such documentation, because the government did not want us in the country. A few times, the police raided the construction site to arrest illegal workers like Naji and me, but we had been trained beforehand by Sardar what to do if the police officers—or, as they called them, the *shortehs*—came. When we heard

they were coming, all of us illegal workers had to go into the building's
basement, a vast space, quite tight and dark, with such a low ceiling that
we had to bend down, and we could do nothing once we were in the
room but lie down. We first had to swarm there, dashing anxiously into
that hole in the ground, crowding through the doorway like rats running away from savage animals. After entering the absolute darkness,
we had to blindly tap the ground to find a spot to lie down. We had to
stay there for some time, an hour or two. The officers, with their handguns and batons, searched the sites for trafficked laborers; they even
asked the builders to show them the passports and official resident permits of the workers who were still up on the sites. The documents were
presented. The officers counted the workers and the documents, and
they never asked how such a huge building was being built with so few
workers? We later learned that the police, too, knew what was going
on, but they had to play that game so that others did not take their
country for a lawless one. They truly needed us; if we weren't there, who
would construct all those monstrous buildings? There weren't enough
young people in the country's workforce, so they needed migrants but
didn't want to grant us residency, because then, when they were done
with us, they could simply kick us out, exactly as they ended up doing,
though not at the end of the construction job, no. That was an easy
move for them to make, but one that would knock Naji and me out,
with humiliation and disgrace, along with a scar for me, a scar that I
still have.

It was my own fault, but maybe I can also say that he caused it,
because it was he who left first. Every Friday morning, a car would pick
him up. He would clean up as much as he could, pick up his instrument
case freely and proudly, and go to meet the car. The other workers said
that it took forty to fifty minutes to reach the city in a truck or minibus,
but the car that picked Naji up could drive that distance in only twenty
minutes. I didn't want to hear anything about it. Nothing. But Naji recounted it all to me. "First, we arrive at Yadi's house. We stay there for
a few hours until a few other people join us. I practice my violin a bit.
Then we all go to a kabob house, where the workers are all Iranian,
from the owner to the workers, but they speak Arabic so well that if

they don't tell you, you can't guess they are Iranian. We eat lunch there, then head to Sheikh Saleh's house. The entertainment room is so big that it can hold a hundred people. On Fridays, only his close friends come over, around twenty to thirty people, sometimes less, sometimes more. There are also one or two singers who sing Arabic. Most of their songs are familiar to me, so I can tune myself with them quickly. The sheikh is a more or less young man, handsome, friendly, quite nice. You'd like him if you met him."

I got mad, feeling hotter and hotter without realizing it. "It seems very important to you that he is handsome, because you keep repeating that over and over."

"But I just said it once. Well, I don't remember repeating it."

"You know what? What does any of this have to do with me that you have to tell me about them? I'm not ever going to see the fucking guy. Whatever he is. A sheikh or a donkey or a goat. Handsome or ugly. Has he sent for me to come and meet him to like or dislike him? I can tell you, without even seeing him, that I don't like him at all. Whether I ever see him or not. A bunch of people who don't have anything other than money. They rule the world with their money and can buy whatever they want, even other humans; they can buy people like you to entertain them, just for a few unworthy coins."

"Unworthy?" he retorted.

I knew I was talking nonsense. I turned my face away from him and spit at the foot of the wall. "Screw this world, for nothing is of value in it except money. Just those coins." Naji was silent. "Your Agha Yadi thinks we are stupid, telling us he is an electrical engineer. He is just a pimp for the sheiks; his business is not electricity but pretty boys. You can tell him that on my behalf."

Naji still didn't say anything, not that night, not the day after. I didn't show any interest in talking to him either. Even though we had breakfast and lunch and dinner together, it was all in silence, without exchanging any words. He continued with his Friday plans. He didn't inform me how much money he made there. I figured that his heart was not with me anymore. Then one day, he simply started collecting his belongings, telling me that Yadi had found him a job at the site where Yadi was working. An easier job, supervising the workers. It was his responsibility to walk around the site, and instead of working himself, he would watch the other workers to see if they did their jobs right, and if anyone skipped work or didn't do enough, Naji would tell Yadi on them so that he could somehow punish them, for example by cutting back on their wages or even firing them.

"How can you do this? How can you sell someone out just because they are leaning back to take a few drags?" I asked him.

"This, too, is a job. If I don't do it, someone else will. And it's not right to get paid and slack. Do you think it's right?"

"I might not consider it right either, but I'll never snitch on someone and take the bread out of their mouth."

"You think my flimsy snitching can take the bread out of someone's mouth? You think so? Nah. I doubt it."

"There'll be some kind of punishment, for sure. Whatever it is, he'll lose face as he begs and pleads in front of the other workers."

"You're too sensitive. Have you forgotten what blows this life has dealt the two of us? How it has knocked us around until we ended up here? Who did us wrong? These very people." Naji paused before continuing, "Of course everyone prefers to have an easier job, right?"

"Yes, but at what price?"

"Well—"

I didn't let him speak. "Don't you ever forget that, more than others doing us wrong, we did ourselves wrong. There were people who actually helped us out. Good people. I hope you've not forgotten that." The way he turned around and showed no interest in continuing the conversation, I figured he could well remember who I was talking about.

"I must go now." Carrying his stuff, he went off to settle in another building far from our current one, a building I had only seen from a distance, which was, for some reason, being completed sooner than the others. After that, I was all alone. Alone among others. After Naji left, a few workers who were sharing a room with many others and were cramped in that small space asked if they could move into my room, but I could hardly put up with anyone else in my space. I wanted to be alone at night, keep the oil lamp on late, talk to myself or to his memory and share my unspoken secrets with him. He was gone, and I jolted awake from my nightmares at least once every night, sat up, and remembered that he was gone. When I imagined the damned face of that fucking guy Yadi, I was filled with hatred. Was it hatred or jealousy?

More than jealousy, it was the feeling of fear that overtook me after he left. Without him, I felt under attack by other men's vicious gazes. The fear of my body and soul being targeted didn't let up. When I went up the unfinished wet, unsafe stairs with an armful of bricks, a man walked by me and, with a smile that multiplied my pain a hundred times, said, "Well, your friend left, huh?" Which one of them was it who smirked and said, "Now you have to find another one, because boys like you who are that way always need someone to put it in them"? The short man whose job was guarding the warehouse laughed so hard, as if he wanted to show everyone that he only had two teeth left in his mouth. "I myself am at your service, my dearest brother. We, too, have a heart, you know?" I kept sweating and pushing the cart full of thatch upstairs. I could feel the greedy look of a tall man. His eyes were looking at me, but he was talking to the guard. "What do you have to say, Bengali monkey?" He was Sardar's right-hand man. His look terrified me so much that I had no choice but to tell Sardar about it.

"Agha Nosrat, your right-hand man, who I thought would be protecting me against attacks by other men, honestly, he seriously scared me the other day. So I thought I would tell you before it is too late and something bad happens."

Sardar was standing next to a tar barrel with a closed lid, which functioned as a table. He was having bread and cheese and tea. All the workers were resting. He asked me, "What do you mean? What could happen, God forbid?"

I didn't know how to respond. "Many bad things could happen, Chief."

Chewing his bread and sipping his tea, he looked me up and down as if looking at a naked woman. "Mashallah, you are good-looking too. May God protect you." And this rang a warning bell in my ears: I was not even safe from this man's sharp clutches. Our building, which now had a roof, was submerged in silence, illuminated by the white light of bulbs hanging from the ceiling. We knew now that the building would become a covered shopping center. Sardar understood that I really disliked his look. He asked me, "What exactly did Nosrat tell you?"

"What I just told you. He scared me."

Suddenly, he called out to Nosrat, who was walking past us. He joined us. "At your service, Chief."

His mouth still full, Sardar asked him what he had said to me. I was looking down, picking at the dried pieces of mud on my clothes with my nails. Nosrat was shocked, or maybe he only pretended to be. He said he was just joking, said that he would actually punish anyone if he heard anyone had upset me. He put his fingers on my face. His cold shameless fingers slipped under my chin. "Promise me that if anyone causes you any trouble, you'll come straight to Nosrat, okay?"

Sardar said, "Get a roommate from among your fellow countrymen. You'll both save on rent and won't be alone at night, and you'll gain some peace of mind knowing someone is there with you in the room. A shy devout worker like yourself, Agha Jamil. That is your name, Jamil, right? Mashallah, what a fitting name. May God protect you."

He was right about getting a roommate. I had to do it, but I felt bad thinking about replacing Naji with someone else. I thought that if Naji decided to or was forced to come back, then I would have to get rid of the new roommate. I felt more comfortable keeping his space so that if he came back at some point, there wouldn't be any issues.

But after the horrible events of that night, I regretted not having sought out a roommate. Though my regret was brief, lasted a day or two. I had never thought that something like this could happen, and now I was inside a nightmare. A nightmare occurring not in my sleep but while I was wide awake. Three shadows sneaked into my room. Before I could move, they held me tight in their grip, covering my mouth by wrapping a keffiyeh around my face. They had their own heads and faces covered with keffiyehs too. Nobody could hear my screams and cries. Or perhaps they did hear me but pretended not to, because the following morning, I could tell from the way some of the workers looked at me that they were aware of the night's events. They had been aware while it was happening that the man who had his face covered (like the other two) was violating my worn-out body. I could do nothing but cry for myself, cry with sorrow for all the pain that was penetrating my body, burning me from head to toe and to the depth of my bones. My childhood home filled with tiny white flowers. Naneh Reyhan's kind fingers touching the jungle of my hair in the summer. Afternoon strolls on the riverbank with the wind passing over the long grass and my body. Why had I left all that behind? For someone who I didn't even have by my side now. Something that was now nothing but a bitter memory. My past life now seemed pleasant and happy. I just wanted to be there. If God willed, he could, in the blink of an eye, pull me away from the savage body wrapping itself around mine like a carnivorous snake, free me onto the riverbank, set me down among the grass. If only God willed. But he didn't, and my thrashing about under that body brought me nothing but pain. The men wore black-and-white keffiyehs similar to those of other workers. There was nothing different about them, no traits that I could tell Sardar about the next day.

"That's all? They had black-and-white keffiyehs? Nothing else?"

"Nothing."

"All three of them hurt you?"

"No. Two of them were standing guard, paid to tie me up and keep watch while the one did his thing. Then all three of them left. I didn't see where they went."

"How do you know the two were paid?"

"Huh? I don't know. I guess they were."

Sardar didn't say anything. He was kind, gave me three days off, though unpaid. On the fourth day, he told my coworkers to not give me heavy jobs such as pushing the cart full of mud upstairs, which knocked us all out.

There was a mason who told the workers what to do and what not to do. Whenever he got mad at me, he gave me the job of pushing the cart. He got mad at me even though he didn't have any reason to. He pretended to be both hardworking and very religious. Evenings, he would sit on a prayer rug, arrange several prayer beads of all kinds and colors, and pray in a language I didn't recognize. He whispered things and kept bowing down and moving the prayer beads. His room was two rooms away from mine. In my comings and goings, I had often no choice but to walk by his room. He had a few roommates. He would sit in the middle of the hallway, spreading his stuff out and blocking my way, and whenever I passed, while he continued with his prayers, he raised his head and gave me such a disapproving look, as if I were at fault, as if I had blocked his way, not the other way around. One time, as I was passing, I braced myself and stared into his face. I was looking at him from above and saw a man in his forties who presented himself as older, resting on his tangled legs, repeatedly pronouncing words that had no impact on his expression. The only meaningful thing in his face was the hatred of me he wanted me to see. I was staring at him with a curious spiteful look, trying to figure out if he was the man who had abused me that night. No, if it were him, he wouldn't be expressing so much hatred toward me. If it were him, maybe he would lower his head, maybe he wouldn't block my way, unless he meant to make friends with me. Sardar had promised me that he would find that man, those men. He had promised. He then asked me, "Imagine that guy's identity was exposed to you this very day. Well, what do you want to do to him?" I hadn't thought about that, but it wasn't hard to find an answer to that question.

I soon learned that Naji had not taken the handgun with him. He had left it in a bag of our shared belongings. How could I know whether he had done that on purpose or had simply forgotten it? Until the day he himself came over. All cleaned up. He hadn't come to stay with me, had only come to resolve an important matter, fast and quick, and get on his way. That was all.

"I just came to tell you something, Jamil."

"What?"

"That gun."

"Why didn't you take it with you? Did you forget it? Come upstairs, and I can give it to you."

"No. You know that my building is too crowded."

"I thought Agha Yadi had at least given you a room to yourself."

"There aren't many empty rooms there."

"So?"

"That's it. What do you think we should do, then?"

He wore a white shirt with only three buttons. It was long, and he wore it over his pants; it was a good-quality shirt, soft and pretty, but I didn't like it at all, because I suspected someone had gifted it to him.

"You mean I should get rid of the gun."

His face fell. "That would be a shame." He paused. "Don't you think so?"

"What, then? I should risk keeping it because your majesty might someday need it again?"

"Okay then. All right. Just get rid of it. That's all. Throw it away. Lose it." He said this and left. I called after him, but he seemed to not hear me anymore. And in my mind, I came to the conclusion that your beloved is not always there to protect you. Sometimes, destiny leads him to act otherwise, throwing the ball of danger in your court. Whatever reasons Naji had for leaving it with me, I was now happy I had a gun. I began to look for the man I wanted with clearer intentions. I was sure he was one of the men I came eye to eye with every day. Maybe he had brought the two guards from elsewhere, two traitors whom the workers didn't know. They were certain that none of the workers would stop them, knew that they all would be asleep when I became a mouse trapped by a cat. The exhausted workers would be fast asleep or simply lying in their beds, wrapped in their blankets. Living men, wide awake, who knew a young man was being hurt a few steps away from them, was crying out for help, but who preferred instead to listen and stay in their own rooms. Perhaps some of them had lit up cigarettes while in bed and wondered what to do. It was obvious that you should not risk your job. If you got up from your bed and angrily protested that savage attack against the young man, then who knew if you might come to blows with the builder or even the employer? Someone who had the power, with a simple no, to take away your livelihood and that of your family, who was waiting in your faraway village for you to travel back to them with money, even after a long while. So the best decision you could make in the wind was to hold on tightly to your own hat. And the best decision for me was to once again check to make sure the gun was in the bag and to make sure the religious head mason, with all those prayer beads and all the spitting and praying under his breath, would not have dared to have been the man on that night. There was both fear and hatred of me in his face. No, he didn't seem able to hire two men to be at his service like torturers all night long.

By that age, I had realized that if men's sexual needs were left unfulfilled, they would lead to hatred. I could clearly see that poison in his face, which he wanted to spew onto me. By that age, I had realized that I was surrounded by men filled with repressed sexual flames burning them. It was true that I, too, was a man among those men, but the flame was different in me. It wasn't greedy. It wanted to join someone whom my heart desired. So I kept repeating to myself that I didn't have that sexual greed. It was as if I were Naneh Reyhan, who was married to the memory of her dead husband, and I was happy with myself; but there were others around me who were not satisfied and kept hurting me one way or another, all the time. Especially after Naji left, because most of the workers, even the employers, were kind of intimidated by him, as they thought he was bullheaded, and they couldn't predict how he would react. Naji had also made up stories from some old fights that I didn't remember, recounting in detail how he had ripped his enemies apart. Naji thought it was because of those stories that the men were on the lookout for him, and I only laughed at him.

I had fallen in love with that gun. I secretly checked on it once or twice a day, touching it through the fabric of the bag to make sure it was still there. My love for it intensified when I found out that the man who had attacked me that cursed night was Nosrat, Sardar's right-hand man, who made Sardar's life easy. He was a big man, and his face showed signs of fistfights and all kinds of blows. His nose was broken and beaten flat. Because the workers wanted to stay out of trouble with him, they did their jobs well and on time. We hadn't seen this with our own eyes but had heard that some workers who slacked had even been beaten up by him.

Nosrat paced around the building, talking loudly: "We are at the service of those who do their work on time and well, who do whatever they are asked without arguing, but we have to be honest with each other. We want nothing to do with those who want to slack off and still be paid for nothing. Here, we don't pay anyone for nothing, my brothers. But we'll give you free kicks in the ass, as many as you want."

A few of the workers laughed at his words to make him think he had said something funny. He was standing there, outside a newly built mud shed, checking it closely to see if he could pick on whoever had built it. Everyone knew that he would eventually find some fault with it. I was in the hallway of one of the building's higher floors. I was looking at him from up there, but, in my mind, I was imagining the moment I would shoot him. The bullet leaves my gun and hits him in the chest. The sound of the shot echoes strangely in the air, as if the bullet is still roaming around in the hall after being shot. At first, Nosrat doesn't believe he is shot. It's said that it takes a while for the person who is shot to realize the bullet has entered their body. Shocked, he looks around. With one hand on his chest, he turns to see who has shot him. He spots me, or I show myself to him with the gun in my hand. I don't have anything to hide. I am done hiding—myself or the gun. I have thought about everything in advance, about being arrested in the dungeon of this foreign, tough, masculine country, about the worst things that can happen to a murderer like me, who has neither a residence permit nor someone to support him, nothing. I am even prepared to be taken to the gallows, because Nosrat is a citizen, and based on the country's laws, if you killed one of its citizens, you would be executed. So my death is a sure thing. Nosrat collapses in the middle of the pile of mud, turning and twisting like a snake. Finally, he becomes motionless, like a mud statue, but his blood is still mixing in with the mud, in the mud.

Just then, the workers cheered in unison. "Say a salavat," one said. The workers, who had stopped working, joined together in saying a prayer to the prophet.

Sardar was standing at the door of the building. He asked, "What is going on here? Who are you saying a salavat for?"

Seyyed, an older worker who had a good relationship with Sardar, said, "For the health of our angel, our blossomed flower, your newly born child, Sardar."

Sardar looked around him with surprise. A young man I had never seen before was standing next to him. With a smile as wide as his face, Sardar asked, "Where did you hear about it? The baby was just born last night."

The workers laughed.

Seyyed said, "How could we not learn about it when it's news of Chief's happiness? How would that be possible, my child? How could we not learn that the child is a boy? Thank God."

Sardar grew even more joyous. Looking to the ceiling, as if looking up at God, he murmured, "Thank God." He then asked, "Where is Nosrat? Has anyone seen him around?"

A voice said, "I saw him walking to the bathroom, Sardar."

Sardar glanced around him and noticed me. "Jamil, please come here. Let me introduce you to this fellow countryman of yours."

One of the workers said, "What about sweets for the occasion, Chief?"

"They should wait until later. We must now get back to the hospital to take mother and child home. Sweets are in order, I give you my word, brothers; I won't forget."

I put down the tools I had in my hands and went to Sardar. He introduced the young man standing next to him as Javad. He was handsome and olive-skinned; the collar of his shirt was open, revealing some of his chest hair. Sardar said, "Javad Agha is a very good loyal young man, but he doesn't want to work here anymore. He wants to go back to Iran, but he won't be picked up until three days from now. He has already given his room to another worker, before knowing he had to wait a few more days. Javad used to work on another building. He worked for us for many years. He is quite honest and reliable. In short, since you are by yourself, I thought he could stay in your room for these few nights. Of course, he'll pay the rent, and he is very prim and proper." Without asking me whether I would agree or not, he turned to Javad and said, "Go bring your stuff, dear boy. It's not more than a backpack, is it?"

"No, Chief. Just one backpack. That's all my life's assets," he said and laughed.

"Are you sure it's just two or three nights?"

"It should be only two," he responded to me and went to fetch his backpack.

Nosrat came back. "Congratulations, Chief. You had a son. Thank God."

"I'm God's servant, truly," Sardar murmured under his breath, as if talking to himself.

Nosrat was buckling his belt. I imagined that I would surely have shot him if I had had the gun in my hand just then.

He told Sardar, "Chief, you have to admit, you never have had a worker as good as Agha Jamil here, because not only does his mind work well, but his body is also strong. Honestly, any builder who has such a worker is pretty lucky. You should appreciate him."

Sardar, however, was not listening. He was counting a bundle of bills, from which he handed me a few. "This is Javad's rent for the room. Here you go, brother."

"But he hasn't come yet."

"Well, he is on his way."

"But also, why are you paying for him?"

Nosrat jumped in, took the money from Sardar, and quickly put it in my pants' pocket. "When Chief says do something or don't, you don't argue anymore, son. You just do it. Okay?"

He didn't take his eyes off the depths of mine until I said okay. There was a smile on his lips that suggested he had known me for many years. He had narrow eyes. They were not as horrifying up close as they were from a distance. His eyes seemed to want to assure me that he would have my back against the violence of other men, but it didn't seem that there was a large brain in that huge head of his. Not only his look, but also his smile was childish. And still, maybe because of his large build and wide chest, I suddenly felt like throwing myself into his arms.

"Okay then, so you keep watch on the workers," said Sardar. As he started walking toward a white car waiting for him, he told me, "I don't think there is much more at the site for you to do. For now, it would be best if you just work with Nosrat. You hunting down the lazy good-for-nothing workers will benefit us more than you taking a couple of bricks upstairs." He reached his car and left.

"Your roommate is a good kid. He is one of the seasoned ones here, but now he is leaving. Has he told you that he is leaving?" Nosrat asked me.

"Yes, he has."

"Just because this Agha Javad is a bit suspicious, I thought he might not have told you that he's going back to Iran to become an officer there."

I turned to walk toward the building. "That's why he is coming to be my roommate. Only for three nights. Otherwise, I'm not one to take roommates."

Nosrat started to walk with me. "But you did have a roommate before. Is it because of him that you are not getting a new one? What was his name?"

I told him Naji's name and demonstrated that I had no interest in talking about him. I felt Nosrat wanted to tell me something. Had he sensed that I had wanted to kill him? If he asked me, should I tell him the truth or not? Now that I didn't want to kill him anymore, I thought I should tell him the truth, but the problem with telling the truth was it always threw you into new webs of trouble. Telling the truth always raised more questions, many more questions. So I decided to completely ignore the whole thing.

When we reached the building, Nosrat said, "I'm not feeling very well today and have a sore throat, so I can't talk loudly. Please announce to the workers, with a loud voice, that they can take a ten-minute break for tea, only ten minutes."

At first, I felt very good that he had asked me to do this task; I felt I was kind of important. "Everyone! Workers! Brothers! Take a ten-minute break for tea." Then: "Hey, Shacheragh! Please bring tea for the workers."

Shacheragh's voice came through the kitchen, sounding like a kind woman, along with the sound of glasses clicking and clacking. "Sure, my dear one. So thoughtful of you, sir."

The workers started to lie around next to each other, rolled cigarettes, and looked at me in a way I had never seen before. They seemed to think Nosrat was teaching me how to be his right hand, so when he was not there, I could order them around, but I hated giving orders to others.

Nosrat said, "I've heard you got some delicious cookies. The guy who bought them for you from the city told us." Then he burst out laughing.

I was headed to my room to get it ready for Javad. Nosrat was following me. I said, "He bought them with my own money. I hope he's told you that as well." I pointed this out to him because I knew the workers gossiped behind each other's backs, especially behind my back, making up things that were not true, which I tried to let go in one ear and out the other.

Nosrat was laughing and, followed by the suspicious eyes of the workers who were lying around in the clear light of the day, walked with me toward my room. A loud happy voice said, "Tomorrow, Chief will bring us all sweets, because he's got a son in the house now, a baby with a dick. After all those years waiting."

Several voices cheered, "God bless him."

Shacheragh first brought tea for Nosrat and me. I offered him a few cookies, which he took but didn't eat, put them in his pocket, said thanks, and went to offer tea to the other workers. Even though he knew I didn't smoke, he offered me a cigarette. He said, "The worst thing about your friend is that he is so cocky. That's why I don't like him, and if I want to give him a hard time, I definitely can, and can do it so well, but I won't, because I know he is your old friend."

"Why do you want to give him a hard time?"

"I don't like cocky people. I can hand him over to the police in one second, but for your sake, I won't have anything done to him."

He was bluffing. No one wanted the police to show up there, especially the employers and the builders. "Why are you so cross with him?"

He looked at his watch quickly, then got up, went to the balcony, and shouted, "Okay, brothers, get back to work, there's not much time left until lunch. Mashallah, you guys. The Sunnis say Ya Omar and get up; the Shiites, Ya Ali."

Some workers burst out laughing. Nosrat came back to my room and took another cookie. "I ate all your cookies. I'll get you some more on Friday when I go to the city." He picked up the cookie box and looked closely at it to memorize the information. "Chief really likes you to have given you this new role. Do you know how long you have to be here and how trusted you must be, like me, to get such a role? But you, in such a short time —"

I cut him off to understand what he was talking about. "I think Chief meant that I should accompany you just today, since he had to go back to the city."

Nosrat laughed. Shacheragh once again brought us tea. This time, there were only two glasses of tea on the tray. In that whole building, only Nosrat and I could lean back now and continue drinking tea, without anyone questioning us.

He said, "Such a pity that you don't have a residence permit, otherwise Chief would take you to the city, to some nice places there, to good hotels. Unlike what some believe, this place has lots of fun entertainment spots. Actually, it has all the nice places and beautiful hotels you would want. A pity that your permit is not in order. If the police arrest you in town, you'll be deported directly to your own country." He went and sat on the stool, which was close to the bag with the gun in it. I knew he was shameless, and since he considered it his job to know every nook and cranny of all the workers' lives, he might have decided that very moment to search through that bag; but if I panicked and went to move the bag, he might have gotten more suspicious, so I just stayed there, anxiously following his smallest moves.

I said, "But Chief already has two wives and so many kids. When would he be able to take me to a hotel?"

"God knows that he just married the second wife so she could give him a son. And thank God that she just gave birth to one. Chief has live-in servants, so there's no need for him to be at home in the evenings. Okay?"

I said okay but kept wanting to speak about Naji. How come he could go to the city every Friday, even though his residence situation was like mine, and he, too, was there illegally? But I didn't say anything, not wanting to cause him any trouble.

Nosrat continued, "But there is a big house around here. Not a house, but a mansion belonging to Asad. Everyone calls him Sheikh Asad, but Chief and I simply call him Asad, because we are quite friendly with him. Near here, before you reach the city, where there is still no sign of the police, and even if they show up, they don't dare cause any trouble, for fear of Sheikh Asad. They say he is originally Iranian. Whenever he is not around in the mansion, he gives the key to me so that if Chief wants to go there or take guests there or do whatever, he can do it there at Asad's mansion. By the way, Chief told me to ask you whether you have ever had caviar."

I got what he was implying, but I was speechless and couldn't protest. I was afraid that my smallest mistake could cause him to search that bag and find the gun.

I asked, "Does the mansion have a pool too?"

"I'm sure it does. I haven't used it myself, but I have used the huge bathroom there, which has a very large round tub, always full of water. Have you ever had whiskey? Chief told me to ask you that too. You have no idea how much fun it is to lie down in that tub, like this, keeping your head out of the water, smoke a cigar, and gulp down the whiskey. Don't be afraid of whiskey. It's not like arak that can make you drunk and topple you over with just one shot, no, whiskey is not like that. It gets you drunk, but very slowly and softly, and what a great drunkenness."

He was waiting for me to say okay again, but I didn't, and he kept asking, "Okay? Everything okay?"

I got up and stood in the middle of my room to make him get up from beside the bag.

He looked my body up and down a few times. I asked, "What about you, man? How many wives do you have? Officially and unofficially? How many total?"

He liked my questions and burst out laughing. While he laughed, he kept checking me out. "I don't have a wife, brother. I didn't get a wife when I was young, and now it is too late. No one will put their daughter's hand in mine."

I could keep him around for myself. Crazy but kind, he seemed the kind of guy who would go out of his way to do no matter what for you. Hanging out with him could rid me of many of the annoying things there, like my problem with taking showers; whenever I took one, there were several pairs of greedy eyes checking me out from over the top and under the bottom of the shower curtain, which was full of holes, and I could do nothing about it, because whatever I did, any objections or protests, they just made things worse. I could ask him to bring me beautiful things from the city: mirrors, hats, brushes. But now, all the glory I had built up around him in my mind a few moments ago dissipated. His embrace suddenly seemed the most useless place in the world, and his big hands, which for a quick second I had imagined as warm supporters, now seemed like the cotton-and-fabric hands of a scarecrow. He was sitting there on the stool and pimping me for his boss with a meaningless smile.

At that moment, even if I were certain that he was not the man who had abused me that night, I still wanted to shoot him, to empty all the bullets in that gun into his empty brain. But thank God I was a logical person, and, before it was too late, I imagined being tortured and killed for having killed someone whose life or death was not that different to me. If I still carried the hatred I had felt a few hours ago, I would have perhaps leaped forward and pulled the gun out and *bang bang* right at that moment while he was sitting there on the stool.

Finally, Javad arrived with a large bag on his back. He put it down and breathlessly complained, "You didn't tell me you were on the third floor. I was checking the rooms on the second floor one by one."

Nosrat got up and went toward Javad. "Man, you carried this huge bag all by yourself? Why didn't you ask your uncle Nosrat to send someone to help you?"

Javad looked at me with a smile on his face. "Whoever doesn't know what is going on here might think how kind and lovely this uncle Nosrat is."

Nosrat took a step closer to him. "I'm not kind? I who have done you so much good? Good thing that Jamil is one of our own, otherwise, if he were a stranger, he might think you were telling the truth and that I really am unkind."

Javad laughed. While laughing, he tilted his head up, revealing the underside of his chin and his neck. He had a long neck and a big Adam's apple, that bump that always took me to a safe place. All men had it, but it was only protruding and obvious in some people. It was as if it were a red apple giving me a sign of familiarity, a sign of trust. And I could see it in the middle of Javad's throat. Now I was hoping for Nosrat to leave the room. An hour or so ago, I almost felt he could be my savior, but now I just wanted him not to be there anymore.

He said, "I'm going to go check on the workers. Get your things put away, and at lunch come to Shacheragh's kitchen." He looked at Javad's body with desire and added, "Now that you are leaving us, you've got some good weight on you."

Javad jokingly pushed him away with the tips of his fingers. "Bite your tongue! I'm wearing loose clothes, that's why I look fat."

"This boy has totally lost his mind. All the men want to gain some weight, and this one wants to lose some," Nosrat said as he was leaving the room. Both of them laughed. Nosrat left.

"It's because you, sir, are just a peasant, a hillbilly from nowhere, who doesn't understand such things," Javad said, loud enough for Nosrat to hear.

I went and picked up the gun bag to move it to the other side of the room. Suddenly, Nosrat returned to the room. I felt alarmed, didn't know what to do.

He turned to Javad. "I forgot something important. Remember not to hook up with our friend Jamil here. His friend in the other building

168

is possessive and has a handgun. He has said that if anyone gets close to his friend, meaning this Agha Jamil right here, he would shoot them in the head. I just had to tell you, man." He said this and, with the loudest laugh I had ever heard from him, went on his way.

Javad was standing there startled, staring at me. "What did he say? This motherfucker Nosrat?"

"It seems you are on pretty intimate terms with him, right?" I asked.

He glanced around the room, looking for a place for his backpack. "With Nosrat? He's funny, I like him. Though he can be such a dick when he needs to be."

"How come?"

"I've known him for a long time. I've been coming here for work for years. Before, it was easier to come and go, no one checked you. It wasn't like this at all, because they knew you were coming to slave away, couldn't really do anything else, so there were no issues, especially for leaving the country. But now, it's all trouble. I want to leave here and go back to my own country, but I'm afraid. As simple as that. At least if I had a gun or something that could keep me safe on the road, it would be a different story."

I was trying to put the bag in a safer place. "Why do you even want to leave now? Why do you want to go back? Why don't you stay, now that you have learned the ways of living here? And do you think things are still the same back there? No, I don't think you could join the forces and become a pasdar as easily as before."

"To become a pasdar?"

"Nosrat said you were headed to Iran to become one. It's not a bad job at all."

"What a motherfucking bullshitter he is!"

"Well, these days everyone is."

"Isn't that funny?"

"What?"

"How about I put my backpack here in this corner?"

"That's fine."

He pulled his bag to that corner of the room. "Well, back then, right after the revolution, I thought of going back to Iran and becoming a pasdar or something. I had heard that there would be a great future for it. Anyone who got into it from the very start now holds some kind of position, but this is not something I can do, my dear Jamil. I can't arrest the women of my own town for improperly wearing hijab and the men for phony excuses like walking or talking with women, to handcuff them and take them to the station. It's none of my business what kind of clothes people want to wear. With hijab or without hijab. Long sleeves or short ones. The news from Iran made me reconsider becoming a pasdar." He paused for a moment before asking me, "Is Nosrat right that your friend has a gun? Do you know how much he might want to sell it?"

Perhaps the time had come for me to get rid of that gun. It was of no use, neither to me nor to Naji. No use and even trouble. It could be big trouble for us.

"What do you want a gun for? You are going somewhere that's full of guns. I've heard that even kids carry guns these days. You want to take a gun with you from here? Are you kidding me?"

"I don't want it for myself. I know someone who is looking for one."

"Who?"

"One of the Afghan kids. Do you have one?"

"No, I'm sorry."

"Are you sure?"

"Yes, I am."

"Why do we even keep talking about it then?" He pulled the stool forward and sat on it. "Why are you not working today? Are you on break or leave? Or what?"

"Chief has asked me to be Nosrat's right-hand man today. I don't know why he did this, but he did. And it seems that means doing nothing and just wandering around the building or sitting and chatting with others."

"Can I take one of your cookies?" He did, and as he was chewing, he added, "Maybe Sardar likes you."

"Do you know where Asad's mansion is?"

He laughed. "Is he taking you there too? It's a funny big house. It seems it belongs to a sheikh who lives there only two or three weeks

out of the year. I've heard he has a Japanese wife and only takes her
there two or three weeks out of the year. But there's something really
iffy about that house. Sardar's wife, I mean his first wife, has discovered
the location of that mansion, and, because she very much loves her
prick of a husband, she might show up there at any moment, like a
djinn, with her guards, and cause you awful harm. I have, for example,
heard from her rivals, the young men who have had something going
on with Chief Sardar, that she has hurt one with a knife and another
with pellets from an air gun. Recently too, her brother wanted to hit a
pretty young Pakistani boy on the head with his sword, but the guy was
informed and escaped Chief's wife and her brother's sword in time."

I got worried (even though I had no plans for getting involved with
Chief) that I would be caught in the grip of this wife and her guards.

"What would you need a gun for?" I asked him.

"I already told you."

"Yes, you did. You'd feel more at peace if you have a gun with you
when going over the border, especially these days."

Standing there in the middle of the room, he gave his body a twirl. I
told him the story of the bandits ambushing us and Naji pulling out his
gun. Javad wanted to know where the gun was now. I gave him a useless response. He checked himself in the mirror, asking me to appraise
his body too.

"You have an awesome body, boy. Both your height and your build.
A body better than yours they can only find up above."

He laughed. "Who do you mean?"

"The ones who choose the Mister World champion."

He kept telling me how funny I was. It seemed he had just learned
the word *funny* and used it for everything, enjoying just saying it.

"So you know how to work with it?" I asked.

"Work with what?"

"With the gun."

"If it has a bullet inside it. Does it? Have you seen it?"

"I don't know anything. It surely has."

"So you haven't yet seen the gun."

"Which gun?"

"The one your friend owns. The guy who works with Yadi."

I responded in a way that let him know I had more information but didn't want to give it to him. "I have to move my stuff around so there is space for your things in the room."

Javad was not working anymore. He and two Afghan guys were waiting for a smuggler to come get them the day after, which was a Friday morning. I was trying to come up with a plan to make him take the gun and rid me of it, though I was smart enough to not give it to him directly, because if that were the case, I could sell it to him and make some money too. I had to be very careful so that if anything happened, neither Naji nor I would be pulled into the mess.

That night, Javad told me about his hard past, how his stepfather had sent him out to bring home money when he was just a kid, and he had to do all kinds of inappropriate jobs just so that he and his sister and mother could stay safe from the stepfather's violent beatings. When he was fourteen, a truck driver took him on as a helper. Javad said that the first days and weeks had been pretty good because the truck driver paid him good wages, and he ate delicious food at eateries on the road. Best of all, he was away from home two or three nights a week, not having to tolerate the stepfather's constant nagging. But then that very good job turned into a horrifying nightmare filled with pain. "Then, there was pain and nothing but pain."

A few weeks after Javad had started the job, one night, the driver stopped the truck on the side of the road, pretending something was wrong with it and that they had to sleep right there overnight. He then started talking elaborately about the sexual pleasures between two men, but when Javad did not give in to him, the driver had raped him right there and then, and he could do nothing except break down in tears and scream and cry, but, on that freezing midnight in the middle of nowhere, who was around to come to the rescue of a teenager all by himself? "Then, the driver sat behind the wheel and turned the engine on. I was sitting there next to him with my face drenched in tears, wishing I could leave and never come back there, but I did come back, because I had no other way. The driver increased my wages, so much so that I could buy a lot of new clothes for my sister and me for the new

year; my sister and I were even able to go to the theater some week-
ends. After that, I spent less time at our house and mostly stayed with
the driver. After many times of doing that thing, it wasn't as painful
anymore. Little by little, I sometimes even began to want it myself. Can
you believe it?" He burst out laughing, but his laughter was like crying.

Not that day, but today, as I'm remembering him, I'm crying, for
him and for how one person had changed his sexual destiny by force
and threat. Such things have not been rare in this world, men constantly
raping young boys, leading their bodies to want that kind of sex after
it is repeated enough, the victims even becoming addicts, their lives
fucked up after their sexual identities are ruined.

I murmured, "Someone else deciding one's sexual destiny."

But he seemed to have a hard time accepting this idea. "Maybe there
was something in me that was different from others. Even before I was
trapped under the body of that pimp. No. Let us not curse him. He
wasn't a bad guy. He was just a motherfucker. The first days, he caused
me a lot of pain. A few years later, when I spread my wings, I didn't stay
with him. My aunt found me a better job, and I became a tailor's assistant at a sewing shop. The guy taught me a lot, but he also took advantage of me a lot. He was a single fifty-year-old man who loved young
boys. I was good for him, but he wasn't good for me."

I noticed that he was beginning to praise himself and complain
about others, and I was in no mood to listen. Not that I don't like listening to other people's life stories, but I want to throw up when someone just wants to present themselves as innocent, playing the role of a
duped victim, saying that they have ended up in that wretched place
because of others, and that everyone is at fault for their misery except
themselves.

I said, "I should find my new pair of socks. These old ones are worn
out. I think they are in this bag."

He was lying down on his own blanket, reading an Arabic newspaper. Or maybe he was just looking at the pictures. Some of Naji's stuff
was in that bag, a few pair of pants that he hadn't worn for a long time
and a few pairs of work gloves that were of no use to him anymore. I
pulled all those things out slowly and put them to the side. A water jar

and some glasses for tea and teabags that he had left for me. He had left almost all the food for me, not taking anything that he knew I could use. For the first time since he had left, I was seeing all the boxes of the delicious cookies he liked left behind in the bag. The colorful fabrics, too, were to stay with me. We had said we were keeping them for the day we could once again have a house of our own to live in at peace. It didn't matter how it was, as long as the kitchen was big enough for us to put our little table in there, every week throw a new tablecloth over it and arrange plates and glasses and a bottle of wine on top. We bought those bits and pieces from sellers who sometimes came to the construction sites with their vans. They were usually people close to the employers, because random people were not allowed to visit our exile encampments.

During the time when Naji was nice to me and still considered me a close friend, he used to sometimes buy me beautiful gifts from those sellers. One day, he bought a huge bundle of flowers, a colorful bundle of plastic flowers that I hung from the wall of our room for several weeks, arranging them as if they were in a vase. Every Friday, I dusted the bouquet of various types of beautiful flowers with a wet piece of fabric.

One day, one of the workers told him, "We thought you had bought the flowers to take to your wife when you went home, not to hang these girly things here, you tough guy." The other workers roared with laughter; they did that whenever something was even a little funny, as if they were looking for any excuse to laugh. Naji then told me to take it down, so I washed the bouquet and dried it and put it inside the bag. Whatever I brought out of the bag now, I put it somewhere around me. Javad was sitting behind me. I could feel his shadow lying across the blanket, silently evaluating my belongings. I pulled everything out except the cold heavy gun, but when I got up on the excuse of going to the bathroom, it was protruding from under the fabric of the bag, tempting anyone to look and find out what it was.

"Hey buddy, can you keep an eye on my stuff while I'm gone to the bathroom?"

"Sure thing. Go. I'll be here."

I was trembling with fear. The bathroom was outside the building. What if, while I was gone, he saw the gun and panicked and let everyone know about it? He didn't.

I thought his stay with me might be prolonged because smugglers usually arrived later than planned, but that didn't happen in his case. It was Friday noon when the smuggler came and took them with him. Several hours before he arrived, Javad had packed his backpack and joined the two Afghan guys who were to leave with him. He wanted to be away from me. He wanted to escape the weight of my gaze, and I knew why. Then I saw them getting in a van, which started and disappeared into the desert, out of our sight. Javad had said, "I'm going to find my aunt, who's such a good woman, and spend the rest of my life with her. She is alone, and I am alone. I'll work in a sewing shop for a while to save money and eventually open my own shop, a shop in which I can make all kind of clothes, for men and women. I'll get rich and keep bettering my life." He told me these things on his last night in my room, before taking the gun—I mean stealing it—from my bag. He thought he was stealing it from me to defend himself and save his life on his way back, not knowing that the gun would end up taking his life.

We heard the news the following week. One of the trafficked migrants who arrived from the other side of the border gave us the news. Apparently, near the border, three men had approached Javad and his fellow travelers, and they got frightened but had no choice other than to let the men approach them. Instead of waiting to see what the issue was, he immediately pulled the gun out, and one of the three men killed him right there by shooting one bullet at him. Afterward, it was discovered that the men were border patrol agents in plainclothes and not too dangerous at that phase, because when you were leaving the country, they didn't bother you as much, only to make sure you are leaving. Seemingly, they hadn't even intended to search Javad and the Afghan travelers, but after he pulled the gun out and was killed, the patrol lined them all up and did a body search. Then it was revealed that the gun was empty, with no bullets. I hadn't known that, or else I might not have given it to him. I mean he didn't ask anything, and I didn't say anything, so when it came to Javad's death, I didn't find myself feeling guilty. No. I had just wanted to get rid of that gun, get that vicious tool away from Naji and me. At the time, life had made me so tough that I said to myself, "You shouldn't worry. Each person is responsible for their own happiness and misery."

I kept brooding about Chief Sardar's message delivered to me by Nosrat. If I got involved with him, I would be freed from all that nasty heavy work. Six days a week, I had to wake up at dawn, gulp down a few bits of bread and cheese with two cups of tea, then start slaving away, moving weights, bricks and mud and cement, from one floor to another. Sometimes I broke down in tears under the heavy weight of the cement container. As I walked up the stairs, I wondered what sin I had committed to deserve such heavy weights, such disasters? I, who had once upon a time dreamed of studying and going to university, how had I ended up here? I wondered if I wouldn't have been better off if I had stayed in our village, in my father's house, doing what he said, what he asked me to do. No. That, too, would not have been the life I wanted, but that would have at least been better than living in exile, under so much weight. Exile. My hardest life experience had been living among people who themselves lived and felt in exile, and, for that very reason, were angry, angry with everyone and everything. Among people whom you soon realized didn't care whether you were alive or dead, because they had not built any relationship with you as a living person. And you had no choice but to keep your distance and during workdays turn yourself into a robot that walks and moves things from one place to another, constantly following orders from the worker ranked higher than you. At night and on Fridays we had time off, and I locked myself in the small space of my room, shedding tears, away from the eyes of others, for what had befallen me. What sin had I committed in my short life to deserve this?

And now that my shoulders could not bear the weight anymore, Nosrat implied that I could have an easier job that did not require carrying any more loads around. Just roam around the building, up and down, supervise other workers to make sure they were working well, and if I noticed any wrongdoing, I had to report it to Nosrat so that he and Chief Sardar could decide how to punish the worker. The key punishment was to cut the wages for that day, but if there were several reports of slacking from a worker, he could be fired, and those who lost their jobs on that account could hardly find a new one at other construction sites. I had now crossed a bridge and didn't have to worry about such punishments. The only ones who could tell me what to do and what not to do were Chief and then Nosrat, even though Nosrat had lost his power over me, he really had.

The first few days after I was given this new post, I remembered my conversation with Naji: *"How can you do this? How can you tell on someone just because they were leaning back to take a few drags?"*

"Well, this too is a job. If I don't do it, wouldn't someone else do it? Well, of course someone else will do it. And it's not right to get paid but keep ditching work. Do you think it's right?"

"I might not consider it right either, but I'll never give someone away and snatch the bread out of their mouth."

But now, I was trying to chase those thoughts away. Naji was right. If an opportunity comes knocking on your door, why not answer it? Especially when it's a lucky break like moving from shitty grunt work to a clean fancy job.

Every morning, I woke up at the same time as before, but I didn't have to wear my muddy clothes. My new work clothes were clean. When the workers started their day and were busy sweating, I went to Shacheragh's kitchen, and he served me hot bread with cheese, and tea. My tea ration was not just two cups in the morning anymore; no matter how many I asked for, Shacheragh had to serve me, and no matter how long I stretched out my breakfast, he couldn't complain. Then I got up and did my rounds. Sardar said that as long as I walked around and the workers noticed me, they would do their work without slacking off. Sometimes I watched over one or another from a hidden spot to see if they really worked or not. It was such a good feeling. A feeling of superiority, having more power than others, being able to easily lead a worker to his downfall. It was also a good opportunity to take revenge on the ones who had bothered me any chance they got. For example, the motherfucker Abdol Malek, who bullied me so much. I knew he liked me; he had tried to give me hints with his vulgar looks, but I hated the way he looked at me. Once or twice during showers on Fridays, I had noticed him pushing the door open a bit, examining my naked body. When I asked him what he wanted, he got the jitters and quickly said, "Pretty." He spoke in a mixture of Arabic, Persian, and English, each word in a different language. One day, before my position changed, I was standing in the desert looking into the distance. Maybe I was listening to Naji, who had so easily left me for other people, me, who had remained loyal to him all along, who had not left him in the worst days, in the hardest conditions, but he had easily left me for an easier life. I was probably deep in these thoughts when I sensed a heavy shadow behind me. It was Abdol Malek, wearing an ugly brown suit, which he thought was the most beautiful thing in the world. He pulled a bundle of American dollars out of his pocket, flaunted it in front of my eyes, indirectly telling me that I could have them if I wanted them.

I said, "No, thanks, I'm not the type."

But he didn't understand what I was saying, or maybe he didn't want to understand, and tried to make sure I understood the real value of those bills, comparing them to both the local money and Iranian money. I, too, tried to make him realize, in his own way, with all three languages, that my answer was still no. He suddenly attacked me, grabbed the back of my collar, and pulled me toward him with a mixture of resentment and hostility. I let him know that if he didn't leave me alone, I would tell Chief Sardar that he had attacked me. Even though I knew Chief would not take my side, because Abdol Malek was a great mason, and Chief wouldn't want to lose him. Whatever complaint I took to him about Abdol Malek, nothing would happen, except increasing the curiosity of the other workers, resulting in their bullshit questions. Eventually, I was able to pull myself out of his grip and leave. Following that day, his attitude toward me grew even worse. He sent me to do hard things in vain, trying to get under my skin, as if he wanted to take revenge. Sometimes he would order me to go downstairs and bring him a big container of mud. After I struggled to bring the mud up, he would say he had asked me to bring cement, not mud. I then had to go down again, over all the slippery little bricks, and come up once again with yet another heavier load.

When this happened, I could do nothing but curse Naji under my breath, he who, in my eyes, was the reason for all my misery. But honestly, was Naji the reason behind all my misery, or was it love? The very love that many wished for. The very love that poets had described in all its grandeur and beauty. It was love that had thrown me into this exile, among these sex-deprived men who prowled around you, waiting for a chance to rape you. I was sure the man who came to my room that night and abused me was not Abdol Malek. It wasn't him. He didn't have the strength and wouldn't have dared to do it. I kept telling myself not to think about that night anymore. Be done with it. Now I told myself that I must adapt to my new situation, one that I still hated but was better than slavery and humiliation. Now I had to put up with Sardar.

Some Fridays, Nosrat took me to the house they called a mansion. It was a big house in the desert, with no other houses around it. On Fridays, a group of men who seemed wealthy gathered there to enjoy themselves. Sometimes there would be a group of musicians, singers, and dancers to entertain them. The men drank, ate delicious food, played cards, and laughed. In their gambling, you saw all kinds of bills, from dollars to pounds to Arabic money, all kinds except Iranian. The mansion had many rooms, with comfortable beds and clean sheets. You could tell that whenever we were not there, the mansion was cleaned from top to bottom. I loved its big clean bathrooms. They were stocked with many expensive colorful towels, and I could use whichever I wanted. The first days of being with so many people joking around and laughing and having fun didn't allow me to think about my deep sorrow. I mean, I talked myself into thinking everything was fine and happy, and I just had to enjoy the situation, which many of the workers dreamed of and was mine now. While gambling, Sardar threw some bills to me. "Play with us. Have fun. Enjoy yourself."

"What if I lose?"

"Don't even think twice about it. Money is to be spent, to be lost, or else it's just a bunch of paper."

He tried to make me feel fully comfortable; he wanted me to be happy. There were a few other men there, too, who sometimes brought younger men with them. These young men were often either Russian or Eastern European. Beautiful tall young men whom I could easily have fallen in love with, but I did my best not to tread in that territory, because it could be a dangerous game. If the guy sponsoring the young man learned about such a side relationship, it would be really bad for me, worse than I could even imagine. Arab men are pretty possessive in these situations. For some of them, the boys under their wings were their pride and honor, so if they sensed that someone was distracting the affections of their boys, there could even be bloodshed. All those men also had another thing in common: they were all afraid of their wives and wanted to make sure news of their affairs with the young men didn't reach them. Many said that the wives knew about their husbands' Friday trysts but had no way of cornering them. In short, our fear was neither of the law nor of the police but of the men's wives. This was exactly what Javad had warned me about, but I had not taken him seriously back then. Honestly, I had forgotten all about it, or maybe I had wanted to forget about it, so exhausted had I been of slaving at the construction site, so painful had my shoulders become under such heavy weights, the pain constantly increasing. I was just looking for a way out. For some peace, even if it were temporary.

That's how I welcomed Nosrat's invitation and slipped into Sardar's arms. He wasn't a bad guy at all and tried to be kind to me. Without thinking about the dangers of the situation, I thrust myself into his hands, and eventually, because of him, I ended up where I am today. I mean not because of him—I led myself here. I am the sole reason behind my miseries. I knew I should have stayed away from him from the very beginning. But do you see how I betrayed myself? How I betrayed my emotions? Especially since my first time there in the mansion with Sardar, with the first touch of his hands, his getting closer and closer to me, I suddenly realized what I didn't want to see. I didn't want to realize it, because a long time had passed since that night. I was beginning to forget its doomed memories, but he brought them back with the touch of his rough hands. The way that feeling entered my body, so suddenly and violently, and the attack of fear. I turned into a fish slipping out from under his limbs, escaping somewhere, I don't know where. I just know I had to be somewhere away from him, to escape his grip, but he leaped toward me with laughter, assuming I was playing around with him. His hands held me firmly and took me back. I had no choice but to surrender, and today I have no choice but to write the events that shaped the worst season of my life, and, because it was the worst, I must write it down to reveal myself to myself, to see how wanting to free myself from my heavy job and how yearning for more comfort threw me into a tunnel of filth. Anyway, I remembered the night he so violently came to my room in the building, accompanied by his two guards. After that night, I thought I would be taking two steps. Step one was to identify the guy, and step two was to kill him. But how? I had not given that detail a thought; it was simply that my anger was dictating to me in that moment that I would kill him. I had to kill him. It didn't matter to me where and when I would identify him and what role or position he held. I just wanted his death. Now he had come forth of his own will, not knowing that I could identify him from the touch of his hands. So the first step was taken without my having to do anything. Now, it was time for the second step. Would I take the second step?

From the very beginning of the affair, Chief Sardar approached me with kindness. Fridays in that mansion, he was soft and considerate, making sure I had a good time. The man who was the host—or pretended that he was—wasn't a real sheikh but liked it that everyone called him sheikh. The young men he brought with him wore makeup and tight T-shirts with sexy slogans displayed across their chests. During the gatherings, while listening to and watching the musicians, the sheikh signaled the boys to sit around him, lean on his knees, and keep caressing him. Especially during the gambling, when the sheikh was more excited, the boys had to constantly fondle him and fake laugh to keep him from getting frustrated.

The sheikh's boys kept changing. He said he had brought the new ones from Korea. The guys seemed happy with their situation. Chief Sardar, however, never expected me to act like them. He had no problem with my beard, which had grown long, and said that it looked good on me. In short, I didn't feel the pressure to humiliate myself with him; the great humiliation of my life was the fact that I was not with Naji. He had left, and instead of him, I was involved with Chief simply so that I could live and work under better conditions. There was a huge difference between having to carry heavy containers full of mud and cement up and down the stairs, versus having my hands in my pockets all day and just walking around the building. I sometimes did leave the building to look around for workers who had ditched their assignments to hide in a corner and rest for a bit. And sometimes it happened that two workers, holding on to their shovels, stood there chatting away, forgetting they were still on the clock, and I had to give them a warning. Or if there was a dispute between two workers, I was the one who mediated to resolve it.

Was Naji happy with his job too? For my own sake, I tried to stay in the dark about him. It was better this way. I had no news of him, his happiness or his sadness, either of which would hurt me. If I heard that he was having fun, I would be jealous. If I heard he was having a hard time, I would be sad for him and cry when I was alone at night, so no one could see my tears. I would cry both for him and for myself, left behind after having gone through so much trouble for him. The fact was that I was there in that encampment in exile because I wanted to be with him. I tried to calm myself down, telling myself that I shouldn't always expect good from others in return for my own good deeds; honestly, no good deed goes unpunished. I talked myself into accepting that that was just how life was, how the universe worked.

Of course, there were also some enjoyable days in my new position. Some of the workers who wanted to tease me called me boss. In response, I simply smiled. I knew they acted out of jealousy; they thought they were making fun of me. I told myself that they should just go fuck themselves, let them say whatever their hearts desired. Despite all this, the flames of revenge kept rising and burning my heart from time to time, before cooling down again. Some nights, I spent the hours until dawn planning to kill Sardar. Other nights, I argued with myself that I had to think about my future and, instead of such thoughts, find a way to free myself from that barren desert. Especially after one of the workers found a way to escape, I was, more than ever, determined to do the same. Every day, I repeated to myself dozens of times that I, too, would leave soon. At night, in the twilight of my room, I looked at myself in the mirror and repeated, "You'll leave. You'll fly away from this cage. You'll fly toward freedom." But when?

The young man was called Shahab, and he arrived and then quickly left again. I had seen him at the construction site and wanted to get to know him, but we hadn't yet gotten the chance to talk. I thought he would be there for a long while, and there would be time. Then one evening at sunset, I saw him sitting, facing the desert, staring at nothing.

"Do you, too, like watching the sunset?"

He turned toward me. "Huh? No. Sunset? Sorry, can I ask you a question?" I looked at him, waiting. He continued, "I'm so sorry, but do you have a cigarette? I'll give you one back tomorrow."

"There's a Somalian guy who—"

"I know, who sells cigarettes. In that other building. I went looking for him, but he's gone to the city and won't be back until tomorrow. I'm really craving one, but I'm shy asking people."

"I don't smoke myself, but if you really crave it, I might be able to get you one or two from Shacheragh, if you can replace them by tomorrow. Okay?"

"I can't thank you enough. You're not a smoker to know what a draw this beast has."

"I know."

Shacheragh said, "Do you swear you don't want them for yourself, my dear boy? You are still too young to smoke, my dear boy. I just don't want to have to carry the guilt of your smoking." We laughed together, and he gave me three Indian cigarettes, which Shahab told me were quite strong.

While coughing through the first few puffs, he asked, "Do you watch the sunset?"

"Sometimes, when I'm in the mood."

"What are you looking for in the sunset?"

"Nothing. I just watch the sunset. Just that. The sunset itself."

"I'm waiting. They're supposed to pick me up soon. An ambulance is supposed to come take me away from here."

"An ambulance?"

"Maybe the guy meant a UN car. I guess that's it, because some of their vans look like ambulances."

"But who are you to have a UN car come pick you up here? Where did you say you were going?"

"My sister said they will pick me up and take me directly to Australia."

"You didn't say who you are. Why would they do that?"

"It's because I'm of a religious minority."

"Nice. I had great friends who were Christians. Such good people. I miss them so much."

"I'm Bahá'í. I've spent a lot of money to make this happen. My sister in Iran has contacted some lawyers who are trying to get me out of here."

"Why did you leave? Didn't you like Iran? Was life hard for you there too?"

"I actually loved Iran, still love it a lot."

"So why are you here?"

"You know, after the Islamic Revolution—" He suddenly stopped talking. "You are Muslim, right? I mean Shi'ite Muslim?"

"Yes, a Shi'ite Muslim. Why do you ask?"

"Does that mean you agree with the current regime in Iran? I mean, do you think they are righteous?"

"Frankly, I don't know much about that and don't really want to know either. The only thing I believe is righteous now is that I must find a way to get the hell out of here and go to Europe, anywhere in Europe."

"Why? Did you also have issues there in Iran? Or you just didn't like living there?"

"I don't want to talk about it. Sorry to be so direct, but if you know someone who would take money to get my freaking body out of here . . ."

"But I love Iran."

"Yes, you mentioned that."

"I loved living there."

"Good for you."

"I loved everything about it. Our neighborhood. The tree-lined green backstreets. The neighbors' daughters. My colleagues at work. I'm too sad to have to run away from a place I love so much, a place where my sisters still are." He wanted to tell me why and how he had come there, and even though I was not in the mood to listen to his love story about the homeland, I still invited him back to my room and offered him tea and cookies. It was better than doing nothing. Listening to his life story could keep me busy for a bit, distract me from thinking about my own misfortunes, and I also hoped I could get some information from him about how I, too, could fly away from that cage. He lay down on a blanket and told me his story: "I keep saying this to my lawyer too. I tell him that my crime is not just being Bahá'í. Even being branded like this, I could still stay and live there, because I love everything about it. Just in the past few weeks that I've been separated from everyone, I realize how hard it is to be away. I never thought that one day I would have to run away from my own homeland.

"When the revolution was happening, my father sensed something bad was afoot. He didn't want me and my sisters to participate in the protests. He warned us against the mullahs, but we didn't listen to him, went to the protests, and shouted out death-to-the-shah slogans. Only my older sister understood what my father said and agreed with him. My father told us the mullahs had been enemies of Bahá'ís since a long time ago, that even in the Qajar era, we had been under the threat of extremist mullahs and Shi'ites. He said that the murderer colonel, Mirza Taghi Khan, the so-called Amir Kabir, had been an expert at killing the Bahá'ís, priding himself on our genocide. He said that the mullahs were of the same clan.

"We didn't pay attention to his words, until finally the Islamic Revolution was over, and the new regime sat on the throne. A few months after the victory, they started to persecute the groups they loathed, and apostates and the Bahá'ís were among the first to suffer. News kept pouring in about revolutionary officers attacking Bahá'í neighborhoods and setting the houses on fire, or about Bahá'ís being executed on the pretext of having collaborated with the monarchy and the SAVAK.

"When my father heard these reports, he summoned me.

"'Come here, Shahab Allah.'

"I went to him. 'What is the matter, Agha joon?'

"He said, 'Go find Feiz Allah Khan the gravedigger, and tell him your father wants him to dig his grave in the next day or two.' Father had bought the plot next to my mother's grave for himself so that he could be buried next to his wife of fifty years.

"I said, 'What are you talking about Agha joon? You are not dead!'

"He said, 'Better safe than sorry, son. Please go and do this for me.'

"I couldn't turn a deaf ear to his request. I went to Feiz Allah and, in his pickup truck, the three of us headed to the Bahá'ís cemetery, called Ahl-e Behesht, People of Paradise, which is just outside of town, among fruit orchards, and he dug Father's grave. Father then sat by my mother's grave and talked to her, as if telling her he was going to join her soon. He had foreseen the future, knowing that he couldn't bear the chaos that the revolution had unleashed. He thanked God that Tahereh, my mother, was not alive to see the situation.

"Each piece of news about the attacks on and executions of our youth caused Father to age dozens of years, and every week we witnessed his sudden decline, until, finally, he died. He asked us not to take him to the hospital and let him die on the porch of his own home, where my mother had also died. But Father died at the worst time possible for a Bahá'í person in our small town. When Father was still alive, some unexpected bad news circulated around town. Aunt Ghadam Kheir brought the news, handing it over directly to Father, who was on his deathbed. She said, 'Do you know what has happened, Fath Allah Khan? Just yesterday, a family whose grandmother died took the body to Ahl-e Behesht to bury her there. They noticed that the wooden gates of the cemetery that had always been open were now locked and chained, with two armed guards standing by. No one knows who they are and where they have come from. They had also put up a sign that read, "Welcome to the burial ground of the cursed and the doomed. This location is closed until further notice." The guards didn't let them take the body of the deceased into the cemetery and bury her. The people's pleading was of no use, and they were told that the orders had come from the capital, and that from now on, the Bahá'ís should take their dead to be buried at the main cemetery in town. People explained to them that they had already bought their grave plots there and wanted to be next to their family members, but their imploring got them nowhere, and they were forced to return home with the body.'

"The next day, Aunt Ghadam Kheir brought the news of two other old men dying whose bodies had also been left unburied, whose families didn't know what to do. The news caused Father's condition to deteriorate. At night, he asked me to come to him and said, 'Shahab Allah, you are my only hope. I want to be buried in my own grave next to your mother and nowhere else. Remember this.' He said, 'Remember that if you bury my body somewhere else, I won't forgive you.' With these words, he put such a big responsibility on my shoulders, because he asked me to promise him, and I did promise him that, no matter what happened, I would bury his body in the grave next to my mother's.

"In the following days, Feiz Allah Khan went to the icemaking factory and bought big slabs of ice for households that were still holding on to the bodies of their loved ones. We had no choice but to keep our dead covered in ice until the issue with the cemetery was resolved. Using some big thick plastic plates, we made a container like a coffin and kept our dead in it under a big pile of ice. It was such a hard thing to do, especially because the human dead decompose and begin to smell faster than other animals, but I kept pouring ice over Father's body, not letting its smell spread around. During those days, that was all I dealt with, ice and more ice. Father's chalk-white face under the pile of ice made him look like a thousand-year-old mummy. At night, I sat next to him and wondered for what crime his dead body and those of other Bahá'ís had ended up like this. I knew for sure that Father not only had not wronged anyone during his life but had also always tried to be a good person, not harming anyone. Then I told myself that perhaps that was the very sin my father and his people had committed, that they had tried to be good and not harm others.

"My sisters were afraid. Some of the families could not tolerate those conditions, were disheartened, and went and bought new graves for their dead in our town's main cemetery and buried them there, in the hopes that, one day, things would go back to normal, and they could move the bodies to their final resting place in the Ahl-e Behesht cemetery. But I could not do that, because I had made a vow to my father. Father had toiled for us his whole life and was the best father I knew of; I had made a promise not just to him but also to myself, that I would do everything to bury him next to his wife. My sisters, who were tormented by the presence of the body in the house, said we should bury him in the main cemetery. My younger sister, who has leftist beliefs, said, 'Father is already dead. What difference does it make where he is?' But I was afraid. What if the dead could actually tell where they were buried? Then I would have to suffer until the end of my life.

"While having these thoughts, suddenly I had an idea. One of the advantages of living in a small town is that most people know each other. I went to look for Agha Abdi, who worked for city hall. He drove the water tank truck, which meant he filled the tanker up with water, drove around town, and watered the trees. He also had a helper who jumped off the truck and placed the water hose at the foot of each tree. Agha Abdi knew my father and had good memories of him, so I was able to talk him into helping me carry out my plan in exchange for some money. My plan was to hide my father's body, which my sisters had wrapped in a shroud, in Abdi's truck cab, under his seat, then together enter the cemetery, on the pretext of watering the trees, and bury my father's body in the grave waiting for him. I finalized the plans with Abdi. The following day, very early in the morning, he filled up his tanker with water and came to our house. Together we stowed the body in the cab of his truck and drove to the cemetery. There was only one guard at the closed gates. He was not a resident of our town, so we didn't know him, and he didn't know us. He asked us where we were going. Abdi jumped down from the truck to talk to him. He told him that he was on a job to water the trees in the cemetery and introduced me as his helper. The guard didn't want to let us through at first, saying that the municipality was to bring bulldozers to raze the whole cemetery to the ground, so why would it want to water the trees there? Abdi argued with him that they wanted to keep the trees. Then the guard asked for an authorization. Abdi came back to the car and took the papers for his truck's gasoline ration to show him, and the guard believed him, since he was illiterate, and let us in.

"When we reached Father's lot, I pulled the body down and hurriedly buried him, throwing soil on top of him and filling the grave. Abdi kept watch to make sure nobody saw us. I leveled the top of the grave so as to not raise suspicions, but apparently someone had seen us fidgeting around the grave, and when we left, they checked the site, and we were exposed. I was at peace, because I had kept my promise to bury Father's body where he had asked me to, and I knew that no one would exhume it, and yet I was sure that the authorities would look for me to arrest me, because they had already gone to Abdi and forced him to give them information. That day, I didn't go back home and went instead to my extended family, who hid me in a safe space in the house. The officers kept checking my parents' house, looking for me. My sisters feigned ignorance. Then my older sister arranged for my escape, before she herself was arrested. A guy picked me up and took me to Lengeh Port and from there, I came here. The officers had told my sister that if they found me, they would send me to the firing squad, because I had acted against the town imam's fatwa. Abdi was freed a day or two later, but I don't have any news from my older sister who was arrested. That is the story of my escape. My unwanted escape. And I know now that I must stay away from our homeland for years and simply be consumed with desire and sigh for it, but I'm happy that I for one didn't succumb to their nonsense and instead fulfilled my vow to my father. You know how happy this makes me? What peace it brings to me?"

And the following week, they came for him, though not in an ambulance, but on a motorcycle. It was quite early in the morning when a motorcyclist wearing a keffiyeh came to the site and asked one of the workers for Shahab, then told him he was there to fetch him. Shahab collected his stuff and, after a rushed goodbye with everyone, hopped on the motorcycle and rode off. How happy he was. What joy spread over his face as he sat on the passenger saddle and looked at me with a smile. I waved to him, wondering whether there would be a day when I, too, could fly away from this cage.

Nosrat asked, "Where in Europe are you thinking about going?"

"It doesn't matter. I've heard you just need to reach the borders of Europe, and then you'll eventually find one place or another to settle."

"That's right. And because of the commotions in Iran, you'll definitely be able to seek and get asylum."

"The guy you said you knew, where could he take me?"

"If I find him. If he is around. With all the different passports he possesses, who knows in which country he is now?"

I turned away from him. It seemed he had simply babbled something to win my heart.

He continued, "But I'll ask around to find him. We don't want you to leave us, but, well, I'll ask around."

He asked me not to talk about my plans with anyone, even with Sardar. He said if Sardar knew I wanted to leave, he would find a way to disrupt the process, not letting it go through, because he liked me and wouldn't want me to leave. However, I didn't really trust Nosrat. I could sense a veil of lies over his eyes. But since I didn't have any support, I had to follow through quietly with him to see where my request would lead.

"I'd let you know when it's time. I'm still asking around. He'll soon make an appearance. He always does this, gets lost for a while before showing his face again."

The two feelings of belief and disbelief in Nosrat's words moved in me along parallel paths. The benefit of belief is that it brings with it dreams, dreams of reaching Europe, finding security, and starting a carefree happy life; dreams of wandering freely in the streets with new friends; dreams of entering a dance college, going on stage, the audience's rowdy cheers. I decided to be nice to Nosrat, so much so that he would think that, if he had access to it, I would go to the mansion all alone with him. The Friday events were ongoing, with one occurring every few months. Going to the mansion and being with Sardar and the rest of the stories. All the men had their own boys, except Nosrat, who didn't have anyone, who always looked at others with envy and tried to entertain himself by overeating and drinking to excess. I was noticing that he looked at me strangely. He seemed to imply that he longed to be with me but didn't dare step out of line with Sardar. I was kind to him so that he would follow up with the smuggler to Europe.

Finally, the time came for Nosrat to meet up with the smuggler on my behalf. Sardar had said that he had to go somewhere to take care of some important business, so he wouldn't be going to the mansion the following Friday—no one was going there on that day. Nosrat said he might be able to bring the smuggler to the mansion that Friday to resolve my departure drama. I asked him why not plan to meet somewhere else.

"The poor guy is not someone who can appear just any place. For security reasons. He has said that he will come if the place is safe and no one is there except us. I don't know any place safer than the mansion. Do you? If yes, besmellah, tell me and we'll do that." He knew I didn't know of any other place.

"What if the mansion guard sees me with you there and reports back to Sardar?"

"First of all, Chief Sardar trusts me more than his own eyes. Rest assured. Second, I think the guard has gone to his village and won't be back for a while. So rest even more assured." He laughed. For me, none of that mattered anymore. All that mattered was that he help me leave, to fly out of that cage, and that I could fly toward my freedom as soon as possible.

"Okay, whatever you say, Agha Nosrat."

Three days before that Friday, Naji came to see me. The sun was setting, and the sky was clear. I had gone to the back of the building, where the workers didn't usually gather and there were no passersby, where Naji and I used to go together, staring at the sky, waiting for the moonrise. Same on that evening, when a golden light pulsed every few moments on the blue surface of the sky, as I fixed my gaze on the horizon. In one corner of the sky, a patch of pale gold was appearing, as if the ball of the moon had been thrown into the depths of a pool and was now rising little by little, until it would all of a sudden pop up above the surface of the water. In a flash, a soft breeze moved over me and continued on slowly, spreading a familiar scent around me. Then a familiar shadow, a very familiar one, appeared next to me, and I turned and saw the circle of his face. He smiled. I had to hide my enthusiasm, so he could not tell that I was so excited to see him that my knees were shaking. I had to show him that I, too, was now an important figure in that building and had an important job, but whatever I was showing him in that moment was nothing but lies. The truth was that my heart was pounding, and I didn't want anything in that moment but to hold him tightly in my arms, lay my head on his chest, and silently enjoy his presence.

"Why are you panting?" he asked, then continued, "Anyway, for God's sake, listen to what I have to say and don't hang out with this fucking guy. I mean Nosrat. I've heard that he is something like Hamed. Excuse my language, but he's of that same breed of motherfuckers."

"Hamed did you wrong, I agree, but he didn't do me wrong."

"Well, because he was your brother-in-law, you were family after all, so he couldn't hurt you that much, otherwise he would have if he could. But this venomous snake of a eunuch has no family ties with you, so—"

I burst out laughing. "Eunuch?"

He, too, laughed. "I swear on your life. I've heard that he is a eunuch. I mean, when he was young, he had hernia or something that had to do with his dick and balls, and he went to the hospital for surgery, but they fucked up and zapped it all, making him a eunuch."

I just kept laughing. I couldn't stop. It was as if Naji had come there solely to make me laugh. I didn't hear the depth of his words at all, I just heard that he was saying funny things to make me laugh, exactly like the old days, when we walked home from work, when I was exhausted, and he made me laugh. But now I was not exhausted, and Naji did not laugh anymore. He lit a cigarette and waited for my laughter to subside. I was curious what the heavy thing in the pocket of his shirt was, but I preferred not to ask. I kept laughing at him. "Did you want to tell me something important?"

"Just that. I wanted to say I've heard a lot of things about your Agha Nosrat, so you should not hang out with him, for your own good. I wanted to tell you to be careful with him."

"I, too, heard bad things about your Agha Yadi. This for that."

"Nosrat is a miserable lowly traitor who sells people out for cheap. This is what I've heard about him. Be careful that he doesn't sell you out too."

"What value do I have, though, to be sold out? Why do you speak nonsense?"

Not paying attention to what I said, he pulled out what he had in his pocket. Something wrapped in shiny gold-colored paper. "I saw this in a shop and liked it, so I bought it for you, hoping you would like it too."

He handed it to me. It was heavy.

"Well, is there anything else you want to say to me?" he asked me.

"What is this?"

"Is there anything else you want to say? Take care of yourself. People have become such assholes," he said and left.

"What is this? Where are you going?"

He didn't want to stay with me; it even seemed he was running away from me. I wanted to run after him, give him back whatever it was he had given me, but my curiosity got the better of me. I unwrapped it quickly. It was a small mirror, and when I brought it up to my face, it gave my sad eyes to me.

The promised Friday arrived. I was dressed and ready early in the morning, staring out at the desert, waiting for Nosrat. It was noon when he came in a car. He parked far away, because we had decided not to let anyone see us. This time, he was driving a luxury car. Cautiously, away from the eyes of other workers, I approached his car, got in, and we started off on a dusty road toward the mansion, a road that, with so many cars coming and going over it, had actually become packed hard, but even now, as I turned and looked behind us, I could see a messy cloud of dust running behind the car. "What is behind us that you keep looking there, Agha Jamil?"

"Nothing. There's nothing. You said that the smuggler is definitely going to the mansion today?"

"Please, don't call him a smuggler to his face, because he would hate that. His name is Mullah Mohajer."

"Is he a mullah?"

"Do you mean the type who wears a cloak and turban?" He laughed and continued, "Actually, he always wears a suit and tie, and carries a very expensive leather briefcase. But since in their region *mullah* is a title of grandeur and trust, and he is grand and trustworthy, people call him Mullah Mohajer."

"Has he mentioned how far he can take me?"

Nosrat didn't have any information. Whatever I asked him, he said we had to ask Mullah Mohajer. We reached an asphalt road, and I still was suspicious of him. I wondered if he was just going to take me there to sit and kill time while no one was coming at all. What if he was planning to rape me? I thought of what Naji had told me and wondered if I was doing the right thing going to the mansion with him. Wasn't that utter stupidity?

"Is Mullah Mohajer supposed to get there first or are we?"

"What difference does it make?"

"It does make a difference."

"You are so anxious. Let me turn around and take you back to the building to your own room."

"Take me back? Now that we've come all this way? Did you just learn that the guy is not coming?"

"I didn't say he was not coming. I said if you are anxious, I could take you back, so you can stop worrying."

I tried to calm myself down. We had come most of the way. I looked at the desert, and Naji's words kept swirling around in my head, not letting me feel at peace.

I said, "Do you know that someone attacked me one night? In the middle of the night?"

He asked, "Who was it?"

"I don't know. He had his face covered. The faces of his two guards were also hidden with keffiyehs. I didn't see them."

"When was that? Recently?"

"No, not recently. It was a very cold night. I thought you knew who it was. I told Chief Sardar about it. How come he didn't tell you?"

He shifted in his seat and aimlessly moved the rearview mirror. He didn't turn to look at me. He didn't want me to continue the conversation. "He might have said something. I can't quite remember. How was it that you couldn't see their faces? Why didn't you push the keffiyehs away to see who it was?" With a meaningless smile—or perhaps a terrified one, though I didn't know what he would be terrified of—he turned toward me and added, "You naughty one! You yourself know who it was, but you are now pulling my leg. Or you are attempting to make me spill the beans? So good that you've shaved your mustache and beard. Well done. It was time."

"What do you mean it was time? Is something coming up?"

He got agitated again. "No, bro. Nothing other than the fact that we are going to have some fun." He giggled. "Like loads of fun." He kept laughing.

"And discuss the details of my trip to Europe with Mullah Mohajer. The pricing, the timeline, the itinerary of the trip."

"Right on. May God bless the pure milk that fed you, the young flourishing Iranian man that you are."

The road was narrow. Whenever a car sped toward us, I closed my eyes out of fear, thinking about what would happen if the cars suddenly hit each other and everything came to an end in one second. Everything. That would be the real freedom. In some moments, I also felt delighted, imagining that the planning for my trip was complete and that I, like Shahab, was saying goodbye to everyone. I was not sure if I would go to Naji, too, to say goodbye to him. Maybe I would. That could be an excuse to see him one last time, while also proving to him that I could have a good life and future without him too.

I was leaning my head against the back of the seat, enjoying the cool of the air conditioner when we reached the mansion. Nosrat's eyes kept searching for a car or a person. There were no cars or people around the mansion. He told me to sit right there in the car so he could go inside and check everything. He knew that Sardar was pretty far away from there. When he got out of the car, he continued to carefully check around especially in the direction of the few newly finished buildings nearby that were clearly still empty. It seemed that Nosrat was delaying going inside the mansion, until he finally put the key in, unlocked the door, and went in, leaving me there in the car all by myself. Five minutes, ten minutes, fifteen minutes, and I was getting tired of aimlessly sitting there. I was about to get out of the car and knock on the door when I saw a black car approaching. I thought the smuggler had arrived. There were one woman and two men in that very expensive car. It stopped when it reached me. All three passengers got out. One of the men stayed right there next to the car and kept looking around him. The woman and the other man walked toward the car in which I was still sitting. The man motioned for me to lower the window. I pushed the button for my own window, but all the windows went down. A vapor of heat and fear sprayed over me. The man asked me who I was and what I was doing there. I told him I was there with Nosrat. The woman recognized Nosrat's name and asked me for my own. I told her. She asked if I was the Iranian Jamil. I told her I was. She asked if I was the same Jamil who worked for Chief Sardar. I confirmed it. She asked if I sometimes came to the house with Sardar on Fridays. I said no.

The woman, who was tall and big, was wearing black from head to toe, and both her arms were covered with gold bangles. She instructed the man, "Go ask Nosrat if this is the boy."

The man went and buzzed at the door, then spoke to the person inside through the intercom. I knew that there was no one in there except Nosrat. I heard that the man was speaking Arabic, but I couldn't hear what he was saying or hearing through the speaker. He returned and told the woman, "It's him."

The woman turned to me and said, "You are the faggot, right?"

I didn't say anything, just wished Nosrat would come back as soon as possible.

The woman said, "You are the one who has stolen our Sardar from us."

"I think there has been a mistake." I was watching the man's hands. He was wearing a pair of black leather gloves. I thought the next step would be for them to pull me out of the car and beat the hell out of me, and that was why he was wearing the gloves.

The woman said, "Aren't you ashamed to call yourself a man?"

I didn't know how to respond. The man's right hand had brought something out of his coat pocket, and now both his hands were busy fumbling with it.

The woman said, "You are even less than a whore." She turned her back to me and said something to the man that I didn't hear. She stepped away from the car.

I was dumbfounded, not knowing what was going to happen. Suddenly, the man's quick hands drowned in darkness, and before I could turn my face completely away, the man threw a liquid in my face and immediately stepped back. Then, darkness. Half of my face was burning in darkness. A fire that I could not see but only feel its heavy horrific burning, my screams under all that burning, and the woman's voice cursing. A little bit later, someone took me in his arms. The woman's voice stopped. I heard one car leaving, but the car I was in was still parked there. Nosrat's voice kept repeating, "What happened? What happened?" I couldn't see anything anymore; I could only hear. Now the woman's voice sounded frightened. Nosrat had gotten in the car. "We have to take him somewhere."

The woman got in too. "You should go to a hospital."

The car started off, with Nosrat driving. There wasn't anything in my head except an onslaught of pain and the hurting voices of the woman and Nosrat, who talked with each other in anxious broken words.

"You said you would just give him a slap."

"It was Mohammad. My brother. He can't bear hearing these things. He's edgy."

They took me to a small quiet hospital that seemed to be for keeping dead people. When we arrived, everything was covered in a white fog, and little by little, I lost consciousness in that fog, and there was nothing anymore. Nothing. Not even pain. It seemed they had injected me with something. Yes, they had put me under. Hours later, I woke up amid white sheets. A dark-skinned man in white clothes was looking at me. It felt like a pan full of burning hot cement had been put on half of my face. The brutal itching of the skin on my face was the most excruciating pain I had ever experienced. Intending to scratch my face with all ten fingernails, I tried to raise my hands, but they didn't move, because the nurses had tied my wrists to the bed. It was the doctor's order since he knew that, after coming to, I would want to scratch my skin, and that was the worst thing I could do at that stage, the stage at which my face was covered with bandages and medication. Acid had burned half of my face. I had to stay in the hospital for a few days so the doctor could ensure my wounds wouldn't become infected.

My bed was in a large hall, but there was no other bed next to mine. I just saw that there were a few other beds at a distance from mine, and men who came and went amid the whiteness. There were no women around. The doctors and nurses were all men. A nurse brought me some water and untied my hands from the bed, explaining why they had restrained me, telling me that now I could decide whether I wanted my hands to be tied down or not. I told him to leave them untied. He once again warned me that scratching my skin at that stage would immensely delay the healing process. I promised him I'd be careful not to do it. It was the cleanest hospital I had ever seen in my life. The first day, I had contact only with the doctor who was attending to my burns; after that I was just in touch with nurses.

No one asked me who I was and what had happened. It seemed that they already knew everything. I don't know when it was that a police officer in uniform arrived and sat on the couch next to my bed. He looked at me, but what could he see of me other than a bundle of white fabric with two black bullets moving amid them? I was told I was lucky that the acid hadn't hit my eyes. Lucky? Anyway, the police officer's job was to watch over me. He told me that the following day some people would come to interrogate me. He stayed the whole night on the couch, and every time I got up to go to the bathroom, he did too. A young nurse, who said his mother was Iranian, sympathized with me, and seeing how much pain I was in, he went and brought some strong medication.

The following day, three officers came to see me. Two were in uniform, and the other was a plainclothes officer. One of the uniformed officers spoke Persian too. I preferred to talk only in Persian and for him to translate. Most of the questions were asked by the plainclothes man, who kept jotting down notes. The questions kept coming at me until they got to my relationship with Chief Sardar. I told them there hadn't been anything strange between the two of us. They asked, "If that was the case, why did Sardar's wife attack you like that?" I told them I had never seen the woman before, didn't know her, and had no idea about her intentions. The plainclothes officer, though, with the look he and his colleagues gave me, showed that he did not believe what I was saying. I was afraid, but I knew that my face was not visible to reveal my lie and my fear to them. Anyway, my whole life had been exposed to them already. Worst of all, my residence in the country was illegal, and they had surely reported me to the immigration office, and I was sure those were to be the last days of my stay there, unless I was first to be their guest for a while in prison. I imagined that the next day Chief Sardar and Nosrat would come visit me in the hospital. My eyes, the only parts of my face that were in good shape, were glued to the clean shining hallway floor, with all kinds of reflections leading to the entrance. I wanted to see their bodies, together or each on his own, in that hallway, walking over the reflections, approaching my bed, and asking me how I was doing. But they didn't come; they didn't ask. Neither Nosrat nor Sardar.

The saddest afternoon of my life in a foreign hospital in a foreign land passed slowly and heavily, leading to the saddest night of my life. The lights gradually dimmed, but there was no full blackout. There were still some scattered lights on here and there, but it was now too late for visitors. Even if they came, the hospital guards would not let them in, so they would have to leave and come back the day after. They didn't come the day after either. The next day, my eyes had once again been glued to the floor since early dawn, and the hallway looked different now. The nurse gave me eggs and cookies. Then he helped me drink milk. He told me that small hospitals in the middle of the desert were solely for border guards and employees. He said he assumed they would either move me from the hospital to the prison or to the prison hospital. His words made me tremble from head to toe, drilling fear into me. Imagining prison and having to bear all that misery intensified the pain of the wounds on my face.

There were many workers whose residence situation was like mine, because no one considered entering the country illegally a big crime; everyone thought the worst-case scenario would be that you would be arrested, taken to the border, and let go to return to your own country. That was all. But my wounds were not yet healed, and as the nurse explained, the hospital was obliged to keep me there while I was still healing. I wished I could escape from there. Now that I was certain that I didn't have anyone to come visit me. No acquaintances, not even Sardar, who had been so kind to me. I wondered why Nosrat had been so unkind. What if I had listened to Naji, who had warned me against getting close to Nosrat? But I had not listened to him, because I was sad and upset with him and was not really even hearing what he was saying; that was why I had broken into stupid laughter and had only been able to focus on his Adam's apple moving up and down while he talked.

In the hospital, too, when he sat at the edge of my bed, I foolishly and slowly moved my finger over his Adam's apple, and he looked around, alarmed. That morning the nurse had been helping me drink my milk, because my hand trembled with fear and couldn't hold on to the glass. I was afraid of everything, everything that was worth being afraid of and everything that was not. Finally, a familiar presence came down the hallway toward me. Before him, I had seen a few women wearing thick black cloaks over their heads and bodies arriving and walking past my bed. My eyes were fixed on the hallway. He walked slowly and with uncertainty, because he didn't know the way and perhaps assumed he had to turn somewhere, but in that big hall, there was no way to turn, and you had to keep going straight ahead. He walked in and closely looked at each and every patient lying or sitting on the beds. He was looking for me. He didn't know that he would not find me easily. The nurse had stepped away from my bed and was now at a distance when Naji reached me, with his clean white shirt, wearing a keffiyeh over his head like most of the men there.

"Hey, Naji! Where are you going?"

With his whole body, he turned toward my bed. He couldn't tell where the voice had come from. He stared at the bundle of bandages hiding my face. He had not yet looked at my eyes. It was the bundle of fabric he addressed. "Jamil?"

I smiled, but I don't think he saw my smile. "Come closer." Suddenly, I noticed joy spreading across his face. He bounded toward the bed until he stood right in front of me.

This time when he said "Jamil," his voice was full of tears. He was crying. "What happened?" As if stopping himself from collapsing to the ground, he suddenly dropped onto the edge of my bed. He took my hand in his, squeezed it, kissed it, and moved my palm along his own face, and my fingers felt the wetness on his cheeks. I sensed he knew the story, so I didn't explain anything.

"How did you learn? Who told you I was here?"

"Nosrat. He said he didn't know much, said he had heard from someone that this had happened. He didn't say from whom. He then gave me the hospital address. There is a guard at the door especially for you who asked me a hundred questions when he learned I was here to see you. He wrote down my name and information. I have to go present myself at the police station afterward."

"You got yourself into trouble too, for my sake?"

"I doubt it's going to be anything hard. The guy said they'd just ask me a few questions about you, that's all. Well, he didn't say more."

For those very few questions, they kept him in the station for a whole day, until they figured out that his residence situation was problematic like mine. I was kept for three more days at the hospital. Then they removed my face bandages and gave me some medication and some ointment to put on my wounds several times a day. The nurse, whose mother was Iranian, also gave me some bandages and disinfecting liquids and quickly taught Naji how to wash my wounds. When Naji was attentively listening to the nurse's instructions, I watched his animated face. I had a strange feeling at that moment, as if someone had kissed my heart.

Then I still had to deal with the police. This time I was not alone; Naji was with me. A long line of questions, one after another. About my relationship to Sardar, I repeated the same things I had said earlier. The rest of the questions concerned my relationship with Naji. We told them we were cousins and had come there for work. At the police station, they wanted to know why Naji had come forward, when he could have stayed in hiding and continued with his job. Naji said he had come because of me, because he could not have abandoned me under those circumstances. He said he wanted to take care of me, no matter what. Once, he noticed Sardar and his wife outside the police station. They, too, saw us but didn't exchange any words with us, just got into their car and left. Naji said he had seen Nosrat driving the car. We never found out what the law did to Sardar's wife, who had caused me that catastrophe. Naji told me to not think about it, because perhaps they had easily shaken it off, because, after all, they were wealthy citizens of that country, and I just a poor illegal laborer. I thought about Sardar and Nosrat's relationship and could not figure out its nature. I could not understand why Nosrat had exposed me to Sardar's wife. Was it out of jealousy for Sardar? Or had she promised him good money? Was it my own fault for having looked down on Nosrat?

Naji said, "Why is it so odd to you? I already told you Nosrat is a cheap betrayer, but, well, you didn't believe me, so." He spat on the ground with disgust. "If we were on the other side of the border, I would definitely kill him. But well, tough luck, we are here, and my hands are tied."

The head of the station kept us there for a few hours and said he had to contact the central office about our situation. That same evening, we were informed that, the following day, two guards were to take us to the border and release us so we would leave their country for Iran. The officer told us that they had pitied us and didn't want to rub salt in our wounds. They made us sign something that said if we were arrested ever again on their soil, we would be sentenced to maximum punishment. We spent the night in the station. They didn't treat us badly. They gave us food and a place to sleep. The next morning, two police officers put us in a four-wheeler and took us to the construction site to collect all our personal belongings and head to the border. The workers who were illegally there had already gone into hiding, and those who were legal didn't even come forth to exchange a word with us. Some of them were staring at me in disbelief. I had hidden the half of my face that was covered in bandages under a keffiyeh. Only Shacheragh came forward, looked into my eyes, and I saw his own eyes fill up with tears. He had heard the story. "You're a good boy. I'm sorry this happened. But don't worry. Life is not all nice and beautiful like your face. You are young with a beautiful heart no one can reach, so make sure you take care of your beautiful heart." Poor Shacheragh had no clue that my heart, too, would one day receive such heavy blows that the pain would not leave me alone until the end of my life, leaving a wound much worse than the one on my face. In any case, he took me in his arms and squeezed me hard with such affection. An officer stood there staring at us. The other officer had gone with Naji to collect his belongings. Shacheragh said, "The world has become ruthless. It's dog-eat-dog these days." He let me go. He pulled out his handkerchief from his pocket, dried his eyes and nose, and gave me a box of koluchehs. "You have a long road ahead. This will come handy. May God protect you."

The four-wheeler carrying Naji and the officer arrived; the other officer and I got in, and the car drove off to the border. Naji and I were facing each other. He kept trying to smile at me, and I could, every time, see tears welling up in his eyes, and he just tried to stop them with his smile.

I asked, "Why did you show your face at the hospital only to be deported in such a humiliating way?"

"For your sake, stupid."

One of the officers snapped at us. "Hey, boys! Stop talking Iranian."

I didn't want to hear anything anymore. It was enough that Naji had left his good life for me, had come to my aid and stood by me to the point that he was being deported from the country, to return to a place where nothing other than danger awaited him; his gesture was worth the world to me. Danger was actually awaiting both of us, but maybe less for me, because my face was not clearly recognizable. As he looked at me, Naji extended one of his arms and put his hand on mine, transmitting the warmth of his body to my heart through his touch. His fingers seemed longer and more delicate, and now they were moving on my hand with a kind touch. Suddenly, the officer in the passenger seat turned his head around, and it seemed that even before turning, his eyes knew to go after our hands. His eyes were fixed on our hands for a few moments, and we didn't make any attempt to separate them for his sake. His eyes moved up and stared into ours before turning to stare back at the road ahead, which was nothing but the desert and a very narrow asphalt road that stretched into the desert. We reached another police station, a very small one, built at the foot of a high hill. We realized that behind the hill, there was the sea. The police officers got out of the car and told us to get out too. We saw three or four other officers there. They accompanied us over the hill and stopped us near the water. There were five other arrested men, too, in handcuffs. A large boat without a motor was parked at the shore. The officers were waiting for another boat to arrive to pull the motorless one that would hold us, the seven criminals. But to where? We didn't know. The officers went and sat down on the slopes and lit cigarettes. The other five prisoners were Iranian too. One of them turned to the officers. "Brothers, can you please unlock our cuffs so we, too, can smoke cigarettes?" At first, the police officers didn't understand what he was saying. This time, the man gestured with his hand to tell them what he meant. The officers rejected his request and made him understand that we had to wait until we got on the boat to smoke. The Iranian man looked at us and said, "How come your hands are free?"

"Because we are good kids," Naji said, and we both burst out laughing.

The man didn't like that. "Ha ha ha. I hope you choke on your hideous laugh!" He had thought we were making fun of him, but, really, we were just laughing for our own sake, to forget for a few seconds our pain and fears.

The man said, "I'll show you when it's time." He angrily sat down next to the other four men.

"Sorry, we weren't laughing at you. We were laughing at ourselves," Naji explained.

"I know you weren't, or I would have pushed you both into the water by now."

Naji moved away and gestured to me that the guy was not open to conversation. The two of us went and sat on a corner of the hillside and stared at the sea. It was the ugliest stretch of water I had ever seen. It was the color of moss, flowing forth ripple by ripple before flowing back away from us. We knew there was a village far away, out of sight for now but soon to become visible. A random piece of land in our homeland where we would be kicked off the boat, and then we just had go and see what awaited us.

One of the men who was lying down on the slope, staring at the sea, exclaimed in a loud voice, "Oh homeland, where are you so that I can give my life for you?"

The officer who had just finished his second cigarette threw the butt down, walked toward us and the other men, and asked what the guy who had just shouted was saying. The men all tried to explain to him in Arabic, but he didn't get it. Naji translated for him. The officer laughed and went back to where he came from, once again lay down next to his colleague, and explained to him what the story was. They both laughed. The stupid laughter of the officers made Naji and me laugh too, but we tried to hide our laughter so as not to trigger the anger of the officers or the men in handcuffs. Finally, the motorboat came. The officers unlocked the men's handcuffs. Two armed officers were standing watch on top of the hill, pointing their weapons in our direction. We were transferred to the boat. It had two oars on the sides that were of no use for now because the motorboat was dragging us. We all waved at the officers staying behind land. They just kept looking at us. The man who, from the moment he set eyes on us, was looking for an excuse to pick a fight turned to Naji and said, "Well, you see, we both have our hands free now."

Naji showed him his backpack and said, "Well, my hands are not yet free." I wanted to laugh at his words. Naji could be really funny when he wanted to be, and he could so calmly pull other people's legs that I would just die of laughter, something he actually often did to just make me laugh. All those days and nights I had laughed as a result of his words and felt thrilled. But the guy didn't much like to see us laugh, so this time around I did not laugh at Naji's words. Our boat kept being pulled through the water.

The man told Naji, "What has your naughty friend here done that they have shoved his head in the oven and burned his face like this?" A few of the men laughed at his words, as if he had said something quite funny, or they were simply looking for an excuse to laugh, and now they had found it. I could see in Naji's eyes that he was angry and might attack the guy any moment, so I put my hand on his and caressed his skin with the tips of my fingers. I wondered what it was that made Naji's skin so lovely and desirable to me. I wondered what would happen if it were just the two of us in the boat and no one was dragging us behind them. We could continue over the water in whichever direction we wanted to go, to whatever country, a European country, where no evil person could find us, and the two of us could live together quietly until we died.

The silence in the boat stretched on. Even the wicked guy didn't say anything more. Then we spotted a small water police station. We were being taken there. There were a few boats and barges parked in a row, along with a few fast motorboats. The officers who had brought us there talked to the ones in the station and decided to send us, while we were on the boat, to the land we could spot. The officers made us understand that they were not going to accompany us any farther and that we had to row ourselves until we reached the land on the other side. They also explained that they would continue to watch us all the way there, with their guns pointed at us, so if we did anything wrong and tried to steer the boat off in another direction, they would shoot at us, and we were the ones responsible for our own lives. They wanted to know if any of us knew how to row. The wicked man, who seemed to be the head of the group of four, said he knew how to get the boat there, though when he took hold of the oars and began rowing, it was obvious he had lied and had no experience whatsoever. The more he rowed, the more the boat turned around itself. The officers stood in their own boat and laughed at his rowing. The man cursed the oars and said the boat was broken and there was no way it would move forward. The officers asked if anyone else knew how to row. I told them Naji had been an expert, many years before. The officers laughed once again and ridiculed us and asked Naji to sit at the helm. Cautiously, Naji handed me his backpack and sat down to row. He got control of the boat in only a few moments. The officers didn't laugh anymore. They waved at us. The other men stared at how Naji rowed the boat with its seven passengers toward land. What calm, what pride I was feeling that Naji was steering all of us now. As he continued rowing, he took off his shirt and continued with a bare chest. I took his shirt from him and smelled it; it smelled of his sweat. One of the men looked at me strangely. "Are you two brothers?"

"We are cousins."

"You really have each other's back. Good for you. Not all cousins are like that."

One of the men, who wore a white fabric around his head, added, "My motherfucker cousin ripped us off and led us to this hell. He said you'll pay the smuggler, but when you get there, you'll be paid so much that you'll make up for it in only one week. Anyway, he cheated me big, and now I'm going back belly-up."

A big wave came our way, almost toppling our boat and throwing us all into the water. The men screamed out of fear. The only people feeling safe were Naji and me, because he was steering the boat. The boat found its balance again. We all gave a sigh of relief. The man who played the role of their group head, whom we learned was called Mostafa, said, "You're having a ball making us shit-scared, you two pretties."

Naji was on the verge of getting angry once again, but I stopped him and told Mostafa, "If you want to get to our destination safely, please be quiet and let him do his job." I expected the guy to attack me or say something vulgar, but he just sat down on the wooden beam that spanned the middle of the boat and didn't say anything else, just tried to light his cigarette. It was windy, and the most beautiful naked chest was stretching and flexing in front of me. The chest I imagined would be the safest place in the world for me for the rest of my life. For my defenseless head, for my forsaken body of which nothing remained but a burnt piece of log.

Naji said, "We'll go abroad, and they'll fix your face and return it to what it was before. Did you know? Exactly like it was before. You can't believe it."

"Why should I believe you?"

"I swear I saw the ads in the newspaper myself."

"First of all, nothing will restore it to what it was before. Second, if you knew how to read, you could've read the ads you are talking about, and you would see how much that costs. You have no idea."

"Money doesn't matter. We'll work and make enough. Just promise me that you won't worry. Okay? Will you promise me not to be sad?"

That was all I really wanted. His words spoken so gently were enough for me to feel happy and strong. His words were life's affectionate smile at me. Our boat reached the land in silence. They had told us to leave the boat behind right there in the water, without tying its rope to anything. The other five men just wanted to get off the boat as fast as possible, and their rushing caused the boat to almost topple over once again, and if Naji had not been quick in handling it, we would have definitely fallen into the water. Anyway, we were finally on land. We knew we had to walk for hours to reach the first town. There was a light breeze, carrying with it a little bit of dust here and there. We carried our stuff on our backs. I felt bad for Naji for having to carry such a heavy backpack all by himself. I asked him a few times to let me do it, but he wouldn't accept my offer. His backpack was not too heavy, but it was hard to handle, because of the violin, a few clothes, and a lot of cigarette packs. I could see how the misshapen bag was slowing him down. The light breeze had turned now into a heavy wind, blowing even more dust around.

Naji said, "I'm worried about your wounds. We must wash and cover them with ointment. In this bloody dust that constantly sits on one's skin."

I remembered the third red-and-white keffiyeh Naji had gifted me some time ago, to replace the one he had asked me to give to that young woman so long ago; I never wore this third one, because I was mad at him, but now it could serve as a comfortable strap for his instrument. I pulled it out from the depths of my backpack and asked Naji to take out the violin from his. He asked what I wanted to do. I only told him to be patient. The other men were lying around and smoking, waiting for us. When Naji pulled it out, I told him what I wanted to do, and together we tied the keffiyeh like a rope to the pins at the top and bottom of the case; now we could take turns carrying it. Naji said, "Mashallah to your brain, boy."

We kept walking, and the men trudged along, huffing and puffing, cursing everything under their breath, themselves and their country and the guards and God and whatever else they could name, and this became the source of our secret jokes and laughter, softening the suffering of the road. Naji was still wondering how to protect my wounds against the dust, especially now that the wind had gotten stronger.

He said, "I bet you still have your needle and thread with you, right?" I asked him why he needed it. He mocked me by telling me to be patient. One of the men, who was overweight, had to pause often to rest, and we others had to follow his lead and lie around on the ground. Maybe it was because they were all older than the two of us. The next time we stopped, I took out the small sewing kit from my backpack and handed it to Naji. He was looking for something in his own backpack. A long white shirt gifted to him by I don't know whom, which I didn't like. Then he took out his heavy bag of metal stuff, full of knives and scissors, and quickly cut the shirt from under the sleeves from one side to the other, and the shirt turned into a bag with the two ends open. He threaded the needle and sewed one end closed with wide stitches. "I'll put this over your head for a second to measure something." I brought my head closer to him, and he threw the bag over it and pulled down; my face disappeared under the white fabric of the bag, and I could not see anymore, then I felt the touch of Naji's fingers around my eyes. He pulled the bag off again and began to cut the two points he had marked to create two holes for my eyes. He had created a mask for my face, to prevent dust sitting on my wounds. "Okay, now is the time to wash and put ointment on them." He then shouted to the men, "Sorry, gentlemen, we'll take a few more minutes, excuse us." He showed them the ointments and cotton pads and, as if happy with hearing this, they all lit cigarettes again. Even lighting cigarettes in that wind and dust was a challenge. I was the only nonsmoker in the group. "I swear, I'm itching for one," said Naji.

"So have a smoke first."

"Stop babbling nonsense and come a bit closer," he said jokingly.

He first washed my wounds with the disinfectant, then put the ointment on them with cotton pads. I stared into the depths of his eyes, a clear bottomless sea that invited me to keep going without ever reaching the end. He closely examined the wounds and covered them with medication. I remembered that I had a small mirror in my backpack, but when I began to look for it, Naji said he had thrown it away because he didn't want me to feel sad looking constantly at my wounds.

"But I loved that mirror. You knew that, right?"

"As if I didn't. But it's of no use to us now, Jamil. Trust me. What bullshit are mirrors anyway?"

If I were not in that situation, basking in the ointment being applied to my skin with his hands, I would have gotten angrier, would have shouted at him and forced him to say he was sorry, but now, as his hand approached my face holding a white cotton pad, I calmed down. First, the sudden touch of the ointment—a cold moment. Then the slow movement of the cotton pads over my skin with some tolerable pain, while I drowned in the sea of his eyes. All these details kept me from acting harshly, invited me to quiet and love.

We started off once again. Now, I was wearing a white mask over my face, a bag I had pulled over my head, with two holes for my eye sockets. The men laughed a bit. I told Naji he should not get mad at them for laughing at my mask, because they were exhausted and were probably looking for any way to have some fun. They were not bad people, just terrified. They had left Iran only a week before. They had paid big sums of money to a smuggler, only for the inept smuggler to lead them, in the end, to the police station right at the center of the officers' nest, so the guys had been arrested and were now being returned to Iran after a few days and nights of detention and interrogation. One of them believed the last smuggler was an Arab spy, and one had another hypothesis. In sum, they had different opinions about the reasons behind their arrests, and it wasn't clear which one was true. The wind got stronger every moment, bringing with it more dirt and dust. Some of the men were wearing sunglasses; what joy I felt when I noticed Naji still had the sunglasses I had bought him.

We sat down and ate something. At the station, we were each given a big homemade piece of bread stuffed with cheese and dates. Naji had some chocolate, and I had Shacheragh's koluchehs, which we both shared with everyone. Mostafa had made some guesses about the relationship between Naji and me. He asked us a few times whether we really were cousins, and each time we confirmed it, but he didn't believe us anymore and was trying to flirt with Naji. "I swear on my own life I've never seen such a quick, clever, handsome boy." Naji just smiled. I wanted to punch the bastard liar in his muzzle; he first wanted to violently attack us and was now singing Naji's praises. Every now and then, he held out his water bottle to Naji and said, "You know, I'm not much of a water drinker. I mean, I'm worried that I'll have to piss a lot. You can drink from my water bottle, as much as you want. I know that the youth get thirstier because of their young bodies."

Gasping for breath, Naji smiled. "Thank you. We do have water. Keep it for yourself; you'll need it. We still have a few more hours to go. And the weather is just getting hotter."

Mostafa realized that he had to offer water to me too. He turned toward me and said, "And you too, even if you want to wash your face, the water is pretty clean." My face was still under the mask. He advanced toward Naji and pulled him to the side, and the two of them walked together for a bit. Shoulder to shoulder. The other men dragged their heavy bodies along, scattered around, some ahead of us, some behind us. Naji and Mostafa got ahead of me. I could not hear their conversation. I saw Mostafa throwing one arm over Naji's shoulders, as if the two of them had known each other since childhood, as if they were lovers. I wanted to run forward and furiously pull the dude's hands away from Naji's tired shoulders. Naji stopped for a second and calmly took Mostafa's hand and softly brought it down from his shoulder. Smiling, he threw me a look, gradually stepped away from him, and came toward me.

"What did he want?"

"He was wondering where we would spend the night. He wants to help us. If we don't have any place to sleep tonight. And we don't, right?" He was right. I remained quiet, since I had not thought about this.

A short while later, when we all stopped to rest and so that the smokers could smoke, Mostafa told everyone, "Friends, if you have a place to stay tonight, great, but if you, too, like me, have nowhere to go for now, we can all spend the night in my nephew's cowshed. That is, if we get there safely, of course." We all laughed. He liked it and kept going with more bravado. "When he wakes up and sees all these big men lying next to one another in his shed, he probably won't like it that much, but who cares about him. I'll take care of it, being an uncle should get me some privileges."

Two of the men said they had their own places to stay. Two others besides Mostafa himself were not from that town and had to stay overnight in the cowshed. Naji and I, who also didn't know what to do, accepted his invitation. Mostafa told us about his nephew. His name was Meysam, and although he was just in his thirties, he already owned a big cow farm. He had been a religious revolutionary since his teenage years, and he had had to leave and move there because he was hunted by the SAVAK forces in his own hometown. He had been so active during the revolution that he had faced death several times, surviving by a hair's breadth. He was such a devout religious follower of Imam Khomeini that there had once been an assassination attempt on his life by some anti-revolution People's Mojahedin members. He hadn't died, but he had had a limp in one leg ever since, though he was now one of the high-position members of the Hezbollah Organization and was becoming quite wealthy.

"What is the Hezbollah Organization, brother?" one of the men asked, laughing, and repeating the name out loud.

"I'm not sure. Whatever the name, it's now the most important organization in the country, and our Meysam is one of its high-octane people there."

While Mostafa was talking about his nephew, I was leaning on my backpack, watching Naji smoke, the masculine way his lips blew the smoke out. I was not sure if I liked Naji smoking or not. I didn't like it at all that he took so much smoke into his lungs, that smoking made his full burgundy lips dark-toned. But I enjoyed his smoking gestures, the way he skillfully tapped on his cigarette butt to shake off the ashes, the way he sometimes raised his hand holding on to the cigarette to push his hair back behind his ear, startling me into thinking that the ember might burn his earlobe, though his hand always came down without harming his ear.

When Naji said, "We too would be grateful to spend the night in a corner of the cowshed," Mostafa was happy. Perhaps he imagined he would be able to spend the night close to Naji.

He said, "Okay, so let's get moving." He got up.

"We have one other thing to do before we leave. We have to hide this instrument inside the bag again," I explained.

"Why do you want to hide it?"

"Have you had your head in the clouds? You seem to think everything is coming up roses in this country, Agha Mostafa." Naji and I started putting the violin away inside the backpack.

Mostafa watched us for a while, murmured, "Well, I guess I don't know what's going on," and started off. We, too, got up one by one and followed him. On our way, we noticed Iranian guards passing by in the distance in their four-wheelers. In those moments, we lay down on the ground so as not to be spotted. Our arrival in our homeland was getting harder and more terrifying. We hadn't felt as frightened up to this point. We had heard that the border patrol officers were the most fanatical Hezbollahis, and if we were arrested, we would either be sent blindfolded to the noose for the crime of spying, or we would be tortured until we would confess to crimes we had never committed. As evening fell, things got better, as we were able to reach the palm groves and move through the trees in darkness. From here on, only Naji and I knew the way, and if we hadn't been with the group, the rest of the men wouldn't have found their way to their destination. We reached a road. Two men separated from the group. They said their goodbyes and stayed on the shoulder of the road, waiting to hitchhike. We crossed the road and entered another part of the palm grove. When a passerby walked by us from time to time, I removed the mask from my face so as not to appear too weird and scary. We asked Mostafa for the cowshed's exact address. By his preliminary directions, we realized he was talking about the very pig farm we had worked at. "But that place belonged to George. A Christian guy."

"No more Christians, bros. The country is now Islamic, and now not only Christianity but also all other religions have pulled over and parked their cars for now." He burst out laughing. "Look who has really had his head in the clouds!" His laughter gradually subsided. "Now the farm belongs to my filthy nephew, who, with all his reach in the regime and its organizations, refused to find a job for his own uncle so I wouldn't be forced to spend so much money to make my way to a foreign land and suffer so much. For them to throw me out after only a few days, with such humiliation. That's why when you two said you were cousins, I could not believe you, because I know relatives who don't have each other's backs so well. The dude keeps making excuses, that I'm a drunk and that if he were to introduce me anywhere, then I'd cause him shame, because the drunk are thorns in the eyes of devout Muslims. I told him what nonsense that was, I mean Zakariya Razi, who discovered alcohol, was Muslim himself. Hadn't he seen pictures of the man wearing a turban? But who has an ear to listen with, brothers? Anyway, we should be grateful that we can at least spend the night in his cowshed." We asked who the caretaker of the farm was these days. "I just saw the place a few days ago. I had to stay there for a few nights until the smugglers came to fetch me. There was a bulky man there who was deaf but as loyal as a dog to his owner." That was a fitting description of Zaal. He added, "He had an interesting name, too: Zaal."

We no longer had any doubts. The pig farm was now a cow farm. We asked him if he had any news of George, but he didn't know him. Now Naji and I were wondering what to do. Did we continue with him or reconsider and find another place to sleep for the night? But where? On a night when the full moon was sitting on the throne of the sky, shedding its light all over the palm groves? The worst thing we had heard was that these new police officers were a completely new breed compared to the old ones; they were the guards of the revolution. If they busted you, they treated you as revolutionaries, so you couldn't bribe them with a few bills like before. No. We had heard that once they arrested you, no one, not even God himself, could free you from their grip, and it was this fear that led us to decide to stay in the cowshed that night and find ourselves another place the following day.

We reached our destination. Zaal opened the gate for us. He knew Mostafa, stood there staring at him in shock for a few minutes. Until Mostafa decided to throw himself in Zaal's arms and begin crying. It was fake crying. While holding Mostafa in his arms, he looked at Naji. Naji smiled at him. Zaal looked at me too, but then seemed to decide to turn away. We knew, despite his imposing figure, how kind he was. Maybe looking at another person's wounds hurt him. Finally, Zaal shook everyone's hands and kissed their cheeks as was tradition, but the wounds on my face kept us from kissing, so we just touched our shoulders together. The farm garden had changed. A few rooms made with cement blocks had been added around the garden, creating an ugly scene. And yet Naji's weeping willow was still there in the middle. Naji walked to it, knelt in front of it, and for a while got lost in himself.

"I didn't realize this was a sacred tree," said Mostafa. He thought Naji was praying in front of the willow.

I explained to him, "He planted the tree himself. Everyone working here called it Naji's willow." Naji got up and embraced the tree. He cried. Zaal took us to a room at the end of the garden, turned on the only lightbulb hanging from the ceiling. It was a room with no windows.

The floor was covered with a few faded pieces of carpet. There was a pile of blankets in a corner, gray army blankets. Zaal simply talked to us with his eyes, and he was now telling us that we could each grab a blanket and lie down in any corner we wanted. Mostafa told the guys, "Be at ease, boys. Lie down and rest. We can relax, brothers."

The men lay around on the floor. One of them stretched his legs up on the wall and explained to his friend, "This way, blood circulates back from your feet to your heart." Zaal was still fixated on us. He recognized me, too, but couldn't really ask any questions. His eyes were filled with sorrow. Without making a sound and just by moving his lips, Naji asked Zaal if George was there too. Zaal moved his head with regret from side to side, signaling no. His eyes kept going back and forth between us. I felt there were a lot of things that he could tell us, but he either didn't want to or couldn't; maybe if he had wanted to, he could have.

Mostafa said, "Don't underestimate Agha Zaal just because he doesn't hear and speak; he understands a lot and is super kind. Last week he took very good care of us. God bless him." He also gestured to Zaal that we were exhausted and needed him to go. Throwing a last look at me, he left the room. Mostafa was now busy planning our sleeping arrangements so that he would be close to Naji, but Naji made it clear to him that he had to be close to me because I might wake up in the middle of the night and need him. The other two men didn't say anything but kept an eye on Mostafa, from time to time whispering something in each other's ears and chuckling. Before bed, Naji washed my wounds and put medication on them, put a clean piece of fabric under my head, and recommended that I sleep on my back and try to not turn my face to the sides to avoid making my wounds worse. I held his hand in mine and squeezed it. "I'll try, doctor."

We both laughed. Naji got up and asked if we were ready to turn the light off. Two of the men and I said yes. We were all drowned in total darkness. Mostafa's voice said, "Oh . . . but I haven't finished my cigarette yet." One of the guys said, "It's like a tomb." The despairingly lustful ember of Mostafa's cigarette continued to burn in the darkness. Our bags were next to us. Naji had put the bag containing the violin

next to him to prevent anyone from stepping on it during the night.
My hand reached out in the darkness and found his. Our fingers locked
into each other, and I fell asleep peacefully.

But I woke up anxiously. It was just getting light. The other men were
still asleep. I walked out of the room. A man was moving around the
cowshed, working. I noticed him taking a pack of fodder inside and
coming back with a few empty buckets to wash under the faucet outside. In another corner, Zaal was gathering white pieces of fabric hanging on a clothesline. I walked to him quietly. He stopped and looked
at me. He tried to smile, but I saw tears welling up in his eyes. But I
laughed and walked out of the garden. They had built fences all around
the farm, using palm and other tree branches and leaves. The sky was
clear, summer on its last legs. The light breeze signaled the arrival of
the fall. It had been years since I had heard dogs barking and roosters
crowing, and they sounded delightful to me now. Behind the cowshed,
there was a palm grove that extended all the way to the river; in front
of it, nothing but an empty desert that led to the road, a desert we had
walked through so often. The road led to the town and meandered a
thousand times, one branch of it separating and heading toward the
village where my father's house was. A place that embodied the homeland for me in all the years of exile. Often during the hard moments
of misery, I wished I could grow wings and fly toward it, the "it" that
belonged to me, the place I wanted to return to. I had convinced myself
I preferred it with all its hardship, no matter what it was, to the horrifying alienness of the foreign land. Well, I had returned now, but still, I
was not sure this was what I wanted, what I had wished for.

I heard a car honking behind the fence on the desert side. Opening the gate early in the morning for the truck to enter the farm was
still Zaal's job, but how did he learn of the truck's arrival despite his
being deaf? It was, perhaps, his sense of responsibility. I could tell that,
in those early moments of the day, he was so much expecting the truck
that the moment it got close, the ground under his feet let him know,
so he could go open the gate. He was like a preprogrammed robot, as

if created by God only to serve the boss, regardless of who it was; he was loyal to the current one as much as to the previous or the next. I stepped back to hide myself behind the wall of the cowshed. The truck entered the farmyard. The bearded man in the passenger seat had already gotten out and was busy fumbling with a section of the fence that had been tampered with. He limped and seemed angry, grumbling under his breath. I thought he might be Meysam, Mostafa's nephew, but I was shocked to realize he was our own Kavous. I guessed his limping was the result of the face-off between him and Naji, the day Naji had pushed him down the stairs. How much weight he had gained! And he was wearing the clothes of an old man. What if he saw us? He did see me. I mean his eyes fell upon me, but he continued what he was doing, tucking back a few branches sticking out from the fence. I ran to the room to tell Naji so we could get out of there before it was too late. Mostafa, too, was awake and, already dressed, came out of the room.

"Good thing Meysam is here. I'm going to find him before he disappears again." He was tying his shoelaces. "You know, he's pretty busy with a thousand different things." He stood up and winked at me. "I'm going to get some money from him." He looked around, spat out a heavy mix of saliva and phlegm. "This nephew of mine is rolling in money. Bills are like wastepaper to him these days."

I rushed into the room, quietly woke up Naji. The other two men were still deeply asleep, seemingly with no intentions of waking up anytime soon. I whispered in Naji's ear what I had seen. Horrified, he sat up in his bed.

"Are you sure?"

"Yes, unfortunately."

"What should we do now?"

"Don't panic. Just pick up your bag quietly, and let's get out of here." We gathered our belongings in silence. We were about to leave the room when we heard Mostafa and Kavous talking loudly close by.

"Do you think I'm sitting on a treasure trove, Uncle? And you've gone and even dragged along a couple of other suspicious men, too, whom I should perhaps feed breakfast and lunch. No, Uncle Mostafa.

It was wrong of you to even bring them in without my permission. Who knows who they are? What if they are ex-SAVAK? What if they are American or Israeli spies?"

"That's nonsense, my dear. They are a bunch of miserable guys like me who went to the other side just to earn their daily bread, but they weren't lucky enough to stay. Now, if you dish up a little dough to your uncle to pay for his trip to the village, your dear uncle will promise he won't bother you again."

Continuing to talk, they moved farther from the room, and we waited for the right moment to escape without them noticing. Suddenly we heard a quarrel; it was Mostafa and Kavous, who was now called Meysam. The sounds of a brawl and curses traded back and forth. We decided it was a good moment to run. The other two men were still asleep. Cautiously, we headed to the garden. In a corner, Mostafa was holding Kavous's throat between his hands, squeezing it with all his might, aiming to strangle him. There was no one around to separate them. Naji paused for a second, felt pity for Kavous being choked to death by Mostafa's hands. He put his bag down, went and took Mostafa's hands, and pulled them away. Finally, as the result of Naji's actions, Kavous was released from Mostafa's grip and began to cough.

"You should've let me strangle the bastard."

Still coughing, Kavous saw and recognized Naji. "You're his accomplice, then. Two anti-revolutionaries."

Mostafa had now completely retreated. Naji, too, was slowly stepping back. Now Kavous was mainly concerned with Naji and not Mostafa anymore. I ran and picked up Naji's bag. Limping, Kavous rushed into the cowshed. I said, "Let's get out of here, Naji." But Naji seemed frozen. Mostafa was facing the wall, with both hands on the wall, his shoulders trembling, either with fatigue or sobbing.

Kavous came out with a gun in his hands. "You phony faggots," he said as he came closer to Naji. "We revolted to destroy people like you, and you have the audacity to attack me? We even kicked out the shah and his mighty bunch and destroyed them, so it's much easier for us to kick the likes of you in the ass."

I was so afraid, imagining Naji being shot, drowning in his blood, and leaving me all by myself, that I didn't notice Mostafa biding his time behind Kavous to attack him again when the moment was right. And attack he did, aiming to snatch the gun from Kavous's hand. The two became entangled once again. We went out the main gate, toward the desert, to escape to the road. Zaal was not around or maybe was hiding in one corner or another.

Before we reached the gate, two bearded old men in military clothes appeared in the desert, as if the desert had suddenly vomited them on us. We heard someone whistle behind us. We turned and saw Zaal by the door of the long hallway, which once had been a trash room, signaling to us to come in. We ran to him and went in, and he closed the door behind us. The first change we noticed was a big gunny sack hanging in front of the door like a curtain, where there had been nothing but an open door before. We pushed it aside and walked into the long, narrow, dark hallway. We knew that there was another door at the other end that opened on to the palm grove. That door was always locked from the inside, but the keys were always in the keyhole. The smell of human shit is the worst in the world. Behind the gunny sack there was an Iranian toilet, the second change made there, along with a plastic water pitcher in an ugly red color. We jumped over the toilet on the ground, passed beyond another dirty gunny-sack curtain, opened the locked door, and got out on the other side of the hallway. The high walls around the farm separated us and the palm grove from the desert. We cautiously stepped toward the wall.

"You motherfucker, open the door!" It seemed the two old men were still held outside behind the first door of the hallway, since Zaal had refused to open it for them. Then suddenly the sound of the door opening, the sound of running, feet moving closer and closer. We ran into the desert.

At some point, Naji said, "I'm tired, I'm passing out."

We heard a man shouting, "Shoot! What are you waiting for, dickhead?"

"Stop!" We heard the same man shouting toward us. "Stop!"

We stopped and looked at each other. I could read in Naji's eyes what I, too, was thinking. What would happen if we continued running and they shot at us? At that moment, I read in his eyes that things were too bad for us to stop and surrender, so we started running again, not paying attention to the warnings, and the voices of the two old men got quite distant, and we could barely hear them, but the sound of shooting was close and clear. We expected that one of us would stumble to the ground. I kept looking at Naji while running. He did the same. Maybe the sound of shooting came from the garden and had nothing to do with us. The two old men were not running after us anymore. They hadn't run after us at all, and no one was following us now, but we continued running while we still had breath to get as far away from the area as possible, because we were almost certain that the gunshots came either from Kavous or from Mostafa aimed at the other. Whatever it was, we knew we must not be arrested around there. We reached the road but thought that those who were after us would definitely follow the road, so we crossed the road and went into the palm grove on the other side. We sat down, hiding amid the palm trees, waiting for the dust to settle. Then we came back to the road and tried to hitchhike. It was before noon when a minitruck stopped for us. We only had dollar bills with us, and though the driver was alarmed by us at first, the dollars lured him.

"It's none of my business who you are and where you are coming from. If the Hezbollahi brothers stop us, we'll tell them you are passengers, and I'm just a driver. Is that right, you vibrant youth of the homeland?"

"Well, that's exactly what it is."

"Obviously, you are smart kids. You know, in the chaos of these days, it's best to take care of everything right off the bat; like the money that you are paying me right now, please."

We paid him, and he started off. We had discussed where we would go. In our disheveled condition, we felt embarrassed going to George's house. Going to Suren was not the best idea either. So we thought of Amrollah Khan's daughter, Mahin, assuming we could find her and she was in a position to accept us, given all the changes that we noticed around us. The town had become very crowded, as if its population had grown tenfold. The roads seemed narrower, or maybe it was that they were busier. No one followed the traffic rules, the street signs; everyone crossed the street in whatever direction whenever they wanted; the sidewalks were so busy that pedestrians walked in the middle of the street, and the cars cleared their way with constant honking. We repeated the address to the driver. He said everything about the city had changed, even the names of the neighborhoods and streets. He said the main squares and streets had been named after the famous living mullahs or the young men martyred during the revolution or the holy imams. We were ashamed to say that the neighborhood we wanted to go to was the Doub.

The driver finally understood where we wanted to go. He said, "With the directions you give, it seems you are headed to, I should be biting my tongue, the old Doub area." He spit out the car window. "May God forgive me." He looked at us. "But it's not like what it was before, my brothers, as you probably know."

"Of course, of course, we know it's not."

"It's now a normal residential neighborhood with normal people. The city plans to demolish all the neighborhood and build up everything anew. I heard that it will be soon. Only God knows." He sighed heavily and mockingly. "What we were. What we've become."

There were many mothers in the streets with their kids. The driver explained that the new school year was starting in two days, so families were busy with back-to-school shopping. The other recurring scene around us that was terrifying was young armed men standing in groups at every corner and intersection, checking the cars; sometimes they stopped them and pulled the passengers out, did full body checks, and looked inside the cars. We didn't really know what they were looking for.

"Do you see, brothers? The very people who revolted now should answer to a bunch of young kids rising to power out of nowhere. If they decide to, they can even finger you, just because the law gives them the permission." He sighed once again and adjusted the rearview mirror. "Man is his own worst enemy. Who to blame but us?"

We reached Mahin's old street. The neighborhood looked different. There was no sign of the metal gate, of any unusual traffic, of what once had been the red-light district. We found Mahin's house relying on our memory. Two black flags with the names of Prophet Muhammad and his family members embroidered on them were hanging on either side of the door, between them a length of green fabric with its four corners nailed to the wall, marking someone's death or some religious ceremony. We anxiously knocked. Mahin opened the door. She didn't recognize me, which was expected, given the state I was in, but she didn't recognize Naji either. "Hey, boys, who are you looking for?" It seemed as though twenty years had passed since we had last met. She was wearing a brown scarf made of thick fabric, knotted tightly under her chin. She seemed tired and hopeless, and gave us a listless look. She glanced at me for a second before diverting her eyes, the way you do when you see a disgusting thing. Naji mentioned Amrollah Khan's name, and finally Mahin recognized us. She was happy to see us but still didn't know what to do, standing there in the doorway talking to us with uncertainty. Quickly, we told her where we had been and what we had been doing since we last met. We told the truth about everything except the scars on my face; we said they were caused by a workplace accident, and so we also had to lie about why we were back in Iran.

From Mahin's gestures, it was obvious she didn't intend to invite us in. When we finished telling our story, she told us to wait for her at the door. She went in and came back wearing a black veil. "Let's go." She told us she was taking us to a friend's house on the same street. She said it would be easier to talk there.

Habib had a straw mat spread in the courtyard. He clearly was a drug addict; he was quite thin, with protruding eyes; he strung out his words and shuffled around. His house was just a small courtyard and one room. He didn't let us sit on the mat but went inside, brought out a checkered blanket, spread it on top of the mat, and then invited us to sit. "Friends of my dear Mahin are the light of my eyes." Mahin introduced us as Amrollah Khan's best friends, didn't fall short of giving us the highest praise. Habib kept saying, "Good. Good. We are at the service of Amrollah Khan's friends." He also teared up remembering him. He just talked and said pleasantries.

Mahin said, "Instead of all these empty pleasantries, go make some tea for your guests," and winked at us, showing she was teasing him. "Of course, sure, right now," Habib said and went inside.

Asking indirect questions, Mahin wanted to know how we were doing financially. We told her how much we had in dollars and how much that would be in Iranian rials. Her eyes sparkled hearing those numbers. She said she knew someone who could help us exchange the money but added that she first had to go back to her own house, find his number, go to the phone booth around the corner to call him, and then bring us back the news. She explained why she couldn't take us to her own house, that the house belonged to her sister-in-law, whom she called Ammeh Zari, and that she had to first check every move with her, but Zari was not home at the moment. Mahin said that by the time we took care of the money issue, Zari would be back too, and after quickly consulting with her, she would take us home with her. She also asked us to not reveal to anyone, especially Habib, how much money we had.

When Mahin and Naji left to exchange our money, I stayed with Habib, because we didn't want to drag all our stuff around. Mahin had suggested that it would be better this way. Habib offered me tea and dates and told me the story of his life, the story of his relationship with a woman named Banoo. Habib looked disheveled, but he had a kind heart, and even though he was an addict, I liked him. He was aware of what was going on around him and what kind of people had gained power; he knew that he and his kind were nothing but victims of political games. He said, "If you really want to gain something from this huge spread, you need to show that you are violent and ready to shoot not only the enemy but also your own compatriot; even if you can't really do it, you have to pretend. Do you get what I'm saying, young man?" He talked until Naji and Mahin got back. They had exchanged our money. Mahin advised us to take good care of it. She left us once again with Habib to go talk to Ammeh Zari about the possibility of us staying with them temporarily and returned saying that she would allow us to stay for two or three nights, until we could rent a room somewhere. We thanked Habib, and I gave him two packs of Naji's cigarettes as a gift. He cheered up seeing the American cigarettes. He held one of the packs in front of him and started talking to it. "When will you come to our rescue, my beloved?" We laughed. Mahin said Habib made everyone laugh with such nonsense talk.

Mahin's house was small too: a small courtyard and three rooms on top of each other, connected by a narrow staircase. She took us to the top floor and asked us to not pull the curtain to the side, because people who were not supposed to might see us. She made a comment about how it was an unsafe time, how people had become untrustworthy, ratting on each other for no good reason. She said the town's prison was overflowing with inmates, so they had even turned some schools into lockups. She said her husband, Teymour, was in prison, but since every time she brought up his name, she burst into tears, we didn't ask her questions, letting her talk about him whenever she felt like it. We had not yet met Ammeh Zari or Mahin's six-year-old daughter, Hasti. "My daughter was so unhappy today, because she expected me to take her school shopping since schools open in a few days. She wanted to go get stuff like the other kids. But I swear to God, I'm strapped for cash. So Ammeh Zari just took her out to entertain her for a while today."

We were taking a nap when we heard a girl crying, saying things we could not pick up in between her sobs. Mahin brought her to our room. "Say hi to these two nice guys. This is Uncle Naji and the other is Uncle Jamil." Hasti stopped crying. She was wearing clean but very cheap clothes. Her hair was disheveled. She was hiding behind Mahin and kept sneaking glances at me, at the half of my face that was appalling to her. Mahin told her we were friends of her grandfather. Hasti had never seen her grandfather, just knew him through pictures that Mahin had. Amrollah Khan playing music, at the peak of his life, on the stage. Naji still had some chocolates left in his bag and gave them to Hasti. I also gave Mahin some money so she could go grab us and the rest of the household sandwiches and sodas. That night, we told her we had decided to get Hasti her school stuff and other necessities. Naji had suggested we give the money to Mahin to do the shopping, but I fancied going to the bazaar, window shopping, feeling the joy of shopping.

Mahin suggested we all go together. Naji excused himself and said he was exhausted, but actually he was afraid of being recognized by the very men he had befriended once upon a time, his mutual friends with Kavous, men who had now become one or all of those guards we had seen in every nook and on every corner of the town.

The next day, after lunch, we set off to the town center, Mahin, Hasti, and I. When I was heading down the stairs, I heard Ammeh Zari making a fuss about why Mahin had not told her one of us had a burnt face. I didn't hear Mahin's response but heard Ammeh Zari continue, "Well, it goes without saying, letting a burnt person into one's house is a bad omen." I preferred to turn a deaf ear, because at that moment the most important thing in my mind was doing the school shopping for Hasti.

There was much hustle and bustle in town, like the day before. The bazaar selling stationery was swarming with people, girls and boys holding on to their parents' hands. I wanted to buy all the little and big notebooks there were for Hasti, but Mahin kept saying, "No. That's too much." Still, we got a good number of notebooks of all colors and shapes. Some black pencils, paper and colored pencils for drawing, books teaching alphabet through stories, books introducing animals and flowers. Hasti got a kick out of each purchase, and it just melted my heart to see her.

Mahin said, "Hey, you two! Why are you getting so much stuff? How many years of school are you shopping for here?"

Then we went to another store and bought Hasti a new set of clothes for school. A navy-blue manteau and a maghna'eh. "It's wicked to make these poor kids wear these clothes in such hot weather." Hasti, though, was excited to wear her uniform. We also got her some shirts, T-shirts, pants, and underwear. I told Mahin to get Hasti whatever she needed right then.

She disagreed. "No, that's enough for now. We can buy the rest later; we got the whole bazaar today." Then she turned to Hasti. "Have you even thought about where you are going to put these?"

"In Ammeh Zari's closet."

The shopping area was roofed and dedicated to clothing stores. After the kids' stores, we went to the women's. The women around us were all wearing scarves and maghna'ehs. Hasti started to run out of excitement, but she tripped on another woman's foot; Mahin reached out to grab her, and her scarf slid down from her head.

Suddenly, a terrifyingly harsh masculine voice snapped at her from behind. "Fix up your hijab, sister. Having some modesty isn't a bad idea, especially for you women."

I began to turn slowly, following the voice.

Mahin alerted me, "Don't look at them, or they'll come arrest you."

I noticed a tall bearded young man in military uniform, but with no badges or hat or guns. I had noticed many of them, men in military uniforms but carrying no guns. We also saw many men whose only weapon was a club, though they held them so methodically, as if they were indeed guns.

"They are basij forces," Mahin clarified.

"Just laugh them off. Come see these," I responded.

The first thing I noticed and thought it would be nice to get for Mahin was a long turquoise dress shown on a headless mannequin; it was made of see-through lace, revealing the pink body of the mannequin. "What do you think about this?"

I also pointed to a pair of black shoes made of thin leather straps, through which you could see the naked feet. "And these, too, would suit you, I am sure."

She laughed. "Where am I going to wear these under current conditions?"

"If you have them, you'll surely find an occasion to wear them."

Hasti jumped in. "He's right, Mom. They will be pretty on you. Buy them, please!" She had warmed up to me, wasn't afraid of my scars anymore, even held my hand from time to time while we were walking. She would raise her head and, with her round black eyes, look at me with such a smile that I felt she was mirroring my own childhood, when I was happy. Was I happy during my childhood? I had to stop thinking about the past, had to instead think about how I could make Hasti happy now.

"I want makeup too. Don't forget," she said.

"What use do you have for makeup, little one?" Mahin asked her.

"I'll tell you later."

There were some cosmetics in the store window. Hasti noticed them before we did.

"This store seems to have nice things," I pointed out.

"I know a better place for makeup," Mahin said.

"Let's go there quickly," Hasti said.

"Let's first look at this store and see what nice things it has. It's not good to rush shopping," Mahin replied.

It seemed she wanted to distract Hasti from buying makeup, but she didn't know I, too, was on the lookout for it. We kept looking at the store's window. It displayed only products for women. There were some pairs of summer shoes and two shorts, up to the knees, one khaki-colored and the other cherry-red, hanging on the two sides in symmetry. A narrow but tall shelf that went from one side of the window to the other was full of cosmetics, including lipsticks of all colors, blotting powders, tiny tins of eye makeup. In the middle of the shelf there was a picture of an alluring pair of eyes, the eyes of a woman, looking at you, following you wherever you went. There were blinking lights in every corner of the shop window. I was so spellbound by the beautiful display that I didn't hear the angry voices of a few motorcyclists entering the shopping center. Mahin grabbed my sleeve and pulled me to the other side of the store. She didn't know exactly where she was pulling me, just wanted to keep me safe from the sudden violent invasion of the motorcyclists, who had alarmed not just Mahin, Hasti, and me but everyone there, all of us backing up, pressing ourselves against the wall. There were two men on each motorcycle. When they reached us, they slowed down, almost stopping, and, suddenly, the rider in the passenger saddle moved his hand through the opening of his shirt and pulled out a big stone. He shouted, "Allahu Akbar! God is Great!" and threw the stone toward the window of the store. The big glass pane shattered, and the stone knocked the makeup shelf down, scattering the lipsticks and powders. The motorcyclists left. Then we heard another store window shattering. People gathered in front of the store, whose owner had come to the door, standing there in shock, unable to believe his eyes. "Why? What was that for?"

A man passing by said, "You are wondering why? Can't you see what kind of immoral things are sold in these stores?" As he continued on his way, he added, "Some of these people seem to be clueless about what has been going on in this sacred nation of ours."

I was one of the people who was clueless about what had happened in that sacred nation. I had just noticed that a lot of things had changed. You couldn't see any more girls or women showing off their hair; it had all been plunged into darkness.

Mahin said, "Let's go. We're done shopping." She grabbed Hasti's hand in one hand and the shopping bags in the other and rushed toward to the exit. Hasti was afraid. I followed them.

A man called to her, "Hey, Sepideh!"

Mahin went toward the man and greeted him. She introduced Hasti, and me as one of her relatives. The man was the owner of one of the stores. The man joked with Hasti and laughed, asked Mahin what she was doing there. Mahin explained that we were done shopping and were making a quick exit for fear of the men.

The man laughed. "Come in and check out my store too. You might be tempted to buy something. You can find anything you want here." But there was nothing in his store window except a few navy-blue women's manteaus, a line of maghna'ehs, and a few small carpets with the names of the imams woven in circles on them. The carpets were of the same design, just in different colors. The salesperson was a woman dressed in a long black manteau and a black maghna'eh covering her hair. When we entered, she welcomed us with a smile. The man, still laughing, walked toward a small wooden door at the back of the store, opened it, and entered. The three of us followed him inside. A large space with no windows, full of lights of different colors.

All different kinds of clothes hung around the room. A few women, whose scarves had fallen almost off their hair, turned and looked at us, then immediately lifted their hands to their scarves to fix them. Hoshyar, the store owner, said, "Don't worry, ladies. They're with us." Smiling, the women continued examining the clothes.

There were rows of makeup in another corner. I was itching to check them out. And I couldn't wait to head in that direction.

"What are you looking for?" Hoshyar asked.

Mahin gave me a subtle glance. "Well, we were just window shopping."

I jumped in. "We're looking for a beautiful pair of women's shoes, a dress, and some makeup."

He took us first to the shoes section.

"What if the guards discover this place?" Mahin asked him.

"Do you see anything out of the ordinary here? These are all women's clothing and accessories, and, based on the law, it's legal to sell them, but to pay respect to the blood of the martyrs of our revolution, we are not showing them off in public. Just out of respect for the martyrs' blood. Who wears these? Don't the martyrs have sisters and mothers? The gentlemen running the government, too, have wives and daughters. And these days, all girls put on makeup. So, you see, what we do here is moral and legal." He laughed. "Here you go, here are our shoes." He showed us a few rows of women's sandals.

I picked a red pair that I found more beautiful than the rest and put them in front of Mahin's feet. "Try them on."

She did, but she needed one size smaller. The young woman working there brought her a smaller size. Mahin slipped them on and checked how they looked in the mirror. "I agree, they are pretty. What do you think, Hasti?"

"They're very pretty. You should buy them, Mom."

Hoshyar was right. All the women, even the younger ones, who were in his store—or I had better say in his backroom—were wearing heavy makeup. On the one hand, I showed Mahin sheer and even short clothes to buy, and on the other, I wondered where women could wear them when they had to appear in the public completely covered.

"At private parties," Mahin explained. She showed me a few women in that backroom who, under their long navy-blue manteaus, wore sexy short clothes, similar to the ones I had insisted Mahin buy but she hadn't because she either didn't want me to spend too much money or didn't think it would be proper to wear them. It seemed even strange to the store owner that Mahin had enough money to shop like that. He asked how her husband, Teymour, was doing. She said a few words, but, clearly, she didn't want to speak of him again, because the mere mention of his name was enough for her to burst out crying, and she didn't want to cry in front of Hasti.

Hoshyar asked me about my face scars. Mahin told him it had happened at work. Hoshyar wasn't like the others, who looked at me with pity; instead, he smiled and said, "These things happen to men. You just have to take good care of it so that it heals, little by little."

When saying goodbye, I just shook his hand. Then, he cautiously looked around him, stepped closer to Mahin, kissed her on the cheeks, and caressed Hasti on the head. When paying, we realized he had given us a good discount. Mahin told me that Hoshyar was one of her good old friends.

"Thank God you have good kind friends in this town."

We then went and bought some food, some cookies, and chocolate too. I told Mahin it would be nice to get some alcoholic drinks for Naji. Mahin laughed, told me I clearly didn't know anything about how things had changed in the short time since the revolution. "It's illegal."

When we were abroad, I had heard from a few of the guys that the new regime had banned alcoholic drinks, but I had never imagined you couldn't even buy them from stores to take home. I said, "Regardless, it would have been nice if I could cheer Naji up with a bottle of whiskey tonight. He loves whiskey."

"You definitely can't find whiskey, but maybe Habib can find you some arak for tonight, the ones people make at home."

"But that could be dangerous, mess up your gut, or I've heard that bad alcohol can harm your eyes."

"Nothing to worry about there. People drink gallons of homemade arak every night."

We got a taxi to head back home. In the car, I could see how Mahin's mood had changed; she was feeling delight, a childish joy. Every few minutes, she grabbed my hand and smiled.

"Mom, how come that guy called you Sepideh?" Hasti asked Mahin.

"Because when I was young, I had very fair skin, so the neighborhood kids called me Sepideh, for my white face. Agha Hoshyar is an old friend from my childhood days, and, for old times' sake, he calls me Sepideh."

Hasti laughed. "So, Sepideh Khanoom, how come you are not fair anymore?"

Mahin laughed too. "Because life happened, making everything about us dark and gloomy." She put her hand on mine.

The taxi driver noticed us in the rearview mirror. I had noticed him watching over us. "Excuse me, sister, what's your relationship with this guy?"

"Why?"

"Well, you keep fondling each other in my taxi, in my car where I make my life."

Mahin smiled and gave me a glance. "This gentleman is my son, sir."

"You don't come across as having such an old kid. No, not at all."

When we got out, Hasti asked, "Mom, how come the taxi driver said you don't come across as having an old kid?"

"He meant your mom is pretty—young and beautiful."

"Of course she is. But was the guy blind to not see me?" She then turned to me. "Right?"

"Right about what? That the guy was blind and couldn't see you? Or that your mom is very pretty? Or did you mean both? Well, both are true, anyway."

"He was blind not to see a big girl like me sitting there and how pretty my mom is."

"Just hold on to that and remember the rest of the story."

Mahin kept laughing at the conversation between Hasti and me. She honestly looked more beautiful. With the excuse of testing the makeup (that's what she told Ammeh Zari), she put some on. She wore her new clothes and showed them to us.

Hasti, too, wore her new clothes. She showed all her stationery to Ammeh Zari, who was busy washing a handwoven carpet in the yard. The sun was setting. Ammeh Zari, too, looked happy from Hasti's joy, but she was still suspicious about us. Mahin had told her lots of great things about us, told her how much we had helped her father, trying to gain her trust. While Ammeh Zari was washing the carpet, her food kept boiling in the pot on the outdoor stove, its smell filling the whole house, a smell I was inhaling after many years. Hasti wandered around the yard with her new clothes, every moment bringing one of her new things to show off to Ammeh Zari. She kept showing her affection, with words, hugging her, giving her big kisses on her cheeks. "Ammeh loves you so much." The two of them had a strangely good relationship. Mahin explained that Ammeh Zari loved Hasti like her own child, as she had never married and had her own child.

When Ammeh Zari finished washing the carpet, Naji and I went down to the yard to help her put it up on the terrace fence to dry. Hasti lingered around us and instructed us on how to put the carpet up. She made us laugh; we called her "Ms. Student," and her eyes lit up.

She said, "Come with me, then, and I'll show you my school."

We could see a long street from the window of our room. There was a school at the end of the street, and that was the one Hasti was going to the next day. We could not see the building from our window, but Hasti stretched her arm and pointed to it as if she could see it herself.

"Right there, at the end of the street. That building with red bricks."

At first, we kept asking where, which one, but soon realized we had better follow along, otherwise she would not let us be. "Oh, yes, that school, the building with red bricks. We got it."

"But that red building is not our school; our school is the one behind it."

Because Hasti had to go to bed early, we had an early dinner. But out of excitement for her first day of school, she didn't feel sleepy or just pretended she wasn't. She had decided to make me up as a bride with what we had bought, and no matter how hard they tried, Mahin and Ammeh Zari could not dissuade her.

Exhilarated by the possibility, I said, "Mahin Khanoom, it's a good game. Please let her do her thing for a bit." I was both excited by the prospect of wearing makeup and by the good feelings I got from Hasti. A six-year-old girl who not only wasn't alarmed by my face scars but also was trying to console me with her gesture and not heeding the very scars that made the adults turn away. Or sometimes their eyes would stay fixed on my face for a bit, but with a sullen look, out of either disgust or empathy. And now, Hasti, this little angel, who had met us only yesterday, wanted to sit in front of my face and first put some pink lipstick on my lips. She did so. Then brushes of various colors around my eyes and eyebrows. She could put powder only on one half of my face; I noticed her checking the scars, perhaps wishing those ugly things were not there. But they were. Then, suddenly, it seemed that she made up her mind to concentrate all her efforts on the normal half of my face. She also painted a red circle on my cheek. Naji and Mahin laughed. Naji was slouching back in a chair, and Mahin sat on the floor close to the door so that if Ammeh Zari said something in protest she could hear. Hasti also brought a piece of white tulle to throw over my head. When she finished, she held the mirror in front of me. "Take a look and see how beautiful you are."

My lips pink, the cheek that was not scarred red and round, around my eyes black, my eyelids green and blue, and my forehead several colors. I took the mirror from her and stared at my scars. They were in patches, only a few of them on one side of my face, but they had completely changed it. I was looking at the ugliest person I had ever seen. How come Hasti was not afraid of me? I myself was terrified of myself. Now the three of them were looking at me and laughing, and I felt the tears welling up in my eyes.

Mahin noticed and quickly got up. "Okay, tonight's show has come to an end, ladies and gentlemen, please leave. Let's go, my love. It's time for bed. You have to get up early for school. Your first day of school."

"But I haven't yet showed Naji my school uniform."

Mahin took Hasti's hand. "Tomorrow, before you leave for school, everyone will see your uniform. It's time to go to bed now. Say goodnight. Goodnight, uncles."

"Goodnight."

"When you wore it to show Ammeh Zari, I saw it from up here. It looks good on you. Very good," Naji said.

"So you two will wake up early tomorrow? When I'm going to school? That early?"

"Of course, we will, what do you think? Tomorrow is an important day for us."

Hasti smiled. The most beautiful sleepy smile I had ever seen. She yawned. "But men don't wake up that early in the morning. They should sleep till noon."

"We are not that kind of men."

"Okay, goodnight then."

Mahin said, "Make yourselves comfortable. If you're not sleepy, leave the light on; just be careful not to get too close to the window. Just that. Having the light on is okay." She smiled and left the room, holding Hasti's hand in hers.

"Why did you tell them to keep the lights on? Aren't they sleepy?" Hasti's voice came through the hallway.

Naji and I were now alone together under one roof after a very long time, without greedy curious eyes watching over us, and I spent one of the calmest nights of my life next to him.

I woke up hearing Hasti getting ready for school. Naji was still asleep. Her voice was coming through the window. I sneaked a look at the street through the curtains. A few women and young girls waited for Hasti and Mahin to join them, and when they did, they all started off in the direction Hasti had showed us: "You go straight down this street below our window, then take a turn into another street you can't see from here; it's a long street with green boxwood bushes on both sides, like walls. Real walls, but green. And if you push your hand against the wall, all your fingers will go through the wall. Can you believe it? If you don't, I can show you so you can put your fingers through the wall. You go until the end of that street to reach that building. Look. The red building that has no windows. Why doesn't it have windows?"

It was a strange building. As Mahin explained, no one really knew what the place had been before it was a school. It had something to do with the army; people had seen high-ranking military personnel sometimes going in there. There were always some armed guards around it too. Early that morning, Hasti and her friends were headed in that direction. It was the first day of fall, and as always, the new school year had begun.

Naji said, "I've never gone to school, but I can tell what a strange feeling it must be."

"Very strange. Both exciting and terrifying. You are suddenly thrown into this new situation and then the teacher comes in, and you have no idea what you should do."

The group of women and girls turned into the long boxwood-lined street and disappeared out of sight. The schoolboys were headed to school in the opposite direction. Now my point of reference was that red building they said was fifteen minutes away from the house. That was not a short walk for kids that young, but they were so excited that they probably didn't notice. Around two hours later, Mahin returned. "We were told to leave so that the kids could get used to the environment. I came quickly to check on you and see how you're doing. Have you had breakfast?" We said yes. She slouched on the floor. "I'm really craving a cigarette." Naji gave her one, and the two of them filled the room with smoke. Mahin kept an eye on the door, out of respect for Ammeh Zari, who hated cigarettes. She said that in the worst days of her and her husband's life, it was Ammeh Zari who had looked after Hasti, so she preferred that Ammeh Zari didn't see her smoking. She said anytime she wanted to take a puff, Ammeh Zari nagged, pointing out, directly or indirectly, cigarettes' harms and how the smoke was bad for the kid and how cigarettes were the source of all decadence. She even sometimes said it was smoking that had led her brother Teymour to end up in prison. Mahin spoke of Teymour, her husband, Hasti's father. She said his crime had been hanging around in the former red-light district; drug trafficking came up as she spoke too, but she quickly veered away from it. She brought up the brothel once again and explained that six months before, a few newly turned Hezbollahi guys, who back then frequented the brothel, had seen Teymour in the street and identified him and turned him in to the police. Mahin had only been able to visit him once since then.

"I know they will execute him. You can't imagine how bloodthirsty they are. Killing people is much easier for them than killing cows and sheep."

"For what crime?"

"For the crime of moral decadence and a false drug charge," Mahin cried. "They haven't even let me take some cigarettes to him."

"You mean he hasn't had a cigarette all this time?" Naji asked.

"They've told me I can go visit him one more time on the fourth of Mehr. That's in just three days. If they allow it, I'll take Hasti with me."

Naji pulled out three packs of cigarettes from his bag. "Try getting these to him. Maybe they'll let you this time."

Moved by Naji's gesture, her eyes filling up with tears, Mahin got up and kissed him on the cheeks. "How kind you are. Both of you. From where has God sent you to me? For me and for Hasti. Dad called you the boys of love."

"I, for one, am not a boy of love anymore; as Ammeh Zari says, I'm a boy of bad omen."

Mahin squinched her eyes. "How come? But Zari doesn't dislike you; she actually really likes you."

"I heard her telling you it's bad luck to have a burned person enter one's home. She said it brings one misery. Well, she is right."

Mahin felt embarrassed. I regretted what I had said, though I also wanted to let Mahin know I had heard Ammeh Zari.

"No, she didn't mean you," she explained.

I smiled.

She cautiously glanced at the door. "She is a bit superstitious, but she is not a bad woman. Not at all. She actually has such a pure heart. But she loves Hasti so much, she is afraid of something bad happening to her." She wiped her tears away. "I'm sorry if that's what you took her words to mean."

I felt ashamed. "No, not at all, I didn't mean that."

Naji jumped in. "Let's forget about what Ammeh Zari said. Tell us about Amrollah Khan. Do you visit his tomb at all? Have you cemented the grave, put up a tombstone?"

"Honestly, no. I haven't been there forever. I don't even know how things are there. Glad that he's gone and not seeing all that is happening these days."

"We should check up on his tomb, say hi to the Great One."

"The Great One!"

"He was and still is for me," Naji said.

"Anyway, that's a great idea. I'm so glad you two came and found me."

Ammeh Zari called Mahin from downstairs. Mahin hid the cigarettes in a plastic bag and put them under her arm. "I'll see you later at lunch. I guess Pari has come, so it's time for us to go back to the kids' school. Her daughter Samaneh is Hasti's classmate. Do either of you two have kids?" We said no. "Good for you." She laughed. "Make yourself at home, I beg you. You can lock this door from inside. Look, like this. Goodbye for now."

She left. Naji pulled out his playing cards and sat down to play solitaire. I pulled a chair to the window and sat there, watching the street through the thin gap between the curtains. Only a long narrow line of sight. Such a strange calm. After all the hustle and bustle of the kids, a heavy silence had now spread around the streets.

"I felt Mahin's comment about making ourselves at home was weird, wasn't it? Was she implying something?"

Naji was sitting behind me. I could hear him shuffling the cards. He said, "She's a good woman. I hope her husband is released soon, so they'll be rid of this poverty."

"That is if he is allowed to get a job afterward."

"He will eventually. From what I see, the country is still in shambles. He has to mix up with this new crowd and somehow find a way into their nooks and crannies."

I wanted us to talk about ourselves. We both fell silent for a long while. I sank further into my chair, closed my eyes, and reminisced about the good old days of meeting Naji. The day he had washed my muddy feet. He poured water from the jar over my naked feet, pushed the mud away with his hands, and how lovely it was to feel the touch of his hands. I heard Naji locking the door. I heard the wind; it whooshed over the grass fields and reached us, bringing with it sprays of river water, splashing the drops on our faces. Was that real or just in my imagination? Whatever it was, it was so enjoyable I didn't want to open my eyes for fear of losing it. Then I felt those familiar hands on my shoulders. They touched the skin of my neck. I was leaning back in the chair with my eyes closed. The hands were rough and full of little cracks. They circled around my ears, returning to me the pleasure I had lost. The fingers were busy, moving farther down and through my shirt's buttonholes. I did not need to ask God for anything else other than what I had right then, right there. My body's peace, the body that was in need of peace. His warm breath on the part of my hair. I was taking flight, suspended in the best place in the world with the best pleasures.

Suddenly, the sound of an explosion outside made us jump apart. Another huge explosion that shook our room. Screams were heard all around. I pulled the curtain aside a bit more. I saw a few warplanes in the sky, one so close to the earth that I could even see the pilot's figure. They left a few targets smoking and left. They retreated but left behind the black smokes of their bombs. They had bombarded a few locations around town, including the one behind the red building. Smoke rose from Hasti's school. People poured out into the streets, screaming, "The school! The girls' school!"

We heard Ammeh Zari call out to the holy imams. "Ya Abolfazl! Ya Seyyed Shohada!"

We didn't know what to do. Naji said, "Mahin was going to the school. We should leave, too, to see what is going on."

We went out and, with all the other people running toward the girls' school, set out in the direction of the street Hasti had talked about so much. How well she had described that boxwood wall. The greenery came along with us, or was it the greenery that took us along with it? But we were headed toward total darkness. We reached her school. Many others had gotten there before us. The mothers entered the school perimeters hitting themselves over the head. There was a huge hole in the middle of the schoolyard. Ambulances arrived. We found Mahin looking for Hasti, dazed and screaming. Each mother shouted her daughter's name. A few army vehicles arrived too. Officers pushed the people out of the schoolyard so that the medics could get to the wounded. We held Mahin's arms to stop her from slapping herself relentlessly. The medics brought out a group of girls, and seeing their daughters, the parents ran forward and took them in their arms. But there were families who still had no news of their kids, including Mahin. Including Naji and me.

One of the medics shouted, "Those of you who have not found your kids, come to Shir o Khorshid Hospital!"

With Mahin and many others, we went to the hospital. It was only on our way there that we learned a war has broken out. Iraqi planes had suddenly attacked the town, and, in their mind, they had bombarded sensitive government and military spots. They had hit the airport and parts of the oil refinery. Many workers were killed in those explosions. The central department of education offices were another target on that first day of the war, killing many teachers. The other target had been the girls' school—no, that wasn't the main target; apparently the planes meant to bomb that cursed suspicious red building but had mistakenly dropped the bomb on the school and the little girls who had just started school with all the joy and excitement we had witnessed. Now we were witness to something completely different. In the hospital area, people were screaming, hitting themselves in the head, running around at a loss.

"For God's sake, do you know where the wounded workers have been taken? Do you?" or "The wounded teachers. Where are they? I beg you on your mother's grave, tell me where they are." Groans that were far from human voices, sounded like the howling echoes of a group of jackals fallen into a trap, with no way to get out. "I'm looking for my daughter. Have you seen her?"

We were all sitting around on the grass, desperate and exhausted. Mahin, who wore a tight black headband around her forehead, was sitting next to us, rocking back and forth, moaning Hasti's name over and over.

Several men walked out of the building. One who had a piece of paper in his hand jumped onto a bench and shouted, "Brothers and sisters! Pay attention. The names I'm going to read are alive and in the hospital ward."

We were all ears. He started to read out the names. But no matter how far down on the list he went, there was no sign of Hasti's name. There were many other families who, like us, had not heard their missing person's name on the list.

We asked, "What should we do now?"

Another man jumped up onto the bench and said, "Brothers and sisters whose kids' names were not on this list should go either to the Missing Persons Unit or, unfortunately, to the cemetery office."

The women's collective scream filled the air. Mahin fainted in our arms. We lay her down on the grass of the hospital yard, and I went and found some water to splash on her face.

The moment we saw the young men in military uniform, we would hide ourselves, because we were afraid of Kavous and his men recognizing us.

The Missing Person's Unit was just an office with one door atop a long cement staircase. A fat man stood at the half-open door with a board in hand, holding too many pieces of white paper. Two police officers still wearing the old regime's uniform, carrying batons, kept going up and down the stairs. Their job was to not let people climb the stairs.

"Anyone who wants to know about their missing person's situation should just stand down there and wait for this brother to read the names."

We stood there, as if a flock of starving slaves begging for food. Each person shouted a name, all the names blending into the air, and no response coming our way. Until, finally, the fat man by the door came out and said, "I still don't have any names here to read to you. We are waiting to receive the missing persons' reports." People asked why we were there then. The man said he didn't know, said we had to ask the person who had sent us there. The police officers just realized what was going on and stepped back from the crowd and disappeared.

Once again, we heard several explosions. Some people said the enemy troops had entered the town, were surrounding the area, and their radios kept warning people to evacuate the town as soon as possible, because they intended to demolish the whole town. Our attempts to find Hasti were hopeless. Her name did not appear on the list of either the wounded or the killed.

"Thank God, sister. Your child has not been martyred. She is just missing."

"What do you mean Haj Agha? What should we do?"

"Just be patient. Have some revolutionary patience."

We patiently waited for hours, until the afternoon, until the sun set, until the night. We waited on our way to the hospital, on our way to the cemetery, and on our way back again. The ones who had found the names of their children on the wounded list were in a better situation, because at least they still had some hope. Now, even those whose loved ones were among the dead seemed calmer, perhaps because they did not have any hope anymore; they were just spread out on the ground, full of sorrow and with heavily trembling shoulders. But the families like ours, which was not finding any signs of our Hasti, were, like birds whose heads were cut but were not yet dead, restlessly flapping, hitting ourselves all around, trying to find something. And we didn't find anything that night and had to inevitably go back home without her, without Hasti, to continue the search again the next day.

Ammeh Zari was so furious, she could not tolerate seeing Naji and me. She felt it was the curse of our arrival in her home that had brought them that disaster. Maybe she was right. She was right, because we all knew how she had predicted misfortune from my face scars. That night she told us that if we didn't leave her house right then, she would call the guards on us. Mahin failed to change her mind no matter how hard she begged her. Mahin wanted us to stay with her and help her find Hasti, and we, too, wanted to stay and help find that innocent girl, but we were alarmed by Ammeh Zari's threat. We really didn't want to deal with the guards, so we gathered our stuff and left immediately. The town was filling up more hour after hour with soldiers who were not carrying any arms. They said a military unit with the latest military ware was headed to the town, but no one knew when they would get there.

The enemy planes were still able to fly above the town with no trouble and bomb wherever they wanted. Sometimes the helicopters, carrying men with machine guns, came so low in the sky that you could see the figure of your murderer before he shot you. The neighborhood youth had started digging trenches to sleep in at night in most parts of the town. Walking around, you could see in every nook and cranny shadows who, like gravediggers, moved with shovels and scattered soil around. You could see women, kids, and old men sitting by most trenches, ready to crawl in the moment they heard the planes or the wheezing of the mortar bombs before they hit the ground. As we walked, looking for a safe place to sleep, we noticed a group of people lying down in a dried-out gutter. We joined them, lay down next to them to sleep.

The next morning, we decided to leave the town no matter what, leave that island of death surrounded by water and fire. There were only two ways to leave. You could either find a boat to get yourself to the other side of the water, then walk through the desert to another town forty kilometers away. Or you could cross the only open bridge in town to get to the other side of the river, where, for some money, cars were waiting to get people to other towns. Since we had bad memories of traveling on foot and were fed up with it, we decided to try the bridge, hoping we could convince a car to give us a ride somewhere safe. There was only one bridge people could use for leaving and the other two were under the control of the regime, open only to government or military vehicles, though there were as yet no signs of them. The street by the bridge was overflowing with a crowd trying to find its way to the bridge. The queue moved at a snail's pace. As we joined the others, we could no longer see anything but a mass of flesh in front of our noses and a blue sky above us that was being covered by a veil of black smoke. It was so busy, we couldn't take any real steps, had to simply drag our feet forward while our bodies were hauled by other bodies of flesh pushing against ours. It was so humiliating. Everyone felt this, but we had no other choice. If you wanted to escape from that slaughterhouse and save your own life, you had to bear with it.

We heard there were guards on the other side of the bridge, deciding who could leave or not. We asked what that meant. Nobody knew at first, and we, stuck in the middle of the crowd, couldn't find out until we reached the other side. There were not too many guards. Some of them stood at the head of the bridge, wearing fabric bags over their heads and faces. Bags with two big holes for the eyes and one for the nose. How terrifying they were, those two black bullets moving amid the khaki bags, the two eyes whose most important job is to watch the beauties of the world, but now they were busy with a vicious act. I remembered wearing a bag over my face while we crossed the desert. I could see now why the other men had been so afraid of me, how ugly and terrifying I must have looked wearing that weird mask so similar to the guards'. But these guys' intentions were different from mine; they wanted to avoid recognition while they were identifying others. One of them seemed to recognize Naji. Did he? Or were we imagining it? The guard was standing behind an army Jeep. He didn't have a gun, and it was just him and his mask and the two terrifying holes for his eyes. I was the one who felt the weight of his eyes through those two hideous holes.

"We're done, Naji. Just don't look at him."

Those eyes zoomed in on us. "Hey, you, brother, you step out."

He meant for Naji to leave the crowd, but instead we turned around and pushed even farther into the crowd. It was tough. The crowd was moving in one direction, and the two of us were trying to move the opposite way. Everyone was so afraid and in such a rush that nobody paid any attention to us. The guard who had recognized us, recognized Naji really, and maybe me too, shouted a few more times, but we had decided not to look behind us. We didn't hear him again, until a while later, another voice shouted, "Arrest him!" But there was so much noise among the crowd that no one heard him. Or maybe people pretended not to hear him. People were frustrated by the guards and didn't want to cooperate with them; even some who had figured we were running away from something tried to open the way for us to move in the opposite direction. Those were horrifying moments, or maybe, as Naji said,

I was overreacting. I just didn't want to be taken in by them. Maybe Naji was right, and I had created a terrifying imaginary mountain of this fear.

"Why did we even run away? The guy didn't have anything to do with me."

"He didn't have anything to do with you? Didn't you hear him keep saying, 'Stop. Arrest them'?"

"At first, he didn't. But when he saw us running out of fear, he thought we must've done something wrong, have something illegal on us." And he threw such a glance at my face to imply that my scars had raised the guard's suspicions.

I didn't object, because I didn't want to exude even more fear. When we got out at the other end of the crowd, we didn't see any more guards, but we kept rushing on. A cargo truck was parked facing away from the town, and several men were jumping up to get in the back. After making sure the truck was headed out of town, we got on too. The co-driver charged us a fare, then went and took his position in the passenger's seat, and we started off. On the road, the driver had to stop several times because warplanes kept appearing overhead. Some of them were our own and some the enemy's, but it wasn't easy to tell them apart, so the driver got alarmed by all of them. I did too, and this made Naji laugh at me. "But this is one of our own, Mr. Educated Idiot!" Whenever our conversation got to joking and teasing one another, I felt relieved, because I knew we had moved past quarreling and were once again there for each other.

Once again, we had to plot to get out of town, because wandering around for folks like us had become more dangerous than ever before. The guards were looking both for spies and for supporters of leftist parties. It was the best opportunity to identify and pick up young members of unwanted parties, because the town was now like a naked body, like the palm of a hand, which you could see wholly with one glance, the doors to all houses, all closets, opened to the streets. The guards kept patrolling the town with their fast lightweight Jeeps, stopping and questioning any young person who did not look like the Hezbollah members or the soldiers, and if they figured they had leftist beliefs, took them to the station. We certainly were neither spies nor leftist, but there was a saying I remembered from Naneh Reyhan when she warned me not to do something that might get me taken to the station for questioning.

I told her, "But Naneh, I hadn't done anything wrong. I was just walking by the shore."

Naneh Reyhan said, "When you are taken in, it'll be hard to leave there, my dear one. As they say, before you can prove to them you are not the water boy, they've made you do forty rounds to carry and bring them water." She burst out laughing. "Do you get what I'm saying, my dear?"

The folks Naji hung out with before the revolution were now all guards, and it would be the end of us if any of them saw us. Unfortunately, Naji's face was hard to forget, because of his beauty, even though now he had a long beard. He suggested we head toward our birth village, with the hopes of finding someone there who could help us get to the other side of the water, blend in with the people who were escaping on foot through the desert. I was so tired and helpless and hopeless that I agreed with whatever he said; I mean, I couldn't think of anything else either. We tried to not use the town's thoroughfares and instead moved through the backstreets. We arrived at a grass-covered playground square, but now there were no kids around. A family of three sitting by one of the trenches invited us to lunch. An old man and woman and a fat young girl. They had fried fish for lunch. When we first saw them, they were laughing loudly.

The man called us over, "Come, kids. Come eat some red snapper with us. I've caught them myself at Khark Island."

We were quite hungry, so we joined them. When they saw my scars, they stopped laughing, asked me if it had happened in the war. I told them the story I told everyone: "We worked at a power plant, and my face burned when the plant caught fire."

The old man looked at me carefully. "This is not from fire, my son. This is acid burning."

Naji tried to change the topic of the conversation. "How come in these conditions, you have been laughing your hearts out? Has your lottery ticket won or something?"

The old woman cracked up again, as if hearing a joke. The girl laughed too, in response to the woman's laughter or to Naji's words, I couldn't tell.

The old man said, "This beautiful, charming young lady here is my daughter, daddy's love. Do you think she'd be frightened by the moron Saddam's bombs?" He laughed.

The girl mumbled through her laughter, "The moron Saddam."

The old woman served us two big pieces of fish, and we devoured them.

"How cleanly dug is your trench." Piles of soil were pushed back from the edge of the trench, so you could easily sit there and have your legs dangle in.

"Our dear son-in-law, Eskandar, dug this with his friends. He's gone to take his wife and kids to a village and will be back to take us too."

"God has bestowed on them five kids, each finer and fairer than the other."

The old man said, "Oh, my old woman, you keep praising your grandchildren, okay?" They all laughed. Apparently, the old man was just trying to make his daughter laugh. He kept tapping her shoulder with his to signal her to laugh, and the girl laughed.

"His car didn't have enough space for us. It was him, his wife, who's our daughter, and five big kids. Mashallah. But he said he would be coming back soon to get us too. All three of us. And this young lady is going to be the one sitting in the passenger seat. All by herself." The girl had beautiful brown hair, but her face was puffy, like she suffered some kind of abnormality.

The area the trench was dug in was a vast one, surrounded by rows of unified-looking houses. Each eight houses created a row, and each two rows facing each other, a street. From that square, there were streets leading to others. Every now and then, one or a few people came through the streets, passing the square, and the old man called to them, "May you not be tired. Come join us."

And whenever we saw men in military uniforms, we felt alarmed, so after lunch we decided to leave, but the old man kept insisting that we stay, not letting us go on our own way.

"I swear you on your mothers' graves, stay with us until Eskandar arrives. It won't take long."

He gave us a few blankets to sleep in a corner with them. The sound of explosions was nonstop, but they were still coming from farther away and so not too terrifying. Too exhausted, we slept above the trench. They didn't want us to leave because they were afraid, and we were hopeful that when Eskandar came, he would give us a lift to our village too, because the old man told us that he moved passengers with his own car, and the way things were, finding someone who would agree to do that was nearly impossible. The men who had cars were moving their own families around. The other cars were military ones and didn't give anyone rides unless they were arresting them.

The sun set behind the gable roofs of the houses. The stars rose one after another. But they were soon covered with the thin veil of my tears. I turned my face so that no one could see me. I thought how nature could be beautiful if there were no war, how much peace we could have if we were somewhere that was not war-torn, wherever it was, as long as there was no war. Then I could ask Naji to pull out his violin from his bag and play on and on, if there were no war.

The old man told Naji, "You haven't yet told us what is in this beautiful bag of yours."

"Nothing but some regular odds and ends."

"How about a gun? Do you have a gun in there too, you smarty-pants? You do, right?"

His wife and daughter were running after one another a bit farther away from us like two little girls. The old woman bent down and picked up a pebble, or pretended to, and threw it toward the girl, and the girl ran away, continuing to laugh.

"No, sir. What gun, what weapon?"

The old man laughed. "Okay, I know what you have, then."

He looked around him and brought his face closer to Naji. "Arak. Is it homemade or factory-made? Apple or grape?"

Naji said, "So you have gone through our bags when we were asleep, sir? What else did you find there?" With a sullen face, he turned around and lit a cigarette.

The old man turned to me. "Why is your friend so fiery? You know what, I give you whiskey, factory-made, black label. I hid it in that flowerbed inside that flower bush so that the guards couldn't find it. I'll give you a few full shots. And you promise to play some music for my little Manijeh, whichever of you two plays it. You see how the bombardments intensify with the fall of the night, and my dear girl gets so terrified, her whole body trembles like the branches of a willow tree, and we have to do all we can to distract her, but how would that be possible? See what destiny God has bestowed upon us in these final days of our life." He blew his nose and wiped his tears with a napkin.

Naji said, "When your Eskandar comes to take you to the village, everything will be okay. It's so unfair that the government has left people to themselves, helpless and without shelter. The right thing would be to send cars to gather people from around the town and transfer them to safe places."

"You're still wet behind the ears, my son. This government cannot even pull up its own pants, how can it come to the people's aid amid this chaos?"

For dinner, we had bread and cheese and watermelon. The old man had many things hidden in the flowerbed behind us. He brought us three glasses of whiskey, and we drank together. The sound of explosions was getting closer and closer. We were mainly surrounded by darkness, and the only lights around us were the few scattered stars in the sky and the reflection of the oil refinery flames, flames that ebbed and flowed, rekindling and rising to the hazy sky the very moment you thought it had died down.

The old man gave Naji another glass of whiskey. "Knock this back too. Hopefully, Eskandar arrives soon too."

Naji drank that glass too. I was getting concerned. "Please don't give him another one, you dear old man."

"Yes, dear doctor!" said the old man, and the three of us burst out laughing.

Naji gave me a long kind look, and, with the same smile on his face, asked the old man, "So, dear doctor, can we go into the trench now? Can we?"

"Yes, sure. Go see how well-organized it is. We have spread a few blankets on the ground so that its dampness doesn't bother us. Go ahead, go inside."

Naji pulled his instrument out of the bag and crawled into the trench. He first made a few low sounds to tune the violin, and then slowly started playing. His music caressed my heart as if it were a cool, delightful breeze. The old man sat the girl on the edge of the trench, her legs hanging down. The old woman sat at a different corner, staring at an unknown spot. I lay on my stomach by the trench, placing my head near the edge, above Naji's shoulder, while he was huddled up and played his violin; and his music was waves reaching me one after another, waves my heart was floating over.

The old man, who was keeping watch to make sure no guards would notice us, walked closer to the trench and said, "Play louder, a little bit louder."

The girl laughed. Continuing to play, Naji turned his head and looked at us, as if from the bottom of a deep well. The old woman was in a different world too, seemingly in the far distance, a world she was looking into with a smile on her face. What did she see that held her attention that way? It must have been something beautiful to make her smile like that. Life is full of beautiful things you can stare at with pleasure for long hours.

The difference between the white alarm announcing the end of an attack and the red one announcing the start was just in the opening sounds, otherwise they both were the same, both like blows of death. The old man knew each alarm, so the moment the red alarm started, he gently guided his daughter into the trench, and the girl slid in and settled next to Naji. Her eyes were looking up; she was terrified and on the verge of screaming, but the old man smiled at her and told Naji, "Play louder. Louder."

We heard the wheezing of a mortar bomb. We were told that that was a good thing; to hear the wheezing meant that it was passing above your head, and so you were safe. But the people who were farther away and didn't hear the wheezing, didn't hear any sounds (neither the wheezing nor the explosion), those were the ones who were killed by the bomb. Then shredded bodies. No. I should not let those images enter my mind again, ugly agonizing images that sometimes force their way into my mind. My ears were filled with the sound of the violin; perhaps the girl's ears were too. Naji was playing a fast happy rhythmic tune, and the girl moved herself with it, her big body rubbing against Naji's. My elbows on the ground, my chin leaning on the cup of my hands, I watched them. The old man, still standing above the trench, clapped and acted joyously, doing his best to entertain the girl so her ears could not focus on the explosion that might cause her to scream— even though you could, if you wanted to, still hear the sound of the ex- plosion over Naji's music. The old woman was still sitting there, as if a statue in black robes. Naji played all the happy tunes he knew, until the explosions began to subside. Then they stopped, and Naji began a lighter tune. My favorite song got mixed in with the sound of the white alarm.

The old man sat down. "Thank God."

Naji stopped playing. The girl cheered Naji with her clapping and laughter.

Inside the trench, there was enough room only for the mother and daughter to sleep, so Naji and I slept outside the trench with the old man. We were not too anxious, because there were no tall buildings or walls to crumble on top of us overnight. An autumn night and cold winds. We each had two blankets, one to spread under us and one over. The old man was lying next to us but seemed to stay awake all night.

In the morning, as we were finishing our breakfast, a scrappy car appeared from a backstreet and headed toward us. All three members of the family got up excitedly and shouted in unison, "Eskandar!"

Naji and I were surprised how the car had found its way there in that chaos.

"Eskandar knows the area like the palm of his own hand."

Eskandar was a short overweight man with a thick pair of glasses. He started talking the moment he got out of his car. "You have no idea what is going on on the other side of the water. Everyone is looking for a hole to hide in. I dropped the kids at Marzieh's and came to pick you up. We'll be delayed a lot on the way, just telling you. Both at this end of the bridge and at the other. A group of people on this side beg the soldiers to let them out, another group on the other side beg them to let them in. I told them there's nothing in town to come to, and they asked me why I myself was headed here. I told them half of my family is left behind back there. I was talking about you. I promised the girls I would take you to them as soon as possible."

The old man said, "These two young men are our friends. They are good kids and want to leave." He turned to us and asked, "Where are you headed?"

We told them the name of our village, and Eskandar recognized it. The old woman and girl were gathering their stuff, getting ready to leave.

"You won't find a car to get you there," Eskandar said.

We were also getting ready to leave. "We'll go bit by bit."

"Even if you find a car, do you know how much you have to cough up to get there?" We said an amount, and Eskandar ridiculed us. "Brothers, are you serious? Who would get you there for that price?" The lenses of his glasses were so strong that they made his eyes look too round and big and funny. We asked him what we should pay.

The old man said, "That's Eskandar's job."

Eskandar was tempted to charge us and get us to our village.

"Do you know someone who might take us there?" Naji asked him.

"If you pay good money, why not."

"Who?"

"How much do you want to pay?"

"You tell us how much. Isn't that your job?"

Eskandar said an amount, and Naji agreed. Eskandar then turned to the old man and said, "The whole thing won't take more than an hour. While you are gathering your stuff, I'll take them and come back, and we'll be out of town in no time."

The girl said, "We've already gathered our stuff."

"By the time you, beautiful bride, wash your face, I'll be back."

"But I've already washed my face."

The old man interrupted. "Let this good fellow go earn some dime and come back. We've been here for two days now, one hour won't kill us, right? What disaster could befall us from the skies in an hour?"

Eskandar laughed. "Whatever it is, it's already happened." He pointed to the sky. "Look. What worse can happen?"

Black smoke was ebbing and flowing above our head, veiling the blue of the sky. We said our goodbyes to that kind family. The old man and woman embraced both of us. Their arms felt warm, and I didn't want to leave them, but I had to, because Eskandar was already at the wheel waiting for us. On the way, he told us he'd been lucky to run into us, otherwise he didn't know how to pay for his gas. He told us how invaluable the money we paid him was. He took the bills and put them in his shirt pocket, securing the top with a safety pin. His honesty made me feel very close to him, as if I had known him for years, no, forever. Naji, too, was happy that he was helping Eskandar and that family while also helping us with that money. Eskandar also talked about the hardships of our journey, of its danger. He said if he didn't give us a ride, we would have to walk all the way. He showed us how all the cars were headed toward town, and none in our direction. He asked us why we were headed to the village. We explained that we wanted to find a boat to take us to the other side of the water. When we were almost there, several enemy planes appeared above our head. They turned around. It seemed they didn't have a specific target and were simply looking for something to hunt. Then we heard a big explosion. Eskandar hit the brake. "I told you these areas would be dangerous. Did you see that?"

Naji said, "These are just patrol planes. They do a round and get back to their base. They aren't supposed to drop bombs." We were the only car on that road surrounded by the desert.

Eskandar said, "They'll go back to the base only after taking the lives of our young so that they have something to gift to the motherfucker Saddam."

Naji responded, "Whatever it is, it's best to move. It's more dangerous to just stop here."

Eskandar was frightened. Another plane was headed in our direction. "Where to? Am I crazy to sacrifice myself and my car for nothing, especially with these blind eyes of mine?"

"But you can't just leave us in the middle of nowhere, brother. With all that money you got from us, you must take us to our destination."

"Let's sit quietly for a bit and see what happens."

The plane passed overhead. Apparently, Eskandar was right. It was safer to stop than to move. When he felt there was no risk anymore, he started the car once again. The sound of explosions didn't stop at all. The car kept moving amid its passengers' heavy silence. We moved past a few familiar brickmaking furnaces. They were off, and no one was around. We reached the border of the desert and the palm groves. The car could still go farther, but we asked Eskandar to drop us off right there. The moment we got out, Eskandar made a U-turn and left us without saying goodbye. The place was empty of people. We knew the hill close by. When I was a kid, I used to come there a lot with my sisters, standing on top and watching the desert. It was especially amazing to watch at sunset when the furnace laborers finished their work for the day and headed toward their homes while singing. We watched the sun gradually setting and getting lost behind the desert horizon, the colors of its remaining light changing a thousand times. The wind blew.

Naji said, "I have to sit by this wall and smoke a cigarette. I'm craving one like crazy, I don't know why." He slouched down by a wall remaining from a ruined house and lit a cigarette. There were so many ruins around, I could not yet locate my childhood house through them. A plane appeared from behind us. I lay down by the wall, but Naji kept puffing at his cigarette as if there was no sign of an enemy plane above us. We heard a few explosions very close by, so close, I felt everything was demolished right on top of me. I placed my head in Naji's arms. How much time passed?

"Okay, you can get up. They're gone now."

A young boy appeared out of nowhere, ran above the hill, and pointed to the road. "That's where they hit. Look, the army vehicle is burning."

I, too, ran up to see. Two cars were burning in flames. I called Naji to come and see, but he didn't show any interest. A bit later, a fire truck approached them from far away. Then an ambulance arrived. Some people gathered there, too, to watch, and they blocked my view. I could now only see a mass of people from a distance, and I was worried about Eskandar. I asked a motorcyclist coming from that direction whether he had seen an overweight man with glasses in a red Peykan.

His motorcycle was a tiny and sloppy moped, looking like he had attached a motor to a child's bike. He said both vehicles were burned, an army vehicle and a private car. He asked, "Was it a Peykan?"

I asked, "Was it or not?"

"It was red. A fat man was looking for something on the desert ground. He kept crying and saying, 'Oh, God, my eyes, my eyes.' I wanted to go close and help him, but suddenly Saddam threw another bomb right there, because the motherfucker had figured I was there, so I ran away, chanting my slogan, 'My moped kinda loathsome, but my only way to freedom.'" He said this and burst out laughing.

I asked myself how he could laugh under such conditions but then immediately realized there was not much else he could do except laugh and talk nonsense to push fear away for a bit.

"You know, Saddam himself has sent some agents to find me. He has announced a prize for my head."

I asked him why, and, once again, he spoke some nonsense and giggled.

I thought about the old man and woman and their fat daughter. Who would get them to their destination? How hard it would be for them to sit there waiting tonight under the bomb attacks, and waiting for what? What if Eskandar's car had burned up? What if the fire the firefighters had put out by now had already devoured the whole red Peykan and simply spit out its remains into the desert? What if Eskandar had not yet found his glasses? I could not stop blaming myself.

"Why should we feel guilty? He brought us for the money. You saw that, didn't you?" Naji said.

"It was because of us that he came on this dangerous drive."

"It wasn't because of us; it was because of the money."

I realized there was no use talking to Naji. I sat alone and cried for Eskandar and that family. To calm me down, Naji said, "Thank God, he is still alive. Well, didn't the motorcyclist tell you he had seen Eskandar? He did, right? So?"

I was agitated and impatient. "I don't know. I'm not sure. I didn't get what he was saying. I'm not sure of anything anymore. Of anything at all."

We started off toward my father's house. We got there. The door was closed, but there was no lock in place. I gently pushed it open, and we entered. A woman sat by the jasmine tree. The wind was blowing, and a shower of dried little flowers poured over the woman's head. As we entered, she raised her head and asked, "Who's there?" It was Naneh Reyhan. She was blind now and seemed a hundred years older. I noticed the circles of her eyes moving, but she didn't see us and just kept moving her small head to the left and right. "Who are you?" She was wearing black. The black gauze of her dress was covered with dust.

"Naneh Reyhan?" I said.

She turned her head and held her ear to the direction of my voice. After a moment of silence, she asked, "Jamil? Are you back?"

I dropped my bag on the ground, went and sat in front of her, and took her in my arms. She smelled my face, and her tears wetted mine. She smelled of dust. A few flowers were stuck in the gauze of her dress. A mixture of the scents of earth and smashed jasmine filled my nostrils. I asked, "Where are the others? Why are you here all by yourself?"

She said, "Is someone with you? Tell them to put their bags down and rest. If you are hungry, there's some yogurt and cheese in that ice box there. The fridge doesn't work. There's no electricity. Bread is in this bag here. Eat something and rest. Your father will be back soon."

"Is Haji still here?" I asked.

"He brought me here from my own house to sit here and watch over the house to stop any strangers coming in. Everyone else is gone. They first crossed the water with a boat, then walked to a distant village to stay safe. Haji said he'll stay to see what he can do about the cows."

"Where are the cows?"

"The government took them. They said it was because Haji supported Saddam Hussein. Five or six months ago. They said it was morally right to take foreigner's properties. They thought Haji was one of them. All these troubles are stirred up by that Hamed, who denounced Haji to the new government."

"I had imagined Hamed would be helpful to Haji these days, would remain loyal to him, at least it seemed so, at least he—"

"No, they are each other's enemies now. Hamed became a supporter of this non-Arab imam. He told Haji he was a foreigner's Muslim and had to be turned in to the guards. He told the guards he had brought here that Haji was the head of anti-revolutionaries."

"Where is Hamed now?"

"He's gone to town. It's a long while, my dear boy. When the shah ran away, he, too, left, taking his wife and kid with him. He was given new clothes. A big motorcycle. A full gun. Now Haji has gone to tell the government people that his cows are as old as God himself." She coughed. "Maybe that way he can get them back."

"I don't want to have anything to do with any of them. I just want to go to the other side of the water as soon as possible."

"Seyyed. The one who planted herbs. He has found a small boat with which he takes people to the other side for some money. When he comes back, I'll tell him to take you two. What's your friend's name?"

Naji was now lying in the shade of the wall. We had some bread and yogurt. Naneh Reyhan told us that after I left, no one brought her her eye medication, and, little by little, she lost her sight. It didn't matter to anyone, because everyone had their own problems and couldn't bother with hers. Yesterday, when they all left, they didn't take her with them, because they knew it wouldn't be easy for her to walk across the desert, and she would need help.

"But we will take you with us, Naneh. The moment we find a boat to help us cross the river, we'll take you with us."

"You should wait for Seyyed to come back."

"Do you know when he's going to be back?"

"The sun has not set, has it?"

"No, not yet."

I was glad I thought about taking Naneh Reyhan with us.

"But I can't walk. I mean I can, but I can't see in front of me, so I'll just be a burden to you."

"Don't think about that, Naneh. Even if I have to carry you on my back, I'm going to take you along."

When I was saying these things to Naneh, Naji gave me a mocking look, as if knowing they were just empty words and none of it would come true. But I felt differently. The sense of guilt that I had about a few people pushed me to want to do something for someone. People like Javad to whom I gave the empty gun that caused his death; like Hasti, whose disappearance followed our arrival in their house and the curse of my burned face; and now Eskandar and that helpless family. I felt that pulling Naneh Reyhan out of that pit of fire and taking her to safety might alleviate some of my guilt, maybe.

"Where do you want to take her?"

"I don't know yet, but wherever we go, we're taking her with us, until we reach somewhere we can settle her."

"You've gone crazy. You're talking nonsense."

Naneh Reyhan said, "It's late for today. You have to leave early tomorrow morning. Seyyed will take you. Why hasn't Haji returned yet?" And she answered herself. "Maybe the thing with the cows has taken long. He'll be back eventually."

I wasn't sure if I wanted to talk face-to-face with my father or not. Either way, we had no choice but to wait for Seyyed's arrival. Naneh Reyhan was happy that we were there with her.

"Whether you like it or not, you are staying in the village tonight. You must find somewhere to sleep."

We told her we would find something close by. She insisted that we must sleep in trenches and asked me to take her to the palm grove. I did as she asked. There were only a few rows of palms still standing.

"What happened to the palms?"

"Because Hamed made them believe Haji was anti-revolution, the government ordered the center of the grove to be flattened and a mosque to be built instead for the villagers. They haven't yet built it, just brought down the palms. And now the war has happened."

In the middle of that empty space, there was a trench Naneh wanted to show us. She explained that Haji had paid to have it built by a few of the young villagers, but he had slept in there only the first night before being scared to death by the experience. "But you are young, there's nothing for you to be afraid of. May you stay healthy and safe. It's better to sleep in there than be hurt and paralyzed by shrapnel outside the trench. Don't fear anything. It's totally safe there, my dear."

Haji's trench had a roof too. But Naneh herself was afraid of sleeping there.

When the sun set, Seyyed came back from the river. He was surprised to see us but acted friendly with us. We told him we wanted to cross the water, and he told us we had to wait till the next day. He told us how much he wanted for taking us, and we agreed. I told him we wanted to take Naneh Reyhan with us, but he acted as if he had not heard me. He was quite tired and wanted to rest. He said he would come after us the next morning. He left without telling us where he was sleeping. He had his own trench somewhere else. We went back to Naneh Reyhan, and she began to tell us stories of things that had happened while we were gone.

"The first day of the war, Haji was very pleased. He said Saddam was coming to save our people from these mullahs who have just come to power. He thought Saddam's men would take over and that would be it, but instead of sending his troops, Saddam has been dropping mortar and bombs on our heads. You have no idea how many innocent people perished that first day, how many women and children. What suffering. The bombs almost fell on Haji a few times. Finally, he realized Saddam doesn't care about our people. God only knows what's wrong with him, getting so violent, attacking our defenseless people. That very first day, I knew God loves me so much to have taken my eyes from me so I didn't have to see how women and children were being ripped apart.

What disaster, what suffering." She told us we had to be very careful to avoid coming face-to-face with government officers. She said they arrested anyone who seemed like a stranger around here and took them to the station for being enemy spies. Finally, a night darker than any night I had ever seen arrived. Naneh Reyhan said we had to hide the burning tip of the cigarette, otherwise the enemy planes would know there were humans there, and because they were against humans, they would drop bombs on us. She kept wondering loudly why things had turned out like this, why Saddam had suddenly decided to kill everyone, why he wanted to destroy everything. We told her it was because he had always been a violent crazy person who enjoyed killing people. Naneh Reyhan gave us a bottle of water and some dates mixed with sesame seeds. They were both delicious and healthy. We knew those few pieces of date would keep us full until tomorrow.

There were no stars in the sky. The sky had turned into an ugly tight roof that kept moving lower and lower, putting more and more pressure on us. That night Haji did not return home. Naneh Reyhan was worried for him. I went through the rooms of the house and found some blankets. We said goodbye to her and told her we would see her the following morning. We went to the trench she had showed us. They had covered the trench with a big metal sheet, leaving only a hole for entering and leaving. First, I crawled into the trench and spread two of the blankets over the bare dusty ground, then Naji came in with his and my backpacks. There was nothing but darkness. Mere darkness. We put our bags beneath our feet and lay down right next to each other.

"Aren't you afraid of this tar darkness?" I asked Naji.

"We have no other choice."

"What if we went out and slept outside in a corner or by a wall? Wouldn't that be better?"

It seemed like a bomb had been waiting for me to finish my question to suddenly fly toward us and explode all around us, followed by yet another, and a chain of horrifying sounds. Naji and I lay there face-to-face in a silent tomb of fear. After a long sequence of explosions and sounds of horror, silence surrounded us once again. A silence more horrifying than those other sounds.

"See?" Naji noted.

"What if one of them explodes right above this trench?"

"Well, that's why we're in here. Even if it falls a dozen meters away from us, we are still safe, because there's nothing around here to fall over us and lock us up here. Right?"

His words made me imagine being buried alive. An attack of images I didn't want to see but couldn't get rid of either. I saw the two of us being buried in a grave, with no one knowing we were there, and no matter how hard we scratched the roof above us, we found nothing but layers and layers of mud weighing on our chests. There was no hope for us to reach the light.

"How long do you think it'll take us to die?"

"When? Where?" Naji asked me.

"If we are buried alive and have no way to get out, how many days will it take for us to draw our last breath?"

His laughter filled the trench. His mouth was close to my ear. "You, Mr. Educated, you are the one who should know these things, not me."

But I was just afraid and didn't know anything anymore. I did not want to stay in that grave and kept looking for excuses to go out, but it seemed that the enemy had decided the real war was to happen at night, that very night, with explosion after explosion. Then Naji's hands wrapped around my body and pulled me even closer, and his lips started moving over the scars on my face, slowly and gently, from one scar to the next, his lips getting wetter and wetter.

"Aren't you afraid of my scars? Don't they make you cringe?"

"Which scars? Where are they?" His tongue slid over them, and I stopped thinking about death. I let myself go in his hands, trusting his long fingers looking for the buttons he unfastened, one after another, and I began, little by little, rolling from coldness to warmth, from fear to safety. He kept rolling me, taking me along, along on a boat he was rowing.

The barking of dogs replaced the sound of explosions. They were far away, were horrified. I could not remember ever having heard so many dogs barking in the middle of the night. Those dogs were there to alert their humans of dangers. They barked to announce another bomb coming soon, and with every bomb falling, it seemed that a thousand tons of metal were being scattered around.

Naji's lips moved around on my neck. "Why do they want to kill us?" I slid down and put my forehead on his chest. "Maybe Ammeh Zari was right that all of this is because of the curse of my face. Well, a burned face is bad fortune after all."

He laughed. "Mr. Superstitious Intellectual, you weren't like this before." And to make me happy, he laughed once again, and I felt a bit happier hearing his laughter.

Darkness gave way to moonlight, and suddenly we were in the midst of the most luminous spot, on the wet muds of the shore, and we rolled around each other in the wetness and the mud, with such pleasure I had never before experienced, and the only sound I could hear from outside was the sound of the wind wheezing over the trench, giving way to the next wind to wheeze over us, and the sound of the branches and the leaves. Was it real, or was it just in my ears? The sound of two bodies intertwining, the sound of breaths, the sound of whispers in the ears.

"We'll leave here for somewhere where we're free, where we don't have to be afraid of being together. We'll then get a house with big windows facing east, so that the sun wakes us up every day, shining its light onto our bed. Something tells me we'll get there. Very soon."

"How are you so sure?"

"Someone who knew the way well shared all the details with me. Tomorrow, I'll take you right to the border, and we'll be on the other side in no time. Step by step."

"I'm so thirsty."

He didn't mind my interrupting him. He sat up and found the water bottle Naneh Reyhan had given us. When he unscrewed it, the scent of rosewater filled the trench. Naji found my hand in the dark and put the bottle in it. I drank the water. It reminded me of my childhood days. When I was scared of something and couldn't do anything to calm myself, I would run to Naneh Reyhan's house, and she would give me water with drops of rosewater in it.

Outside the trench, there was darkness and silence. We could see the big barks of palm trees in the distance. Naji lit a cigarette and cupped his hand to hide the ember. If it wasn't for my fear and insistence, he would just smoke it normally, because he believed the enemy's planes could not detect the burning tip from up above. Once again, the planes started throwing bombs in our direction. "Hurry up. Put your cigarette out. It's getting ugly."

He carefully put it out on the ground. We crawled back into the trench and fell asleep calmer than any other time.

A rooster's crowing announced the arrival of the day. Then we heard a few men talking. I opened my eyes. Rays of sun crawled inside the trench through the holes in the roof. A harsh voice shouted, "Who is in there? Get out!"

The sound of a breechblock made our hair stand on end. We didn't dare leave the trench and show ourselves. We stopped breathing, imagining they would think no one was there and leave if we didn't respond or make a noise. Suddenly, the roof above us was peeled away, pouring pebbles and soil over our heads. A few pairs of eyes were staring down at us. A few guns were aimed at us.

"Put your hands on your heads and slowly step out."

Whatever orders they gave, we followed. They were three young armed men in khaki clothes.

"You didn't find any better place for this, you faggots?"

Naji, who had his hands on his head, said in a low voice, "We were just sleeping here, brother."

"Sure, on your mother's grave, you were just sleeping." The sun had not yet completely risen. The wind was blowing. "Take them to the car. You, bring their stuff from the trench." Their car was parked behind the wall of our house.

Naneh Reyhan, holding her arms in front of her and finding her way toward us, said, "Let them go. They're my kids. It was Haji's fault for calling you. I wish I were deaf and hadn't told him you were back, my dear Jamil. Wish I could cut my tongue out. I thought your father would be happy."

"Push the old woman inside the house and stop her from babbling so much."

One of the guards went to her and violently pulled her arm, took her inside, and shut the door. Naji and I were taken to the back of their Jeep. I saw my father standing there, as if he had just come back from the land of the dead only to stay here with the living for a few minutes before going back to his death.

"Hang them. Especially the one with the burned face, my own son. The doom and disaster we're in are all on them, officer. Hang him so that calm and security might be restored. I should've taken him out myself all those years back to stop our catastrophes. It's all that useless Hamed's fault. Good thing they are now trapped together. Promise me you'll hang them both together, right here." He seemed to be talking in the air, with the wind; they seemed to be not even hearing him.

Seyyed was standing farther away, watching us, unable to do anything. The guards threw Naji's and my stuff into the car in front of their seats, and the car took off, driving us away from our home, our birthplace. Haji just stood there, not talking to anyone. The car reached the main road. Many army vehicles were passing by, young soldiers at their wheels, singing and laughing. We were taken to a station in town, held in a cement hall. Someone came and asked who the musical instrument belonged to? I said it was mine. Naji said it was his. The guard looked from one of us to the other, confused. "Well, which one? Yours or yours?"

"It's mine," Naji said.

The guard took the violin out of its case and handed it to Naji. "Break it. Smash it. Right here. Put it down on the floor and stomp on it."

Naji put the violin on the ground.

"Now step on it and crush it like this." The guard himself stepped on the violin. Its wood breaking sounded like human bones breaking. "Now your turn. Exactly like I did."

But Naji didn't move.

"I said smash it, you motherfucker."

Naji looked at me. Some time passed.

"What are you waiting for, you little boy?" From the look on Naji's face, it was obvious that he was not going to smash his own violin. "I'll make you do it. I'll force you, faggot, to bite your instrument with your own teeth into bits and pieces." He hit Naji on the back of his shoulders with both hands. "For now, kick it a few times, until later." Naji seemed not to hear him. He seemed not to hear anything, as if he were in another world. The interrogator himself took yet another step toward the instrument and stamped on it once again. The heart-wrenching sound of the violin breaking tugged at my heart. "Do you get it now? See what you need to do, you dirty dog? Come on."

He was addressing Naji, but I stepped forward and stood in front of the violin, bringing my foot down on its body as strongly as I could. Once again, the sound of the wood breaking, the echo of the screams of the strings. My next kick ripped the strings apart, causing them to hang loose. Kick after kick after kick, in a bout of madness, as if that instrument was at the root of my misfortunes. It was a curse I had inherited from my ancestors, a curse that first took my mother's life and was now taking my own. Once again, with another heavy kick to the fallen body of the violin, I unloaded some of my hatred.

"You step away. I want him to come."

But no matter how hard the guard tried to push Naji to kick the violin, he didn't. He himself was kicked by the man, slapped, received an onslaught of horrible swear words, but he did not follow his orders against the violin, though it was now nothing but a crushed piece of wood with loose strings. The guard broke the bow into half with his hands. The broken sticks didn't fall apart, though, because they were still attached to the strings. He kept shaking it until he freed them from the strings. He then dropped them down on the broken violin. Naji kept staring at it with wet eyes.

"I know what to do with you, you stubborn little homo, but being such a bullhead won't do you good here. You'll see."

A big hall was awaiting us. We were taken there blindfolded. Through the small gap underneath the blindfold, I could glimpse it. It was big and made of cement, and some others wearing blindfolds like us were spread out in limbo on gray blankets. Horrifying sounds could be heard coming from a nearby room. The harsh sound of the interrogator who kept cursing someone, forcing them to say something. The voice of a man whimpering in pain, crying, and saying, "That was all. I beg you." Imagining that I might soon hear Naji's cries, I felt my whole body trembling. I wanted to die before hearing such sounds. But that day, none of us ended up in the interrogation room. At night, there was nothing but silence. We had been told that we were not allowed to utter a word. If we needed to use the bathroom, we had to raise our hand until finally a guard would come and take us. For breakfast, they served us each half a piece of bread covered with a little bit of butter and jam. We were also handed a plastic cup of tea. We ate our breakfast while blindfolded. I don't know how long it was after breakfast, when a guard came for Naji and me and told us to follow him. He took my sleeve and pulled me after him. Naji was holding my hand and following us. My hand in his trembled out of fear, and he kept trying to calm me down with the soft touch of his fingers.

"Guys, you all listen carefully to what is being said, so you only do what you are told, not one bit less or more, exactly as you are told." We were a group of blindfolded prisoners in a room. The guard continued, "We'll make each one of you stand at this doorframe and tell you to remove your blindfold. I mean only the person standing there, not others. Guys, be careful to not remove your blindfold without being told, or you'll be getting a good beating, both on your head and your neck, so good you'll feel your brain in your nostrils. But, God willing, no one will remove their blindfold unless they're ordered to. Then, without your blindfold, you hold your head straight and walk all the way to the end of the hallway into another room. There, you put your blindfold on again. You got it?"

The prisoners called the hallway "the recognition hallway." A group of masked people were standing there looking at us as we walked by. We didn't see them, but they saw our faces clearly and could identify us. Some of them were guards and some prisoners who had given up and were cooperating with the guards, ratting out other party members. Naji and I were not part of any parties or organizations, but Naji's hanging out with Kavous's people threw us into their trap. One of the masked guards recognized Naji, who was primarily accused of carrying out a terror attempt on Kavous and who had also stolen his gun. I was his accomplice in the case. They separated us. A few days later, I found out that he, too, was thrown into one of the small cells I was thrown into for solitary confinement. A long narrow hallway with cells lined up on both sides that I failed to count. I could hear the sounds of others in their cells. Sometimes they were shouts of Allahu Akbar. Sometimes they were protest shouts. When someone cried out Allahu Akbar, that meant they were now fed up and were shouting either for help or for more beating. Then, through the gap under the door, I would see someone being dragged out of a cell and down the hallway. That day, too, the moment I heard someone entering the end of the hallway, I bent down to see their movement through the gap. I saw him. It was Naji. It was him being taken by a guard. I recognized him from his ankle, which was the only part of his body I could see. He was probably being taken for interrogation.

"Well, well, you haven't yet told us how long you've had a sexual relationship with one another."

"We were just friends. Friends and nothing else." My eyes were covered, and I could not see the interrogator, who had a soft feminine voice.

"Why am I even asking you? That friend of yours, with whom you were just friends, has confessed everything and written here that that's not true. Just friends, yeah right!"

I didn't tell him Naji was illiterate, didn't know how to write. He hit me hard on the head several times. I started crying. At that moment, I hated everything and everyone in the world, most of all myself. I wanted to die right there and then, not to go through all that humiliation.

"It'll all be cleared out in the court."

A few days later, they sat Naji and me face-to-face in a room. I didn't know what was going on. The guard came and took me to a room. A voice I had not heard before ordered me to remove my blindfold, and I noticed that Naji, too, was doing the same in front of me. The man who was next to us had covered his face with a khaki sack, and only his eyes could be seen through the holes in the bag. I felt I was meeting my death, and we were being taken to the firing squad. I could feel the bullet suddenly hitting me. I could hear my bones shattering. Naji's face was covered in bruises from punches and slaps. He had a big swelling under one of his eyes, so big it seemed like it was about to burst and pour out pus and blood. He looked at me as if through a grave he was drowning in, looked at me as if he was waiting for me to pour a fistful of dust in his eyes so he could not see me anymore. His look seemed sick and ashamed.

The guard hit him in the shoulder and in a hideous voice said, "Tell your friend you've told us everything. Tell him that you told us you two have had sex for the past five years." There was no room for us to protest and say we hadn't even been together for five years. "Come on, tell him. What are you waiting for?"

In a hoarse voice, as if his throat was blocked by a cough, Naji said, "I've told them everything."

"Okay, now put back your blindfolds, you motherfuckers."

"But, brother, I'm one side of this situation, and I'm telling you there's been no such relationship, if it were—"

"Shut the fuck up, you."

The next time I saw Naji, his face looked a bit healed, even though the bruise around his eye was still there when I saw him for only a few seconds in the courtroom. When they brought me in, he was sitting in a first-row seat. They took me and sat me down next to him. Our arms touched, and he rubbed his fingers against mine on the seat. The judge ordered a guard to separate us, and he came and stood between us, and with a humiliating smack on Naji's shoulder, pushed him away from me. He hit my shoulder too, but then raised his hand and slapped me in the face, before suddenly pulling his hand away with disgust and throwing a glance at my face, then at his own palm; he then rubbed it on his other sleeve, as if cleaning up the nothingness that was stuck to his hand, and sat down on the seat between Naji and me.

Another guard pressed the play button on a small stereo on the judge's desk, and a Quran recitation started broadcasting. Seven or eight men were sitting around the room. I hadn't seen any of them before. The judge was a clergyman. The court secretary read our charges. It was a long list. When they got to the charge of our relationship, the judge said we had confessed to that crime ourselves, adding that, based on evidence provided by a group of adult sane men, we'd had a sexual relationship with one another. He said the witnesses were our own family members as well as old friends and acquaintances we'd frequented for a long while, but he didn't name anyone. He also noted that we were arrested while committing the crime. When he asked us if we had anything to say, I responded that we were not committing a crime when arrested and added that we had never committed a crime. I cried. I didn't mean to. Naji felt ashamed of my tears. He wanted us to pretend that we were strong, but I couldn't carry on this pretense, because I was not.

"Your friend here says you were," the judge said, then turned to a man (who we later realized was our lawyer) and asked, "Do you want to add anything?"

"Haj Agha, my clients here are young and naive, and they've already repented too," said the lawyer, then turned to us and asked, "You have repented, right?" We nodded in confirmation. The lawyer continued, "I request the honorable court to please have mercy on my clients' youth and naivety and consider reduced punishments for them in the final verdict."

That day no verdict was announced. We knew for sure that we would be hanged, but we didn't know when. And when we asked them, we were told our verdict was not yet announced. We knew postponing it was meant to torture us further. The other prisoners awaiting execution said the same. It was a brutal torture, knowing that you were going to be hanged but not being told when that final day would be, so every day you expected the guard to open the little aperture on the door and call out your name.

After the hearing, we were taken to the public ward, a hall with several rooms. I was transferred to room seven, and, a few days later, I found out Naji was in room three. Every twenty-four hours, we were allowed to leave the room only four times: an hour per day for a break in the fresh air and three times for bathroom use and prayer ablutions.

After lunch, a guard came and took us to the yard. The number of prisoners kept in the ward varied between thirty-five and forty, and we had to sleep side by side for lack of space. Upon entering the yard, some of the prisoners immediately started a game of volleyball, others sat down to the side to smoke, and I crouched down in a corner, a deep sorrow weighing on my heart, wondering if anyone there was more miserable than me. No. All those people had at least someone on the outside, a beloved who awaited them; everyone except me.

"Get up, boy, and find yourself a spot somewhere else. Come on. Get up. Don't want to be seeing you here."

I came to myself and looked up to see who was speaking. It was a man with harsh features, an old scar on his eyebrow, squatting and smoking. "Excuse me, who are you talking to?"

"To you. Don't argue with me. Just get up and go sit somewhere else. I beg you on your mother's grave."

He obviously was low-spirited, ready to burst into tears, but I felt he didn't have the right to talk to me like that. "See, my friend, we both are prisoners here, with a shared misery. You don't have the right to talk to me like that." Even though I was scared of the guy, I felt at least in there I should not be afraid of anyone, otherwise I'd be done for good.

"I don't like the scars on your face. It was the curse of someone like you that set my life on fire the other day," said the guy bitterly.

I felt like, fuck it. If I let him say whatever he wanted, then I had to suffer in my loneliness, swearing at myself for not having stood up to him. Anyway, my situation couldn't get worse than it already was. I got up. "I won't let you speak to me like that. Do you feel because I'm young and scarred you can say whatever you want? No. I'm not afraid of you."

He got up. He was much taller than me. He seemed to want to attack me. Suddenly, he yelled, "When I tell you I don't like you, I mean I don't like you. Now instead of standing here and bragging about stupid shit, get the fuck out of here before I do something both you and I will regret."

Two prisoners came toward us. A few others were watching us. I was getting ready for a fight.

270

"May you be healthy and happy, Agha Teymour. What's going on?" one of the prisoners asked the guy.

"Nothing. Just get this burnt-up kid out of my sight before I jump and strangle him against my own will. I just don't want to see his face right now."

"Strangle me? Do you think the law doesn't apply here?"

Another guy, also tall and big, put a gentle hand on my shoulder. "Actually, the law doesn't apply here, my dear boy; to tell you the truth, it's worse than that." He pulled me away to another corner of the yard, sat me down, and offered me a cigarette. I told him I didn't smoke. He lit one for himself and said, "You haven't yet gotten to know Agha Teymour. He's one of the kindest, most loyal fellows here."

"Of course, he did a great job showing me that side of himself," I said sarcastically.

The man smiled, trying to calm me down. "If I tell you what happened to him only a few days ago, you'll sit down and cry for him right here. I'm sure of it, because you seem to be a sensitive boy. I can tell from your eyes."

I remained silent and kept looking at him so he would continue. "A few days ago, his wife was supposed to come for a visit. She was supposed to bring their daughter too, but on the day of the visit, they didn't show up. Instead, his sister came with horrifying news about his daughter. Do you know what happened to her? Actually, no one really knows, because on the very first day of the war, Iraqi bombs targeted her school, killing many innocent girls and disappearing many others. Do you know what that means? It means these innocent girls are lost, and no one knows what has happened to them. Agha Teymour's daughter was one of them. So his wife didn't dare come visit and give him the news. When his sister came, she told him that his wife, the girl's mother, was at fault, because the woman had allowed one of her old friends into the house whose face had been covered with horrible burns and nasty scars, not like the small few on your face, no, not at all. Anyway, the curse of those scars caused the death of the six-year-old. I'm not superstitious, but poor Agha Teymour has had so many horrible things happen to him in the past two years that he has become superstitious, and too much so at that, like it or not. It's mainly his sister's fault, because she keeps whispering nonsense in his ears. So when he saw your scars, he was reminded of his own daughter. Now, you be a gentleman and don't take it personally. If you have a kid yourself, you'll understand how much he is suffering. Do you have a kid?"

"No, I don't."

"But you understand our Agha Teymour's pain, right?"

"Yes, I do."

"You're a good, kind boy. May you be healthy."

"But he and I are living in the same room. What if he keeps being harsh and swearing at me in front of everyone every day?"

"He won't. Don't worry. I'll talk to him and make him realize that you are different from the guy his sister has talked about. I'll tell him the scar on your face is not a curse. Now take this tissue and clean up your tears. Mashallah, you are a wise, educated big boy. A man like you should not be crying."

I didn't tell him my tears were for lost Hasti.

A few days later, two new prisoners were sent to our room. One of them was our own Amir the Troublemaker, and the other a man in his fifties with a thick mustache, hair full of gray strands, and slumping shoulders. He had obviously been beaten and tortured, with no visible signs of torture on his face.

Amir the Troublemaker recognized me after a while. We talked a bit about the past and laughed about a few of the people we knew. He then told me about his own charges. "In this hot weather, I was just strolling around when suddenly a Komiteh car with three morality police officers stopped in front of me. Why? Because I was wearing a short-sleeved T-shirt and Ray-Ban sunglasses. You remember how I always wore colorful T-shirts when it got hot. What's the problem with loving foreign-made T-shirts? I asked the officers who was bothered by my T-shirt or glasses. I told them how everyone knew that I'd been wearing short-sleeved T-shirts for years. One of them said things had changed, and I asked him what had changed, and he said, 'We're mourning our martyrs now, young men who've sacrificed their lives for this revolution so we can live in peace today.' He said, 'You should be thinking about them and how their bodies will tremble in the grave and their spirits will be tormented when they see that people like you are still wearing American-made T-shirts in the street.' I told him, 'Well, brother, look! First of all, I've been one of the main fighters for the victory of this revolution. If I and others like me had not been in the streets bringing down the shah's throne with our shouts, people like you would still be in your villages running after sheep.' The guard ordered me to speak more carefully, but I added, 'Second of all, the martyrs are having fun in heaven with the nymphs and fairies, my friend. Why would they care about me wearing a short-sleeved or long-sleeved T-shirt or sunglasses?' Some people standing close by listening to our conversation started laughing and clapping for me. The officers were offended, but they couldn't arrest everyone, so they threw me in the car and brought me here. And I kept cursing them all the way here. When we got here, they told me they'll keep me here as long as it takes for me to repent and beg them for forgiveness. But I don't have any intention of repenting for now." He laughed loudly. "They think I'll give up soon and start begging them."

I laughed too. "They didn't know your nickname is Amir the Troublemaker."

"I swear on your life, this time I wasn't the one starting the trouble. No. It was them who stirred it up."

His being there was good for me. We talked, and, during the fresh-air breaks, we played games and entertained ourselves. But I witnessed how he once again got himself into trouble, ending up in the ward's interrogation room, where he was beaten for hours. The story was that some prisoners made things by hand to keep themselves busy. For example, they turned old unusable socks into threads. Two people worked on one sock and, after a while, had pulled a handful of colorful threads from it, which were then used for various handicrafts; some people did embroidery with them, creating images of flowers or houses, or sewing words into cloth. Amir the Troublemaker, too, spent a few nights sewing something on the back of his T-shirt using those colorful threads. I noticed that he was busy with his T-shirt but didn't pay much attention to what image or words he was sewing. Until that day when we were out in the yard playing volleyball together. I was facing the door and the two guards, and Amir had his back to them. Suddenly, I saw the guards walking over to where we were playing, all the time staring at Amir's lower back. They stopped our game when they got there. The older guard held Amir's shoulders and made an effort to read what was written on his shirt. It was in English. He hardly read it. *"Freedon?"*

"This is not *Freedon*, officer, no." Amir grimaced.

"Is the last letter an *N* or an *M*?"

"*M*, Haji," the younger guard said.

The older one tried reading it once again. "Okay, then, it's *Freedom*. What does that mean?"

"You don't know, sir?"

The younger guard pretended they did. "Of course, we do, bro, but we want to hear it from you, to see if you know what's on your back after all the trouble you've gone through to write it and show it off."

"*Freedom* means liberty, officer. That's what it means in English. Liberation," Amir said and continued mockingly, "Do you remember the slogans we chanted? The only way to freedom is—"

The younger guard stopped him midsentence. "Who has ordered you to write such nonsense on your shirt? Is that a party order?"

Amir realized from their attitude that they were getting infuriated, so he looked down and remained silent. The younger guard said, "Do you think we are like the foreign countries where you can do whatever the fuck you want without anyone bothering you? No, bro. Here, we'll skin you alive for writing this bullshit on your T-shirt. You'll see."

When we were taken inside, one of the guards took Amir to the ward's interrogation room and returned him four or five hours later. He had been beaten, and his face was completely red from the slaps. He had also been forced to pull the threads of the words out of his T-shirt with his teeth and nails to mess it up. After that incident, Amir changed. He would sit in a corner without talking to anyone. He was traumatized. If you paid attention, you could still see traces of the word *Freedom* on the lower back of Amir's T-shirt.

There was another prisoner who was brought to our room at the same time as Amir, and his only crime was having been a communist and a political prisoner during the shah's era. He said he had spent seven years of his life in various prisons, transferred from one city to another, until finally ending up there again. He said that a month before, his house had been raided in the middle of the night, and he had been arrested. The whole month he was tortured to confess what communist party he was working for, and no matter how much he swore he had put politics completely aside and had no interest in it whatsoever, they had not believed him and had told him they would keep him there as long as it took, until he confessed what party leadership he was a member of.

His eyes filled with tears when he was talking to me. "I swear to God, I'm not anymore. I swear on the Prophet, I'm not a member anymore. But no one listens, no one believes, my dear boy."

Every room had its own boss, chosen from the prisoners, who then assigned chores to others; for example, one prisoner was in charge of cleaning the room, another of receiving the food rations, another of distributing newspapers, and I was in charge of taking care of and watering the plants in our room, and had a special little bowl to do that. We had about a dozen different plants put together by the prisoners themselves, on the windowsills around the room, that I had to check on every day. One evening, when everyone was sitting around in groups of three or four playing different games, I started attending to the plants. One of the things I liked about my role was that, since the plants were on higher shelves, I had to pull myself up onto the windowsill to reach them, and when I did that, I could glance at the city through the gaps above the sill. A long street frequented by cars. Sometimes I saw people, free people who strolled along the sidewalks, alone or together, hands in their pockets. The tall streetlamps that were now off because of the war and were not to be turned on. I wondered whether those people were aware of the taste of the freedom they had. Right, there was the war, and everyone was caught up in that miserable event, but at least they all had the choice to roll into a trench or take cover in any safe space when an air raid happened, but we, the prisoners, had nowhere to go other than our room, which could be blown up at any moment by one of those heavy explosives coming from the other side of the river, turning all of us in a split second into ashes spread out in the air, and then we would be nothing but dead people with no corpses.

There is no horror worse than hearing enemy planes flying in the sky overhead, aiming to drop bombs, and not even having the choice to run and take shelter. I kept telling myself not to think about it. Thinking about some events is more painful than the event itself. I had already made all the leaves of the plant in front of me shine with a wet piece of cloth, so I jumped down and went to the rest of them. Some prisoners had placed pictures of their mothers or friends or children among the leaves. Now that I'm writing this, I, too, have a few coleus plants, but no pictures of anyone to place among their leaves. The plants are right here on the windowsill next to my desk. The same color as the three plants on the windowsill in the prison room. Among the leaves of the plant, in the middle, there was a picture of Hasti placed securely enough not to fall. I took better care of that one. I watered them three or four times every week and tried to cut their stems to shape them beautifully. When we shook the blankets in the mornings before folding them, the air filled with wool dust, part of which entered our lungs and the rest of which sat over everything in the room, especially the leaves of the plants; so in order to clean the leaves, first I had to move the pictures. I removed Hasti's picture, but instead of getting to the leaves, I got lost looking at Hasti, staring at her laughing eyes, remembering her putting makeup on my face, explaining to us how to get to her school, and the joy of listening to the way she pronounced her words.

And now, staring at the picture, I couldn't tell if I was laughing or crying, maybe crying in my heart, but there was a smile on my lips, and perhaps it was that smile that irritated Teymour. Suddenly, an arm rushed toward me and snapped the picture out of my hand. Then there was silence. Everyone in the room noticed Teymour's move, but no one dared say anything; they all just looked at us, and, as my eyes filled with tears, I continued cleaning the leaves. I couldn't sleep all that night and cried under my blanket. I couldn't tell Teymour how much I loved his little daughter, no, I couldn't, because he might have strangled me right then and there. So I had no choice but to remain silent and cry all by myself. I had started to believe that the reason behind that disaster was the presence of my scarred face in that house. If it weren't for the curse of my scars, Hasti would still be around, with her aunt and mother, and, sometimes, her father.

Naji's face was scarred now too. I noticed traces of beatings and torture on his face when I saw him in the prison yard one day and stepped closer. Usually, the prisoners in different rooms were brought out separately; each room had an hour, then they would all go back, and it was the next room's turn. The rounds started in the morning and continued until the afternoon, but that day the guards had decided to finish them all before noon and be done with them. The prisoners said it was because the Iraqi radio had announced the bombings would start at around 1 p.m., and the guards wanted everyone to be back in their rooms well before one o'clock that day so they themselves could go hide in the shelters peacefully and not be targeted by the bombs. They had brought both of our rooms out at the same time, and when the guard guided us to the center of the yard with his stick, as if we were sheep, the yard was already busy. Some prisoners started running around the area. Others started running after one another and laughing. I noticed Naji in the crowd, squatting in a corner.

The moment I walked toward him, a guard shouted, "Room three prisoners hurry up and come over here."

Naji was a resident of room three and had to go. Their guard was standing by the door and kept calling them and sending them into the hallway one by one. "Hurry up, your time is up, brothers."

Naji stopped short, seeing me.

"What happened? Why did they beat you?"

"They're looking for Suren and his friends. They want to know where they are."

"Well, you know where they are!"

He stared into the depths of my eyes. "No. I don't anymore. I know nothing."

The guard shouted once again. "Are you deaf? Hurry up. I'm closing the hallway door. Hey, you faggot, I'm talking to you." He was pointing at Naji.

Naji simply smiled and left. He was gone, and now, only we the prisoners in room seven remained in the yard. No matter how hard I tried to erase the image of his beaten-up face, I could not; his face was in front of my face, and the ring of his last word in my ears: "Nothing."

That day, both the Iraqi radio announcement and the prisoners' guesses about the guards wanting to hide in the shelters turned out to be true, except that the bombings started at two instead of one. The building we were in trembled every few minutes, and we all shouted out of fear, but there was no one around to hear us but the prisoners in the other rooms, whose shouts we could also hear. Our screams of terror were expressed with the same words that once were the words of victory shouted in the streets, Allahu Akbar, a repeated reminder of the greatness of God.

That day I woke up earlier than others with the sparrows making a lot of noise behind our prison room window. Maybe they were singing a song or something. It seemed no one heard those sounds other than me. Everyone was still deeply asleep, so I felt that the birds had a message just for me. There was no good news to be found there, so I had to expect something doomed. Death that could lead to freedom. Freedom? Am I free now? Have you ever felt yourself being trapped by your own betrayal?

"Don't think about it as betrayal, bro. Think about how you're first helping the revolution and second helping yourself. You'll get a good prize for it. A prize of being alive, of life, and what's better than that in this world?" the man told me.

I didn't have anything to say other than what he asked of me.

After breakfast, the little aperture on the door opened, and a set of eyes looked around the room, then the lips attached to the face called my name, and I was sure then that the sparrows had had a message for me. A message or a warning? Whatever money I had, I had already stowed away in my pockets and my clothes. The guard guided me blindfolded through the hallway and took me to the interrogation room.

I did not recognize the interrogator's voice. "There's no need to remove your blindfold," he said, then told me what he wanted from me. "I've heard you are smarter than your friend. We should've come to you from the very beginning to ask. We're not going to harm them or anything, 'cause their party is allowed to have its activities, but, well, some of them are the roguish type. When you lead us to them, we'll just ask them some questions and that's it. Okay, now let's get to it. You two have been there and know the address."

Even though I did not believe his promises about reducing my sentence and the rest of it, I cooperated with him, because I didn't want them to do to me what they'd done to Naji. No. I was dead tired of being beaten and tortured. He then sent me to wait in the hallway with my blindfold on while they prepared for the mission. I sat there for hours. At noon, a guard put a plate of rice and stew and a plastic spoon in my hand. A bit after lunch, our group, consisting of seven guards in two private cars and one Komiteh Patrol car, left the prison. What a nice feeling it was, sitting in a car and moving through the town, until we arrived at the town square. I remembered the night the shah's statue was brought down. How excited Naji was. He kept bouncing away from me, running into the crowd and trying to help with the rope. One end of it was around the shah's neck and the other down there in people's hands as they pulled and jubilated.

"Do you know how spiritually rewarding it is to touch the rope, give a hand in bringing down the statue?" Naji asked me.

And now, that statue was not up there anymore, and nothing else was there except an infinite void. The guard sitting in the passenger seat asked the driver to stop in the square. People were gathering in the middle of the square, where there was no grass anymore. I noticed five corpses wrapped in gray blankets at the foot of the stone pedestal. The guard got out and said he would be back soon. A few other armed men stood there too, as if waiting for someone. People looked happy, didn't seem to be worried about bombs. From the conversation between the guards, I figured the bodies belonged to those responsible for the theater fire; they had just been executed. I had seen scenes from their court hearing on the prison TV, so I knew that one of those bodies belonged to one of the theater workers, another to the owner of the building, and another to a police officer from the shah's time.

Our guard returned, and the caravan set off once again. He recounted that during the execution, the bullets from a guard's gun had ricocheted off the pedestal and hit one of the onlookers, a villager. He added how fortunate the man was to become a martyr at the scene. Everyone in the car laughed except me, there with them only because I was going to betray Suren, who had been so good to Naji and me. I kept telling him, in my heart, how sorry I was and asking him to forgive me, that I had no other choice. The guards were aware that I knew their hideout. I told Suren that the interrogator had told me they wouldn't do anything to him and his fellow party members, just ask some questions. Suren himself had once said that their party and the new regime shared similar beliefs, and none would harm the other. So why had they kept their party base hidden?

"What are you whispering to yourself?"

"Me? Nothing, brother."

"Which direction should we go now?"

"Toward the grain silo."

We were driving away from the town center, which was full of wandering soldiers with no weapons in their hands, army soldiers and volunteer forces. The incessant sound of explosions filled the air, and it was not clear where they were coming from. The last time I had passed this road I had noticed the electricity poles lining up on the two sides, their shadows lying down on the pavement. Back then, we were in the Jeep driven by Suren. He talked of politics, and I was saddened by the shadows run over by the car tires.

"Are you listening to me, kids?"

"Yes, Agha Suren."

"I noticed you were looking behind you, and I thought you were not listening."

"No, Agha Suren, I was with you."

"Anyway, socialism aims to free humans, similar to what religion does; it's just that one has to do with the material world and the other with the spiritual world."

That day when I was in the car with the guards, the shadows were not there anymore, even though the electricity poles were still there on both sides of the road. The car I was in drove ahead of the others because I was the guide. I kept looking for the sun but didn't find it. An infinite gray veil had blocked the sky. Black smoke rose into the sky and blended with the veil.

"Look in front of you, brother, so you don't lose the directions."

"We're getting there."

After several turns to the right and the left, we arrived at that back-street. The public phone booth was still there, even though it was tilted and falling to the ground. The neighborhood, maybe because it was farther from the water, still seemed safe, not as much evidence of explosions and fewer ruins. Above the building entrance, a sign read, "Revolution Nursery." The cars came to a stop. Except for the driver of the car I was in, everyone got out. All of them had guns. They rang the doorbell and went inside. I didn't want to look in that direction. I didn't want to. I just wanted to be dead. I wanted to not be at all, or to be anywhere but there. I wanted to at least be blind and not see that Suren's beautiful yellow Jeep was parked there at a corner of the street. What could I do other than put my forehead on the back of the front seat and push my eyes against it so hard that my eyes popped out. But I kind of knew I would see that Jeep there, a car filled with the good memories of laughing with Naji, of Suren's kindness. I could understand now why Naji had not given the interrogators the location—because he knew what horror would befall him. I felt like a truckload of soil had been emptied on top of my body, or perhaps I should have written a truckload of shit.

The location was much more important than I had thought, and the guards knew this. They knew that important documents were printed there and that key figures of the party who were still in town met there. They had stayed behind because they wanted to stand against the enemy in a war they called a war against the homeland, organizing their own forces to fight side by side with the soldiers. Now, some of the guards were inside the building, and some were on the lookout outside. The driver and I were at a distance. The driver had his hands on the steering wheel and stared at the door of the nursery, like a cat ready to bounce, but I was trying not to look. Fear had taken over my body and mind. Hunkering down in the backseat, unable to feel the passage of time, I felt nothing but horror. I couldn't tell how long it took until they started to bring women and men out of the building. A photographer who was among the guards took a picture of each person, and then another guard pushed that person into the Patrol. I had never felt so degraded and ashamed. All of them were in trouble because of me, even though the interrogator had said they just wanted to ask some questions. What was going on now revealed that it wasn't only that but was much bigger than that.

"Do you see how many condoms they've pulled out of there? Condoms and birth control," said the driver. I noticed a guard standing next to the door of the building, holding several boxes that I couldn't recognize in front of the photographer to take pictures of.

I asked, "Excuse me, but why did they have so many condoms and pills there? What's been going on there?" The words broke down in my throat.

The driver laughed and glanced at me, giving me a smile, though one filled with disgust. "It seems you are clueless. These communists have no issues whatsoever with sex, and anyone can fuck anyone, but because they don't want to get pregnant, they, mashallah, use a lot of condoms. Those who want to enjoy it more give the women the pills instead." He then pointed to a woman just brought out by a guard. "Look, that's one of those women."

Suddenly his attention was diverted to something at a farther corner of the street. "Oh, that guy seems to have come from the back of this same building and is leaving. Look, look, none of the brothers is noticing it. Look, he's gone." I could see a man who, away from the eyes of the others, rushed toward the end of the street. The driver was alarmed. "Stay here. I'll be back in a second."

He got out of the car, locked the door on his own side, and ran to the end of the street, and I was left there in a car no one was paying attention to, but I didn't have any hopes, because I thought he had locked all the doors, but he hadn't; the back doors were open. When I started thinking of escape, my fear multiplied a thousand times. I quietly opened the door, got out, and stood there next to the car for a bit to see if anyone said anything. But no one did, because no one was paying attention to me. My eyes stopped seeing anything other than shadows moving back and forth. I started walking away from them, toward a narrow side street full of trees. There was no one there. I kept walking without knowing where my hands and legs were and what they were doing. I felt a shadow following me, the heavy thick metal of the tip of a weapon pressing against my temple. I kept getting more and more distant from those streets. Then a large barren empty lot guided me through to a row of newly built beautiful expensive houses. After some roaming and searching with horror, I finally dropped down on the ground next to the wall of a house. It was obvious that the residents had left the house behind. I didn't have any more energy to get up and move; I didn't even know where I could go. I guessed that several guards were now looking for me in the area. I was a crumpled heap on the ground and had my head between my knees when I felt the heavy shadow of someone's eyes fall over me. I looked up. An old woman came out of the house and stared at me, as if staring at a trapped animal. I looked back at her beggingly. She went in and closed the door. I thought she was calling the police or the guards, informing them of my suspicious presence there, and that I had to get up and continue running away, but I was no longer in charge of my legs.

I thought, "Well, this is the end of the line, and now you have to get back to your cell, this time enduring even more pain, a hundred times more than before, until you are hanged, and the pain ends forever." The door to the house opened again. A young tall and sturdy woman came out, a club in her hand, followed by the old woman. The young woman asked me who I was and what I wanted. I broke down crying and told them I was a prisoner on the run but that I was innocent and had been arrested for no reason and was going to be hanged. The two women talked with each other in the Gilaki language, which I didn't understand. Then the young woman turned to me and told me they would give me shelter. They guided me inside to a small storage room at the back of the yard and gave me water and food. The old woman cried and said her son had recently been executed by the regime. She said he had been a simple officer during the shah's time, but he had been arrested for the crime of collaborating with the shah's security forces, endured several months in prison, and last month, the mother and sister, the young woman, had been informed of his execution. I asked them why they had not yet left the town.

"Do you mean to leave my beloved behind here and go? No, I can't," said the old woman.

"But we have to eventually leave. There's no other choice," said the young one.

They offered me food and safety, and who else other than God could I be grateful to that there were still kind people in the world. If everyone was like the guards and the traitors I had seen until then, what filth would take over the whole globe. If everyone was simply a spectator to the events, like the ones who had sold their souls and the ones who had a seal of silence out of fear, even smiling out of fear, a smile that then turned into hypocrisy, finally transforming into neighborhood and public betrayals.

George, too, had remained in his house all by himself and didn't intend to leave town. He had sent his wife and girls to a distant town. "If I, too, leave, who is going to check on our young man in these circumstances?" He meant Ararat.

"But he's now resting there peacefully, free from any disturbance," Suren replied. Suren, too, had found refuge at George's house. I didn't think I could find George, and yet the day after my escape and taking shelter at the women's house, I headed toward George's house, because that was the only place I knew in town, the only place whose owner I hoped would take me in if I found him.

"The party base has been exposed. Did you know?" Suren asked me. And I looked at him and felt how lucky I was to be there. "No! What? When? What happened to your Jeep, Agha Suren?"

"My Jeep? Which one? How so?"

"Nothing really. I was just asking."

"He didn't sell it to me, went ahead and sold it to the comrades," said George.

"That car wasn't good for you, monsieur. Take that from me," said Suren inattentively.

"When I think that you, too, might have been there and gotten arrested, I get pretty sad, Suren. Who knew which black hole you were in now," said George.

"Black hole? No. It's not like that. I'm sure everyone will be freed one of these days. Our party is not in conflict with the regime. Do you know what the prints were that they confiscated? I mean our last bulletin. It was about this war being one against our homeland and that everyone in the country had to serve the war in whatever capacity they have. In that bulletin, we remind people that each person should do as much as they can. Do you know what that means?"

"Yes, my dear Suren, yes, you've told me that a hundred times so far, but I'm talking about you, your own body."

Yet Suren didn't pay attention to George at all and once again said, "We meant that anyone who is young and can carry a weapon should do so, of course under supervision and military command. And if someone is a doctor, they should go to the front and help the wounded."

George mockingly continued what Suren was saying. "Those who are mothers should sit by the oven and bake bread for the soldiers. Opium traffickers should go to the front and provide the trenches with supplies."

I burst out laughing, and as I saw George light up, I laughed even more, but Suren lit another cigarette as an objection to my laughter, so I stopped laughing.

"Well, now what are you implying by all this, Monsieur Suren?" asked George.

Suren didn't say anything, simply kept puffing at his cigarette. Intending to lighten the mood and tease Suren, George said, "So tell me, how come your party used so many condoms and birth control pills in its office?" He laughed again. Even though I wanted to join him in laughing, I stayed silent out of respect for Suren.

"What a ridiculous show . . . What lies!"

"I'm asking a serious question."

"You mean you don't know that such tricks are used to smear the party's reputation?"

George kept laughing. His laughter made me feel better, decreasing my fear. We were hiding in a corner of George's house, under a staircase, that, based on his calculations, was the safest place in all the house, kind of functioning like a trench. The space had been the storage room before, where they kept work equipment and various odds and ends, but now George had turned it into a small room by spreading a carpet on the floor and placing a samovar in a corner. George, too, had picked up smoking.

The sound of explosions didn't stop in the town for one second. They asked about what I had gone through, and I told them my whole story, from the time we left them up to the present moment. No, I'm lying. I didn't tell them about my arrest and how I had escaped but instead told the story in a way to make them think that only Naji had been arrested, for having had a physical fight with Kavous.

I could feel that even though Suren pretended to be optimistic, he was pretty scared and was glad he had not been at the party base during the raid. And I was even gladder. I had figured out that he aimed to leave the country, and even though he had an official passport, he could not go through legal routes for two reasons: one, that airports and other official departure modes were shut down, and two, that he was afraid of being recognized and arrested. His being Christian could be another cause of trouble for him. So members of the party in Tehran were helping him leave through clandestine paths along the western border, reach the neighboring country, and from there head to the US.

In the past two years, almost all his family had migrated to the US. He said that on the other side of the border, human rights organizations would help him out, because he was both of a religious minority and a political activist.

Away from Suren's eyes, I showed George the money I had with me and asked him to ask Suren to take me with him, at least to the other side of the border, and George discussed this with Suren. Suren didn't know what to say, and George kept trying to talk him into it. "Look, the boy has his own money to give the smuggler. Also, you'll be heavily guilty if you can take him and don't."

"Why would I be guilty, monsieur?"

"If he stays here and is arrested, and is hanged along with his friend, then who would be guilty for that?"

Suren remained silent for a bit and then said, "I should talk to Nasir. If he agrees, I have no problems. I'd love to help. And it's not bad to have a young man accompany you under these circumstances."

He asked me, "How much money do you have?" I showed him all the money I had. "I must talk to Nasir. He'd know if it's possible or not."

Now George was doing all he could to send me away with Suren. He wanted Suren to give him assurances that he would try his best.

"Only if you promise me that you're going to leave town soon and go to your kids. You must promise me."

"I promise, monsieur. I promise you."

Nasir was a short, thin, and agile Kurdish man, and he had a minibus. When we got into his minibus, wearing the Kurdish clothes he had given us, there were already several other men and women there too. He had taught each and every one of us what to say if we were stopped and asked questions by the patrol guards. For example, he had told Suren to say his son was a soldier serving in Kurdistan and that they hadn't had any news from him, and because the boy's mother was restless, he was now going to look for his son. He had told me to say I was from Khoram Shahr and worked there, but my family lived in

Kurdistan, but now that the war had started, I was headed there to join them. But at the checkpoint, I was stupid and said other things. I couldn't remember what Nasir had said and told the guard some other things by mistake. Nasir also picked some travelers who were really headed to Kurdistan; he wanted to pretend he was a simple driver transferring passengers.

A young man around my age got in who had several scars on his body: a big gauze on his chin, some scratches on his forehead but no gauze covering them, and one hand bandaged. The seat next to me was empty because everyone seeing my facial scars preferred not to sit there. Suren, too, had said it was best that we pretend not to know each other at all and not sit with each other. The scarred side of my face was toward the window and could not be seen from the aisle, especially if I looked straight ahead. The young man was Kurdish and said his name was Omar. During the ride, he told me about his life. I was full of fear, and he full of stories to tell. He said he had been a porter in the previous regime in Khoram Shahr and Abadan, hanging around the river with other Kurdish porters and transporting the loads from the boats to the land on their backs. He said even though it had been a hard job, he had good days in those towns.

As he talked, he ate almonds he pulled out of his bag, which he shared with me, and I munched them to take my mind off the risk of being arrested. He said when the revolution happened, he returned to Kurdistan, hoping to find a good job in his own town and stay with his family, because he imagined the situation would improve in the country, but with the victory of the revolution, Kurdish political parties attempted to gain independence from the central government, causing the new regime to enter a war not only with the parties and political entities but also with all people of Kurdistan province, a brutal merciless war. The guards sent from the capital wanted to terrorize the locals so that no one would wish for independence anymore, so they started killing people in the streets, holding public group executions, and then bombing the villages with planes. As he described it, there was nothing but fire and death all over the region, so, upon his mother's advice, he left Kurdistan for Abadan again, to at least be away from danger, but then the Iraqi attacks on Abadan started, and once again he found himself amid violence and rampant fires. He said the scars on his hand and face were due to fires. He told the story of a family whose house was on fire and, passing by, he learned that a little girl was stuck inside; none of the men watching had the courage to go inside, but Omar, like those in action movies, took the risk and went into the house, saved the girl from the fire, but injured himself. I told him I had seen the exact same scene, in which he was the hero, in several movies. He remained silent for a bit, then asked me what kinds of films I was interested in, and I told him Indian movies with dance and music. He said he liked detective movies and loved the Kojak series. He then threw me a suspicious look and asked if I was sure I liked Indian movies. I asked him what the problem was with that. He laughed and said Indian films are made for girls, adding that it was the first time he had met a man my age who liked them. Anyway, he kept babbling on until we arrived at a patrol station on the road.

The soldier at the side of the road signaled the driver to stop. The minibus stopped, and the soldier told Nasir to wait until his superior came, before running to the newly constructed building of the station. A little bit later, a police officer came out. The road was not busy, and only our car had been stopped. There were a few military Jeeps and a Patrol car parked around there, but no one was in them. The officer got in.

"Brothers, may you not feel tired of the road," he said, and each of us gave him one or another response. He was thin and so tall he had to stoop, because the roof of the minibus was too short for him. His eyes kept moving between us and the building. He kept looking at each and every one of us as if he was looking for something we didn't know about. He asked Omar who he was and where he was headed and what the story of his scars was. Omar told him what he had told me, and the officer asked him to show his identity card. Omar brought out a birth certificate from his bag and handed it to the officer, who studied the picture and checked it with Omar's face. "Are you sure this is your own certificate, boy?"

"Yes, officer. Doesn't the photo look like me?"

"It seems you took it in your old age, you young boy."

Omar laughed. "Are you teasing me, Officer?"

"What are all these stamps on your certificate?"

"For voting, Officer. Don't you vote yourself, Officer? Aren't you aware of these stamps for voting?"

"It's none of your business whether I vote or not. Here, put this back in your bag. Haven't they taught you that talking too much might get you in trouble, young man?"

Omar got his documents back and responded in a low voice, "They have, sir."

"Thank God you understand some things, then," said the officer. He then turned to me and asked, "How about you, young man? Why are you headed to Kurdistan? What's your business there?"

"I'm going for work," I responded, my voice trembling, my mouth feeling dry.

"Going to Kurdistan for work?" He bent out of the window and called out, "Kheir Allah, hey, Kheir Allah," and then continued toward me. "But there is a war going on there. Everyone is running away from it, going to safety, but you are headed there to make money?"

An old man who was sitting behind me, whom I hadn't noticed before, said, "Oh, dear officer, don't you know? War is to make some people rich. Haven't you heard our supreme leader say war is a blessing? What does that mean? That means there's a lot of money to be made in war."

The soldier was running out of the station building toward us. The same soldier who had stopped us, stopped when he reached the minibus and tried to do a proper military salute, but he seemed to be tripping on a pebble and was almost about to fall. Eventually, he held his hand to his temples. "Yes, sir."

The officer talked to him through the window. "Don't let him take the women. I'm not yet done with them. Hurry up and tell them I said they should hold on until I come. I have work to do."

"Yes, sir," said the soldier, then turned around military-style to go, but suddenly an army Jeep sped past us on the road, and if Kheir Allah had not paid attention, he would surely be hit. He stood there scared, looked in both directions, and then headed to the red building.

The officer told the old man, "That's not what the leader meant, dear man. He meant spiritual blessing, not materialistic." He turned to me and asked, "How about you, my boy, do you have your birth certificate with you?"

"Yes, sir."

"Look at me. Turn toward me so I can hear you and get what you are mumbling." He had his eyes on both inside the bus and outside around the building. I hesitantly turned toward him, and he saw the scarred side of my face. "Oh, oh, were you, too, in that fire, my dear boy?"

"No, sir."

"Where's your birth certificate? Please pull it out and show it to me."

I looked through my bag for the certificate I didn't have. The old man said, "A blessing is a blessing, dear officer, whether it's spiritual or materialistic. It doesn't matter. Any blessing offered by him is welcomed because it comes from him."

But the officer was not paying attention to what he was saying anymore, because he was staring at the building, where two men in military uniform were now taking three women wearing colorful Kurdish clothing out of the building and toward their Patrol. All the women were blindfolded, had their hands on each other's shoulders, and were walking cautiously. He told me, "Hurry up and find your birth certificate. Soldier Kheir Allah will come to you," and hurriedly left the bus, running toward the women. Before he got there, he called Kheir Allah. He came and once again gave a military salute. The officer told him something and pointed to the bus. They were far from us, and we couldn't hear their conversation. The soldier got on the bus and said in a loud voice, "The scarred boy." He looked at Omar, looked outside and called out to the officer to ask him something, but the officer just made a gesture and turned toward the women again. Forming his hands into a handcuff, he had hinted that the soldier should arrest me and take me out of the bus, but he thought he had to arrest Omar, so he ordered him, "Let's go, bro, with all your belongings. Your bag and everything else, all of it. Hurry up, we are late, and military work should be on time. Come on."

Omar threw me a glance, but I had my head down and didn't want to reveal any expression. "I'm sorry, but I think you've made a mistake, officer."

The soldier spit outside and turned to Omar again. "No, you're the one who's making a mistake, bro. Aren't you scarred?"

"Yes, but . . ." Omar said this and looked at me, and I was feeling the weight of his eyes on me. "Don't forget your birth certificate," ordered the soldier and hopped down, waiting for Omar, lost in watching the women. The officer was not paying any attention to us, was busy talking to the military people standing by the blindfolded women. It seemed they had a disagreement about taking or not taking the women. Scared, Omar hesitantly took his bag and, while his heavy look was still on me, headed to the bus door and left. The soldier took his hand and pulled him away. No one spoke. A horrifying silence had overtaken the bus, and I was dying of fear. Everyone knew the officer had meant me and that the soldier had taken Omar by mistake. I could not see anything but darkness. Then I realized the bus was moving slowly. The officer was still negotiating about the women. The soldier was taking Omar to the building, and I could not do anything but close my eyes to not see anything. And I didn't see anything, and I remained like that until I felt the bus moving along the road. When I opened my eyes, there was only the road and nothing else. The road and silence. Then there were dirt roads, and we didn't come upon any checkpoints.

For a long stretch of the road in the mountains of Kurdistan, we were transported by donkeys. It wasn't just Suren and me, but several other families too. When we were crossing the border, Suren kept sobbing, "Why should I leave my own country? Why should I run away?"

Everyone looked at him in silence. He seemed to be changing his mind and wanting to go back, but it was too late. In Turkey, our group was divided. Everyone had someone who was waiting for them, everyone except me. A man and woman came after Suren and took him with them. He kissed my forehead and asked me to take good care of myself and not to be fooled by anyone and everyone. He apologized for not being able to take me with him, because the rest of their trip was planned just for him. He held me in his arms and cried and said he hoped he would see me in one or another corner of the world again. He wished me health and happiness, leaving me behind while looking at me through a veil of tears before disappearing with that man and woman.

After two months of wandering in hopelessness, I finally found some people who helped me figure out the rest of the way. Those were good days, and Iranians outside the country still loved each other and tried to help each other out. Thank God things were not like today back then, otherwise, I would still be roaming around adrift, looking for a way to get here, to this land far away from the terror of being hanged and dying.

So, Naji, I finally made it, reaching what I had wished for all my life, a wish both of us wanted, with each other and for each other; I mean music and dance classes. But you were not with me anymore, or perhaps I should say you were with me but out of reach. You were always a ghost and a ray of light, and I knew that if one day you could see that I have become a professional dancer, you would be very happy. And this was the reason I continued, because it wasn't easy at all in that foreign land. In the beginning, I thought about the possibility of your return, imagining the door to my room opening and you stepping across the threshold, wearing a smile on your face. "Do you see, I eventually came." But later, when I finally accepted that you were dead and there was to be no return, I thought about your spirit being at peace (if your murderer could allow you any peace). Anyway, I worked hard and kept myself motivated, and after many years, I finally got on stage and can now dance in front of people—but only for you.

But the pain is still here with me, Naji. Pain is always here, the pain of thinking about you and unwillingly seeing, and not being able to make it disappear, the damned scene in which the crane with the hanging rope pulled you up, dragging that beautiful slender body of yours all the way up to the black well of death. The pain of thinking about my own betrayal of Suren. A thousand other incurable pains lining up in my head, each day one of them showing itself off, and I try to write them down, thinking maybe they will let me have some peace. The very miracle of writing so deeply entangles me with you that I hope afterward I can move away from you, free myself from you, shifting you from the intimate *you* position to that of the distant *he*.

I don't mean harm, my beloved, but sometimes it is necessary for me to take the opportunity to survey my present home, to see where I am and hear the voice that is now calling my name in the street facing my window, a muffled voice that seems to be passing through a tunnel to reach me. This is the voice of my neighbor, a man who has no one except three dogs that he brings early every morning to poop and pee and take a walk to the green area in front of the building, while he himself loiters around in the cold, looking for a neighbor or passerby who would pause for a moment and listen to his words, his never-ending repetitive words. All he says is that God intends to punish humanity on account of the crimes and betrayals of some of us, and soon he'll explode half of planet Earth (still unknown which half) from within and without, destroying it forever.

And that's the end of our story . . .

Glossary

Abolfazl: Half brother of Imam Husayn, the third Shiite imam, who was killed during the Battle of Karbala, fighting alongside his brother.

Agha: When used on its own, simply as *the Agha*, throughout the book, it refers to Imam Khomeini, founder of the Islamic Republic, who lived in exile in France and returned to Iran in 1979. When used next to proper names, it simply means *Mr., sir.*

Agha joon: Literally translates to *dear sir*, but it is used in addressing fathers and grandfathers.

Allahu Akbar: Literally translates to *God is the Greatest* and is used in various contexts, for example during daily prayers, funerals, and protests.

apostates: People who are nonbelievers or have renounced Islam.

arak: An alcoholic drink made of grapes and aniseed. In Iran the term is used for vodka or any alcoholic drink in general.

Azan: The Islamic call to prayer.

Bahá'í Faith: A monotheist religion that originated in Iran in the nineteenth century. Its followers, Bahá'ís, have been considered infidels and faced persecution since the establishment of the Islamic Republic regime.

basij: A militia unit working under the Islamic Revolutionary Guard Corps, with responsibilities covering domestic security, particularly in relation to religious and political issues as well as moralities.

besmellah: Literally translates to *In the Name of God*. It is used as an encouragement phrase when initiating a task, similar to *Let's do it.*

Bibi: A term of respect and endearment used for women, especially women of older age. It often is used as part of the name of an older woman.

Chelo Kabob: A dish of rice and kabob. Chelo is the term used for cooked white rice when not mixed with any other ingredients.

djinns: Invisible mythological beings, capable of assuming human or animal form and said to have extraordinary powers.

Fateheh prayer: The prayer recited at funerals. Fateheh is the title of the first surah of the Quran, which is part of the prayer used at funeral rituals.

Fatemeh el-Zahra: The daughter of Prophet Mohammad and wife of the Imam Ali, the first Shiite Imam.

fatwa: An Islamic ruling made by a religious authority, often with regard to contemporary issues that need interpretation of Islamic laws and texts.

haram: Forbidden or unlawful according to the Islamic law. It is used in relation to certain acts and foods; for example, eating pork and drinking alcohol are considered haram.

Hezbollahi: Hezbollahis are conservative religious people who organize and act in response to what they consider assaults to the Islamic law or the leader of the Islamic Republic. Historically, they have stood above the law and not been persecuted for their actions even when disrupting social order. Not to be confused with Lebonan's Hezbollah Organization.

hijab: Islamic dress code for both women and men, though the rules are stricter for women, who are forced to cover their hair and most of their body parts.

Imam: A term used for Muslim religious leaders. In Shiite Islam, it is used for the twelve religious leaders succeeding Prophet Mohammad. In the case of Imam Khomeini, the term refers to his religious leadership and is simply used as part of his name.

Imam Ali: In Shiite Islam, Ali ibn Abi Talib is the successor of Prophet Mohammad and considered the first imam. He was also married to the Prophet's daughter Fatemeh el-Zahra.

inshallah: From the Arabic phrase *in sha Allah*, with a slightly different pronunciation but the same usage and meaning of *If God Wills*.

kaka: A term used to refer to an older brother or a person who feels like an older brother.

keffiyeh: A traditional headdress worn by men in southwestern regions of Iran, providing protection against the sun and sand. Different varieties are worn across the Middle East.

kolucheh: An Iranian cookie, varieties of which are made in different regions of the country.

Komiteh: In full, Komiteh-ye Enghelab, or the Islamic Revolution Committees, was an organization founded in 1979. One of its main duties was street patrols to oversee public adherence to Islamic morality codes, public demeanor, and anti-regime activities.

maghna'eh: A specific form of women's headscarf used as the compulsory hair hijab in schools, government offices, and some private workplaces.

mashallah: From the Arabic phrase *ma sha Allah*, with a slightly different pronunciation but the same usage and meaning of *God willed it*. Used to express awe and congratulations, with a wish to protect against evil eye.

motreb: The term is used mainly for a musician, but also for a singer or dancer, someone who performs to entertain audiences. It, however, implies the speaker has contempt for the artist, considering them lowly and not of high artistic value.

mullah: Someone who has studied the Islamic religion and laws. A Muslim cleric. After the Islamic Revolution in Iran, mullahs sat in many government positions, ruling the country.

Naneh: Literally means *mother* but is also used to refer to other older women, such as grandmothers, relatives, or nannies, who provide care for a child. It sometimes simply becomes part of the name of the addressed woman.

People's Mojahedin: An Iranian dissident organization that started as an armed Islamic-Marxist group in 1965, which, since the Islamic Revolution, has focused on overthrowing the regime. It is, however, widely unpopular and mistrusted today among Iranians because of its cult-like system, ideologies, and actions.

rial: Iranian monetary unit.

rubab: A lute-like musical instrument.

salam aleikom: The Arabic phrase literally translates to *peace be upon you* or *hello to you*. In the context of Iran and the Islamic Republic, it is often used in more formal contexts, either by religious government people or in addressing them, instead of the more common *salam*.

salavat: An Arabic prayer to show veneration to Prophet Mohammad and his family. In Iran, the prayer is used in celebratory occasions to pray for good fortunes, in funerals to pray for peace for the soul of the dead, or even when trying to break up fights and disagreements between people.

santour: A Persian musical instrument similar to a hammered dulcimer.

SAVAK: The Iranian secret police during the Pahlavi monarchy.

Sepah: The Islamic Revolutionary Guard Corps. It was founded in 1979 by order of Imam Khomeini as a new branch of the country's armed forces to mainly focus on safeguarding the Islamic Revolution and its ideology and rulings.

seyyed: Meaning *sir* or *lord*, the term is used to identify a man who is a descendant of Prophet Mohammad. It is commonly added to a person's name and sometimes used instead of the name itself.

Shah Cheragh: Literally translating to *King of the Light*, it is the title given to Seyyed Ahmad, son of the seventh Shiite imam, Imam Musa al-Kazim. Shah Cheragh's mausoleum is in the city of Shiraz in Iran. Shacheragh, the name of the cook at the construction site, with a slightly different spelling and pronunciation, is a simplified form of this title.

sharbat: The term is used for a variety of nonalcoholic drinks made by mixing water with other ingredients such as juices, sugar, and fresh herbs or fruits.

shorteh: Policeman.

sigheh: Temporary marriage in Shiite Islam.

tombak: Persian goblet drum.

Tudeh Party: Iranian communist party formed in 1941 that supported the Iranian Revolution of 1979; in the 1980s, however, its leaders and members began to get arrested by the Islamic Republic government.

Ya Ali: Literally translates to *Oh, Ali*, calling the name of the first Shiite Imam, Imam Ali, as if addressing him to ask for support. The phrase is used when getting up or starting a task.

Ya Omar: Literally translates to *Oh, Omar*, calling the name of the second Suni caliph after Prophet Mohammad, as if addressing him to ask for support. The phrase is used when getting up or starting a task.

With gratitude to L. for her editorial assistance and sisterhood throughout this project.